ALL THE PRETTY FACES

GRAVEYARD FALLS

ALL THE PRETTY FACES

GRAVEYARD FALLS

RITA HERRON

Montlake
Romance

This is a work of fiction. Names, characters, organizations, places, events, and incidents are either products of the author's imagination or are used fictitiously.

Published by Montlake Romance, Seattle

www.apub.com

Amazon, the Amazon logo, and Montlake Romance are trademarks of Amazon.com, Inc., or its affiliates.

ISBN-13: 9781503950696
ISBN-10: 1503950697

Cover design by Marc J. Cohen

Printed in the United States of America

To Jennifer St. Giles—friend, fellow writer,
and plotter extraordinaire.

Thanks for your insight on the cosmetic surgery business
and for sending my twisted thoughts
down a different path!

CHAPTER ONE

The dead girl stared up at Special Agent Dane Hamrick, her eyes wide with terror, her lips forming a cry for help that had probably gotten lost in the wind boomeranging off the sharp mountain ridges.

It was the tears that got to him. They had dried, but stained with the blood, they created a crimson river down her cheeks.

Dane's gut tightened. She was so young, pretty, vulnerable. Dark hair, dark eyes. She'd been stabbed in the heart with a sharp instrument. The minute he'd heard that she bore a crisscross pattern across her chest, he'd raced to the scene.

The stab wound was almost identical to the one that had killed his sister, Betsy.

Grief for the young woman clogged his throat, yet hope shot through him. For ten damn years, he'd followed every case with any similarity in MO to his sister's murder, hoping to finally track down Betsy's killer. Four young women ages eighteen to twenty-one had been left in an alley—like his sister—except the cause of death varied. Another victim just last year had been marked in a crisscross pattern, but the pattern had been made with a hot curling iron, not a scalpel or knife.

His heart pounded. This case might be the one.

Yet how many times had he been disappointed?

Too many to count.

Still, when Cal—who was on call for his wife because she was expecting a baby at any moment—told him about the case and described the MO, Dane had driven like a maniac from Knoxville to the scene. Betsy's freckled face as a teenager had dogged him the whole way, urging him not to give up.

To find the man who'd stolen her life.

God, she'd been so excited about her future. She'd just enrolled in college. Then she'd taken that trip to visit the campus—

Sheriff Kimball cleared his throat. "Special Agent Cal Coulter said you'd worked cases with a similar MO."

"Yes," he said. He made sure to add an edge to his answer. No need to involve the sheriff in his personal interest in the case.

The guilt he'd lived with since he lost Betsy made his jaw snap tight with anger.

Big brothers were supposed to protect their baby sisters. Not let them get murdered at nineteen.

Did this girl have a brother looking for her? A mother or father or sister? A family who wanted closure?

All the more reason to get to work. Assess the details.

He knelt to examine the stab wound more closely.

Sharp, deep, straight to the aorta. Then the killer had twisted the blade to the opposite side to make the crisscross. She'd bled out quickly. The wound had been inflicted by a sharp instrument—a hunting knife or maybe a scalpel.

Betsy had been stabbed with a common pocketknife. Her wound had been crude, jagged, done in anger.

A crime of passion.

This stab wound appeared planned, the cuts on her even, methodical.

Okay, that was one difference in the MO.

Although it didn't necessarily mean it wasn't the same unknown subject, or unsub. Killers evolved over time. This one could have murdered Betsy in a fit of rage, then lain low and bided his time, afraid he'd get caught. Slowly he perfected his technique.

He'd awakened his thirst for killing when he murdered Betsy.

"Do you have an ID on her?" Dane asked.

The sheriff gestured toward the woods behind the motel. "Not yet. No wallet or purse or phone on her, but I haven't done a thorough search of the area yet. The ME is on his way."

Good. Maybe he could get DNA or dental records to identify her.

They needed a name. Family to contact.

One of them had to make the notification.

His mother's scream of denial the night the police had shown up at their door echoed in his head as if it had just happened yesterday.

He swallowed the lump in his throat. "Who found her?" Dane asked.

"The janitor. He was taking out the trash. Clerk at the front desk said she wasn't registered as a guest."

Wind rustled the leaves, tossing dried brittle ones across the victim's body.

The stench of garbage suffused the air. The fact that this woman had been left near the Dumpster made bile rise to Dane's throat. "Son of a bitch discarded her like she was nothing."

"Yeah, pretty cold." Sheriff Kimball scraped a hand through his hair. "To leave her naked and exposed . . ." He let the sentence trail off, shook his head in disgust, then heaved a breath as if to refocus. "Is this like the other case you worked?"

"There are similarities." A sheen of sweat broke out on Dane's neck as he recalled the photographs of his sister.

Betsy had been left in an alley, but she hadn't been naked, thank God.

This woman was stripped of her clothing. Instead of an alley, her body lay in a tangle of weeds and brush in a ditch, one hand outstretched as if begging for help. Or had she been posed that way for a reason?

The whites of her eyes bulged with broken vessels and had yellowed like an egg that had been cracked, the yolk spilling out. Even more disturbing, tiny slits had been carved beneath her eyes, more tracking down her pale face like the claw marks of a bird of prey's talons etched in snow.

Betsy had a similar marking below her eyes, although the claw marks had been jagged, done in a fit of rage, not as detailed or perfectly drawn as these.

What did those carvings mean? Was it some kind of signature, or had the bastard simply wanted to inflict more pain?

Ten years was a long time. The killer had aged, maybe become more selective. More sadistic. He could have practiced his skills, perfected the claw marks.

He could be killing for the fun of it now.

Either way, Dane would find this woman's killer and get justice for her.

He wouldn't stop until he got it for Betsy, too.

◆ ◆ ◆

Coming back to Graveyard Falls had been a mistake.

The tightening in Josie DuKane's chest clawed at her, a sign of another panic attack.

She closed her eyes and forced herself to take slow, deep breaths. To fight through the terror. But the Bride Killer case had been her first personal contact with murder. Then she'd become one of his victims.

Except she had survived. The other girls had died, been strangled with a garter by Billy Linder because they hadn't lived up to his expectations as the perfect wife.

Images of Billy tying her up—taunting her, ordering her to cook for him and his sick mother, then threatening to kill her when she failed—flooded Josie.

God. She'd worked so hard to overcome the trauma of the past two years. Therapy and staying at home where she was safe, surrounded by her family. Pouring her heart out into the journals that described her turmoil over being held hostage.

At first her entries had been almost incoherent, ramblings about the nightmares that refused to let her sleep through the night. The other victims' faces had floated toward her like ghostly images, their cries to be saved piercing her ears. *Why did you survive? Why didn't you save us? We didn't deserve to die so young.*

Guilt made her question herself. Was there something she could have done?

Logically the answer was no. She hadn't been involved in the case at the time. She'd met Billy Linder at church when she'd gone to pray for her mother and grandfather. Billy had seemed shy, harmless, had talked about taking care of his ailing mother.

The woman was barely alive when Billy carried Josie to his house. A house filled with dead animals Billy had preserved.

Even months later, at night when the lights went out, the eyes of those dead animals stared at her, haunting her with their piercing, vacant looks. Sometimes those eyes blended with the dead girls' eyes. Their horrified eyes accused her of letting them die.

Those nights she'd wake up screaming.

Her sister, Mona, and her mother had encouraged her to see a therapist, and that had helped. Then she'd started the journals.

She gripped the door handle of her car, tears pooling behind her closed eyelids.

She had to get out of here. Couldn't face the town today.

Even if they had come to see her.

Her phone buzzed, jarring her, and she glanced at the number.

Mona. Thank heavens. Mona must have sensed she was in trouble. Her sister had a knack for understanding people, which made her a great therapist. It was the reason Billy had called Mona for advice on finding the perfect mate.

Mona's compassion and understanding had helped get through to Billy at the end, and then Mona had saved Josie's life.

Josie punched Connect and whispered her sister's name.

"Josie, are you all right?"

"No." Her heart stuttered. She hated being weak.

"Ah, sis," Mona said softly. "I'm sorry. I knew it would be difficult for you."

"I shouldn't have come back. You and Mom and Johnny were smart to leave this town." For some reason, Josie thought it would be cathartic if she told her story and talked to residents and the victims' families.

Some had been supportive. Sympathetic. Had readily agreed to interviews.

Others had been furious about the book and accused her of taking advantage of them.

She hadn't wanted to hurt anyone.

"I'm not sorry I left," Mona said. "Even though Mom inherited Grandfather's house, neither one of us wanted it. There were too many bad memories."

Josie mumbled agreement. "Trust me, I don't plan to stay here any longer than necessary." She wanted to make sure they portrayed the story accurately. This was a true crime film, not fiction, and she didn't want them embellishing the story too much. Or disrespecting the victims' memories.

"I think you're brave to go back and face everyone," Mona said. "After all, the people have to sympathize with you. You were abducted by the man who tore apart their lives. You helped bring him to justice."

Mona's calm voice and reassuring words helped to tamp down the panic.

"I'm proud of you for writing the book," Mona continued. "Now that movie production company is turning it into a film, everyone who watches it will understand the victims' and their families' suffering."

Josie dabbed the perspiration from her face with a tissue. "Thank you. I needed to hear that."

Worry reverberated in Mona's sigh. "I still wish you'd let me come with you, sis."

Renewed strength swelled inside Josie. All her life she'd felt alone, but now she had a sister. Had it not been for the murders, she would never have known that Mona existed. Her mother had kept that secret well.

After the abduction, she and Mona had bonded over their shared experience with Billy. No one else truly understood what it had been like to listen to his sick ranting, to pretend to go along with him until help could arrive. To see that homemade wedding dress hanging on the door waiting for his wife.

She shivered at the memory. "I appreciate the offer, but you have to take care of yourself and rest. That baby you're carrying needs you."

"He needs his aunt, too, so please be careful."

Josie's lungs squeezed for air again. She had received some hate mail after the book launch—some people thought she was sensationalizing the murders. A couple of complaints sounded sinister, bordering on threatening.

She wasn't sensationalizing the murders or the victims' lives. She wanted to speak up for them.

"It's just a press conference," Josie said. "What could go wrong?"

Dane greeted the medical examiner, Dr. Wheeland, while Sheriff Kimball went from room to room at the motel canvassing the guests. Wheeland had helped Cal with the Bride Killer case and was a by-the-books, detailed doctor. Dane could use his expertise now.

With the small size of the motel and its location on the outside of town, at least he didn't have to deal with rubberneckers driving by or other locals cluttering the scene.

The skies were darkening, though, adding to the somber mood. They needed to work quickly before the rains started and washed away evidence.

"Do we know who she is?" the ME asked.

Dane shook his head. "No ID yet. The way he posed her could be significant. Her body is contorted at odd angles." Could be he wanted her to look macabre because she reminded him of someone else. Someone from his past who he hated or who'd hurt him. "Look at the broken compact mirror in her hand."

"What do you make of it?" Dr. Wheeland asked. "She's not wearing makeup. No lipstick or eye shadow either."

Dane shifted, contemplating the ME's observations. Wheeland had grown up in this area and worked intensive murder cases. "In his eyes, maybe mirrors symbolize vanity. So he stripped her bare of clothes and makeup to expose the real girl beneath." Dane inhaled a strong odor, almost sweet. "Her skin smells like some kind of hospital soap, like he cleaned her before he dumped her body."

The ME sniffed her hand. "You're right. He probably wanted to wipe away DNA."

"That's possible." Dane considered profiles of killers he'd studied. "Or maybe he thought she was dirty for some reason."

"Think she was a hooker?"

Since he had no knowledge of the victim at this point, he had to consider every possibility—but it didn't sit well with Dane.

The police had the nerve to question him about his sister's sex life and wanted to know if she was promiscuous. Their theories had infuriated him.

"We'll know once we ID her." Dane studied her hands. "Look at her nails."

They were short, neat, but not painted. The killer could have removed polish, but a prostitute would probably have had longer nails, even fake ones.

Dr. Wheeland turned her hand over to look beneath the nail beds. "If she fought back, she might have some epithelial under the nails. I'll let you know."

The ME lowered her hand, then examined the claw marks on her cheek. "Good Lord, look at this, Hamrick."

"I saw." Dane winced at the brutality. "He carved her face."

Although small cut marks had been made beneath his sister's eyes, they were superficial. These were deeper and resembled track marks down her cheek.

The difference could mean the murders were not related at all.

Despair threatened at the thought, but he fought it. He wouldn't give up yet. This was just the beginning of his investigation.

Maybe, just maybe, he was onto something this time and he finally had a link.

"It gets even sicker." Dr. Wheeland gestured toward the deep groove the killer had carved in the victim's cheek. "He removed a sliver of bone."

"What in the hell?" Dane noted the point where the unsub had snapped the bone in two. Why take a piece of bone?

Had the bastard kept it as a trophy?

Josie's legs wobbled slightly as she climbed the steps to the podium to address the crowd who'd gathered outside the courthouse. More than a hundred locals were present, along with the press and strangers she didn't recognize. Whispers and voices rumbled through the group as if they were eager to hear her talk about her book and the upcoming film.

Mona had helped her through her earlier panic attack, but the sight of various victims' family members staring at her made her breathing grow pained again.

Sara Levinson, one of the Thorn Ripper victims' mothers, didn't look happy at all. Neither did Doyle Yonkers, the brother of another victim. Their scorching scowls reeked of disapproval.

The mayor tapped the mic and introduced her. A few boos mingled with the clapping.

Shaken by the animosity, she gripped the podium, then lifted her head to face the crowd. Didn't these people understand that she wanted to honor the dead?

"Miss DuKane, we're delighted to have you," the mayor said. "We understand you suffered at the hands of the Bride Killer just as many of our locals did, and we're glad you returned to share your book."

Josie schooled her nerves, determined to maintain control. She'd fought too hard to recover to fall apart in front of these people. She wanted to be a role model, to prove that she refused to let fear keep her from living her life in hopes that others could do the same. She'd also insisted on being part of the production process to make sure the producers kept to the truth. The last thing the families needed was more pain.

"Your book *All the Little Liars* is based on the story of the mother-and-son serial killers Charlene and Billy Linder?" one of the reporters asked.

Josie nodded. "Yes. During the course of the police's investigation into the Bride Killer murders that occurred two years ago, Special Agent Cal Coulter uncovered the truth about the Thorn Ripper case that took place thirty years prior to that, and the connection between the cases."

"The mother taught the son to kill?" another reporter asked.

Josie hesitated over the question. "She definitely encouraged him to get rid of the young women he brought home because they didn't measure up to her expectations. The family history of abuse played a key role."

Another reporter piped up. "She killed three teenagers when she was young and then told her son about it?"

"Yes. Charlene Linder framed local football star Johnny Pike because he'd rejected her. At the time she was pregnant, and later delivered a son named Billy." Josie paused, still processing the fact that her mother, Anna, had been in love with Johnny at the time, and that she'd given birth to Johnny's baby.

Solving both cases had led to Johnny's conviction being overturned, and now her mother and Johnny had finally married.

They'd also reconnected with the baby her mother had given up.

Mona had been Josie's lifeline during therapy. When she'd shown Mona her journals and mentioned she was interested in criminology, Mona had encouraged her to take classes in criminology.

Coupled with her journalism classes, one of Josie's instructors had suggested she use her own experience and write true crime stories. With her journals to go by, she had begun the next day and found writing as a reporter covering a story had helped her view the events that had happened with a different perspective. Understanding Linder's background and the psychology behind his actions enabled her to realize that she wasn't to blame.

"Billy Linder was the Bride Killer?" the reporter asked.

"Yes." Josie's voice broke. Billy's name still had the power to make her heart flutter with panic. Irritation followed at having to recount details that these reporters should already know. Hadn't they done their homework and read her book?

Although, the media fed on the gory and were probably playing her, hoping for a reaction. The public also thrived on the drama.

Doyle Yonkers waved a copy of her book in one hand. "This is the way you're presenting the story." He flipped the book over and read the back cover copy.

"Two decades ago, the town of Graveyard Falls was terrorized by the Thorn Ripper, a vicious and unforgiving killer who targeted young, beautiful girls. This merciless murderer tossed the girls from the top of the town's beautiful waterfall, relishing their screams. The local sheriff arrested all-American high school senior Johnny Pike, sentencing the wholesome boy to a life of misery in prison. The killings stopped, but the town's terror wasn't over yet . . .

"Two years ago, three more brutal slayings tore apart the fragile peace in Graveyard Falls. This time, the victims were found savagely dressed in macabre wedding gowns. The Bride Killer showed no signs of stopping his rampage of terror . . .

"Josie DuKane bravely survived an attack by the Bride Killer, and this book details her harrowing tale. Not only did her instincts keep her alive, but they helped uncover the truth behind the Thorn Ripper and the Bride Killer, a twisted mother-son killing team now safely behind bars where they belong.

"Soon to be a major motion picture, this firsthand account of ruthless killing is a must-read . . ."

"Don't you think this is sensationalism?" Sara Levinson shouted.

Josie swallowed hard. "I'm sorry it if appears that way, but marketing was in charge of the copy. The goal is for people to read the story and understand the truth."

"He used a Taser?" one of the reporters interjected.

"Yes," she said, grateful for the diversion, "Billy subdued them with a Taser, tied them up, and kept them at his house."

She fought revulsion at the memory. God, she'd been so gullible.

She'd felt sorry for Billy that day at the church.

She hadn't seen beneath the surface. Hadn't seen that Taser coming . . .

He'd misread her compassion as a sign that she'd make the perfect wife for him. In his mind, that meant she'd obey him, cook for him, take care of his mother, and service him when he wanted.

The reporter moved closer to her. "Miss DuKane, you wrote that Mr. Linder was looking for a bride. Why was he obsessed with finding a wife?"

Getting into Billy's mind-set had helped her cope before. It would help her now. She would just stick to the facts. "His mother's illness triggered him to start killing. He wanted to marry before she died, because he was afraid of being alone. Once he subdued his victims, he took them to his house and forced them to pass tests proving they were worthy of being his wife."

"What kind of tests?" one reporter asked.

Determined to maintain control, she clenched the podium to keep her hands from trembling. "I describe more about that in the book," she said, grateful her voice didn't falter. "Essentially, though, his tests consisted of basic chores like cooking and cleaning. Being . . . obedient." She'd played into that, pretended she wanted to take care of him, offered to pour his mama tea, to make biscuits and gravy for them.

She couldn't even think about a pan of gravy now without it turning her stomach.

She cleared her throat. "Billy's mother, Charlene, was abused by her father, and she repeated the cycle by abusing her son. Billy's bedtime stories consisted of tales about the teenagers she'd killed and left at the base of the waterfalls. She referred to the victims as *little liars*."

Another reporter waved her hand. "Why did she call them that?"

Josie blinked as the flash of a camera nearly blinded her. The sky was darkening from the threatening storm, the trees shaking with its force. "Charlene was disturbed and didn't fit in with the other teenagers. Her victims were popular cheerleaders who shunned her. According to her journals, she saw them as Goody Two-shoes who lied about being virgins. Apparently the three victims had made a pact to sleep with Johnny Pike, and she was jealous because he paid attention to them and not her."

"The girls she killed bullied her, didn't they?" another reporter shouted.

Josie bit her tongue. This was a touchy subject. She certainly didn't want to imply that the teenage victims had done something to bring their deaths upon themselves. Their parents and loved ones didn't want to hear the girls disparaged. "I wasn't there, so it's hard for me to say they bullied her. According to teachers, Charlene was quiet, withdrawn, an awkward girl who didn't make friends easily. She was obviously affected by her father's abuse."

Sara Levinson crossed her arms. "So you're saying she was a victim?"

Josie hesitated, surprised at Sara's vehemence.

"She was a victim of abuse," Josie said. "I'm not defending her actions, though, or the pain she inflicted on the families in this town. I'm simply explaining the circumstances." She gave Sara a sympathetic look. "I completely understand how trauma like that can affect families. It's not fair and nothing can change what happened, but maybe if we understand how and why Charlene and Billy resorted to such violence, we can accept it and move on."

A male reporter in the shadows raised a hand to get her attention. He looked familiar, but she couldn't place him. "Have you visited Billy in the psychiatric unit?" he asked.

Josie fought another shiver as she recalled walking down that long, cold hallway. A guard had escorted her into a large sterile-looking room with a table in the middle. Billy had shuffled in, handcuffed and shackled, his eyes vacant and glassy with drugs. When he'd sat down, he twisted his hands together, picking at his nails, which he'd bitten to the quick.

When he'd finally looked up at her, he'd asked if she'd brought his tools.

He wanted to open his taxidermy office again.

"Miss DuKane, you did visit him." The reporter consulted his notes. "I spoke with the nursing staff and they confirmed it."

So he had been baiting her. "Yes, I talked to him. He's a very disturbed man."

"That doesn't justify the fact that he killed three of our local girls," someone muttered.

"He should be put to death like they were," another woman said.

Josie schooled her reaction. As much as Billy haunted her nightmares, she didn't know if she believed he should be given the death penalty.

Although *she* would be dead if Mona and Cal hadn't shown up. She'd failed Billy's tests and tried to run. He'd caught her, tied her up, then said he had to kill her.

A raindrop fell and plopped against the podium, lightning zigzagging across the sky. More whispers and rumblings of protest echoed through the group.

Josie lifted a hand to signal them to let her speak. "I didn't write this story to condone what Billy and his mother did or upset any one of you. Understanding what drove both of these individuals to commit these heinous crimes will hopefully help the victims and their families in their recovery. I also hope it raises awareness of the cycle of domestic abuse." And maybe teenage bullying. Although the mothers of the teenage victims resented the suggestion that their children had treated Charlene unfairly.

"Nothing will bring back our daughters," one woman cried.

"You should let them rest in peace," another local added with disdain. "Not cause more agony to their families by making them repeatedly relive the sadistic crimes."

Sara stepped to the front. "Every time I see your book and think about watching my daughter being murdered on screen, I feel sick."

Josie tensed. Sara had talked to her freely during her interviews.

Apparently she regretted that decision.

Josie felt for the woman. She couldn't treat her like a stranger or dismiss her emotions. "I'm sorry, Sara," Josie said softly. "I understand your grief and pain. This is not easy for me either. I still have night terrors about being held by Billy Linder myself. This book is meant to honor those we lost. I hope you'll see it that way as well."

Tension escalated as a cluster of folks in the back shouted disagreement. Someone yelled at her to leave town.

Others called out support, excited that the filming would boost the town's fledgling economy. Already the inn had been refurbished, and a local builder had renovated cabins on the river for production crews and others involved in the filmmaking process.

Cameras flashed, recording the scene. Reporters began to comb through the crowd, taking notes as they questioned individuals.

She should have kept up her distance. Letting down her guard with Sara had opened her up to being vulnerable.

Josie backed away from the podium, her breathing labored. The heated stares and shouts seemed directed at her. Tempers were rising.

The air grew hot around her, cloying. Stifling.

She had to escape.

"We don't care about the money." This voice came from someone in the back. "We want our nice quiet town back."

She wasn't sure Graveyard Falls had ever been a nice quiet town.

Nerves on edge, she scanned the group, then the street, searching for the sheriff. Although he was supposed to be on guard in case of problems, he'd texted earlier that he was meeting Agent Dane Hamrick from the FBI. She'd interviewed the federal agent for the book.

Neither of them were here now, though.

Judging from the mixed reactions, tempers were spiraling out of control.

The wind stirred again, and the hair on the back of her neck bristled as she inched down the stairs. She had the uneasy feeling that something bad was going to happen.

Or maybe it already had. That could be the reason Dane was in Graveyard Falls. He certainly wouldn't be interested in the movie.

Her phone beeped with a text.

Horror washed over her at the photo that appeared. A young woman lying on the ground. Naked. Blood soaking her chest. Her cheek carved out.

Dear God, was it real?

♦ ♦ ♦

He walked amongst the locals, invisible to their eyes. They were all caught up in the past. In their grief and anger and pain.

In the injustices and the need for someone to blame.

Reporters ran through the throng, taking notes and asking questions, hoping to find the spotlight for their bylines. The movie producers had arrived in their fancy cars and trucks with cameras and makeup artists and talent scouts.

The actors and actor wannabes were coming in droves.

The vision of the girl he'd left by that motel surfaced, spiking his adrenaline. He lifted his hands, the scent of soap and the woman's skin mingling with the fresh scent of blood.

Ah, she had been so beautiful.

But she'd had to die.

Someone brushed his arm as they hurried past. Another pretty girl. Another fake smile.

He trembled with excitement. Yes, Graveyard Falls was the perfect hunting ground.

And the perfect place to hide.

CHAPTER TWO

Dane wiped his hand over his forehead, sweating in spite of the chill in his body. He couldn't help but think about this poor woman's family and what lay ahead for them. About the last few minutes of her life. Had she been terrified? Begged for the man to stop tormenting her?

Those were the same questions he'd asked about Betsy. Questions that still made him wake in a sweat. And the ones that had finally driven his mother over the edge. A few months ago, she'd fallen into such a depression that he'd had to commit her to a mental health care nursing home called the Loving Arms. The people were nice, but he still felt guilty every time he left her there.

The home was close to Graveyard Falls.

Dr. Wheeland scratched his head. "I can't believe we've got another murder in town. Folks around here are barely getting over the nightmare of those Bride Killings."

"I know. I heard they're making a movie based on Josie DuKane's book."

"Damnedest thing." Dr. Wheeland checked the victim's feet. "Charlene Linder probably thinks she's going to be a celebrity."

"Maybe that's what this creep wants, too." All the more reason for Dane to analyze the scene carefully. Details would help find the unsub.

Once again, he studied the woman. Her long hair had probably looked nice earlier, although now it was dotted with blood and lay in a tangled mess around her face. The leaves and debris from the ground weren't embedded in the strands, suggesting she was probably killed in another location. Or that she was dead when she hit the ground. If she'd been alive and fighting, her hair would have been filled with dirt.

"TOD?" he asked.

"Judging from her body temp," Dr. Wheeland replied, "I'd say she died sometime last night."

Anger heated Dane's blood as he studied the sharp marks on her face. As many times as he'd seen death and the pain one human inflicted on another, the cruelty still bothered him. "How about the talon marks? Postmortem?"

The ME's lips stretched thin. "No, look at the blood splatters. He did that before he killed her."

Despite his disgust, Dane tried to get in the mind of the killer. "So he wanted her to feel the pain, to know that he was marking her. Scarring her."

"Probably." Wheeland examined the woman's chest more closely. Bruises marred her torso as if he might have knelt on her to hold her down. "This stab wound was quick, to the point. Straight into the aorta."

"He knew what he was doing," Dane said. "So he could work in the medical field."

Dr. Wheeland shrugged. "True, but anybody with basic knowledge of the human body would know that a wound like this would cause death."

Dammit, the medical angle could have narrowed down their suspect list. "What else can you tell from the body? Sexual assault?"

Dr. Wheeland examined her thighs and lower extremities. "I don't see bruising or visual signs of rape, but I'll know once I do the autopsy." He lifted her hands to look at her nails.

The medical examiner used a tool to pull back a small layer of skin around her areola where the killer had slashed her skin diagonally. "She has implants."

Dane narrowed his eyes. "Those cuts aren't deep, maybe a quarter of an inch."

"They have nothing to do with cause of death," Wheeland said, his voice laced with disgust.

"So he was just playing with her, inflicting pain," Dane commented, a picture of a sick man forming in his mind. Sadistic eyes, a wild, crazed look. "You think he intentionally wanted to expose them?"

"Could be." Dr. Wheeland took off his glasses, rubbed his eyes, then put them back on. "We can use them to ID her."

The wind picked up, shaking the trees and raining brittle leaves down on the ground. One landed on her cheek, sticking to the dried blood.

Dane picked it off. He wanted to know more about her. "Considering the film people descending on the town, she might be one of the actresses or part of the crew."

"You can start there," Dr. Wheeland said. "Meanwhile, I'll run her prints and DNA."

The CSI team arrived and introduced themselves, then began to comb the woods behind the motel for evidence. Dane surveyed the area surrounding the body as well.

"Any security cameras?" Dane asked the sheriff.

Sheriff Kimball shrugged. "Naw, owner said he's been meaning to install some but hadn't gotten around to it."

Dane shook his head in disbelief. Hopefully CSI would find the woman's purse and ID or a cell phone.

His phone buzzed, and he checked the number. Josie DuKane's name popped up.

What did she want? Another interview? Hell, even though Cal had run the investigation, he'd talked to her about his surveillance on the Yonkers man.

Yonkers's sister, Candy, was one of the three Thorn Ripper victims. The man not only owned a pet crematorium, but he was weird as shit.

He had fit the profile of the Bride Killer. He collected those damned dead animals Billy Linder preserved with his taxidermy skills. He'd also suffered a traumatic childhood and watched his family fall apart after her murder.

His mother became depressed, and Yonkers wound up taking care of her. Like Linder and his mother, Yonkers's mother was ill at the time the Bride Killer struck. Yonkers's mother also pressured him to find a wife.

Dane's phone buzzed again. Josie was persistent.

Damn . . . she'd stirred something in him that he hadn't felt in forever. Lust? Hunger?

Things he didn't have time for.

She was too damn tempting. Despite the fact that she was held hostage and had nearly died at the hands of the Bride Killer, she was gutsy and faced the horror with a brave face.

He had to respect her for that. Which made her even more dangerous. Because he liked her.

She made him want things a man like him didn't have a right to have.

If he got involved with her, he might lose focus.

There was no way in hell he'd do that and let his sister down again.

♦ ♦ ♦

The awning of the diner provided a safe retreat while Josie studied the picture of the dead girl. Her hand trembled as she gripped the phone.

She probably should have called the local sheriff, but she didn't know Sheriff Kimball very well, and she'd dealt with Dane before. He was good at what he did.

He was also handsome and tough, all male sex appeal, but she didn't want to think about that. Even if he had been interested, she certainly was in no shape for a relationship.

She would trust him to get to the bottom of this text.

He didn't answer, so she left a message that it was urgent that he call her.

Horror flooded her as she studied the photograph again. The woman looked so young, so pale. Her lips were devoid of lipstick, her nails bare. She was naked, her eyes staring wide in death. Worse, those marks on her face had been carved by something sharp. A knife or scalpel?

Memories of Billy Linder holding that knife to her throat made her tremble. If she hadn't noticed that photograph of Johnny on the mantel and used it to stall until Cal and Mona arrived, he would have choked her with that garter.

She'd been so terrified.

This woman must have been, too.

Fighting another panic attack, she relied on her criminology training to analyze the details.

In one hand, the poor woman held a broken compact mirror.

In the other, she held a Mitzi doll, also naked, the face mangled.

Her breath quickened. The Mitzi doll, a Barbie knockoff, had been popular when she was a kid, and it still was. She'd collected the fashion doll along with all her clothes and accessories, just like most of the little girls her age.

Her nerves prickling, she scanned the crowd and sidewalk, the sense that someone was watching her mounting. If the person who'd sent the photograph wanted a reaction, she didn't intend to give him the satisfaction.

Of course it would be easy to hide among all the people. The town square was packed with locals, reporters, and tourists who'd come to catch a glimpse of the filming.

More voices shouted questions at the mayor, and a few protestors waved signs and yelled for the crew to go back to LA.

Growing more nervous about the text, she decided to go to the sheriff's office. If this picture was real, a woman's life had been taken. It was imperative the police know immediately.

She reached the corner to cross the street to the parking lot, but the sidewalk was clogged with people leaving the press conference.

The streetlight changed, and she blended in with the throng, hoping no one noticed her.

As she stepped into the road, someone shoved her from behind.

She stumbled forward and fell into the street, knees and hands hitting the pavement.

The sound of tires screeching reverberated in Josie's ears. Then she looked up in horror.

A car careened toward her.

A prayer floated off her tongue as she tried to push herself up. Her life flashed in front of her.

She couldn't have survived Billy Linder to die like this.

Tires screeched. People shouted. The car roared to stop an inch from her just as someone helped her up.

A pudgy man jumped from the vehicle and ran toward her. "My God, lady, are you all right?"

Her head spun, the world blurring as she struggled to focus. A woman from the sidewalk rushed toward her. She leaned on the man who'd helped her to stand.

"Are you okay, Miss DuKane?"

Doyle Yonkers.

Josie's legs wobbled as she recognized the voice. How could she forget him? His voice was deep and gravelly. His beady dark eyes made chill bumps skate up her arms. She'd visited that pet crematorium to decide for herself if Dane had pegged the man correctly.

Yonkers might not have been the Bride Killer, but a creepiness emanated from him. He could be dangerous.

The driver of the car halted in front of her. "I'm so sorry, I almost hit you," he said, sweat beading on his face.

"Do you need a doctor?" the woman asked.

Josie shook herself from the shock of the fall. Her hands and knees were scraped, but she hadn't hit her head. "No, I'm okay."

Yonkers and the woman ushered her to the sidewalk.

"Do you want me to call nine-one-one?" the woman asked.

Josie shook her head and stepped away from Yonkers. His touch made her skin crawl.

Other cars slowed, windows rolling down so the drivers could see what had happened. Horns began to honk, the traffic backing up.

She didn't like being in the spotlight. She tucked her hair behind her ear, straightened her clothing, and lifted her chin.

An older couple rushed toward her, the man carrying her cell phone. "Is this yours, miss?"

"Yes, thank you." Josie took the phone with a trembling hand.

The man who'd almost hit her coughed. "I'm sorry, I looked down for a second. You just came out of nowhere."

Because someone had pushed her into the street.

Guilt and terror tinged the man's voice. Josie squeezed his arm. "I'm sorry, sir. I slipped and fell, but I'm fine."

Someone shouted that they recognized her. Another voice yelled for her to leave town. Josie looked up to see who it was—maybe the person who'd shoved her into the street?

The older couple hovered nearby. "Can we drive you somewhere?"

She shook her head. "No, my car is in the parking lot. I'll be fine. I'm sorry for causing trouble."

Anxious to escape before anyone else recognized her, she waved off everyone's concern and darted in the direction of her car. Behind her, more horns blasted, and traffic resumed.

Just as she reached the parking lot, footsteps clattered on the pavement behind her. Fear gripped her. She twisted around to see who was following her—two teenagers heading toward Cocoa's Café.

She sighed in relief, unlocked her car, and collapsed inside, her heart racing.

♦ ♦ ♦

The wind howled off the mountain, and twigs and leaves pelted Dane, a reminder that another winter had barely passed in Graveyard Falls and that the turbulent March winds and storms were setting in.

Dane paced by the creek, one eye on the crime investigators, hoping they paid attention to details.

He reached for his cell to phone Josie, but Sheriff Kimball strode toward him, and Dane held back. Kimball had helped with the Bride Killer case, but something about the man bugged Dane. He was too quiet, distant, as if he had secrets of his own.

The midday sun slanted through the trees. Yet storm clouds rolled above, the sky an ominous gray. They needed to work the crime scene fast before the rain hit and destroyed evidence.

"Six guests in the motel last night," Sheriff Kimball said matter-of-factly. "No one saw anything."

He wasn't surprised. This motel was run-down and off the beaten path. "Anyone seem suspicious?"

The sheriff consulted his notepad. "Not really. Apparently there's a garden club at the local church. Five out of those six guests were middle-aged women here to attend."

"What about the sixth?"

Kimball gave a perfunctory glance toward the van in the lot. "Couple with two kids traveling through. Said their baby was up all night the evening before and they were dead asleep by nine o'clock."

Dane contemplated various scenarios. "Get the manager to open up the rooms that were vacant. The killer could have gotten inside one, stabbed the woman there, then waited until everything was quiet to dump her body."

All business, Kimball nodded. "I'm on it."

The sheriff hurried toward the motel entrance, and Dane went to confer with the lead crime investigator from the county, Lieutenant Ward.

They'd met when Dane was working with the task force Agent Coulter had spearheaded. Having worked together on previous cases, Cal had recruited Dane as soon as he got the assignment. Dane was glad to have the seasoned investigator on the team.

"Have you found anything?" Dane asked.

"No. No signs of a struggle back here. Weeds are not mashed, no clothing fabric or weapon."

Had the killer disposed of the victim's clothes or kept them? "Have your team search the trash Dumpsters and woods for the clothing. How about footprints?"

Lieutenant Ward's mouth slanted into a frown. "A partial by the bushes, but it's not enough to cast."

Dane surveyed the woods, the parking lot, and the exterior of the motel. From his vantage point the manager wouldn't have seen anyone drag the body around to the Dumpster in back.

Sheriff Kimball walked toward him with the manager, a gray-haired man wearing a hearing aid and walking with a cane.

Dane gestured toward two rooms with the lights off. "Let's check those two on the end first."

Together they walked past the rooms that had been rented. The manager pointed to room number four as they passed it. "That one has plumbing issues. I can't put anyone in there."

They reached the two end units, then waited while the older man unlocked the doors.

Dane waved the manager behind him. "Stay outside."

Sheriff Kimball shined his flashlight inside the first room, and Dane gestured that he'd search the corner one.

The scent of cleaning supplies hit Dane as he peeked inside. He shined a light across the interior, but the room appeared to be empty. He paused to listen for sounds that someone was inside. The wind whistled, voices echoed from the crime scene techs, but the room was quiet.

Dane kept his gun at the ready in case someone was hiding in the closet or bathroom.

He flipped on the switch at the door, and bright light spilled through the room, illuminating the dingy walls. The carpet was an outdated rusty brown, the bedspread an orange and green floral that looked like something from the 1980s.

He checked the closet and bathroom, but both were empty. The strong scent of Pine-Sol and bleach that filled the air made him examine the floor and walls more closely. He sniffed to see if it was the same odor on the victim's hands, but that soap smelled sweeter.

He stepped to the door and called one of the crime scene techs to come inside. "See if you can find blood splatters in here."

The young man nodded and went to work. Dane leaned closer to examine the bedspread. Stains darkened the faded fabric, although they didn't look like blood. Of course the bedcovers were supposedly the dirtiest part of a motel room, and no telling where the stains had come from.

He gestured toward the bedding and told the investigator to bag them and send them to the lab.

"So far, no blood," the tech said. "Did you see something specific indicating that the woman was killed in this room?"

This guy must be green around the collar. "No. The cleaner could have been used to cover the crime, though. Process it thoroughly."

Dane excused himself and stepped outside. Sheriff Kimball was exiting the other vacant room. "That one's clear."

Dane poked his head in, but the chemical scent wasn't strong inside that room. His phone buzzed. Josie again. Dammit, he was busy.

"Agent Hamrick."

"I need to see you."

Dane froze. He didn't like the fear in her voice. "What's wrong, Josie?"

◆ ◆ ◆

Josie's stomach churned as she replayed the last few minutes in her head.

"Talk to me, dammit," Dane snapped.

She leaned her head into her hand and did the deep breathing exercises the therapist had taught her after her abduction.

The terror of that night returned anyway. Billy had ordered her to cook for his mother, and she had. His mother hadn't approved, and Billy had insisted he had to kill her.

Then that photo of Johnny Pike had caught her eye, and she'd used it to stall. Billy claimed Johnny was his father. At the time, she'd believed she was Johnny's daughter, so she'd used that relationship to make a connection.

She'd assured Billy he wouldn't be alone when his mother died because they were siblings.

Her plan had backfired. He'd turned on Mona and decided to make *her* his wife.

Tears threatened. If Cal hadn't arrived in time, they might both be dead.

"Josie, talk to me. Are you hurt?"

Dane's concerned voice dragged her from the memory and touched a tender chord inside her. She'd never had a man care about her, just her mother and Mona.

Well, now she had Johnny and Cal, but they were family.

"I'm a little shaken up. I had a close call a few minutes ago and fell in the street. I just scraped my hands and knees. I'm all right."

"You don't sound all right."

She tightened her hand around the phone. In spite of her bravado, her voice had trembled. "I didn't just fall, Dane. Someone pushed me."

"What?" Dane's voice rose a notch. "Did you see who did it?"

"No, a group of us left the press conference at the same time and gathered at the street to cross." She hesitated, self-doubt kicking in. "Maybe someone just bumped me. It was crowded at the crosswalk."

A tense heartbeat stretched between them. Then Dane's voice, low and soothing. "But you don't think it was an accident?"

She massaged her temple, glad she'd called Dane instead of the sheriff. At least Dane knew her well enough to accept that she wasn't imagining things. "No, I don't. But I didn't see who did it. Anyway, I was on the way to the sheriff's office. That's actually the reason I called." An image of the photograph flashed behind her eyes. "I received a strange text, Dane. A photograph. I don't know if it's real, but it certainly looks real."

"What kind of photograph?"

"It's a picture of a dead woman," Josie said with a shudder. "She's naked and was stabbed in the chest."

Dane's sharp intake of breath rattled over the line. "Do you recognize her?"

"No, and I hope it's not real." She closed her eyes on a prayer, then opened them a second later and continued. "Even if it isn't real, I want to know who texted me. If that picture is someone's idea of a sick joke or intended to scare me, I want to put a stop to it. I'm forwarding it to you."

She pressed Send, her pulse hammering as she waited for the text to go through.

"Dammit, Josie."

Dread balled in her stomach at his dark tone. "What?"

"It's real," he said grimly. "I'm at the crime scene with the victim right now."

CHAPTER THREE

Josie lowered her head into her hand again and tried to control the panic bubbling in her chest.

This wasn't some kind of twisted game or joke. Someone had texted her a picture of a dead woman. A *murder* victim.

Dane cleared his throat. "Do you have any idea who sent this?"

She wished she did. "No. The text is from an unknown number."

"Where are you now?"

Josie rechecked the door lock. Good. She was safe. "In my car in the parking lot in town."

A heartbeat passed. "What happened before you received the text?"

"I was at the press conference talking about the book and answering questions. Things got heated. Just as I stepped down from the podium, the text came through."

His voice hardened. "What do you mean—things got heated?"

The memory made her check around her car again. "Some people don't like the idea of the movie. They think it's making them relive the horrible nightmare of the murders, and that I'm exploiting them."

Dane muttered something beneath his breath. "Did you see anyone specific stand out?"

She closed her eyes and mentally pictured herself on the podium. She'd recognized some of the locals. Cocoa from the café. The checkout lady from the grocery store. Sara Levinson. "No, not really. I mean, Sara Levinson was upset, but she wouldn't do something like this."

Dane studied the picture. "There's something strange in the photograph. The victim is holding a doll. But there's no doll at the scene."

Josie's heart hammered. "He must have taken it with him. But why pose her with it?"

"Good question. Does the doll mean anything to you?"

She had a whole box of them in her closet at home. "I collected them when I was little, but so did half the girls I knew."

A second passed. "Jesus, I thought that it looked familiar. My sister had one of them, too."

"Your sister?" Dane hadn't mentioned family before, but then again, they'd only met for that interview to discuss his surveillance on Yonkers.

"Yes," he said. "She got one for her birthday when she was ten. I don't know what happened to it."

"Maybe you can ask her if it has some kind of meaning that I don't know about," Josie suggested.

His breath hissed out. "That's not possible. My sister is dead."

Josie's throat thickened at his abrupt tone. "I'm so sorry, Dane. I didn't know."

"Drop it," he said gruffly. "I don't want to talk about it."

His pain sounded so raw she didn't want to probe. "Where are you? I'll meet you."

"No. I don't want you involved in this murder investigation."

Again, he slipped back to the professional lone wolf.

Josie didn't intend to let him deter her questions about the woman. Her need for answers overpowered the fear that had nearly choked her on the street. "I already am involved, Dane. The killer sent me this picture for a reason."

The question was why?

To taunt her with the fact that she wasn't safe in Graveyard Falls?

◆ ◆ ◆

Dane mumbled an oath under his breath. He wanted to believe that the killer hadn't sent the picture to Josie, but considering the book she'd written about the Bride Killer, he couldn't discount the theory. That damn book had hit lists all over the place and made her name recognizable overnight.

Stars often drew the crazies.

He wouldn't jump to conclusions, though. He had to consider other possibilities. Sheriff Kimball, the janitor, the motel manager, or one of the crime scene workers could have sent it to Josie. Maybe someone close to the scene wanted to give her the scoop for a new story.

Dammit, he hated the media. Swarming reporters stirred up interest from other weirdos. He'd seen it on numerous cases. Freaks wanting to take credit and get their five minutes of fame gave false confessions.

Reporters exposed family secrets and lies.

Just as they had with his sister. They'd dogged him and his mother, asking questions, making insinuations about Betsy's sex life, implying she'd run away. They'd practically driven his mother to a nervous breakdown.

"Dane, what are you thinking?" Josie asked.

He willed his mind back to the case. "It's possible that someone at the crime scene sent you the text. Someone who thought you might want to write about it."

"If there is a story, I'd like to follow it. This town, the people in it . . . It's personal to me."

His fingers tightened around the phone. "Why?"

"You know why. Because the killer has focused on me. Because of what happened with the previous cases." Impatience tinged Josie's voice. "Johnny was railroaded into jail for a crime he didn't commit. Look how many innocent women died because of it. I have to know why this girl was killed, if it had something to do with my book."

"I don't need or want a partner," Dane said. "I work alone."

He had no desire to be used by a crime writer. He especially didn't want to be responsible for her safety.

He'd already fucked up with his sister.

The manager appeared on the sidewalk and walked toward him. "Just go home. I'll come by your place later. We'll see if the IT team can trace your phone to see where that text came from."

Josie sighed. "Dane, I have to do something to help. I can't get this woman's face out of my mind."

"I'll find out what happened to her," he snapped. "That's my job."

"But I've studied criminology, I might have some insight."

"You could also get yourself killed," Dane said through gritted teeth. "Remember what happened before."

Josie's sharp intake of breath punctuated the air. "Of course I remember. Every minute of every day. All the more reason I can't back down now. I can't let these crazies win. Besides, being informed might help keep me safe."

Dammit, she was right about that last part.

He also understood her need not to give in to the fear. She'd had no control when Linder forced her to go with him or when he'd made her cook for his sick mother. For God's sake, he'd chained her to the insane old lady's bed.

Once she'd decided to write the story of the Bride Killer, she'd dived in, and there had been no stopping her. Hell, he admired her guts. He'd read the book, and she'd done a damn fine job of reporting the details while respecting individual family members' feelings.

If the killer had decided to involve her or kill again, he might already have her in his target. Like it or not—and he didn't like it—she needed his protection.

"All right, Josie. Let me finish here, then I'll stop by. In light of what happened today, I don't think it's a good idea for you to be at the crime scene."

She made a sound of frustration but finally agreed.

"Are you staying at your grandfather's?"

"Yes. I'm not crazy about that place, but it's free. My grandfather moved into the assisted living home near Knoxville."

The hurt in her tone tore at him. Cal had mentioned that she and her grandfather hadn't been close. That he and Josie's mother, Anna, had been estranged for years because of the Thorn Ripper case.

He wondered how Josie felt being in the older man's house.

"I'll see you in a bit." Dane ended the call, his shoulders knotted with anxiety as he walked over to question the motel manager.

"Sir, did you take a picture of the victim and send it to anyone?"

The man's white eyebrows climbed his forehead. "Take a picture? What you talkin' about? I ain't got one of them fancy cell phones like all those young kids tote around."

"How about the janitor? May I speak to him?"

"Sure," the manager said. "I can tell you that he didn't take no pictures. He's my brother. He was so shook up when he found that girl, I had to give him one of my nerve pills."

He led Dane inside the motel lobby where a pale-faced man around seventy in work clothes sat slumped on a tattered vinyl sofa. His hands shook as he slurped coffee from a disposable cup.

The manager hobbled over and nudged his brother. "Lemont, you didn't take no pictures of that dead woman, did you?"

Lemont's expression bordered on sickly. Dane stepped back, afraid he was going to throw up

"Pictures? Why would I take pictures?"

"I told you," the manager said with a wave of his gnarled hand. "Why you asking?"

"Just routine," Dane said. The fewer people who knew Josie had been sent that text the better.

He thanked the men, then went to talk to the sheriff. "Kimball, did you take a picture of the crime scene and send it to anyone?"

Sheriff Kimball removed his hat and scraped a hand through his shaggy dark-blond hair. "No, of course not. Why?"

Dane debated whether to trust the man, but he needed help, and the sheriff was on the right side of the law, so he explained about the text.

"Shit." Sheriff Kimball shook his head glumly. "You think the killer sent it to her?"

"Either that or someone here did." Dane studied Kimball for a reaction, but Kimball showed none. "Someone who wanted to let her know that another killer struck in Graveyard Falls."

"Well, hell," the sheriff said. "That's not good. Although if the killer sent it to Josie, we might be able to use that at some point to smoke him out."

Dane's insides knotted. "That is not an option," Dane snapped. "Protecting the town and Miss DuKane are our top priorities. You got that?"

The sheriff's frown deepened the lines around his eyes. For a minute, Dane thought he wasn't going to answer, but then he made a clicking sound with his teeth and muttered, "Yeah, I got it."

Dane silently chastised himself for overreacting. If he didn't know Josie, he might have made the same suggestion.

Only he did know Josie. And he wasn't about to let this sick son of a bitch get to her.

Had the killer sent the picture to spook Josie or as an invitation to play a game of cat and mouse with him?

Would that game turn into a hunt?

Anxiety riddled Josie as she drove back to her grandfather's house. She rationalized that she was being paranoid, that she'd imagined those hands shoving her into the street, but what she'd felt was real.

Determined not to be caught off guard, she scanned the neighborhood and property for strangers.

She'd come to Graveyard Falls two years ago to visit her grandfather because he was ill. As a child, she'd never understood his animosity toward her or the terrible rift between her mother and him.

The moment she'd set foot in the old house, tension simmered in the air. Dark secrets and sadness permeated the walls as thick as the dust that had settled into the weathered wood and crevices.

Even now, sadness lingered as if it weighted the air and made it stale, hard to breathe. Wind whistled through the eaves so sharply that it sounded like a baby's cry.

She flipped on the lights as she entered, the wood floor creaking as she crossed the room to the table where she'd left her notes on the Bride Killer and Thorn Ripper cases.

Staying here was both unnerving and cathartic. She'd wanted to make peace with the fact that her grandfather hadn't wanted her, that he'd put Johnny in jail when Johnny was innocent, and wrecked her mother's life. For years she'd wondered why he didn't love her, if she wasn't lovable.

If he hadn't been so stubborn and sent her mother away, he would have known that she wasn't Johnny's child.

Even if she had been, she hadn't done anything wrong. A decent man would have loved his grandchild no matter what.

She rolled her shoulders.

It didn't matter. What was done was done. All she could do was accept it and move on.

Just like she'd had to accept the abuse in the Linder home and what they'd done to innocent victims.

Although acceptance and forgetting were two different things. The sight of the victims' jewelry hanging on Charlene Linder's skeletal bones was forever etched in her mind.

She studied the photograph she'd received today.

Was this a random murder?

Or would there be another?

Shaken, she went to her bedroom to change clothes, but she froze at the sight on her bed.

A Mitzi doll.

No, not just a Mitzi doll.

This one's face was slashed, blood dotting its porcelain features.

Just like the woman's face was slashed in the photograph.

◆ ◆ ◆

Dane showed the picture Josie had received to Lieutenant Ward. "We need to know if any of your people sent this."

Irritation lined the man's face. "You realize that by asking my team, I'm implying that I don't trust them."

"I'm sorry," Dane said. "It'll take time to trace the text, and if someone on the inside did this, we need to know now. Maybe it's some kind of ploy to get money for offering Josie the inside scoop." Hell, he hoped it was. That would be preferable to the killer having sent it. "Maybe he wants to be included in her next book."

Lieutenant Ward called the team together and explained the situation. "I handpicked you for the team, but for the record and to eliminate the possibility that this was an inside leak, it's necessary to check your phones."

The team consisted of three males and one female.

The female showed no reaction. She handed her phone to her boss.

A tall, dark-haired guy with glasses had been snapping pictures with the team's camera. He set it down on the ground at Dane's feet, then removed his cell phone from his pocket and shoved it toward his boss. He definitely was annoyed. "I haven't sent any photographs to the lab, much less anywhere else."

"I'm sorry about this," Lieutenant Ward said. "Under the circumstances it's protocol."

Dane's respect for the lieutenant rose a notch. He appreciated that Ward hadn't shoved him under the bus.

The other two men exchanged irritated looks but complied with Ward's order.

Dane checked their text history while Ward examined the female's phone. "Thanks," he said as he handed it back to her.

She headed back toward the motel room at the end where Dane had smelled bleach. Dane returned the other men's cells to them while the lieutenant scrolled through the cameraman's phone. Satisfied, he returned it and then waited to speak until the team had stepped away.

"I told you it wasn't one of mine," Lieutenant Ward said.

Dane's gut tightened. He'd been afraid of that. That the text had come from the killer. Now the lab had to trace it so they could track down the bastard.

◆ ◆ ◆

Coming back to Graveyard Falls triggered memories of the past in Dr. Silas Grimley's mind, a past that he'd tried to overcome.

The movie that was being filmed in town had attracted many of his masterpieces. He couldn't help but want to see how far they'd come after he'd made them pretty.

Would they become the stars in this film? Would he become famous for his cosmetic work?

Although he didn't want the fame. He understood the pain of being scarred. Of being laughed at and shunned because of his looks.

Very few knew about those scars. Or how he'd gotten them.

Hand trembling, he climbed from his car and walked through the woods. The scent of animals and blood and raw fear filled the air, taking him back to his childhood.

He knelt by the dirt grave where his father's bones lay and traced a finger over the oval stone he'd put there to mark the spot.

Not that he would ever forget any detail about his father—or his life with the mountain man who'd claimed he was one with the birds.

With a fine sculpting tool, Silas had carved the falcon talons on the rock. He wished he could have carved them into his old man's face.

But it was too late for that.

Only one other person in the world knew that his father's bones lay rotting in this ground.

No one else would ever know.

It was *their* secret.

Yes, this dirt hole in the middle of nowhere was a fitting place for a monster.

Silas arranged the tiny bones he'd collected from his last kill on top of the stone, shaping them like the claws of a raptor. He had a collection of bones at home, small trophies he kept to remember the animals they'd come from, and how he had exerted control over them.

Thunder rumbled above, lightning zigzagging across the mountaintops. It had stormed the night he'd been locked inside the cage with the starving birds.

He closed his eyes, rocking himself back and forth, desperate to drown out the hideous screeches. That was impossible.

The birds squawked and flapped their wings, circling him, then diving down to tear at his skin with their piercing sharp talons.

Instinctively, he rubbed his cheek where the ugly marks had once been. Plastic surgery had erased the visible scars, but his fingers brushed pocked and mutilated skin.

Or at least it *felt* that way to him.

The pain that had seared his nerve endings throbbed relentlessly, making his jaw numb. He welcomed the numbness, except then his cheek sagged and his eye twitched. Then he looked less than human.

Like the monster he'd seen in the mirror after the attack.

Another crack of thunder launched him back in time. He'd screamed and cried to be saved. *The click of the lock on the cage echoed in the dark. The flapping of wings followed. Then the screech of the birds as they swooped down for their prey.*

For him.

Needle-like talons tore at his flesh. He fought and batted at the birds, but his feeble attempts only angered them. They wanted carrion, and he was it. Tears and blood mingled. His voice grew hoarse from screaming.

Seconds floated into minutes. The world spun. The darkness sucked him in. He closed his eyes and prayed to die.

Hours later sunlight blinded him as he stirred back to life.

Sticky blood pooled on his fingers and trickled down his hand as he lifted his fingers away.

A pop of lightning striking a nearby tree jarred him back to the present.

The wind swirled dust around him, the stench of a dead animal wafting in the air. In the distance, vultures swarmed and dipped down on a hill.

It was their nature to feast on the dead remains of smaller creatures.

Just as it was man's nature.

He lifted his fingers to his nose and inhaled. The blood was gone, but the scent lingered on his skin.

The blood of man. The blood of animal.

The blood that made him want vengeance.

CHAPTER FOUR

Ellie Pratt was going to hell.

She knew it as sure as she knew that these hills held evil. She hadn't meant to, but she'd been part of that evil a long time ago.

She wasn't proud of it. But she'd do it again if she had to.

Course some folks thought just because she possessed the second sight, the devil had gotten into her. She'd tried to tell them she didn't want to see the awful things that came in her mind. They just appeared out of nowhere.

As a child, she'd been haunted by strange premonitions. She'd seen kids falling on the playground before they actually fell. Had witnessed a kid being beaten by his mama five miles away. She'd even read minds on occasion. One time when a boy had been thinking about bringing his papa's rifle to school. That had been a good thing.

But other times she'd made the mistake of telling other kids about her visions, and their parents had snatched them away from her like she was a monster. The teacher had warned her she'd better keep quiet and stop causing trouble. The preacher had said she was possessed.

Others called her crazy.

Crazy was the only way she knew to be.

The bones in her knees creaked as she took a dip of snuff, tucked it in her lip, and worked it to one side. The rich tobacco taste melted with the juices in her mouth and sent a rush of nicotine through her, calming her agitation.

The brisk wind chilled the air, hinting at another winter storm, although it was high time spring came to these mountains and warmed up the earth. The old people in this place where she lived needed sunshine and flowers, not more snow and the icy sleet that slashed the roof of the nursing home like nails driving into tin.

Shivering, she wrapped her shawl around her shoulders and dropped into the porch swing outside to watch the vultures swarm a hill in the distance.

It might be cold, but she needed to breathe fresh air. This place smelled like medicine and shit. Like people dying.

She wasn't ready for death.

She was here now, and she'd make the best of her time on earth. She glanced toward the hills, but the sharp peaks and ridges were a gray blur. Her eyesight was almost gone, had been failing for a long time.

It happened the day after she'd done the awful deed. Next morning, when she woke up, the world up and turned a murky gray on her.

God's way of punishing her.

She saw the birds in her mind. The predators.

Each sound they made in the distance painted a clear picture of them soaring across the sky, their wings spread, then diving down to snatch up a bite of carrion.

The vultures always reminded her of *him*. *The monster man.*

Oh, she never spoke his name. Had been scared to say it aloud for years.

Doing so might somehow conjure him up from the dead. Or arouse suspicions from the law, and they'd find her and lock her up for what she'd done.

She pressed one hand to her scarred cheek. He'd torn her face up bad when she'd tried to save the boy, then laughed at her as he licked her blood from his fingers.

He was proof the devil lived in these hills.

One day she reckoned she'd be joining him in hell.

Shoot, she'd been living on borrowed time for a decade now. Soon she'd burn in that fiery pit below.

That's what happened to people like her. People who didn't turn the other cheek.

Her vision picked up a flash of light in the distance. Lightning. God's way of reminding her he had the power. The thunder, his way of yelling his wrath.

Then the world became a fuzzy mixture of gray and nothingness again, and she was being swallowed by the storm.

Losing her sight made her hypersensitive to the sounds and smells around her. The wail of the wind. The snapping of limbs breaking off. The crunch of leaves as the animals scampered through the forest. The scent of crackling wood burning in a fire.

The gnashing of teeth as one animal feasted on another's carcass.

The smell of death.

For a brief second, her vision cleared and she saw *him*. He stood in the shadows of a hemlock, his beady eyes watching her. Her heart began to hammer, and her arthritic hands shook. She pressed her fingers to her chest and fought a dizzy spell, certain her reckoning was near.

Slowly the image faded, and the world slipped into a black hole. She welcomed the dark.

His voice whispered her name as if it was floating from his grave. *"You'll pay one day, Ellie. You'll pay."*

Not a vision but a memory. Although sometimes she got the two confused, lost touch between reality and the images that came to her, showing her glimpses of the future. A future that held ugliness that she didn't want to see.

Lord knew she'd tried penance, had gone to church every time the doors were open the past ten years, and made deals left and right for forgiveness. The deal with the devil she'd made before that would come back to haunt her in the end.

A sharp cry rent the air, and she pivoted to determine where it was coming from. Not outside.

Inside the nursing home. The same cry that had filled the hall so many times this week.

Pain-filled and gut-wrenching, like someone being ripped apart on the inside.

She felt that pain, too. She was an empath, her granny said. Sometimes that pain got to be too much.

Ellie gripped the arm of the swing and pushed off the ground with her feet. To distract herself from the woman's anguish, she began to sing an old hymn, "I'll Fly Away." The nurses had told her to leave the woman in that room alone. That she didn't like visitors.

Ellie couldn't stand that haunted sound. The nurses were wrong. That lady didn't want to be alone.

She wanted a friend.

More dark images assaulted Ellie. Memories or a vision of what was to come?

The birds flying at her.

Then another scream. A young woman crying. Blood spurting from her chest. Her eyes wide in shock. Her hand reaching out for help.

Ellie pressed a hand over her heart and fell back into the swing. Who was that young woman?

What did she have to do with the lady crying in her bed down the hall?

"Yes, Mona, I'm fine." Josie wished she hadn't phoned her sister. She didn't want to upset Mona. But she'd been so shaken over finding that doll that she'd needed to hear her voice.

Because that doll meant that the killer had been inside the house. He knew where she lived.

How to get to her.

"Mom is really worried about you, sis," Mona said. "I told her you were strong and could handle being back in Graveyard Falls. How did the press conference go?"

Mona's confidence grounded Josie. Calmed her. "It was fine," Josie said, although after that press conference, the close call in the street, and the doll, she'd considered running.

"Are you sure you're all right? Because if it's too upsetting to stay at your grandfather's house, no one will blame you for leaving. You can stay with me and Cal."

She jutted up her chin. "Thanks, but I'm not slinking away like a coward. I won't allow what happened to change me." Although it had changed her. Made her paranoid. Distrustful.

She was fighting that fear and paranoia with every ounce of her being. She wanted to be whole again.

Her doorbell buzzed, and Josie hurried to the door. "Sorry, someone's here. I have to go."

"Who is it? Don't open the door for just anyone."

The trauma with Billy Linder had obviously made Mona paranoid as well. "Stop fretting. It's not just anyone, it's Agent Hamrick."

Mona's loud sigh echoed over the line. "God, Cal said he was working on a murder investigation in Graveyard Falls. I can't believe it. I bet the people are frantic."

"It is disturbing," Josie admitted.

"Do you know something about it?" Mona asked.

She considered confiding everything to her sister, but that would only worry her.

She'd protect Mona and her baby with her life. That meant she needed to stay away from them for now. She wouldn't call until she was ready to leave Graveyard Falls.

"He's just starting the investigation. I may use it as my next project," she said instead.

Tension thrummed between them. "Please be careful, sis. I just found you. I don't want to lose you."

Josie's heart swelled with tenderness. "Don't worry. I'm fine. I can't wait to hold my nephew."

She said good-bye, then hung up and unlocked the door. Anxiety bunched her shoulders into tight knots as Dane pushed through the door. His gaze skated over her with concern and a sliver of something that looked like anger.

He'd made it clear he didn't want her involved, but the killer had involved her by sending that text.

"I left investigators processing the crime scene, and I want to see that doll, but first let's talk about what happened on the street." Dane lifted her hands and studied the scrapes from where she'd hit the pavement. "You sure you didn't see who pushed you?"

She shook her head. "No, I wish I had. Maybe I imagined it. I was shaken up over that photograph."

A muscle ticked in his jaw. "Or maybe the bastard is toying with you."

A shudder coursed through her. That was exactly what she was afraid of.

Dane gently touched her shoulder. "Dammit, Josie, you need to get out of town."

The protectiveness in his tone made her want to lean into him for comfort.

She stood ramrod still instead. She had to stand on her own.

Dane was here to work a case. Nothing more.

The dead girl's eyes haunted her. She didn't intend to let him push her onto the sidelines.

She would get the story one way or another.

◆ ◆ ◆

Dane clenched his jaw at the sight of the scrapes on Josie's palms. The damn woman could have been killed today.

He had a bad feeling she wouldn't run from trouble. She'd dive right in, just like she had when she'd decided to write the story about the Bride Killer.

Worse, his body hardened when he looked into Josie's sparkling green eyes, and that pissed him off.

He didn't have time for such nonsense.

An awkward moment stretched between them, and then she backed away and led him through the entryway to a den. The house was old and filled with outdated furniture and antiques. It also seemed dark and depressing, as if it had no life to it. There were no family pictures of the sheriff and his daughter, Anna, or of Josie.

After reading Josie's book, he understood the reason.

Finding out Johnny was innocent had helped reunite Josie's mother and Johnny, but it only widened the chasm between the family and Sheriff Buckley.

"Would you like some coffee or a drink?" Josie asked.

"No, thanks." Dane didn't intend to stay long. "Show me the doll."

Josie pushed her tangled hair from her cheek and led the way to her bedroom.

Dane pulled on latex gloves. Anger seeped through him as he examined it. "He carved the doll's face just like he did the woman's."

Josie swallowed. "That's blood, isn't it?"

"Yes. My guess is it belongs to our victim." Dane was unable to keep the disgust from his voice.

Another heartbeat passed.

"It has to be a message of some kind," she finally said.

Dane rubbed his chin. "The broken mirror, and the doll—you think he's saying he killed the girl because she was like the doll. Not real?"

"That sounds feasible," Josie said.

And very perceptive.

Dane gestured to the doll. "Get me a bag to put it in. Maybe he messed up and left a print. We might even be able to trace where he bought it."

"That's going to be hard. Those dolls are available in every store I can think of, and online."

"True. We'll still look into it." He surveyed the room while Josie hurried to the kitchen and returned with a bag.

"How did he get inside the house?" Dane asked. "Was there a window open?"

She wrapped her arms around her waist. He imagined the sense of violation she must be feeling, and gripped the doll to keep from going to her.

"Josie?"

She startled as if she'd been lost in thought—or fear. "He could have come in the laundry room window. That lock is broken."

Damn. "I'll call a crime team to come over and dust for prints. Tomorrow you should get new locks and install a security system."

She clamped her teeth over her lower lip. "Don't worry, I will."

His gaze swept the room. Had the killer touched her personal belongings?

◆ ◆ ◆

Josie pictured a demented killer roaming through her room and her stomach roiled. This house had always felt claustrophobic, but at least Billy Linder hadn't been inside it.

This killer had.

Dane gestured across the room. "Look around, see if anything is missing."

She forced her feet to move. Her files lay on the table, stacked as she'd left them. Her grandfather had nothing valuable in the house, and she had no expensive jewelry. The only thing of value was her computer, but it appeared to be untouched.

She checked the closet, and her clothes were just as she'd hung them. Then she opened her lingerie drawer, and gasped. He'd rifled through her underwear.

The doorbell rang, and Dane strode to the living room to let the crime team in. Footsteps pounded, then Dane reappeared in the door. "They're going to start looking for prints in the living room and around the doors and windows. Is anything missing?"

Her stomach churned as she faced him. "He took a pair of my underwear."

"Dammit, Josie. He's making this personal with you."

"He wants to frighten me," she said, and it was working. She hated that most of all.

"He's not going to get to you." His voice cracked a notch. "I'll drive you to a hotel tonight."

Josie exhaled. "I couldn't find a room if I wanted. All the hotels within a fifty-mile radius are booked with the film people and actors."

The implications of the murder and film came together in her mind. "This woman could be one of the actresses or part of the film crew." A helpless feeling engulfed her. "What if she came to Graveyard Falls to be in the movie and someone killed her to sabotage the film?"

A firm shake of Dane's head indicated he didn't buy her theory. "That's doubtful. Not a strong enough motive for murder."

Josie curled her fingers into her palms and backed away from her dresser drawer. "Maybe so. But if this murder wasn't an isolated event and he's looking to kill again, he has a whole pool of women to choose from now."

◆ ◆ ◆

Dane couldn't argue with Josie about that point. "Let's not get ahead of ourselves. Hopefully this is an isolated murder, and we'll find this killer, and everything can go back to normal."

The skeptical look she shot him indicated she didn't believe him. He let his comment stand, though. He didn't want to stir up panic.

One of the crime techs appeared, and Dane handed him the doll. "Be sure to dust the dresser and bed. The SOB took a piece of Miss DuKane's lingerie."

The crime tech gave a clipped nod. "No problem. We'll be thorough."

Dane gestured toward the living room. "Let's talk. I want to know more about the press conference and what happened afterward."

Fear darkened Josie's face. "You think the killer was there? That he pushed me into the street?"

His expression was grim. "We have to consider every angle."

She rubbed her hands together, then led him back to the living room. Two crime techs were dusting the windowsills and doorways in the den and kitchen while another handled the laundry room.

Josie walked over to the kitchen bar. "Would you like a drink?"

Yeah, he would. But he was on duty. "No, thanks. Go ahead, though."

Josie poured herself a glass of merlot and sank into the couch. He waited, giving her time to settle down.

"Tell me about tonight," he finally said. "Were there a lot of people at the press conference?"

"Yes. About a hundred. A lot of locals, a few reporters, the mayor." She took a sip of wine. "I talked about the book, then answered questions."

"What was the atmosphere like?"

"Just what you'd expect. Some people were supportive, others complained that I was sensationalizing the murders." She traced a finger along the rim of her glass. "I'm not trying to do that. Everyone in town, even ones who didn't lose a loved one, was affected by the Bride Killer murders. Their sense of security, sense of peace, their trust and naiveté are shaken. I hope that high schools will work with their students on bullying and cliques. That it'll open the doors to communication on those topics."

"Linder wasn't bullied, Josie," Dane said, unwilling to excuse the man's violence for any reason. "Those teenage girls didn't deserve to die just because they didn't allow some girl to join their group."

"No, but tolerance and kindness to others need to be taught."

In theory, he agreed with that. Except Betsy's tolerance and kindness had gotten her killed.

"Anyway," Josie continued, "Billy was molested just as Charlene's father sexually abused her. Unfortunately, it's a vicious cycle—the abused becomes the abuser. The child's concept of love is skewed." She sipped her wine again. "Someone should have noticed and done something to help Billy escape so he could have had a chance at a normal life."

He was a detective—he couldn't afford to let sympathy interfere with a homicide investigation. "Forget the do-gooder lecture," he said, his tone more callous than he meant. "Let's just stick to the facts. What happened after you spoke?"

"Some of the people in the crowd made noises about me exploiting them, so I just wanted to get off stage. I turned the program over to the mayor. He was going to introduce the director of the movie, the casting agent, and the producer and answer more questions."

The attitude of the town toward her bothered him. That push into the street might have been a disgruntled local and could have nothing to do with the murder. "Did anyone approach you? Did you see anyone watching you?"

"No. I ducked under the awning of the diner to compose myself while I looked at the text." She toyed with the stem of her glass. "Then I was upset and wanted to get out of there. I walked toward my car. It was across the street. A group was waiting at the crossing, so I tried to blend in."

"Did anyone in that crowd stand out?"

She shook her head no.

Dammit, he wished she'd seen something to help. "Anyone look familiar?"

"No. Well, not at first."

Her hesitation made him sit up straighter. "What does that mean?"

Josie released a weary sigh. "After I fell, it was chaos. The driver who almost hit me was frantic and apologetic. Another man helped me up."

"Who was it?"

"Doyle Yonkers, Candy Yonkers's brother. I saw him at the press conference, too."

The fact that Yonkers was close by during Josie's fall raised more suspicions in Dane's mind.

"For God's sake, Josie, he could have shoved you then rescued you to make himself look like a hero."

If Yonkers was opposed to the movie or thought Josie had glorified the murders, his anger might have pushed him to murder.

♦ ♦ ♦

Dane could be right. Josie sipped her wine in an effort to calm her nerves. Today's episode resurrected the fear she'd worked so hard the past two years to overcome.

"How dangerous do you think Doyle Yonkers is?" she asked.

Dane took a fraction of a second too long to answer. "He doesn't have a record, but he was traumatized by his sister's death. He also was bitter because his girlfriend dumped him when he was admitted for psychiatric care. You should be careful around him. He might break at some point."

"What about the woman who was murdered?" Josie asked. "Do you have an ID on her?"

Dane's jaw tightened. "Not yet."

She accessed the text again. A mental image of Yonkers stabbing the young woman and then leaving her by the trash made her shudder.

Her heart ached for the victim. She couldn't be over twenty-two. She'd had her entire life ahead of her. "I'll do whatever I can to help find this guy."

She leaned back against the sofa, trying to process how a person could do something so vicious to another human.

Dane made a low sound in his throat. "When you sent the photo, I was hoping there might be a clue as to where the unsub killed her. But that photo is from the dump site."

Josie pushed aside her disgust. Logic and getting into the killer's mind would be the way to find this bastard. "You think he killed her somewhere else?"

"Yes. There would have been blood on the ground if he'd killed her by the trash."

Josie studied the picture again. "She looks wrong—her limbs are twisted at an odd angle. He intentionally posed her like that, didn't he?"

Dane nodded. "He scrubbed her clean, too. Wiped off all her makeup. Hopefully the ME can identify what kind of soap he used. That might give us a lead."

Josie wrinkled her brow, her criminology training kicking in. "Why clean her and then leave her by the garbage? Why contort her body like that?"

Dane scrubbed a hand through his hair. "I don't think it's about her being clean. I think he wanted her face as naked as her body."

Josie's chest clenched. "So we could see what was underneath, what she was really like."

"That's my guess. She also had breast implants. He exposed those as well."

A possible profile took shape in Josie's mind. He was probably midtwenties to early thirties, smart and confident on the surface, but underneath he was insecure.

Dane leaned forward, elbows braced on his knees. "There's something else even more disturbing."

She took another sip of wine, trying to wash down the distaste in her mouth. "More disturbing than carving her face?"

"Yes," he said, his tone darkening. "He removed a sliver of bone from her cheek. I think he took it as a souvenir."

She closed her eyes, trying to eliminate that image from her mind. Impossible. It was so vivid it sickened her. "Dear God. What kind of person would take a human bone as a trophy?"

CHAPTER FIVE

Dane studied the fire as Josie paced over to the fireplace. She'd needed time to assimilate his comment about the bone.

The gas logs glowed and sparkled, warming the room and adding a soft glow, a sharp contrast to the gloomy skies outside and the macabre state of the murder victim.

He'd been wrong about there being no family pictures in the room. There was one on the mantel. A snapshot of the former sheriff with a young girl about seven, probably Josie's mother, Anna.

No pictures of Josie, though. And none of Anna as a teenager.

The former sheriff must be a coldhearted bastard to have treated his granddaughter so badly.

The clock on the mantel chimed, and Josie walked back to the sofa, sank into it, and dropped her hands in her lap. "What if it's my fault this girl is dead?" Josie said. "If she's an actress, she wouldn't have been here if not for my book."

Dane shook his head. "Don't go there. You are not to blame for some madman's psychosis."

Josie stared into the flames, her face strained with worry. She looked so small and lost and vulnerable that he wanted to pull her into his arms and console her.

But that would be a mistake.

A young woman's body lay in the morgue, one who needed justice. Her family had to be told. Clues investigated.

A demented killer had to be found and put away.

That's what he did. He didn't get involved on a personal level with anyone. He had to focus on his job.

This was the case he'd been working ten years for. There were differences in the MO, but those crisscross cuts on the victim's chest and the marks below her eyes were too similar to totally rule out that they'd been inflicted by the same killer.

Nothing could distract him from finding out the truth, not even Josie.

◆ ◆ ◆

Josie rubbed her hands up and down her arms, uncomfortable as she watched the CSI team comb through her house.

"We didn't find anything suspicious," the crime scene investigator said. "We collected three sets of prints and will run them through the system."

"Mine, my grandfather's, and my mother's," Josie said. "The killer probably wore gloves."

"Probably, but run the prints anyway," Dane said.

She and Dane escorted the team to the door. The lead investigator, Lieutenant Ward, promised to contact Dane with the results and any forensics they found on the doll. According to Dane, the bureau's analyst, Peyton, was working on tracing the text.

Dane turned back to her as the others drove away. "Do you want me to stay here tonight?"

She did, but she refused to let fear run her out of town. So she pasted on a brave face. "Thanks, but I'm fine. I'll lock up."

Although he had nailed the laundry window shut, someone could still pick a lock. Only if the killer had broken in earlier and wanted to hurt her, he would have stuck around.

Dane's gaze met hers. He was obviously thinking the same thing.

"I have my grandfather's shotgun," Josie said, determined to hide her worry. "Before you ask, yes, I know how to use it. Besides, if the killer wanted me dead, why didn't he just wait around instead of leaving that doll on my bed? He wants my attention, not to kill me."

"You're forgetting about the street incident."

"I haven't forgotten." How could she when her palms still stung from the fall? "I think that was someone in town who's upset about the filming. They just wanted to scare me." At least she prayed it was.

That it wasn't the man who'd killed that woman and carved a piece of bone from her face.

"I hope you're right," Dane said in a gruff voice. "I'll stay and sack out on the couch if you'd feel better."

Oh, yeah, she'd feel better. Except she'd want to beg him to hold her all night, to keep her warm and make her forget about murder and sadistic men who took women's lives. She wanted him to make her feel safe and alive.

That was dangerous in a different way. "I'm really okay, Dane. Just go home and rest."

A flicker of something like heat—or admiration—stirred in his eyes. A second later, his professional mask slid back into place. "Don't worry, Josie. I won't rest until this case is solved."

Her admiration for Dane mounted. Dane might be a loner, but he was dedicated to his job and protecting innocents.

She clutched the edge of the door to keep from reaching for him. "Thanks for coming over."

Dane gave a clipped nod, although his gaze remained on her face. "If you receive any other communication from this killer, call me, no matter what time of day or night."

She tightened her grip on the door. "I will. Where are you staying?"

"At those cabins on the river where Cal stayed." Dane brushed her arm with his fingertips. "Are you sure you'll be all right?"

Josie took a deep breath. "Yes." Although tonight she wished Mona was here. And her mother and Johnny. She could use the family support.

If she admitted the depth of her fears, they'd insist she come to Knoxville. She couldn't do that. She had to see this movie through and find out who'd sent her that picture of a dead woman.

Dane hesitated, one hand on the door. She mustered up a smile. "Go."

His jaw tightened as he walked down the steps to his SUV. He started the engine, and she closed the door and locked it, then poured herself another glass of wine.

Maybe this one would help her sleep tonight without the nightmares.

Last night her dreams had taken her back to that nasty cabin. Billy was forcing her to put on that wedding dress. Forcing her to bathe his mother and cook for her while he used his taxidermy skills to dig out the eyes of a mountain lion he'd killed.

Sometimes she dreamt she was trapped in a room with those animals, and they were attacking her.

She ran a hand through her hair and sighed. How could her nightmares stop with another murderer stalking the women in Graveyard Falls?

Too antsy to sleep, she checked her computer for messages. A note from the casting director said they were going to hold auditions and interviews for various parts in the film starting the next morning. She was invited to attend if she wanted.

Josie set her alarm so she'd have time to shower and make it to the auditions. Maybe meeting the actors and watching the project come to life would distract her from today's horror.

Still, a woman had been murdered in town. With the photograph fresh in her head, she opened a new file on her laptop and began typing notes.

She detailed where the body had been found, who had found her, her state of undress, and the possible profile she and Dane had discussed for the killer.

As they learned more, she would add to the story.

The MO intrigued her. The talon carving on the woman's face, the Mitzi doll, the broken mirror . . . The fact that he'd removed a sliver of bone from the woman's cheek.

They were clues—she and Dane just had to piece them together and figure out what made this killer tick.

Rain began to ping on the roof, the strong winds making it slash against the windowpanes so hard she thought the glass would shatter. She shivered and checked the gas logs, the house echoing with the turmoil of the past. She could almost hear the arguments her mother and grandfather had had. Taste the ugly words and tension in the air.

Josie had missed having a father and craved her grandfather as a substitute, but he'd hated her before she was even born. Now she understood the reason—he'd thought she was Johnny Pike's daughter and that Johnny was a killer.

Even when he'd learned the truth, he hadn't welcomed her into his arms.

Because he was too caught up in his bitterness and his insistence that he was always right.

No wonder her mother had left town and never come back.

The faces of the Thorn Ripper's victims, then the Bride Killer's victims flashed through her head. Both those serial killers had taken pieces of the victims' jewelry as trophies.

This killer was more sadistic. He took a piece of bone.

The MO had the markings of a psychopath who'd enjoyed the kill and would do it again.

She traced a finger over her mother's high school yearbook and smiled, grateful that Johnny had been freed and they'd gotten justice for the girls.

The young woman who'd been left in the trash deserved the same.

Josie would help Dane find it for her.

And nobody would scare her away.

♦ ♦ ♦

Not ready to sleep and at a dead end on the current case until the lab identified the victim, Dane grabbed a burger on the way back to his cabin. He wanted to review the files on his sister's case one more time.

Two women had been gossiping about Josie in the diner, saying she wasn't concerned about the people she hurt with her movie, that she just wanted the money.

That wasn't true. Josie was kindhearted and cared about the victims. Her compassion had been evident in the way she'd portrayed them in her book.

Small towns always intrigued him. People either gathered together and supported one another, or they turned on their own.

He was so annoyed the burger lost its appeal, but he ate it anyway while he spread out his notes.

How many times had he looked at this file hoping to see something new, a detail he'd missed?

He rubbed a hand over his tired eyes.

Hell, it didn't matter if he'd done it a thousand times. He'd do it again. This time he'd look for clues that the unsub in her case and the current one were the same.

Remembering Betsy should be here now—helping kids, *having* kids of her own—made him renew his vow to find the truth.

The date on the file took him back ten years.

He was twenty-one, Betsy nineteen at the time of her death. They'd lived in Knoxville and had lost their father three years before to a heart attack.

Guilt pressed against his heart.

Betsy was just a teenager when he'd died. After that, Dane was supposed to be the man of the house, but he'd been wrapped up in his own anger and grief. Instead of being there for her, he'd searched for love and comfort from any girl who'd crawl into bed with him.

The school counselor had suggested he and Betsy volunteer in the community. Unlike him, his sister had listened. The next three years while she finished high school, she'd worked at a ranch for troubled kids and adolescents.

Ironic that she'd been murdered when she was the good child. It should have been his body in the ground, not kindhearted, selfless Betsy's.

He opened his desk drawer and removed the folder of photographs he'd brought with him.

Different shots of Betsy through the years. A baby photo, a picture of her playing soccer at five, her first fishing trip with their father, Christmases and birthdays, and her first date to homecoming.

His heart ached as he looked at her sweet face—she was funny and freckle-faced with a laugh that had made him smile even when he was in a pissy mood.

While most girls would have been upset over the scar on her forehead she'd gotten in a car accident, she laughed about it, saying if people didn't like her because of a little scar, they weren't worth having as friends.

He'd been so proud of her attitude.

Grief clogged his throat, and he grabbed a beer from the refrigerator. He walked to the back door. The woods behind the cabin rose into the mountains, thick with trees and wildlife.

The howl of a coyote resounded off the sharp ridges, and the wind roared like a mountain lion, the sound eerie as if a warning that danger lurked in the hills.

He swallowed a sip of the cold beer, then returned to the file and forced himself to press on.

His sister had been murdered in Chattanooga on a chilly spring night when a storm was brewing just like tonight.

Earlier that day, she'd phoned to tell him she'd arrived at the campus and planned to tour the school and meet with the director of social work.

According to the detective who'd investigated her murder, she'd kept that appointment. The hours after that were murky. Notations in her pocket calendar indicated that she'd planned to attend a couple of parties.

The police questioned the girls at the first sorority house, but no one had seen her. The second was a big spring blowout at a frat house. With alcohol and possibly other recreational drugs flowing, the attendees hadn't offered much information at all. One or two claimed they'd seen Betsy around eleven o'clock, but they didn't know who she'd left with.

Police suspected that she'd met up with someone on campus at that party and willingly left with him, but there were no witnesses.

They were wrong.

His sister never would have left with a stranger.

Frustration knotted his belly. He was supposed to be looking for comparisons to his current case. The woman in Graveyard Falls hadn't been in a college town or at a sorority party.

Although it was possible she'd been murdered in another city like Knoxville and then dumped here.

Jesus, he needed that ID.

He looked back at Betsy's autopsy report. No narcotics or evidence of roofies in her system.

What would the tox screen reveal on the girl they'd found at the motel?

Dane rubbed a hand over his eyes again.

Ten years since Betsy's death. That in itself was a problem. Even if someone had witnessed something, memories grew foggy with time.

Although occasionally guilt set in, and a witness who'd initially remained quiet came forward to clear his or her conscience.

He prayed that would happen with Betsy's case. He needed a break, dammit.

Determined to tackle it again, he reviewed the other notes. According to interviews with Betsy's friends at school and the director of the ranch where she'd volunteered, she hadn't been dating anyone. She had no ex-boyfriends; no one was angry with her.

Everyone loved her.

Except for the person who'd killed her.

One detective had theorized that Betsy had an affair with a married man, and that perhaps the wife found out and killed her. That suggestion was ludicrous.

Betsy would never sleep with a married man. She was the most morally conscious young girl he'd ever known.

The idea of a stalker had been tossed around, but they'd found no evidence suggesting one. No notes on her calendar, nothing in her mail, no repeated phone calls from the same number that looked suspicious.

Which put him back to where the case had ended—she'd met someone at the party who'd enticed her to leave with him. Or she'd seen someone she knew and trusted.

Someone who'd gotten away with murder.

The MO had to be significant. The unsub who'd killed Betsy took the silver ID bracelet their father had given her.

This killer had taken the woman's clothes, but as far as he knew, no jewelry.

Although he had taken a piece of bone.

If it was the same killer, had he evolved to the point he needed an even more sinister and personal trophy for himself?

◆ ◆ ◆

Dr. Silas Grimley carefully examined his face in the mirror, one finger running over his skin to make sure the imperfections were hidden.

His face was smooth. Skin clear. Eyebrows neatly trimmed. Eyes focused.

Scars invisible to the naked eye.

He was handsome.

His looks wouldn't last. Soon he would be showing signs. Soon he would have to hide his flaws again.

His hand trembled.

God dammit. It wasn't fair. He'd worked too hard to get where he was to have to give up his career. He'd been so driven that he'd vaulted to the top of his profession faster than anyone expected.

Now he was going to lose it all. His weaknesses would be evident, just like the scars he'd once carried.

His patients, the women who admired him, would run.

Cursing the fates, he slammed his fist against the mirror and watched it crack. Blood dotted his hand, but he didn't care.

He walked to the window and looked outside. The rain that had pounded the earth earlier grew lighter, more distant, the moon battling through the clouds to weave a faint stream of light across the sharp cliffs behind the cabins.

Night was setting in Graveyard Falls.

He had places to go.

He slipped a sport coat on over his neat blue button-down shirt, then carefully combed his hair into place.

The reflection staring back at him looked grotesque in the shattered mirror.

A preview of the real Silas? Of what he had once been?

Because once he had been hideous. Unable to bear the cruelty of others, he'd hidden himself from the laughing faces and ugly remarks.

Then one day some selfless soul had saved him. For a little while he'd basked in the light of knowing what it was like to be one of *them*. The beautifuls.

Just like the models and actresses.

Just like that damn doll.

Shoulders tense, he headed outside.

The thick forests and trees shrouded in clouds cast an ominous gray that looked like a heavy fog across the land.

Yet in the midst of the miles of wilderness and sharp ridges, great beauty abounded. Natural beauty.

Not like the plastics who had flocked to town. Young women with their heavy makeup, implants, thousand-dollar skin treatments, and expensive wardrobes, all dying to be in front of the camera.

Products of his work. *He* made them pretty.

I can make you anything you want to be, he told them.

And he did.

A dark chuckle rumbled from his chest.

Of course, he was a man and he lusted after those beautiful women. What man's body didn't harden at the sight of sparkly sequined dresses tightly wound around luscious hips? At deep cleavage inviting a man to touch, plump breasts overflowing skimpy tops? Short skirts and crotchless panties showcasing endlessly long legs?

What man wouldn't want eye candy on his arm and his cock between a pair of perfect thighs?

He would have that tonight.

Yes, he'd bury himself into a woman's sweet center and live while he could.

Then he'd go back and clean the bones he'd just collected and add them to his wall.

CHAPTER SIX

Dane's phone was ringing as he finished dressing the next morning. He quickly connected the call. "Agent Hamrick speaking."

"It's Dr. Wheeland. I have an ID on your victim."

"Her name?"

"Charity Snow. She was twenty-two years old, born and raised in West Tennessee. No family except for her younger sister, Bailey. The sisters left home for LA to be actresses."

"Current address?"

"I don't have one. But Peyton did some digging. The girls were both in Graveyard Falls to try out for parts in that movie."

Dane was glad to hear Peyton was on the case. She was a top-notch analyst.

"Where were they staying?"

"The Falls Inn."

"Did you notify the sheriff yet?" Dane asked.

"No, you're my first call."

Good. "I'll fill him in, find the sister, and make the notification." Maybe Bailey Snow knew where her sister was the night before and had some clue as to who'd killed her. "Anything else?"

"According to the preliminary background check, she has no police record."

"How about the cleaner?"

"Definitely a strong antiseptic soap," Dr. Wheeland answered. "Peyton is trying to trace the origin now."

"How about drugs or alcohol in her system?"

"Traces of red wine but not enough so she was drunk. But this is the interesting part—we found evidence of pancuronium bromide in her system." The ME muttered a sound of disgust. "It's an injectable neuromuscular blocking drug that causes paralysis. The victim can't move but is aware of what's going on."

Dane frowned. "So she felt the pain?"

"Yes."

"Is that something they would have tested for ten years ago?"

"If it was present, a good ME would have found it," Dr. Wheeland said. "Why?"

"I'm thinking of a past case." Had the ME working Betsy's murder missed something? "How would someone get access to that drug?" Dane asked.

"It wouldn't be easy, but it's not impossible," Dr. Wheeland said. "It's federally regulated and used by physicians, surgeons, hospitals, clinicians, and researchers."

Dane assimilated that information. "That means our killer might work in the medical field."

"True. Or he knows someone who does, or he stole it from a hospital or research facility."

Dammit, that opened up a field of suspects. He could have Peyton check medical facilities nearby to see if any had gone missing. "What else can you tell me?"

"Her last meal was barbecue."

Dane liked the man's attention to detail. "Probably had that at the party. Was she raped?"

"She did have sex not long before her death," Dr. Wheeland said, "although there is no bruising or suggestion that she was forced."

"So it could have been consensual. A boyfriend, then things went wrong?" Dane rubbed the back of his neck. "Or she parted with her lover, then she either met up with the killer or he somehow took her."

"That's possible."

Dane shifted, his head throbbing as he considered all angles. "If it was a boyfriend and he was this violent, he might have acted out with a former girlfriend."

"Peyton is already looking into that angle," Dr. Wheeland said.

"What about DNA?"

"Afraid we didn't find any. The man must have worn a condom."

Dane mentally reviewed the facts. The killer had scrubbed her clean, so if there had been any DNA, he'd destroyed it.

Which meant this kill was planned, premeditated, and the killer was intelligent.

"Okay, let me know if anything else turns up. Maybe the sister can shed some light on what the victim was doing the night she died. If there is a boyfriend and he's our perp, this case could be as simple as tracking him down."

Although that would mean that this case wasn't connected to his sister's. That once more he'd gotten his hopes up for nothing.

That he'd be back to square one, waiting on another call, praying for another lead.

Trying to convince his mother to hang on when he'd reached a dead end again.

◆ ◆ ◆

Josie dabbed powder beneath her eyes to cover the dark circles. Being back in Graveyard Falls threatened to undo all the progress therapy and time had accomplished the past two years. Staying in her grandfather's house hadn't made it any easier either. Her nightmares were back, robbing her of precious sleep.

But she was determined not to let Billy Linder keep her from living. That would mean he still had power over her.

Josie didn't intend to let any man have power over her—not ever again.

She added a little lip gloss, brushed her hair but left it waving around her shoulders, then dressed in a loose skirt, sweater, and boots.

She had no idea what to expect today. The director had explained that the film would use locals for extras, and that they were also looking for Southern talent to portray the townspeople and victims.

He wanted to keep the authentic Southern scenery and character of the town, so they planned to film some scenes on location. Others would be filmed on a set later and edited in.

Josie had suffered from a nervous stomach since the attack, but she managed to nibble on a bagel, then finished her coffee. She stuffed a notepad in her shoulder bag, then hurried out to her Jetta.

Morning sun glinted off the rain-drenched grass, shimmering off the sharp ridges of the mountains. She drove to the community center, where the first round of auditions was scheduled.

Online information had been available for a month, and the casting director had prescreened for several parts, then notified the individuals selected for additional readings.

Traffic was usually light in the mornings in the small town, but today cars jammed the square, and people hoping to be extras had formed a line outside the community center

A small group of locals were clustered to one side with signs declaring that the movie people should go home. She shuddered at one that personally targeted her. She didn't recognize the person holding the sign, but the message was clear.

"Josie DuKane, you don't belong here."

Gusty winds hurled leaves and twigs across the parking lot as she parked, the tree branches swaying beneath the weight of the wind.

Nervous over the animosity in town and the death of another woman, she scanned the area as she climbed out.

Leaves rustled from the right, and she jerked her head around, the familiar tightening of her chest forcing her to breathe deeply to stem another panic attack. Two men in suits walked briskly toward the coffee shop on the corner. A car door slammed, and a group of teenagers jumped out, giggling and talking as they rushed toward the rec center. Then another movement caught her eyes.

A young man in a hoodie darting into the bushes.

Perspiration broke out on her brow. Had the guy in the hoodie been watching her?

A woman strode toward her, angry. "Don't let them talk bad about our daughters. That Charlene girl was strange or they would have been nice to her," Sara Levinson said.

A man, Mr. Burgess, gripped a picture of his daughter Brittany, the third Thorn Ripper victim, in his hands. "You have no idea what it's like to lose a child," he said in a tortured voice.

Josie pressed her hand to her chest, struggling to breathe. "I'm so sorry, I really am. I don't mean to hurt anyone by being here."

Her voice cracked, her emotions on her sleeve as she raced past them toward the community center.

She had the uneasy sense that the man who'd sent her that photograph was somewhere nearby.

She hurried to the safety of the trees near the front and leaned against one. Her breathing was rasping out now, uneven pants that angered her because she wanted to be done with the damn panic attacks.

She balled her hands into fists. She would not give in to that fear.

Her therapist's words echoed in her head.

Take deep, even breaths, focus on your surroundings. The building, the sun shining, the leaves fluttering down, the happy faces of the young girls lining up outside. You're safe. You're alive.

Billy Linder is locked away.

Another voice, her own, intruded.

There's another Billy Linder out there. One who carved a bone from his victim's cheek. One who sent you a picture.

She bit down on her lip so hard she tasted blood. Yes, a killer was out there. Dane would find him.

Until then, she'd be cautious. She needed to stay strong and alert, to put the sicko away.

She straightened her clothing, dabbing away the sweat on her neck. She would do it, too.

Determined, she squared her shoulders and walked up the steps to the front door of the rec center. As soon as she stepped inside, excited whispers and voices echoed around her.

Despite some of the town's animosity about the film, the building was packed with actor wannabes and the film crew and staff.

Two women in suits walked through the crowd, directing people where to go.

Lines were alphabetized and marked for various roles in an attempt to create order. Teenagers clustered together, giggling and whispering as they waited for directions.

A sign in the front pointed toward the director's meeting room. She headed toward it.

Five men and two women had gathered inside and were mingling and getting coffee. The producer, Bruce Landon, tapped his spoon on his coffee cup and asked everyone to take seats around a long conference table. A second later, introductions were made.

Anthony Garry—the lead cameraman; bushy hair and brows, deep-set eyes. Gil Baines—makeup artist; metrosexual, impeccably dressed, manicured nails, hair short and styled. Ulysses Vega—setting and scenery; a rugged, scruffy guy who didn't look as if he belonged in LA.

Olive Turnstyle—the casting director; tall, slightly big-boned, shiny blouse, long manicured nails a startling purple. Emma Leadstone—costume and clothing; red leather jacket and fedora.

Eddie Easton—photographer who worked with the actresses; sharp dresser, thirties, dark hair, a playboy type.

Landon introduced Josie, and she briefly relayed how much she appreciated the attention they were giving to this true story.

The cameraman seemed to be watching her as if he were dissecting her for his camera lens. "You did a good job of describing the town and the people in it. I hope we can find the right faces to portray each of the victims."

"Have you thought about playing yourself in the film?" the casting director asked.

Josie barely suppressed a shudder. "No. I don't want to be in it. Besides, I'm not very photogenic."

"I beg to differ," Easton said with a challenging look. "Makeup and lighting are like special effects. Playing yourself would add an authenticity to the project."

Landon cleared his throat. "Miss DuKane can think about it. Meanwhile, we have a busy day. We can use locals for extras in the bar and restaurant scenes. We also don't need name actresses for the victims since they actually won't be on screen much, but we do want this to look professional." He turned to the casting director. "Olive?"

Olive tapped her notepad. "I've narrowed down the number of actors vying for the parts of Johnny Pike and federal agent Cal Coulter. Also, the former Sheriff Buckley." She directed a smile at Josie. "Maybe you could sit in on some auditions. I'm sure you'd be able to help steer us toward actors who fit the parts."

"Of course," Josie agreed.

Landon angled himself toward the man in charge of setting and scene locations. "Scout out locations for the falls scenes. Let's get those nailed down."

A commotion broke out, voices and shouting erupted from the hallway, and Landon jumped up and rushed to the door. Josie followed and peeked through the doorway to the packed main room.

"Has anyone seen my sister, Charity?" a woman shouted into the crowd. "Please tell me if you have. I'm worried sick," she cried. "I'm afraid something bad happened to her."

Josie dug her nails into the palms of her hands. Was the missing sister their murder victim?

◆ ◆ ◆

Dane climbed the steps to the Falls Inn. As soon as he entered, the scent of peach pie wafted toward him.

Nausea gripped his stomach. That damn scent used to make him smile. His mother baked peach pies on Sundays.

She'd been cutting up peaches the night the police car had rolled into the drive and destroyed their lives.

He hadn't been able to eat it since.

He stepped back on the porch for some air, counted to ten, then pivoted and entered again, this time blocking out the odor.

The owner, Cynthia Humphries, greeted him with a smile. She was middle-aged, dressed in a cream-colored sweater and black slacks.

He sensed she was a down-home country girl beneath the surface, but she seemed nervous as she ran around fussing over the table setting as if she was putting on a show for her guests, most of whom were here for auditions.

The production company had housed the technical teams, cameramen, lighting, sound technicians, and other assorted staff at the lodge by the river.

The producer and a few actors reserved the individual cabins, which had been recently renovated.

"Ms. Humphries, do you have a guest named Charity Snow registered here?"

She flattened an errant strand of hair back into her neat bob and glanced at the guest registry. "Yes, she and her sister, Bailey, are staying in room twenty-two."

A knot pinched his belly. He was about to destroy the sister's world. "Is Bailey here now?"

A frown pulled her eyebrows together. "I don't think so. Most of the young women went over first thing this morning for the auditions." She drummed her nails on the desk. "Come to think of it, she seemed upset. She said her sister didn't come back last night and wanted to know if I'd seen her."

He tried to temper his voice so as not to alarm her. "Have you?"

The innkeeper shook her head. "No. It's been so hectic around here that she could have slipped in and out without me knowing. This place has been crazy. There's a reporter hanging out interviewing all the young girls." She leaned over the desk. "He's been asking them some disturbing questions."

Cynthia seemed to enjoy the town gossip. "Like what?"

"Like why they want to play a dead girl. Who are they beneath their makeup?" Cynthia lowered her voice, her eyes darting around as if disturbed by the questions. "Did they do any research into the Thorn Ripper or Bride Killer before they came to town?"

Probably not odd questions for a reporter. If this man was cozying up to the girls, he might have information that could help Dane's case.

He offered the woman a conciliatory smile. "Who is this reporter?"

"His name is Corbin Michaels. He's not bad looking, although he doesn't quite make eye contact." She removed a business card from the drawer and showed it to him. "Then again, he didn't pay me much attention. He's interested in these young girls, not a middle-aged woman."

A smile teased his mouth. Some females were so sensitive about their age. "I'm sure he simply wants to make a name for himself," Dane said. Which meant he'd probably be questioning Josie, if he hadn't already interviewed her.

Although surely Josie would have mentioned it if he had.

He handed the card back to her. "I'd like to look in the Snow women's room, if you don't mind."

Her eyes widened. "What for? Is something wrong, Agent Hamrick?"

He gritted his teeth. "Ma'am, I'm not at liberty to say just yet, but I really need to find Bailey."

"Then go to the community center," the woman said. "Bailey's probably there. I heard her say she'd do anything to get a part in this movie."

Dane's gut tightened at her statement. Anything?

If the parts had already been decided or two girls were competing for the same role, one of them might have killed Charity to take her spot. But as far as he knew, none of the parts had been cast.

Besides, the MO was too brutal to fit that scenario.

"I'll go there next, but I still want to look in the girls' room."

"All right." Ms. Humphries grabbed a key from the rack on the wall and slid it toward him. "Just bring it back when you're done. If I'm not here, hang it on the hook."

Dane shook his head in disgust. So much for security. Anyone could plainly see the keys and room numbers, snatch a key, and slip into another guest's room.

"You really should do something to protect your guests' privacy," Dane said.

She massaged her temple with two fingers, irritation creating lines around her eyes. "I know, you're right. Normally we're not that busy, and it's not an issue. Now . . ." She gestured around the breakfast dining room, which needed to be cleaned. "I can't keep up."

He took the key, then jogged up the steps to the second floor. The house was quiet throughout, confirming that the innkeeper was right, that all of the guests were at the community center.

First he unlocked the door and stepped inside. The inn was decorated with homemade quilts, stenciling, and themed rooms. A wallpaper border of magnolias accented the green color of the walls.

Two suitcases sat open on the luggage stands, clothes and shoes overflowing. Makeup, hair products, and other female paraphernalia littered the bathroom vanity.

No cell phone or laptop in sight, though.

A photo of two young women hugging in front of a "Welcome to Graveyard Falls" sign was tacked onto the bulletin board above one bed, as if the girls had stopped on the way into town to memorialize their trip to stardom. One he recognized as the victim. The other had to be her sister. They looked enough alike to be twins.

The girls were smiling and holding a sign that said, "Hollywood, here we come."

Dane's stomach clenched. Unfortunately, this trip had led to the end of the victim's dreams just as Betsy's trip to that college had ended hers.

He quickly inventoried the closet and dresser drawers but found no notepads, calendars, or any information about either girl. They'd obviously packed with their goal in mind and only brought along the basics.

Frustrated, he locked the door and descended the steps. The innkeeper and a teenager were clearing the breakfast dishes from the dining table. He hung the key on the board and hurried to his SUV.

On the way to the community center, he phoned the sheriff and asked him to meet him. He needed help canvassing the film crew and actors.

The drive to the community center was short, but it took him ten minutes to park and weave through the throng of people gathered outside.

A young man with dark hair combed stylishly back from his forehead was talking to several of the young women, using a recorder to tape their comments.

That must be the reporter the innkeeper was talking about. Corbin Michaels.

A sob resounded through the air, and a young blonde rushed from person to person, asking questions.

Bailey.

"Have you seen my sister?" She shoved a photograph in front of a group of young ladies. "Do you know where she is?"

Josie walked toward Dane her face strained with worry as if she'd figured out the woman's identity. He paused for a second, dread balling in his gut.

He was about to make the woman's worst fear a reality.

CHAPTER SEVEN

Josie ached for Bailey Snow. Bailey's panic was a palpable force as she searched the crowd for her sister. Her eyes looked puffy and red rimmed from lack of sleep. The poor girl had probably been awake all night worrying about Charity.

"Miss Snow?" Dane said in a low voice as he approached her.

Bailey halted, her face stricken. "Yes?"

Dane flashed his badge and identified himself. "Let's go somewhere a little quieter so we can talk."

Bailey's face drained of color as if she anticipated bad news. Dane gripped her elbow for support, his expression pained. Josie gave him a sympathetic look and walked with them. This girl might need a female shoulder to cry on.

"There's a lounge down the hall," Josie said. "It'll be more private."

She half expected Dane to balk at her intrusion, but he gave her a grateful look as if he dreaded the upcoming conversation.

Bailey's eyes crinkled with recognition. "Wait, I know you. You're the author of the book they're basing the movie on."

"Yes, I'm Josie. Please, Bailey, let's just go with Agent Hamrick. It's important."

Dane nodded his thanks, and the two of them silently escorted Bailey into the lounge. A seating area occupied the first room with a separate door leading to the lavatories.

As soon as they made it inside, Bailey spun toward Dane. "What's wrong? You know where Charity is, don't you?"

Dane reached out a hand to calm her, but she batted it away. "Just tell me, for God's sake. Where's my sister?" Fear made her voice warble. "Is she hurt? In the hospital?"

Josie swallowed back tears. The pain was only beginning for Bailey. She would go through the stages of grief, at the same time needing answers and justice.

"I'm sorry, Miss Snow," Dane said in a low voice, "but your sister is dead."

A choked sob erupted from somewhere deep inside Bailey that spilled into the room like a thunderous roar. Dane squared his shoulders, obviously steeling himself against the woman's anguish.

Josie wasn't so good at containing her emotions. Tears burned her eyes. "I'm sorry, Bailey. So sorry."

"She can't be gone," Bailey cried. "We just got here three days ago. It was her dream to be a star. She thought getting a part in this movie would be her big break."

Bailey's body shook on a sob, and Josie grabbed tissues from a box on the vanity and eased them into the girl's hand.

Dane rested his elbows on his knees and waited, allowing her time to purge her emotions. Josie rubbed Bailey's back, soothing her with low words.

"Tell me what happened," Bailey said brokenly.

Dane and Josie exchanged concerned looks, and then Dane cleared his throat. "I'm sorry, Bailey, but your sister was murdered."

For a long, tense moment, silence fell. Bailey simply stared at Dane, then at her hands, then at Josie, a dozen questions flitting in her tear-swollen eyes.

Compassion filled Dane. No matter what platitudes he offered, it wouldn't assuage her pain. "Is there anyone I can call for you? Family? A friend?"

Bailey shook her head. "Charity and I were pretty much on our own."

An awkward silence followed. He didn't want to pry, but he wanted to help this girl. "Her body is at the morgue. If you want to go, we'll take you to see her. Otherwise, we'll contact you when she's ready to be released."

"What happened?" Bailey asked in a raw whisper. "Who killed her? Did she suffer?"

Dane inhaled deeply. "She was stabbed. We don't know who did it yet, but I promise to find out."

The girlish face aged ten years as reality set in. Violent crimes had a way of changing people. Bailey would never again be the naïve, optimistic girl who'd come to Graveyard Falls chasing her dreams.

"If it's any consolation," Dane added, "she died quickly."

Except the monster who'd taken her life had carved those claw marks into her cheek and stripped a piece of bone from her face before he'd killed her.

She'd felt that and the terror that accompanied it.

Bailey pushed a strand of hair behind her ear, swiping at her tears. "I was so afraid when she didn't come back to the inn. I went out with some of the other girls and got in late myself, so I just assumed she hooked up with someone."

"This is not your fault," Josie assured her.

"Yes it is," Bailey cried. "We should have stayed together."

Dane squeezed the young woman's arm in sympathy. He understood how guilt could eat at you. "Don't blame yourself. Just tell me where Charity went."

Bailey wiped at her eyes. "Some of the actors threw a big party at those cabins on the river."

Dane considered that information. A party with alcohol and possibly drugs would be the perfect opportunity for a predator to strike without being noticed. The same thing had happened to Betsy. "That's a place to start. When was the last time you saw her?"

Her lower lip quivered. "Before she left. She was fussing with her makeup, doing her hair. She was so excited."

"Do you remember what she was wearing?" Dane asked.

Bailey frowned. "A red sequined top and black leather pants."

Except she'd been found naked.

Dane withheld that detail. Once he closed in on a suspect, he'd use it if needed during the interrogation.

Dane softened his tone. "Bailey, I know this is difficult, but bear with me. Did Charity have a boyfriend?"

Bailey twisted the tissue in her hands into a knot. "No. Not really. At least not in the last year."

"What about before? Did she have a bad breakup with someone who might have followed her to town?"

"No." She pressed her hand to her chest as if it hurt. "Listen, we're not like these big-time girls who live in LA and have tons of guys hitting on us. We're from West Tennessee, simple country girls." She hesitated, her voice cracking. "Charity wanted to fit in."

He let the silence stand for a second, but she didn't elaborate. Instead she shifted and looked away as if she was embarrassed. Or was she hiding something? "Is that the reason she had the breast implants?" he asked. "So she could fit in?"

Bailey's eyes darted to his in surprise. "It's not like she was vain, but it's hard out there, competitive."

"I'm not judging," he said quickly. "I'm just trying to be thorough. Sometimes the smallest details can help us find the killer."

"She thought having implants enhanced her looks so she'd land more parts." She glanced down at her own flat chest. "She tried to talk me into it, but I was too chicken. I hate needles."

Dane gave her an understanding smile. "So, no boyfriend. Was she going to the party with anyone in particular?"

Bailey nodded. "Yes. Eddie Easton, the photographer who took our headshots to submit for the casting call."

Dane gestured for her to continue. "Tell me about him."

"We knew him from before," Bailey said. "He came to our hometown and set up at the local mall, said he was looking for the next top model. He really liked Charity. He said she was a natural beauty, that she reminded him of his first girlfriend."

Interesting. "Do you have a photo of Charity that you can text me?"

Bailey's hand shook as she removed her phone from her pocket and accessed her photographs. Dane scrolled through the shots, then forwarded a couple to his phone and then to the sheriff to use for questioning.

"Did your sister call you the night she was killed, maybe from someone else's phone?"

"No, I'm sorry." Bailey sniffled. "I wish she had . . . maybe I could have saved her."

"This is not your fault," Josie interjected again. "She wouldn't want you to blame yourself, Bailey."

Bailey nodded, although she didn't look convinced.

Determined to solve this case as quickly as possible, he forced himself to focus.

If Charity didn't have an ex, then the killer was either someone she'd just met, an acquaintance through the film business . . .

Or a stranger preying on the women who'd come to town.

This photographer definitely had the means to lure women to him. He'd met some of the actors before, so they felt comfortable with him. Then he'd set up a studio right in the middle of the community center to make it easy for his clients. He'd even insinuated himself into the film crew.

That's where he would start.

Easton had the perfect setup. He'd arranged a studio to meet women under the guise of creating professional headshots for wannabe actresses.

Charity had known Easton and trusted him, so she would have willingly gone with him.

Perhaps he wanted to take their relationship to a different level, and she turned him down, causing him to snap.

◆ ◆ ◆

Josie's heart ached for Charity's sister. She was all alone in the world.

"Bailey, did your sister have a computer?" Dane asked.

Bailey twined her fingers together. "We shared a laptop. It's in the trunk of my car. I didn't want to leave it at the inn."

"I need to look at it," Dane said.

"What does her computer have to do with anything?" Bailey asked.

"Maybe nothing," Dane answered. "It's procedure. Charity might have met or communicated with someone online who might have information about her murder."

Bailey ran a shaky hand over her skirt. "You want me to get it now?"

"I'll walk you outside when you're ready." Dane hesitated. "What about her cell phone? I assume she had one."

Bailey looked confused. "Yes, didn't she have it with her?"

Dane shook his head, but he didn't elaborate.

Relief flooded Josie. There was no reason to tell Bailey that her sister was found naked by the trash. At least not yet.

Although if there was a trial, that information would be divulged.

"We didn't find a purse or phone with her," Dane said. "If you'll give me her number, I'll see if we can locate it."

Josie patted Bailey's arm to console her. Finding that phone might lead them to the actual murder scene, and hopefully to more clues to the killer.

Bailey jotted down the phone number, and Dane texted it to the lab to see if they could trace it. He also texted Peyton and asked her to run a background check on the photographer Eddie Easton.

Sheriff Kimball strode toward them, and Dane quickly introduced Bailey.

"I'm sorry about your sister, Miss Snow," the sheriff said sympathetically. "We'll do everything we can to find her killer."

"She was all the family I had," Bailey said, her voice cracking again.

Josie wrapped her arm around Bailey, and Sheriff Kimball shifted on the balls of his feet, looking uncomfortable. "Can we talk for a minute?" Kimball asked Dane.

"Sure."

"I'll go with her to retrieve the computer," Josie offered.

Dane didn't argue, so Josie guided Bailey outside, although she kept her eyes peeled for trouble.

Killers sometimes insinuated themselves in murder investigations or stuck close by to watch the police chase leads.

Josie's pulse jumped as she glanced around.

Sometimes they even hung around to watch their victims' families suffer. Was Charity's killer here watching Bailey cry over her sister's loss, taking pleasure in her pain?

♦ ♦ ♦

Dane's protective instincts urged him to follow Josie and Bailey outside. But time was of the essence, and he needed to speak to the sheriff.

Cautious though, he watched through the doorway as they crossed the parking lot in case the killer was lurking around.

"No chance the sister did it?" Sheriff Kimball asked.

Dane shook his head no. "She was the only family Bailey had left. Besides, they seemed tight. She's pretty distraught."

Kimball jammed his hands in his pockets, sympathy on his face. "Was there a boyfriend?"

"No." Dane's pulse hammered. "I need to check out the photographer, Eddie Easton, who took headshots for both girls."

Kimball perked up. "I heard Easton's name, too. One of the women I talked with said she saw Charity at a barbecue with him."

So the sheriff was on his toes. Maybe he would be more helpful than Dane had first thought. He gestured toward the community room. "Take your deputy and canvass everyone here. Maybe we'll get a break and someone saw something the night Charity died."

Meanwhile, he'd track down Easton. If Easton was a predator of young women, this film had given him a perfect hunting ground.

Dane's thoughts turned back to his sister's case, and hope surfaced. Easton could have pulled the same kind of stunt at the college—played photographer to lure women to trust him. Maybe he'd tried it with Betsy and it hadn't worked.

Dane would get the truth out of him one way or another. If Easton had killed Betsy, he would make the bastard suffer.

◆ ◆ ◆

He stood at the edge of the main community room and watched the ripple effect as the local sheriff wove through the lines of young women and men who'd gathered, vying for a part in this local murder mystery about to be filmed.

Laughter bubbled in his throat. Little did they know that they were mired in a real-life murder mystery of their own.

The women were all fakes. Gorgeous girls on the outside with smiling faces, gleaming white-capped teeth, Botox, implants, and whatever other plastic surgery it took to mold them into a pretty face.

Who would play the next victim in this game?

Soft gasps of shock and whispers floated from one person to the next as that local sheriff and his deputy questioned the actors. Eyes that had been laughing a minute ago now peered at the others in the room with guarded expressions and suspicion.

It would take forever for the sheriff and the Feds to question everyone.

Josie DuKane walked back inside with that pretty blonde, Charity's sister. He didn't care about Bailey.

He had his eyes on Josie.

In spite of the attention she'd garnered from the true crime book she'd written, she was humble.

With those sparkling green eyes, Josie was attractive, too. Not beautiful like the models and actresses or the high-class women who paid to perfect their faces to magazine quality.

Pretty in a natural way. She mesmerized him because she was real, not superficial. She was also smart and used her brain, not just her looks, to get ahead in life.

Yes, Josie was the perfect one to tell his story.

The others, though—they were simply pretty faces waiting to be carved by his hands.

Pretty faces that would look even more beautiful in death.

He lifted his phone and smiled at the photograph he'd taken of the woman, then traced his finger over her face. His pulse pounded as he studied the claw marks. So fitting that she be marked by claws when she'd tried to sink hers into men to get what she wanted.

Josie turned and glanced across the room as if she sensed someone was watching her.

She was looking for him.

He smiled, blending into the shadows.

"This is just the beginning of our friendship and our fun in Graveyard Falls, Josie," he murmured. *Just the beginning.*

CHAPTER EIGHT

Josie stayed close to Bailey as they left the steps of the community center and headed across the quadrangle.

After the Bride Killer had been caught, the town had built the center hoping to create a more positive spirit in the town and bring people closer together as they struggled through their grief.

The center had been designed for a variety of community events with special recreational areas for children and teens, along with rooms inside for classes, arts and crafts, and an auditorium with a stage for community theater.

"I can't believe this," Bailey said in a shaky voice. "What am I going to do without Charity?"

Josie squeezed her arm. "You'll grieve, Bailey, but you have to go on for your sister's sake."

Bailey's face crumpled. "I don't know if I can."

Josie drew Bailey into a hug. "Yes, you can. I understand that you're hurting, and I'm so sorry about your sister. It might not be a bad idea to leave town."

After all, who knew if this killer would strike again?

She stroked Bailey's hair. "Don't give up on your dreams. Charity wouldn't want that."

Bailey nodded against her, although she was trembling when she pulled away.

For a brief second, she considered offering Bailey a place to stay with her, but a small picket line at the corner of the street near the parking lot made her rethink the suggestion. Several individuals waved signs protesting the filming of the movie as they chanted for the outsiders to leave the town alone.

With sentiment against her, her close call in the street, and the fact that the killer had sent her a photo of Charity, having Bailey stay with her might endanger the young woman.

Bailey sighed wearily, and they finished crossing the quadrangle, then the parking lot, until they reached a beat-up VW Beetle. Bailey unlocked the trunk, retrieved a computer bag, and threw it over her shoulder.

"What do you think that agent will find on here?" Bailey asked.

"I don't know," Josie said. "Maybe a clue as to whom your sister might have met up with at that party. Someone other than the photographer."

Bailey nodded. "He has to find the bastard who killed her."

"He will," Josie said with conviction.

Bailey leaned against her car. "I can't go back in there today. I need to be alone."

"I understand." Josie reached for the bag. "I'll give this to Agent Hamrick." She brushed Bailey's sandy blonde hair over her shoulders. Then she slipped a business card from her pocket and slid it into Bailey's hand. "Call me if you need anything, Bailey. Even if it's just to talk."

Bailey nodded, although fresh tears filled her eyes. She swiped at them, then crawled in the driver's seat and started the engine. Josie's heart lurched to her throat as Bailey drove away.

Maybe she should have told Bailey about receiving that picture from the killer. But she didn't want to spook the young girl.

Still, the killer knew her, had chosen her for a reason.

That worried her. She'd barely survived one maniac. She didn't know if she could survive if another one came after her.

The hair on the back of her neck prickled, and she scanned the parking lot and quadrangle.

Was the killer here? Was he watching her?

Small clusters of actors gathered across the lawn, and others were scattered on the steps. Josie shivered as a gust of wind ruffled her hair, and then she hurried toward the building.

Before she reached the steps, a man's voice called her name. She spun around and gasped.

The man in front of her looked exactly like the man who haunted her nightmares—Billy Linder.

◆ ◆ ◆

Dane passed a line of teenagers as he headed toward Easton's makeshift studio. The man had contracted to do headshots for new actresses and also still shots for promotional purposes for the film.

If he was a parent, Dane wouldn't want his daughter to play the role of one of the teens in this film, especially since three of them had been pushed to death off a cliff.

As he walked down the hall, Dane noticed several rooms were marked for auditions, and voices echoed from inside. A room at the end of the hall bore a sign for Easton's Photography. Three young women waited outside the door. Hoping they had answers, he flashed his ID along with a photo of Charity and asked if they knew the woman.

"I've seen her around but haven't talked to her," one girl said.

"Same here," another girl added.

The third girl brushed on lip gloss. "Why, did she get one of the parts?"

Dane shook his head. "No, I'm afraid she was killed after the barbecue. Did anyone see her or talk to her that day?"

Mortification darkened their smiles, but they shook their heads no.

"What happened?" one girl asked.

"She was stabbed to death," Dane said, not bothering to sugarcoat it.

Eyes widened, and shocked gasps followed.

A brunette in the group glanced nervously around the hallway. "Do you think whoever killed her is here?"

"I don't know." Dane hated the fear rippling between the women. Unfortunately, that couldn't be helped. "That's what I'm trying to find out. Were any of you at the barbecue?"

Sheepish, wary looks passed between the group.

"Listen, I don't care what any of you do in your personal life," Dane said, although he hoped to hell they were being careful and traveling in pairs. If only Betsy had stayed with a friend, she might still be alive. "All I want to know is if you saw Charity Snow at the party, and who she was with."

The brunette leaned close to him. "Okay, I did go, but I don't remember her. I got a little too drunk and passed out in one of the bedrooms."

The big brother/detective in him fought a chastising lecture about the dangers of alcohol and parties. Too many ended in sexual assault.

He gestured toward the other two girls. "How about either of you?"

The athletic one of the group shook her head. "I didn't go. I went for a run that night and crashed early."

The redhead fiddled with her hair. "I saw her at the party, but just for a moment. She was talking with Eddie Easton. They seemed kind of cozy."

His adrenaline kicked in. Could he be closing in on the killer? And Betsy's?

Dammit, he was afraid to hope.

"Did they leave together?" he asked.

The redhead shrugged. "I don't know. They went outside, but the dancing started, and I joined in. I didn't see her afterward."

He was afraid of that. "If you think of anything else, let me know." Dane rapped his knuckles on the door and peeked in. Eddie Easton was well dressed with his black hair slicked back.

A pretty brunette was stretched out on a red leather sofa wearing a skimpy bikini.

This appeared to be more than a headshot.

Easton draped a black boa around her neck. "That's great. Tilt your head a little more to the left. Think of something sexy and give me a look that says *I want you.*"

Dane stepped inside, watching as the man fluffed the girl's long brown hair and turned a fan so the strands blew gently over her shoulders. "You look beautiful, doll," he said. "Perfect."

The lecherous way Easton grinned at the girl made Dane's skin crawl.

Instantly disliking him, he cleared his throat.

Easton froze, one hand on his camera as he angled his head toward Dane.

"Excuse me, but we're working," Easton said. "This is a private session."

Dane flashed his ID. "Special Agent Dane Hamrick, Mr. Easton. You're going to have to cut this session short. I need to question you about a murder."

The woman in front of the camera vaulted up from the red leather sofa where she was sprawled. "Murder? Who was killed?"

"One of the actresses." Dane flipped his phone around to display Charity's photo. "Her name was Charity Snow. Did you know her?"

Her face paled. "No. I just arrived this morning. I haven't met any of the others."

Dane narrowed his eyes at Easton. "You knew her, didn't you, Mr. Easton?"

The man opened his mouth as if to argue, but Dane dared him to deny it.

"Don't bother to lie. I talked to her sister. She said you took head-shots of the two of them back in their hometown. Someone else saw you with her at the party."

Easton motioned to the girl. "Why don't we pick back up later?"

"Sure, Eddie." She pulled on a robe, then hurried from the room as if grateful to escape.

Dane folded his arms, sizing up Easton. Expensive clothes, preppy looking, slicked-back hair. Smile a little too flashy.

Definitely a predator type.

Was his photography business a way to lure unsuspecting women into his trap?

He guessed his age to be around thirty, maybe thirty-one or thirty-two, a little older than Betsy would be if she'd lived. Had he been near the college ten years ago when she visited?

Would she have been swayed by his charm? Maybe. Maybe not.

Dane folded his arms and stepped closer, using his size to intimidate the man. "You were the last one to see Charity alive. What happened?" He snapped his fingers. "Or let me guess. You drugged her and slept with her, then when she woke up and realized what happened she got upset and you killed her."

◆ ◆ ◆

Josie broke out in a cold sweat. Had Billy Linder escaped from the psychiatric ward? "Billy?"

"I've been looking for you, Josie."

Josie clenched her hands into fists. His voice sounded different, more high-pitched. On closer examination, his hair was slightly wavier and a lighter shade of brown.

Was this man playing a sick joke on her? Maybe he'd intentionally imitated Linder to frighten her.

She swallowed hard, silently ordering herself not to react. She refused to give him the pleasure of showing her fear.

"Who are you?" Josie asked.

A small smile tugged at his mouth. "You thought I was him, didn't you? The Bride Killer?"

Josie inhaled sharply. "You look like him."

Except there were no scars on his hands. He was slightly shorter than Linder, too.

His eyes were menacing, though, sinister, as if he was looking right through her.

"Who *are* you?" she asked again.

"My name is Porter McCray. I'm auditioning for the part of Billy Linder." A twisted smile lit his eyes. "I visited Billy and studied his movements, how he talks, everything about him, so I can land that part."

A shudder rippled through Josie. The taxidermy tool protruding from the front pocket of his flannel shirt reminded her of the dead animals Billy had on his wall. "You talked to Billy?"

"Yes, he's intriguing," McCray said. "A little subdued, but I suppose that's from medication or being locked up."

Yes, he had been subdued and quiet. Defeated. The nurse had also commented that he was on antipsychotics.

She didn't intend to discuss her feelings with this man, though.

"I want to work with you," he said. "Since you spent time with Linder, you could give me some pointers so I can portray him more accurately." He crept closer. "Maybe we could run through a scene or two from the story."

Josie shook her head as she inched backward.

Images of Billy Linder zapping her with that stun gun then throwing her in his vehicle haunted her.

Then another image—she'd regained consciousness and discovered her hands and feet were bound. Billy's dying mother sat hunched in her wheelchair, her skin a sallow color, her bones poking through weathered skin.

"Mama is dying and I don't want to be alone," Billy had said. To be his wife, she'd had to pass his tests.

She *had* tried. She'd made biscuits and fried chicken and gravy, biding her time until the right moment.

Then she'd flung hot gravy on Billy and run for the door.

He was fast, though, and he'd caught her.

"How about it, Josie? I know you want this movie to be authentic." Her skin prickled as he touched her arm. "Will you show me how he tied you up and what he said so I can do it just like he did?"

Revulsion mushroomed inside Josie. Either the man was the most insensitive person she'd ever met, or he was crazy himself.

It didn't matter, though. She wasn't about to let a Linder wannabe add to her nightmares.

She pried his hand from her arm with a pointed look. Predators thrived on terrifying those weaker than them. This man was stronger than her physically. He must have weighed two hundred pounds.

Physical intimidation wasn't going to work on her.

She lifted her head to dismiss him. "I'm not interested. Now please move out of my way."

Instead of doing as she asked, his hand closed around her arm again. "Are you afraid of me, Josie? Do I remind you so much of him that you think I'm going to hurt you?"

She shot him a venomous look. She didn't intend to give him the chance to hurt her or intimidate her.

◆ ◆ ◆

Easton inched up on his toes in an obvious attempt to make himself look taller and less intimidated by Dane. "Charity is dead?"

Dane met Easton's innocent look with a cold stare. "Don't act like you don't know. You did her headshots back in her hometown and she trusted you, so she went outside with you at that party. You took advantage of the fact that she was young and vulnerable and wanted to be a star."

Easton's lip quivered, a bead of sweat gathering on his forehead. "I take pictures of these girls because I see their beauty and want to help maximize it for them," he said. "Yes, occasionally I get involved with one of them. What man wouldn't?"

"A decent man," Dane said.

Easton cursed. "Dating is not a crime, Agent Hamrick."

"No, but murder is." Dane wanted to slap the handcuffs on the bastard that minute, drag him to the sheriff's office, and force him to confess.

"True, but I didn't kill Charity. For your information, *she* came on to *me*, but I turned her down."

"Sure she did." Dane caught the man's arm as he tried to sidestep him. "Tell me what happened to her."

Easton averted his eyes. When he looked back at Dane, his lips were compressed into a tight line. "I don't know. I went inside for drinks for us, and when I came out, she was gone."

Dane didn't believe him. This guy was a player. He kept fidgeting, which told Dane that he was hiding something. "Where did she go?"

"I told you I don't know. Now, if you have more questions, talk to my lawyer."

"Who threw this party?" Dane asked.

Easton shifted, obviously debating the wisdom of saying more. "A guy named Porter McCray. He's here hoping to land a part, too."

Dane would talk to him next.

Business cards for Easton Photography filled a basket on the table. Another one held business cards from a plastic surgeon group.

Dane gritted his teeth. Charity Snow'd had cosmetic surgery. Did Easton get some kind of kickback from making referrals?

If so, what did it mean in terms of the murder? Did Charity's death have something to do with the group listed on the card?

♦ ♦ ♦

Shaken by her encounter with the Billy Linder lookalike, Josie rushed up the steps to find Dane. She searched the lines in the hallway, relieved to find him walking toward the main room from the photography studio.

His jaw was set in granite.

"Dane, I got the computer."

"Good. Thanks." He took it from her, and his eyes narrowed. "What's wrong? You look like you saw a ghost."

A group of teens entered the room, laughing and whispering, and Josie waited until they'd passed.

Dane kept his gaze on her. She hadn't realized she was so transparent. "I sort of did."

"What do you mean?"

She twisted her hands together. "I ran into a man who looks so much like Billy Linder that it's eerie. For a minute, I thought he'd escaped."

Dane's look softened. "That's not going to happen, Josie."

She nodded. "I know, but this man visited Billy. He's trying to emulate his behavior, speech patterns, his movements."

A dark look flashed across Dane's face. "You think he's a copycat killer?"

"I don't know that he's actually killed anyone, but he gave me the creeps. He wanted me to run through exactly what happened when Billy abducted me."

"Where is this asshole?" Dane asked bluntly.

Josie searched the room. McCray was standing at the edge of a group of young women, watching them with lecherous eyes.

"I'm going to talk to him." Dane's voice was raw with anger. "What's his name?"

A warm tingle seeped through Josie at his protective tone. She'd vowed to stand on her own, but it was nice to know he had her back. "Porter McCray."

"Shit. He's the guy who hosted the party at the cabins."

A chill came over Josie.

That party was the last place Charity Snow had been seen alive.

CHAPTER NINE

Dane studied McCray. Some actors went to extremes to land a part and to fit into a role, but this man looked so much like the Bride Killer that he could have been his twin.

Worse, his suggestion to Josie was disturbing.

Whether or not he was the killer they were looking for was the question.

"I'll have a chat with Mr. McCray," Dane said.

Josie caught his arm before he could walk away. "Let me go with you."

Protective feelings surged inside Dane, reminding him of the way he'd felt about Betsy. Except his feelings weren't brotherly. They were more personal, making him even more unsettled. "I don't like you being involved. This man could be dangerous."

"I know that, but I can't hide," Josie said. "I wrote the Bride Killer story. If Charity Snow's death has something to do with this movie, I have to help."

Dane's heart hammered at the determination in her eyes. Josie was the strongest woman he'd ever met. She'd returned to a town where she'd suffered a horrific attack, and she hadn't backed down when another killer had drawn her into this murder by texting her that photograph. Even the break-in at her house hadn't sent her running.

She was still young and sweet, and she'd already suffered too much trauma.

"You don't have to do anything but stay safe," Dane said. "If we don't solve this murder right away, I want you out of town. Out of harm's way."

Her chin lifted slightly. "I appreciate that. I still want to listen when you question him. He caught me off guard, and I don't like that."

Dane tried to understand her feelings, but the possibility that she might get hurt didn't sit well in his gut.

Not when her mere touch on his arm had his body hardening, taunting him that they would be good in bed together.

"Josie, please just let me handle the situation."

Her eyes softened. They were the damn greenest eyes he'd ever fallen into.

Err . . . seen.

What the hell was wrong with him?

He was getting lost in her when he had a murderer to catch.

Dammit. He pulled away. Letting his emotions into the picture was exactly what he wanted to avoid when he'd first told her he didn't want her involved. "All right. Just let me do the talking. Maybe if he sees you're with me, he'll leave you alone."

He hoped that was true. He'd let Betsy down.

He wouldn't let Josie down.

◆ ◆ ◆

Josie's heart raced. What just happened between Dane and her?

A zing of attraction had hit her when she'd touched him. His voice had gotten low, gravelly, almost possessive when he suggested that he wanted McCray to know she was with him.

He's just doing his job. He didn't mean anything by it.

Dane had never been anything but professional. In fact, when she'd first interviewed him about the Bride Killer, he'd been almost rude.

Cold even.

As if he disagreed with what she was doing, like so many of the people in town.

Yet he'd been the one person she wanted to call when she'd received that text.

He also had a brooding intensity in his dark eyes that drew her. Beneath that rough, lone-wolf exterior, she sensed a wounded soul. She connected with that part of him.

Getting him to open up seemed impossible, though.

Besides, she was damaged and struggling with her own inner demons. What did she have to offer him or any other man?

A group of young women brushed past on their way out the door, chattering about their photography shoots and auditions and their plans for the evening. Someone had posted an invitation on social media to meet up for happy hour at Blues and Brews, a local bar.

McCray was talking to Olive, the casting director, when they approached. Josie shivered at his voice. He must have taped Billy Linder and had adapted a good imitation of his tone.

"I know this man," McCray said earnestly. "I've spent time with him. I can get in his head and become him." His eye twitched just as Billy's had. "Let me show you."

The casting director gave him a wan smile. "You'll have your chance tomorrow. I have to go now."

She started to walk away, but the man blocked her way. "I can be Billy Linder," he said, his tone more sinister. "I can make people see what he was really like. What he was thinking when he killed those women. You know he did it all cause his mama was dying. He loved his mama more than anything, but she was sick. She used to make him do things to her at night—"

Josie instinctively backed away. The vile things Charlene had done to Billy sickened her. Billy was also the product of molestation and inbreeding.

"That's enough." Olive's eyes flared with unease. "Mr. McCray, I will see you at your scheduled time."

McCray reached for her hand. "I can show you how he adorned her with the jewelry he took from his victims. Mama likes sparkly jewels," he said, imitating Billy's voice. "She's happy when I give her gifts."

Dane cleared his throat. "You heard the lady," Dane said. "Step aside."

McCray pivoted, anger streaking his craggy face. When he spotted Josie, an evil glint appeared. "Josie, that was good, wasn't it? Didn't I sound like Billy?"

Josie barely suppressed a shudder. Yes, he did, and his voice triggered the memories she'd worked so hard to forget.

Dane flashed his badge. "Special Agent Dane Hamrick, Mr. McCray. I need to ask you some questions."

The man opened his mouth to argue, but Dane shot him a menacing look and gestured for him to step into an alcove to the side. The casting director darted away, obviously grateful to be rescued.

"Mr. McCray," Dane began, "I understand that you hosted a party the other night."

McCray shrugged. "No crime in throwing a party. It was just a little meet and greet anyway. We were all bonding over the story of the Bride Killer. Some of the guests were especially intrigued by the Thorn Ripper since that was the mama doing the killing."

Violence and incest had bred more violence. A cycle that was hard to break. Not an excuse, though, when lives and families had been destroyed.

Josie's entire family had been affected by Linder and his mother.

Dane flipped his phone around to show McCray the picture of Charity. "Do you remember seeing this woman at the party?"

McCray peered at the photograph, his jagged teeth showing as he smiled. "There were a lot of pretty women there. Next time you'll have to join us, Josie. I bet you could pick out the cast for the movie better than that tight-assed bitch they put in charge."

Josie glared at him. "I don't think so."

"Cut the act, McCray," Dane said, his tone hard. "Did you talk to this woman?"

McCray shrugged, but his posture remained slightly slumped as if he didn't intend to venture out of character. "For a minute. Name is Charity, right?"

Dane gave a clipped nod. "Yes. What did you two talk about?"

"She wanted to play the reporter Carol Little but said she'd take any of the victims' parts." A leer pulled at the corners of his mouth as if the mention of victims excited him. "I offered to practice lines with her."

"Is that all you offered?" Dane asked. "Did you also suggest tying her up and reenacting her murder?"

Heat flickered in his eyes as if the thought excited him. "We could have role-played that, yes."

"How about stabbing her in the heart?" Dane asked. "Did you want to role-play that?"

McCray tugged at his chin. "Where are you going with this, Agent Hamrick?"

Dane ignored the question.

Josie had read about interrogation tactics. Intimidate the man and throw him off his game.

"Did you see her in private?" Dane pressed.

"No," McCray said. "That photographer showed up, and she went outside to talk to him. I lost track of her after that."

"Did you see her leave?" Dane asked.

McCray angled his head to one side. "No, but I wasn't paying attention. I met a couple of the other ladies, and we downed some shots."

"You went out of character, Mr. McCray. Billy Linder didn't drink," Josie said, watching for a reaction.

McCray frowned.

"He could be charming," McCray said in defense.

"Linder wasn't a smooth talker," Josie stressed. "He was awkward with women, shy. That's why the women trusted him, because he didn't come across as dangerous or cocky. He was vulnerable."

Anger reddened the man's face. "I know that and I can play that part." He wiped at his forehead. "But the party did take place after hours."

Dane jumped in. "You said you were with some other women that night. I need their names."

McCray worked his mouth from side to side. He slipped back into character and mimicked the way Billy pulled at his chin.

Josie's stomach knotted.

"This sounds like some kind of inquisition," McCray said. "Did something happen to Charity?"

"Yes," Dane said bluntly. "She's dead."

The man's nostrils flared. "Dead? How?"

"She was murdered." Dane muttered a sarcastic sound. "Don't act like you don't know. You want to be Billy Linder so much that you altered your appearance. You studied his moves. You stabbed her so you'd know what it felt like to murder someone like he did."

McCray lifted his hands, his voice shrill, almost panicked. "I have role-played murder," he admitted. "That's as far as it went."

Dane leaned closer to the man, his jaw firm, his posture aggressive. "I don't believe you. I think you wanted to know what it was like to feel someone die at your hands. You don't just want to play Billy Linder, you want to be famous like him."

Josie curled her fingers into her hands. Maybe her book and this movie had been a mistake. If someone was using it as a blueprint for murder, she should get the book pulled from the shelves and put a halt to this film.

Of course that would mean giving in to her fear, giving in to this latest madman. Overcoming her nightmares was the only way for her to be whole again.

Guilt clawed her, making her chest heave.

Except how could she be whole if telling her story had cost another woman her life?

◆ ◆ ◆

Neesie Netherington had come a long way from Biloxi, Mississippi, hoping to get a break in this true crime film. True, it wasn't a big-screen production with a superstar as the lead, but it would earn her a SAG card, get her foot in the door, and prove to those Hollywood folks she could act.

Not that there was much to playing dead, but there would be the big drawn-out abduction and the kill scene. The way Josie DuKane had described her ordeal, the Bride Killer kept his victims for a while and forced them to endure tests his mama set up to prove they could be a good wife.

Hell, she'd done the wife thing, thank you very much. She'd kissed that bastard Leroy's feet and ass for as long as she could take it.

One day that handsome photographer had come to Biloxi, set up shop at the mall of all things, and invited local girls and women to do photo shoots. He promised to make them look like stars.

She tested the weight of her new double Ds in her hands, adjusting her top to maximize cleavage, and smiled at the perfect face that stared back. That dang scar on her cheek where her stepdaddy had broken her jaw was now gone. No more pancake makeup for her or stares or rude comments behind her back.

She furrowed her brows. Leroy hadn't liked her new face. He'd accused her of doing it to leave him for another man. Then he'd cut her.

She rubbed at her torso where he'd scarred her. No one could see it with her clothes on, but she knew it was there. A reminder of Leroy. Just the way he'd wanted it.

Someday she had to get it fixed.

She'd heard Porter McCray offer to run auditions with anyone interested, and she intended to take him up on it. She'd do everything she could to up her chances. And she could use some acting tips.

First, Eddie was going to do another shoot with her, a private one where she'd dress in a wedding gown like the Bride Killer's victims and pose with a rose stem between her teeth.

Eddie was nothing but a creative genius. He'd also offered to take a couple of the teenagers to Graveyard Falls and shoot them standing on the edge of the falls as if they were about to be pushed over by Charlene Linder.

Her stomach roiled at the thought. She hated heights.

Eddie's photos were so *real* looking, though. This way the director could actually see her as the character.

Her fear of heights be damned. She'd do anything to get this part and not have to go back to Leroy.

◆　◆　◆

Dane didn't trust Porter McCray, but he needed proof before he could make an arrest. "I'll need a list of everyone you talked to at the party."

A chuckle rumbled from the man. "I don't know everyone's names or contact information, Agent Hamrick. It was an informal gathering. Booze was flowing. Everyone was all hyped up, talking about the auditions and Miss DuKane's book."

"Just make a list of anyone you remember. I need to talk to them and verify your story."

McCray's eye twitched. "Don't you mean you need to question them and see if they murdered Charity?"

"Since you're such a study of characters, I'm surprised you weren't more observant," Dane said. "Maybe one of the other guests noticed something you didn't."

His jab hit home. A spark of anger jolted McCray's confidence.

Dane gave him a stony look. "Make the list and get it to me." He shoved a business card in McCray's hand. "Don't leave town either."

McCray waved a hand around, gesturing toward the signs for the film. "I'm not going anywhere. They can't make this story without Billy Linder, and that's me."

The sheer cockiness of his tone set Dane's teeth on edge. Yet he had that wired look about him as if he wasn't quite all there mentally.

McCray angled his head toward Josie. "Let me know if you change your mind about running through some scenes with me."

"I won't," Josie said sharply.

He lifted one eyebrow. "Then perhaps we can have coffee and talk. I have several questions—"

"Leave me alone," Josie said. "I refuse to relive the past for you."

"You asked the victims' families to relive it," McCray pointed out. Josie's face lost its color.

Dane admired her for standing up to the bastard, but he didn't trust the son of a bitch. He inched closer to McCray to block him from touching Josie.

"You heard the lady," Dane said. "Stay away from her or you'll answer to me."

McCray lifted his head defiantly, gave him a sinister smile, and walked away.

Dane ground his molars. He had a bad feeling he hadn't seen the last of the man.

If McCray bothered Josie, his badge be damned. He'd do whatever was necessary to keep him away from her.

◆ ◆ ◆

He knew which ones were bad girls. Which ones were dispensable.

Oh, their pretty faces smiled at him from his wall of photographs. They smiled because they were beautiful.

Some of them even changed their names to become the person they wanted to be.

They had come from dust and bones just as he had. They would return to dust and bones in the end.

Then everyone would see them as they were underneath the façade.

Naked. Ugly. Desperate. Alone.

Crying for attention.

Dying to be loved.

They wouldn't need love once they were dead.

CHAPTER TEN

Josie tried to hide her discomfort around McCray. Men like him enjoyed watching women squirm. She refused to give him the satisfaction.

Dane guided her away from McCray. "If he bothers you again, let me know."

"Do you think he killed that woman?"

"I don't know, but I don't like him. No man in his right mind would suggest role-playing murder to a woman who'd been kidnapped by a serial killer."

Josie drew in a deep breath as they stepped outside. She needed fresh air, but the strong wind made the trees sway and tossed leaves and twigs across the quadrangle. In spite of the heavy dark clouds, locals, spectators, and actors were scattered across the grassy area mingling as if they were oblivious to the threat of bad weather.

Or death.

One couple about her age shared a picnic, their affection for each other obvious. They looked so happy. Carefree. Normal.

Would she ever be normal? Allow herself to fall in love and have a family?

Or would she always be guarded, distrustful, looking over her shoulder for men like Billy Linder?

She searched Dane's face for pity or derision. "That's how you see me, isn't it, Dane? As a victim?"

Not a woman a man would want to be with.

"You were a victim," Dane said matter-of-factly.

Frustration filled Josie. "That's not all I am."

Dane angled his head toward her, his eyes darkening. The whistle of the wind echoed around them, heat brewing between them.

Or maybe she was imagining it. Dane was entrenched in a case. She had to remember that. Just because she was attracted to him didn't mean he reciprocated that feeling.

"I'm sorry, Josie," Dane said softly. "I'm not labeling you. I understand you've worked hard to overcome what happened to you, and that's admirable."

She blinked back tears. Maybe he did understand after all.

"You're right," she conceded, the tension between them making her ache to reach out and touch him. To have him wrap his arms around her and comfort her. Because no matter how much she'd worked to forget her abduction, she hadn't forgotten it and never would. "I don't trust McCray. He may be dangerous."

"Good. You shouldn't trust him." A hint of sadness touched his eyes. "Although I'm sorry for that. I'm sure it's difficult to trust anyone after the ordeal you went through."

Yes, it was. Although she trusted Dane.

At least with her life.

She couldn't trust her heart to anyone. It was better not to love than love someone who didn't return that love.

"I should go," Dane said. "I have more people to question, and I need to carry this computer to the lab."

Josie nodded. He was back to business. They had to keep it that way.

Olive appeared beside Josie, shading the sun from her eyes as she approached. "Josie, I'm getting ready to watch some auditions for the part of Billy Linder. I thought you might want to join me. Of all people here, you know him best."

Josie twined her hands together. Yes, she did. His voice, his mannerisms, his demented eyes and laugh—they were forever etched in her mind.

◆ ◆ ◆

Dane tucked Charity's computer into his vehicle and locked it inside. He spent the rest of the afternoon working with Sheriff Kimball questioning the film production's staff and actors.

Unfortunately, he and the sheriff learned nothing helpful. The few folks who remembered Charity thought she was attractive, sweet, friendly, and that she had as good a chance at landing a part as anyone else.

One California blonde claimed Charity wasn't sophisticated enough for the business, but since the characters in the film were small-town country girls, Charity might fit.

Dane gritted his teeth. Just because a person was born and raised in the South and spoke with an accent didn't mean they were less intelligent, savvy, or sophisticated than that snobby woman.

Just look at Josie. She had grown up in Tennessee, but she was savvier than any woman he'd ever met.

A woman didn't have to have a perfect face or body to be beautiful or appealing to a man.

He would choose Josie any day over a model.

Aware he was thinking of Josie again instead of focusing, he put her out of his mind. She was watching auditions with the casting director.

Josie was safe for now.

Sheriff Kimball strode toward him, scratching his head. "Anything new?"

"I'm going to have the lab look into Porter McCray and Eddie Easton," Dane said.

"Have them run a background check on the makeup artist, Gil Baines. He denied hooking up with Charity, but a couple of women said they saw the two of them walking by the river together. No one saw them return to the party either."

Kimball was actually offering insight, showing initiative. Maybe Dane had misjudged him, and the small-town sheriff was competent after all. "Thanks, Sheriff, I'll pass it on. Keep an eye on him this evening while I carry Charity's computer to the lab."

Kimball agreed, and Dane jogged to the parking lot, climbed in his vehicle, and headed toward Knoxville. He'd check in with Josie again later.

At the moment, he needed to work. He had three viable suspects: Porter McCray, Eddie Easton, and Doyle Yonkers.

One of them might be Charity's killer.

And . . . maybe Betsy's . . .

◆ ◆ ◆

Ellie hated the nursing home, but she'd finally accepted that she needed help. Ever since she fell and broke her hip last year, she'd had trouble getting around.

Although there was that one kind nurse: Precious was her name. She had the sweetest voice, and if Ellie's senses were right, her skin was the color of caramel, her eyes dark chocolate.

Looks didn't matter, though, especially since her eyesight had gone.

The only thing that did matter was a person's heart. Precious's heart was as tender and pure as anyone God ever put on earth.

Some of the workers treated her and the other residents like they were nuisances. Just because their skin was wrinkled, it didn't mean their minds were fried.

Not Precious. She'd devoted her life to helping the down and out. She snuck Ellie an extra fried pie every now and then and brought her the good kind of towel that didn't leave fuzz all over your behind when you dried off.

Sometimes she even visited and stayed awhile.

She didn't mind when Ellie told stories about how she'd grown up in Hell's Holler or the weird things that she saw. She even listened when Ellie relayed what had happened at that ranch where Ellie used to be a house parent. Precious hadn't passed judgment. Precious said that was God's job, and she was not God.

Although Ellie hadn't yet confided about the boy who disturbed her so much. The one with the claw marks on his face.

The one in her nightmares at night. The one who haunted her even when she was awake.

The doctors didn't believe Ellie had the gift of sight. One of the idiots had said she was hallucinating from the pills they gave her, but that was hogwash. He'd said it cause the dumb ass was scared of her.

Why, Ellie had these premonitions just like her mama had and her mama before her.

Granted, sometimes she saw things she didn't want to see, but she couldn't stop it.

Like this morning. She'd been wide-awake when images of dead girls flashed behind her eyes. Dead girls with marks on their faces like they'd been torn apart by a flock of starving birds.

Just like the boy had been.

Lordy, she'd tried to help the kid. Her efforts hadn't worked. He'd hated her in the end just like his father did.

She struggled to get up from her rocker, her bones creaking as she stood. With gnarled hands, she clutched her walker and hobbled to get the herbs Precious had brought her so she could feel more at home. Tonight she'd cast a protection spell around the nursing home, maybe one that would bind the boy's father to his grave.

In her vision, he was coming back from the grave to exact his revenge. She'd seen him climbing from the cold, hard ground, his devil eyes blazing with fire, his bony hands reaching for her, fingers pointed like claws ready to tear her apart limb by limb, his threat reverberating in her ears: "You'll pay, Ellie, you'll pay."

She had no doubt that she would.

◆ ◆ ◆

Dane met with Peyton at the lab outside of Knoxville. "Were you able to trace the origin of that text that Josie DuKane received?"

"I'm afraid not, Dane. It came from a burner phone. He probably used an app to disguise the number and removed the battery afterward, so there's no way to track it."

"I was afraid of that. Thanks for trying." He slid the laptop toward her. "This computer belonged to the victim, Charity Snow, and her sister, Bailey. The sister claims Charity didn't have a boyfriend. We think she met up with someone at a party in Graveyard Falls."

Déjà vu struck him. His little sister had disappeared from a party. There had been dozens, maybe a hundred or more guests attending, but no one had seen anything.

Just like now.

Although alcohol made memories fuzzy, someone could be lying.

"I'll get right on it," Peyton said. "I'll sort through her email and social media and let you know what I find."

"Thanks." Dane scribbled down the names he wanted her to investigate.

"Eddie Easton is a photographer who takes headshots for models and actors. He's in Graveyard Falls doing photo shoots."

"So he had easy access to Charity?"

"To all the women," Dane said with a note of disdain. "Porter McCray is an actor who carries character acting to a new level—he not only looks like Billy Linder, but he's mimicking his speech patterns, mannerisms, and he threw the party where our victim was last seen."

Peyton's fingers were already clicking on the keyboard. "How about the last guy?"

"Gil Baines, the makeup artist for the film company."

She wrinkled her nose. "I thought the victim wasn't wearing makeup when you found her."

"She wasn't. Someone claims Charity was with Baines at the party. No one saw her after that." He raked a hand through his hair as Peyton plugged Baines's name into the computer.

Seconds later, information spieled onto the screen.

"Hmm, did you know that the origin of the name Baines came from the word *bones*?"

Dane's skin crawled. "No, but that could be significant. The killer removed a piece of bone from the victim's cheek."

Peyton rubbed her arms as if chilled, then scrolled further. "Baines is thirty-two, grew up in foster care in Georgia. He got into some trouble as a teen and has a juvie record, although it's sealed."

"Can you unseal it?"

"I'll see what I can do. Meanwhile," she continued, "oh, this is sad. He was trapped in a car that crashed when he was fifteen, sustained lacerations and bruises to his body and face." She moved the cursor down then highlighted a photo. "Look at this. This picture was taken after the accident."

Dane sucked in a sharp breath at the boy's disfigured face. Cuts and lacerations marred over 80 percent. One jagged line ran from right below his eye to his chin, making his cheek sag. Several deep gashes made it appear like a chunk of his chin was actually missing. "How many stitches did he have?"

"According to this, over a hundred."

Dane mentally pictured the man he'd met at the community center. "He looks normal now."

"He's undergone four different plastic surgeries to repair his face," she said. "Living with those scars probably sparked his interest in makeup."

"Interesting that he chose a field where he would surround himself with beautiful women," Dane said.

Peyton nodded. "Insecurities. Once he became scar-free, he thought the women would notice him."

Yet something about that didn't sit right. Wouldn't a makeup artist have wanted to show off his talent by making his victim even more beautiful in death, rather than remove her makeup?

If he'd suffered from being disfigured, why would he want to inflict that kind of pain on anyone? This woman hadn't known him when he was scarred, so it couldn't have been personal.

Although perhaps she symbolized the girls who'd rejected him before his plastic surgery.

He thought about Betsy again. She had a tiny scar on her forehead, but she'd worn it like a badge of honor. She certainly wouldn't have laughed at someone else who'd been hurt. She would have sympathized.

If his motive stemmed from rejection because of his disfigurement, that wouldn't fit his sister. Unless she'd rejected him and he'd misinterpreted her reason.

Disappointment blended with hope . . . He wanted it to be true. He wanted to nail the bastard and finally end the torment for himself and for his mother.

"What do you think?" Peyton asked.

Dane repressed his personal feelings. Peyton knew about his sister's death, but he'd never confided how much it drove him.

"He's definitely a person of interest," Dane said. "So is McCray." He didn't like the way he'd cornered Josie. McCray enjoyed frightening her.

"Let's see what we find." She entered McCray's name and several listings appeared, but the only Porter McCray was deceased. "Are you sure that's his real name?"

Dane worked his mouth from side to side. "No. I suppose it could be an acting name."

She cross-checked his name again with acting schools and casts for other productions, including commercials, but again got no hits.

"He may have changed his name for more reasons than his acting career." If he had, Dane would uncover the truth. McCray could have escaped from a mental home or have a record under an alias. His obsession with Josie could have been what brought him to Graveyard Falls in the first place. Worry knotted his shoulders. McCray could have killed Charity to get Josie's attention. "How about Easton?"

Dane read aloud as the information appeared on the screen. "Eddie Easton was born in a little town near Nashville. His father is a sculptor and hoped his son would follow in his footsteps, but Eddie chose photography. He attended photography school in LA where he first began photographing models and wannabe stars."

Peyton pointed to the police background check. "He has a record. Two DUIs. Lost his driver's license at eighteen, but has it back now. Did some community service. Volunteered at a nature preserve that rescued birds of prey."

The talon marks taunted Dane. "The killer left wounds on the victim's face that resembled claw marks from a bird, and he took a piece of bone," Dane said. "Easton's background fits the profile."

Peyton nodded. "He could be your man."

"He had access to sculpting tools. Is it possible the cuts on the woman's face were made by sculpting tools instead of a scalpel?"

"It's possible," Peyton agreed. "I'll confirm with Dr. Wheeland."

A possible connection, but Dane wanted more. Some sign the guy was violent or psychotic.

"Where was he ten years ago?"

Peyton clicked a few more keys, then frowned. "UT, undergraduate student."

Dane's blood ran cold. Yet hope surfaced again. There were too many coincidences. If Easton attended school when Betsy had visited, they could have met at that party.

His pulse pounded.

Was it possible that he'd finally found Betsy's killer?

CHAPTER ELEVEN

Josie spent the afternoon watching auditions with the casting director.

Olive's demure black jacket and slacks contrasted with her nails, which were painted silver today. She was a take-charge woman with a statuesque frame that caught a person's attention when she entered a room. Josie admired her poise and confidence.

She felt small and invisible in comparison. That was okay with her. She'd had all the attention she wanted since the book hit the shelves. After a piece or two of hate mail had arrived, her publicist began screening incoming mail for possible trouble. Josie had decided not to torture herself with the negativity.

Three teens exited the room whispering about their auditions, and then a gray-haired woman rolled into the room in a wheelchair. Her hair was long and stringy, wrinkles sagged beneath her eyes, and she wore an old housedress. Dozens of pieces of jewelry hung from her thin frame.

Josie gripped her hands together, a panic attack teetering on the surface. She was in costume for Charlene Linder's part. Her age-spotted hand trembled as she toyed with the silver chain around her neck.

Olive glanced at Josie as if to ask what she thought, and Josie swallowed hard, leaned close to Olive, then whispered, "She definitely reminds me of Charlene."

A sinister cackle erupted from the woman, and she shook her finger as if talking to Billy. "She'll never do for a wife. Cut that whore's hair off her."

Josie clamped her teeth over her lip to keep a whimper at bay. The shrill voice, the Southern vernacular, even the insane look in the woman's eyes as they shifted back and forth reminded her of Billy's mother.

"Come here to Mama," the actress said in a hoarse whisper. "Mama will take care of you, son. Mama loves you." She mocked stroking Billy's head as if he were lying in her lap, and nausea ripped through Josie.

The rest of the scene faded into a blur as Josie was swept back to that night. Finally Olive nudged her. "Josie, are you all right?"

Josie nodded, grateful to have Olive anchor her back to reality. *She's just an actress. She can't hurt you.*

Olive laid her hand gently on Josie's arm. "Josie."

"Yes, I'm fine." She forced a breath in and out. "She's perfect for the part."

"Good." Olive stood. "Thank you, Miss Sherman. I'd like for you to read with the male actors auditioning for Billy's part."

The woman agreed, and Josie pulled herself together. But the afternoon presented another challenge.

There were at least thirty men trying out for Linder's part. She'd had no idea that playing a serial killer was such a desirable role. The realization set her teeth on edge.

For the audition, Olive selected a scene between Charlene and Billy where Billy had returned from leaving one of his victims at Graveyard Falls. He was crying, terrified that his mother was going to die before he found the perfect wife.

Billy's relationship with his mother was truly warped.

Charlene had isolated Billy to the point that he'd relied on Charlene for all his needs. Just as Charlene's father had isolated her.

Billy had carried her from room to room, bathed her, fed her, then slept with her as if she was his lover.

By the time the auditions were nearly finished for the day, a headache pulsed behind Josie's eyes. She yearned to go home and soak in a nice tub.

Porter McCray entered the room, looking so much like Billy with his hair, makeup, and mannerisms that her first instinct was to run.

Determined to stick it out, she remained rooted to the spot, her stomach roiling.

Olive spoke in a hushed tone as McCray lumbered through the stage door and settled on the floor beside the wheelchair. His voice sounded almost childlike when he spoke.

"Mama, I wanted her to be the one but she wasn't," he said. "I don't want to be alone. Please don't leave me."

"I'm sorry, son, but I have to," Charlene said. "You have to find the perfect bride."

"I tried," he said in a broken voice. "But she didn't pass the tests. She said she could cook but she couldn't."

"They're all little liars," the woman said in a voice as brittle as her bones.

He laid his head in the woman's lap and clutched at her skirt as he sobbed.

A chill engulfed Josie. The scene carried her back to that horrible night. She could almost feel the heavy ropes around her wrist. Feel Billy Linder's rancid breath on her neck, hear him whispering that she had to please his mother.

"He's disturbing, but he fits the part." Olive tapped her nails on her thigh. "What do you think?"

Josie blinked to remind herself that he was acting. "Yes, he fits."

The crazed look in his eyes seemed real, though. Was he dangerous?

How deep would he go to get into character? Would he kill someone just to understand what it felt like to take a life?

◆　◆　◆

Dane phoned Sheriff Kimball on the way back to Graveyard Falls, but Kimball had no new information. Dane needed hands-on help to cover the three suspects.

"Have one of your deputies keep an eye on Gil Baines, and put another one on Porter McCray," Dane told the sheriff. "Also run surveillance on Easton."

"Sure. You have something concrete on one of them?"

Dane explained about the background checks. "Any one of them is a viable suspect. Easton's father was a sculptor, and he did community service at a nature preserve that rescued birds of prey."

"I'll see if he's still at the community center and follow him when he leaves."

"Thanks." It was getting dark outside, the hours ticking by without answers. He wanted to find Charity's killer so her sister could rest easier tonight.

He pressed Josie's number, anxious to know if she'd heard from the killer or if McCray had bothered her again, but her voice mail picked up, so he left a message.

Pumped with adrenaline from the possibility that he might have a lead on Betsy's killer, he called the nursing facility where his mother was staying. But he had to keep his thoughts on the case to himself.

A year ago, he'd had a lead and shared his hopes with his mother. She'd dragged out all the old videos of his sister when she was young and watched them for hours on end. Seeing Betsy running and playing soccer and strumming the guitar had made it seem like she was still alive.

For a moment in time, he'd thought he and his mother might be close again. That she might emerge from her shell and live in the real world again.

When that lead failed to pan out, she was so disappointed that it broke her, and she'd lapsed into a catatonic state.

Dane pinched the bridge of his nose at the guilt that seared him. Seeing her like that had been damn near as hard as losing Betsy.

All his fault again.

He'd promised his mother he'd make the man pay, but he'd failed. Worse, this time, his mother had sunk so low, he didn't know if she'd ever come back.

When the receptionist answered, he asked to speak to Precious—the one woman there he could depend on to do right by his mother, be honest with him, and make sure his mother wasn't mistreated.

She answered on the third ring. "Hello, this is Precious."

"It's Agent Hamrick. How's my mom doing today?"

"She's had a good day. I took her outside for a stroll. She responds well to the fresh air."

A sharp pang squeezed at Dane's chest. "She used to walk three to four miles a day. She always claimed she had that disorder where she needed the sunlight."

"Everyone needs sunlight," Precious said, a tenderness to her voice. "I'm glad you told me that. I'll make sure she gets out more often, every day when the weather permits."

An uncharacteristic swelling of tears burned his eyes at her kindness. Funny how sadistic people didn't touch him, but the kind word of a stranger could stir his emotions.

"Thank you, Precious. You have no idea how much I appreciate that."

"No problem. Your mother is strong. I believe she can hear everything you say, and that she just needs to rest for a while, but one day she'll come back to you."

He hoped she was right. "Has she spoken at all this week?"

A moment of silence, then a soft sigh. "I'm afraid not. She smiled a little when we took that walk today. I told her that she looked pretty with her perm. We had her hair done yesterday in the salon."

Dane's heart stuttered. "She always prided herself on her appearance." One reason it hurt him to see her go downhill the past few years. She hated hospital gowns and used to have her hair done weekly.

"You are heaven-sent," Dane said, his heart aching as he used his mother's expression. She had been a woman of faith. Even when he'd balked at attending church, she'd grilled her beliefs into Dane until Betsy's brutal murder. Then she'd lost her faith, and he hadn't been able to hang on to it either.

"Please call me if there's any change or if she asks to see me."

"You can visit anyway, Dane. She may not act like she knows you or appreciates your visit, but deep down she understands that you love her."

Dane swallowed the lump in his throat. He wasn't so sure about that. She blamed him for not protecting Betsy.

"Tell her I'll stop by soon." Although he wanted some real information to tell her first. That he'd gotten justice for Betsy.

Then maybe his mother could forgive him for letting them both down.

◆ ◆ ◆

Josie bit back her distaste over Porter McCray. So far, he was the best candidate for Billy Linder's part. He frightened her. Judging from the way Olive squirmed in her seat, he made her uneasy, too.

Worse, Josie's gut instinct warned her that giving him the part would feed his misguided ego, and he might take the role too far.

"Yes, he's studied Linder," Josie said. "He approached me about practicing with him, role-playing. He wants to get into Linder's head."

That meant understanding Linder's dark thoughts and desires. The pleasure he took in carving up animals. His insecurities with women.

His sense of desperation, anger, and power when he wrapped his hands around a woman's neck and choked the life from her.

Olive thumbed her bangs back from her forehead. "Jesus, Josie. If you think this guy is some freak, say so. I've worked on a number of true crime shows and reenactments, and they always draw the crazies."

"I don't know yet," Josie said. "Either he's an excellent actor or he is a little off himself. Then again, I was abducted by the real Billy Linder, so just hearing his words and looking at him reminds me of the night he held me at his cabin."

Olive squeezed her arm. "I know, and I'm sorry. I shouldn't have asked you to sit with me today and watch the auditions."

"No, I appreciate the invitation," Josie said, grateful for a friend. "This is therapeutic for me." She didn't want Olive to fall into the same trap she had when she'd trusted Billy, so she gestured toward McCray. "I may be paranoid, Olive, but I'd be cautious around him."

"Point taken." Olive's phone buzzed, and she answered it while Josie headed outside to her car. Dane had called, so she pressed his number.

When his voice mail picked up, she left him a message saying she was headed home.

Night had set in, the temperature dropping, the winds picking up and carrying the scent of more impending rain. Most of the crowd had dispersed from the quadrangle, the parking lot nearly empty. Although a few protestors still remained, their chant of discontent echoing in the breeze.

A tall man in a dark coat shook his hand at her, and she picked up her pace and crossed the quadrangle.

An eerie whistle rent the air behind her. A man?

Instantly Josie's nerves snapped to alert. She had been caught off guard the night Billy Tasered her.

She wouldn't be caught off guard again.

She slipped her keys from her purse and gripped them in her hand, ready to use them as a weapon, then scanned the grass and sidewalk in search of anyone lurking around.

A couple walking their dog passed. Three women rushed toward a blue SUV and hopped inside, laughing. A man in a dark jacket and hat sat on the park bench with a camera.

Her chest ached with the effort to breathe, but she focused on the techniques she'd learned in therapy and inhaled deep breaths.

She'd met Billy Linder in church. Felt sorry for him. Trusted him.

He'd talked about his mother being ill, and she'd confided about her grandfather's illness, that it had brought her to Graveyard Falls.

He'd interpreted that conversation to mean they were meant for each other.

Then the Taser.

She'd regained consciousness in his house with all those dead animals staring at her.

Her heart thundered as she remembered the terror of thinking she might die. While she'd baked biscuits for his mother to please him, she'd thought of all the things she wanted to do. Places she wanted to go. The family she wanted to have.

You fought back, she reminded herself. *You used your brain and survived.*

She would keep doing that.

Shoulders squared, she hurried toward the Jetta. As she approached the car, she peered through the window in case someone had broken in. But the car looked clear, so she jumped in, locked the door, and started the engine.

The hair on the back of her neck prickled, and she glanced in the rearview mirror and spotted Porter McCray standing behind her car with a sinister grin.

Heart pounding, she shifted into gear, hit the gas, and sped away, phoning Dane again as she drove. Traffic was thicker in town because of the influx of people attached to the movie, and headlights nearly blinded her from an oncoming truck as she turned onto a side road.

She blinked to focus, but more lights from a car behind her fogged her vision. She pumped her brakes, willing the driver to dim his lights, but he sped up.

She veered onto another side street hoping he'd move on, but he turned as well.

Alarmed, she pressed the accelerator and shot forward, then quickly turned down another road. The car followed, the roar of its engine reverberating in her ears as it closed in on her tail.

Suddenly he rammed into her. Josie dropped her phone, clenched the steering wheel with a white-knuckled grip and spun sideways, then made a U-turn, tires grinding gravel as she rode the shoulder. The car did the same.

He was following her.

She swung to the right onto the road leading to her house, taking the turn so fast that her car skidded and she nearly lost control. Desperate to stay on the road, she eased off the gas and managed to yank the car back in line just before she flew into a ditch.

Josie jolted forward, clenching the steering wheel and trying to see the driver in her rearview mirror. His bright lights blinded her.

Then he slammed into her again.

She screamed as her car spun and careened toward the embankment.

◆ ◆ ◆

Dane gripped his phone and punched Connect.

Josie's scream echoed in his ears, sending terror through him.

CHAPTER TWELVE

Josie trembled and lifted her head from the steering wheel. She must have passed out for a minute. What had happened?

Reality slowly returned.

A car had run her into the embankment and she'd stalled out. Heart hammering, she glanced outside for the car, wincing at the pain that shot down her neck from the impact.

A car screeched up behind her, and she searched for the vehicle that had hit her. She hadn't gotten a good look at it, though. Was it the same car?

A car door slammed and footsteps crunched as a man walked toward her. Josie screamed.

Terrified it was the person who'd run her off the road, she scrambled for her phone, but it had fallen to the floor.

"Josie! What's wrong? Are you all right?" Dane shouted over the line.

She didn't dare take her eyes off the man coming toward her long enough to answer. Slowly he emerged out of the beam of his own headlights.

Doyle Yonkers.

She grabbed the Mace from her purse, then braced it between her fingers. Had he hit her so he could kidnap her?

A second later, he rapped on her window. "Miss DuKane, are you all right?"

Josie squinted to see if he was armed. Did he have a gun?

A Taser like Billy had?

He held his phone to the window. "Do you need me to call an ambulance? A tow truck?"

She didn't see a weapon. Or a Taser. Then again, she hadn't seen one with Billy.

"Are you okay? Should I call nine-one-one?" He reached for the door handle to open it. She shouted for him to back away and locked the door. A frown darkened his face, and he raised his hands and took a step back as if to indicate he meant no harm. "Sorry, I didn't mean to scare you. Do you need a doctor?"

She shook her head. "No, I'm okay."

"Josie, talk to me! Where are you?" Dane yelled.

Josie kept her eyes on Yonkers and snatched her phone from the floor. "Second Street."

"I'll be right there."

Comforted that he was on his way, she loosened her death grip on the door handle.

"What happened?" Doyle asked through the window.

Several cars whizzed by without even slowing. Had Doyle hit her or had the driver raced on and left her? "Somebody ran me off the road. Did you see anyone?"

Doyle's thick brows bunched together. "No. You mean someone hit you on purpose?"

She nodded. "Just like someone pushed me into the street." He had come to the rescue both times. A coincidence, or had he caused both accidents, then appeared as if he was her savior?

His eyes flared with shock. "Wait a minute, Josie, you don't think it was me."

"You were around both times," she said, daring him to explain.

He cursed. "I stopped by the community center to see you."

"What for?"

"To convince you to make this camera crew leave town. Can't they film somewhere else?"

"Is that why you ran me off the road? To scare me into leaving?"

"God dammit, I didn't hit you." His wiry hair stuck up where he'd rammed his hands through it. "Someone at the center said you'd already left, so I decided to drive by your house."

Josie kept her fingers curled around the Mace. "How do you know where I live?"

"Everyone in Graveyard Falls knows where Sheriff Buckley lived." He shifted, his gaze swinging sideways as Dane roared to a stop and jumped from his SUV.

"What the hell are you doing here, Yonkers?" Dane bellowed.

Doyle backed away from the window. "I was passing by and saw this car off the road. I stopped to help."

Dane's gaze flew to Josie's. "Are you okay?"

She dropped the Mace, relieved to see him. "Yes, just shaken."

"Did he hurt you?" Dane asked.

Josie shook her head. She didn't know what to believe about Yonkers. He seemed sincere. He'd also saved her in the street.

Billy had seemed sincere, too. And harmless.

She couldn't let down her guard. A killer was on the loose, and Josie couldn't trust anyone.

◆ ◆ ◆

Dane had thought Yonkers was strange the moment he'd met him. The pet crematorium had fit with his hobby of collecting animals that had been preserved. Then Dane had dug into the man's history and discovered that as a kid he'd been obsessed with death.

After his sister's murder, he'd collected articles about other young women who'd been brutally killed. He'd also created his own small graveyard of dead animals that he supposedly found in the woods.

"I'm tired of you treating me like I'm some kind of criminal," Yonkers said to Dane. "You got the Bride Killer and know it wasn't me. So what's the deal now?"

"Another woman was murdered." Dane folded his arms in an intimidating gesture. "Twice now someone tried to hurt Josie. You showed up both times."

Yonkers's eyes flared with surprise. "A girl is dead? Who?"

Dane mumbled a sarcastic sound. "Like you don't know."

A muscle jumped in Yonkers's jaw. "As a matter of fact, I don't know anything about a murder. It was a coincidence that I was on the street when Josie fell. I didn't push her." His voice rose. "I helped her up and stopped that car from running over her."

"I don't believe in coincidences," Dane said bluntly.

"Well, maybe it wasn't totally a coincidence. Like everyone else in town, I attended the press conference because I'm interested in this film. I want to make sure my sister is portrayed in a positive light."

Josie stiffened. "I portrayed all the victims sympathetically."

Yonkers's face reddened with anger. "You made it sound like my sister and the other teenagers were mean girls, that they excluded Charlene and that she had reason to kill them."

"That's not true," Josie said.

"Miss DuKane simply relayed what happened," Dane said. "Raising awareness to teenagers about how they treat others is a good thing."

"My sister wasn't a bully."

Josie folded her hands in her lap. "No one said she was."

"So that's why you pushed Josie?" Dane pressed. "You're angry because you think she made your sister look bad?"

Yonkers cursed. "I didn't push her. I told you I stepped in front of the car that was about to run over her so he wouldn't kill her!"

"Maybe that was your plan," Dane continued. "You pushed her, then jumped in to save her so you'd look like a hero."

Yonkers glared at Josie and then Dane. "If being a Good Samaritan makes me look guilty, then I'm guilty. Now, I'm done here."

Anger flared in his eyes, and he pivoted and headed back to his vehicle. Dane followed him, nonplussed by the man's attitude. He hadn't liked him when he'd run surveillance on him for the Bride Killer murders, and he didn't like him now.

One report Peyton had dug up on the man showed he'd had several fistfights when he was a teen. A girl had also accused him of asking her to play the choking game.

He paused by Yonkers's van, then pulled out his flashlight to search for signs that he'd sideswiped or bumped Josie.

"What the hell are you doing?" Yonkers asked, any semblance of politeness evaporating.

"Looking for paint marks, dents."

"Unbelievable," Yonkers muttered. "You're determined to try to pin something on me, but you have it wrong."

Anger churned in Dane's belly. He didn't see any evidence that Yonkers had hit Josie, but the van was sturdy enough that it probably wouldn't have dented. "Then leave Josie alone," Dane said. "Stay away from her, do you hear me?"

The man's mouth flattened, but his eyes were as cold as ice chips.

"Do you?" Dane asked, his voice harder.

"Yes," Yonkers said in a clipped tone. "If you think you're going to railroad me to jail for a crime I didn't commit like Sheriff Buckley did Johnny Pike, you're mistaken."

"Trust me, I'm not railroading anyone," Dane said. "I will get to the truth. If you lay one hand on Josie DuKane, you'll answer to me. Got it?"

Animosity thrummed between them. Finally Yonkers broke eye contact, muttered a curse, slid into his van, started the engine, and drove away.

Dane gritted his teeth, hoping he'd made his point clear. When he turned back to Josie, his heart pounded, emotions pummeling him. She looked pale but sat ramrod straight as if she was braced for a fight.

She had been smart when she was abducted. She'd fought with her wits and stalled by playing along with Linder until she found the right moment to escape. Linder had still overpowered her, but even then she hadn't given up.

He admired her guts.

Dammit, he couldn't afford to let her get under his skin.

But he would protect her with his life.

◆ ◆ ◆

Josie jammed the Mace back into her purse, relieved Yonkers had left.

Dane walked back to her car and offered her a tentative smile. "If he bothers you again, let me know."

"I will. Thanks for talking to him. I don't know what to make of him."

"I don't trust him and neither should you."

"I don't trust any man," Josie admitted.

A muscle ticked in his jaw. "Not all men are bad, Josie."

Tension vibrated between them, but this was a different kind of tension. Something like desire flickered in his eyes, causing heat to spiral inside her.

She didn't want to be attracted to him, but her heart and body refused to listen to her brain. His strong arms and staunch need for justice made her feel safe and tempted her to fall into his arms.

He jerked his gaze from her to the ditch. "Can you drive your car out? Or should I call a tow truck?"

Josie sighed. His matter-of-fact tone was like a cold shower. So much for desire. She'd obviously misread his concern for something more. "Let me try."

Dane gave a nod, then stepped away from the edge of the ditch. Thankfully, the car had barely slid over the edge, and the impact hadn't triggered the air bags.

She started the car and shifted gears, tires grinding over the dirt edge, slinging dust and gravel. He motioned for her to cut the steering wheel to the right, and she did, then accelerated again. The tires ground and spit dirt, digging her in deeper. Irritated, she cut the wheel slightly to the side and tried again. More tires spinning, gravel slinging and hitting the metal, then another slight turn of the wheel and finally the car eased backward onto the road's shoulder.

He yelled that he would follow her home, and she veered onto the road and drove the short distance to her grandfather's house. Tornado season was in full swing, and the sky darkened with the threat of more storms.

She parked and Dane stopped behind her, then followed her to the porch. Josie's hand was shaking as she unlocked the door.

"Thanks for making sure I got home," Josie said, pausing at the entryway.

Dane cleared his throat. "I'm not leaving you by yourself tonight."

She chewed on her bottom lip. "Dane—"

He gripped her arms with his hands, his look fierce. But his voice was gentle. "Someone tried to hurt you. It's not safe for you to be alone."

Her skin tingled. Of course his job was the reason he'd made that statement. There was nothing personal between them.

I want there to be.

Her pulse clamored. Yet the fierce protective instincts he possessed and his gruff voice soothed her anxiety.

"Dane, I'm home, I'm fine. I don't think anyone will bother me here."

"Get real, Josie. The unsub was in your house before. He left that damn doll."

The wind sent a chill through her. Or maybe it was his words. "You don't have to remind me."

He squeezed her arm. "I'm sorry. But I don't like the fact that this killer may be using you."

"I'm not crazy about it either," she said wryly.

He gestured for her to enter. "Then don't argue. We can talk about the case tonight."

Josie shrugged, then dropped her purse on the side table and walked into the kitchen before she did something stupid like collapse in his arms.

If Dane was going to stay, she'd make dinner.

"Tell me what you know," Josie said as she pulled pasta and ingredients for sauce from the cupboard and refrigerator.

"What are you doing?" Dane asked.

"Making pasta. We have to eat." She gestured toward the refrigerator. "There's a bottle of wine and a beer in there if you want one."

Dane hesitated, his jaw set tight.

"What's wrong?"

"A beer sounds good, but I'm on duty. I'll hold off."

Josie battled disappointment. If he had a beer, he might relax. Might drop the business attitude long enough for them to have a real moment together. But she'd be foolish to invite more when Dane didn't want it. "Suit yourself," Josie said as she heated water in a pot.

He retrieved the wine and a glass from the counter and poured her a glass while she chopped onion and garlic and sautéed it in a pan. She added basil and oregano, dumped in a container of cherry tomatoes, then popped the lid on the pan so they would burst.

"You cook a lot?"

Josie shrugged, deciding to go with the small talk. They both needed a reprieve from the intensity of the case. "My mom and I enjoy cooking together. It's one of my favorite memories as a kid."

Pain flashed in his eyes.

"Did I say something wrong?"

He shook his head. "No, it's nice you're close to her."

"Did your mother cook?"

Another pained look. "Yeah. Peach pie was her specialty."

Perplexed at why that seemed to bother him, Josie sipped her wine and added parsley to the sauce. She dumped the pasta into the boiling water, then pulled out Parmesan cheese and began to grate it. "Tell me more about your family."

His sharp intake of breath made her look up. "Dane?"

He rolled his hands into fists. "My father died when I was a teenager. My mother was devastated, so I became the man of the house."

"Why do I sense there's more to the story?"

Dane must have changed his mind—he took a beer from the fridge, opened it, and took a long pull. "Ten years ago, my sister was killed. My mother blames me." He ran a hand through his hair, walked over and looked out the window, his back to her. "Hell, I blame me."

Josie stirred the sauce, determined not to push him, but sensing he needed to talk. "Why?"

"Because I was supposed to protect Betsy. She was my kid sister, and I let her down."

Josie left the pasta sauce simmering and rubbed his shoulder. "I'm sure you did everything you could to protect her."

He shook his head, then turned to her, his look tormented. "If I had, she would still be here. She would have gotten her degree, maybe been married and had a family by now." His voice cracked. "She loved kids."

Josie's chest clenched. She had suffered herself, but she had survived. She still had a chance to have a family. "What a terrible loss. What happened?"

He dropped his head forward, his shoulders shaking with emotions.

"She was visiting UT and went to a college party. The police don't know what happened, but she was found later. Stabbed to death."

Josie ran a hand over his back. "I'm so sorry, Dane."

"Bastard left her in an alley and just went on about his life like she was nothing. But she was a wonderful girl. She was my funny, annoying, lively little sister. She wanted to save the world, for God's sake."

"It sounds like you loved her a lot," Josie said softly.

He nodded. "She loved me, too, but I failed her."

The guilt in his voice made Josie want to pull him in her arms, but he was so stiff she didn't dare.

"Did the police catch who did it?" she asked.

"No." He shook his head, his breathing raspy. "College kids were partying. No one saw anything. Or if they did, they didn't remember."

"Just like Charity at that party."

He nodded again.

So this case triggered his own bad memories. She rubbed slow circles on his back, massaging the tension from his shoulders, then stepped around to face him. He jerked his head sideways, but she cupped his jaw in her hands. "That's what drives you, isn't it? You didn't get justice for her, so now you have to get it for others."

"That's the reason I joined law enforcement." Emotions darkened his expression. "I will find her killer one day," he said. "I won't stop until I do. It's what I live for."

A wave of sadness washed over Josie. She understood his grief and drive. Although he should have more in his life, someone to care for him, love him.

He looked down at the floor, his shoulders rigid. He was hurting. She desperately wanted to soothe his pain.

Forgetting all the reasons she shouldn't get involved with him, she whispered his name. "Dane—"

He clenched his jaw, eyes glittering with rage and something else . . . Need.

She parted her lips on a sigh, sensing he didn't want words or food—he wanted something else.

Unable to resist, she stroked his cheek, stood on tiptoe, and pressed her lips to his. He stiffened, and for a second she thought she'd made a mistake, that she'd misread him.

That he was going to shove her away.

A heartbeat later, he slid his arms around her, murmured a low sound of hunger in his throat, and fused his mouth with hers, dragging her so close to him that his sex hardened against her belly.

His need for her sparked her courage, and she deepened the kiss and tugged at his shirt. She wanted to feel his bare skin against her fingers, wanted to be in his arms and languishing in his touch so they could both forget about the horror of the murder in this town and the ones in their past.

◆ ◆ ◆

Dane couldn't help himself. Josie's comforting touch softened the ache in his chest.

Talking about his family stirred up anguish. Worse, sharing his feelings with someone made him feel raw all over.

He'd never talked about Betsy or his mother or his damn guilt with anyone. Well, except Cal, and he'd been ass drunk when he'd spilled his guts to him.

Regretting his admission, he started to pull away. Josie threaded her fingers in his hair and traced her tongue around the outside of his mouth, and he tightened his grip instead.

She felt like heaven in his arms, a sweet, blissful relief from the gruesome murder and grisly atmosphere in this town.

Her fingers stroked his hair, her breasts brushing against his chest in a sensual torture. His cock hardened, begging to be inside her. He trailed kisses down her neck and throat while one hand cupped her breast.

She moaned softly. The sound of her pleasure spiked his own. He wanted more.

Heart pounding with need, he removed his holster and gun and laid it on the table.

Fusing his mouth with hers, he kissed her again, his lips forging a path down her neck to her cleavage. Emboldened by her moan, he teased her nipple through her blouse, his breath catching as it stiffened beneath his fingers.

He wanted his mouth on the pebbled nub. Wanted to suckle her until she cried out his name and begged him to take her to bed.

Wanted to be naked and inside her.

Her phone buzzed, jarring him back to reality.

She ignored it and yanked at his shirt. He reached for his buttons, but her phone buzzed again. He glanced down on the table as a text appeared.

A photo.

Dammit to hell. "Josie," he whispered against her neck.

She moaned again and kissed his neck. "What?"

He hated more than anything to pull away from her. God, he wanted her. He needed her. He had to have her.

But the case came first.

The photograph made his stomach seize. A woman's tangled hair, naked body, blood, the broken compact. He set Josie away from him and grabbed the phone from the table.

Josie's eyes widened as he tilted the picture for her to see. She clutched his arm. "Oh God, Dane."

He nodded grimly.

Another woman—dead.

Posed.

Naked.

Just like Charity Snow.

CHAPTER THIRTEEN

Josie staggered backward at the sight of the picture. A second ago, she'd been blissfully in Dane's arms, pleasure replacing the horror.

She couldn't forget, though, not with another girl dead.

Remembering that the killer had been inside her home before, she raced into her bedroom.

Nausea washed over her.

Another Mitzi doll was lying on her bed, its face carved and blood-stained just like the other doll.

Footsteps echoed behind her, then Dane's voice. "Shit, he's been here again."

Josie's legs buckled; Dane steadied her with his hand, then enlarged the photograph. "Looks like she's lying by some bushes. Maybe next to a building." He murmured a low sound. "There's a trash can."

Josie pushed past her revulsion. They needed answers, not for her to be a basket case. She zeroed in on the details in the picture—the leaves on that bush, the gray color of the building. "I think that's at the community center."

Dane frowned. "Are you sure?"

She nodded, the knot in her stomach growing. "We have to go."

She flipped off the gas logs and the stove while he retrieved his gun, strapped on his holster, then punched a number on his phone.

"Sheriff Kimball, it's Agent Hamrick. There's been another murder. I think the body is somewhere around the community center. Meet me there."

Josie grabbed her purse, and seconds later they hurried outside and jumped in his SUV, the kiss between them almost forgotten as he sped toward town.

"I can't believe this is happening," Josie said, fighting the fear. She was being haunted by the dead and the living. The dead from the previous cases had never left her alone, and now two more women's faces were screaming at her for answers. Worse, there could be other victims to come. Victims who needed saving. "Why would he take the chance on getting caught by leaving that doll in my house?"

"I think you were right before, he wants you to write his story." He raked a hand over his jaw. "I'm still wondering why he's choosing the dolls."

Chill bumps skated up her spine. If he escalated, he might come in when she was home next time. She didn't want to be there when that happened.

And he *was* escalating. This wasn't a single murder.

"The doll represents little girls' desires to look like her," Josie said. "Maybe he resents that for some reason."

"He resents beautiful women," Dane said. "It has to be because they reject him."

"Perhaps he's scarred himself. That's the reason he scars his victims."

"That makes sense."

Josie lapsed into silence as he drove, her mind filled with questions about the victim. Was she another actress?

How had the killer lured her into his trap?

Judging from the theory that he wanted to expose women as fake, was he a fake himself? Did he have scars that he'd covered?

Her pulse quickened. Perhaps that was part of it—he hid his own scars, but one woman had exposed him and rejected him because of them. Now he wanted to get revenge and do the same to others.

♦ ♦ ♦

Dane parked at the community center, the winds blowing, another storm imminent.

Two murders within a three-day period, both with the same MO. An MO that had the markings of a serial killer.

That made his job more difficult. Instead of a personal connection to each victim, a serial killer chose various targets, usually with some commonality that reminded him of one person he wanted to destroy.

Personal crimes tended to be more crimes of passion or opportunity. Often the murder weapon belonged to the victim or killer. The crime scene might be messy, and the killer usually made mistakes.

Yet a serial killer was a planner. He was methodical, organized, and although he eventually made a mistake, he'd usually practiced and perfected his crime. He'd studied enough to know how to cover his tracks and avoid detection.

He took pleasure in the actual kill.

The rustle of leaves brought Dane out of his thoughts. He scanned the perimeter in case the unsub was lurking around. The place was dark tonight, the quadrangle quiet, the film crew and actors gone for the day.

Dane pulled up the photo again and pointed to a cluster of oaks and a series of red tips along the brick wall. Josie had to be right about it being around back. The front was lined with azaleas. "This is the area we're looking for. Stay behind me and keep your eyes open," Dane told Josie. "Sometimes killers like to stick around and watch the police work."

A siren wailed, and lights flashed, then the sheriff's police car rolled to a stop in the parking lot. Sheriff Kimball rushed to meet them.

Dane showed the photograph to the sheriff. "It looks like the dump site is in back, but the killer could still be around. Take the right side of the building, and we'll go left."

Kimball agreed, and they separated. Dane lit the way with his flashlight. Cigarette butts and a discarded disposable coffee cup littered the ground. Neither would be from the killer, though—this unsub was too meticulous to leave evidence. The way he'd carved the talon marks and cleaned the body to eliminate DNA proved that.

A screeching noise echoed from above. Vultures swarmed near the back corner.

He pointed to the rear of the building. "She's back there."

Josie inched along behind him as they crept toward the bushes. Leaves and twigs crackled, the scent of death wafting toward him. As he neared the corner, he spotted a foot protruding from the bushes.

"Stay back," he said. "This could be gruesome."

Josie's loud exhale punctuated the air. "Don't worry about me, Dane. Let's just do this."

He admired her bravado, and forged forward, his gut tightening when they reached the body.

She had been posed just like Charity.

He skimmed his light over her, anger churning at the sight of her naked body and the carving on her face.

He yanked on gloves, took a photo, and then swept a strand of hair from her cheek. The woman's face was desecrated, the talon marks stark and brutal looking.

And there was a sharp, deep gouge where he'd removed the piece of bone.

◆ ◆ ◆

Sorrow filled Josie. The poor woman looked to be about her age. Young with dreams ahead of her and hopes for a career—and maybe love and a family.

Sheriff Kimball rushed up, then phoned for the CSI team. "Yes, the southwest corner of the community center. MO appears to be the same as the other victim."

Josie surveyed the ground and bushes in search of a clue, but didn't see anything helpful. No purse or wallet, no cell phone, no clothing. Nothing.

The poor woman's eyes were staring wide open in death, her arms twisted, both legs angled awkwardly. Identical to the way the first victim had been left.

Why contort her body like that? Because it was an unnatural position just as makeup and implants were unnatural?

Leaves had blown down in the wind, and crumbled pieces dotted her hair and body, stuck in the blood soaking her chest.

What had the killer done to her before he'd ended her life?

Dane snapped photographs with his phone. "I'm going to send one to the lab to see if they can run it through the DMV databases and get an ID."

"How long do you think she's been dead?" Kimball asked.

Dane shrugged. "ME will have to give us TOD. Judging from rigor, I'd say she died last night or early this morning."

Josie wiped perspiration from her forehead. "Where did he keep her until he dumped her body?"

"Good question." Dane turned in a circle as if looking for an abandoned place the killer could have used, but there were no empty warehouses or apartments or houses around.

Kimball began to search the area while Dane knelt beside the body. He gently lifted the girl's hand, examined her nails, then sniffed her skin.

"He cleaned her with the same kind of strong soap he used on the first victim."

Josie had moved closer. "Did he rape them?"

"I don't know." Dane paused, wishing they had evidence one way or the other. "There were signs that Charity had sex, but the ME said it didn't appear forced. She could have hooked up with someone before the killer got her."

"Maybe the kidnapper held her against her will, and she thought if she slept with him, he wouldn't hurt her." She'd never understood that kind of desperation until she'd been abducted herself. Although the thought of sleeping with Billy had revolted her. When she'd seen Johnny's photograph and thought she and Billy were related, shock had seized her. She would have fought Billy to the death if he'd tried to get physical with her.

Thankfully, rape hadn't been on Billy's mind. He'd wanted a wife— a *pure* wife—and wouldn't have touched her until after the wedding ceremony.

Tears burned the backs of her eyes as she imagined this woman's frantic attempts to save her own life.

"That's possible," Dane said darkly. "Or perhaps this guy is charming and seduced her, then turned on her afterward. The poor girl probably never saw it coming."

Josie's chest squeezed. "That could be true, too." She considered their suspects. "Eddie Easton fits that profile. He could easily lure the women to go with him. He can be charming. His father is a sculptor, so he knows his way around a scalpel. He has also volunteered with raptors."

She hesitated. "Doyle Yonkers and Porter McCray would have a harder time attracting women."

"True. Yonkers cremates animals for a living. He could be a psychopath," Dane suggested. "He has some history of violence and killing animals. And we can't forget that he showed up both times you were nearly hurt."

Josie fidgeted at the reminder. "If he killed these two women, why not cremate them instead of leaving them for you to find?"

Dane worked his mouth side to side. "Maybe because it's about you—he wants to impress you with his MO like the Bride Killer did."

"I suppose you could be right. Sometimes serial killers actually want to get caught."

Another siren wailed, and seconds later, the CSU's van pulled up. Lieutenant Ward exited the van along with his crew.

"We should warn the women in town that a serial killer is loose," Josie said.

"No. Technically it takes three murders to constitute a serial killer." Dane scowled. "Creating panic won't help."

"The women in town have a right to know, Dane. Maybe we can save a life or catch him if they're on the alert."

"First let me identify this victim and notify her family. We don't want anything leaking before they're informed." His gaze met hers. "I also don't want the details of the MO revealed."

An image of the mutilated doll on her bed flashed back. "Of course I won't say anything. I intend to help you lock up this sicko."

Maybe she'd talk to the producer about putting production on hold until they had the man in custody.

The town was swarming with beautiful women—caked in stage makeup and desperate for any chance to stand out. If the film went away, so would the killer's hunting pool.

Dane spent the next couple of hours overseeing the crime scene investigators. Josie handled herself well, patiently waiting, asking appropriate questions, yet staying out of the way.

"Tomorrow we'll canvass the film crew and actors again to see if anyone saw anything. Maybe someone will come forward with information."

"You think the killer is part of the film crew?" Sheriff Kimball asked.

Dane shrugged. "Could be, but we can't discount a local either."

"I can't stop thinking about Billy Linder and his mama holed up in those mountains," Kimball said. "A few years ago, a prison was flooded.

Some folks think that not all of the prisoners died, that some are still hiding out in the hills."

"If so, why start killing now?" Dane asked.

"I don't know. He could have been biding his time, lying low, then all the hype from the Bride Killer and this movie stirred up his desire to kill again." Kimball jammed his hands in his pockets. "I thought I'd look at the list of prisoners and see if any have an MO similar to this."

Maybe the sheriff was onto something. It certainly wouldn't hurt to explore every angle. "Good thinking. If you find anything, let me know."

Kimball agreed, and Dane went to find Josie. She was talking to one of the investigators who'd been searching the interior of the building.

"We have an ID." Lieutenant Ward indicated an album of photographs. "We found this in that photography studio. It contains pictures of all the women who modeled for Easton."

Ward flipped through the pages, stopping at a picture of their latest victim. "Patty Waxton is her name. She's from Jackson, Mississippi."

"She came all this way to try out for a part." Josie's voice broke. "She died because of it."

"I'll find her next of kin and copy you on the information," Lieutenant Ward said.

Dane thanked him. "We'll question everyone at this place tomorrow. Someone has to have seen something." He paused. "Did you find a schedule for Easton in his studio?"

Lieutenant Ward shook his head no. "He may keep it on his phone."

"I'll question him. Maybe I'll catch him disposing of the murder weapon or he'll slip up and confess."

"What about Porter McCray?" Josie asked.

"Let's pay a surprise visit to him, too."

He studied the headshot Easton had taken of the victim—she looked picture-perfect. Smooth complexion, makeup in place, a sultry look in her eyes as if she was playing to the camera. She was downright beautiful.

Yet the unsub had destroyed that beauty by not only stripping her of makeup but also brutally carving her face until she was almost beyond recognition.

He wanted to make sure that even if she'd lived and used makeup, she couldn't hide the disfigurement.

Why? Because someone had exposed his own?

♦ ♦ ♦

Ellie cried out as the birds flapped their wings and attacked the boy again. He screamed and covered his face and head with his hands. It did no good, though. They pecked and tore at his hair and hands and the back of his head.

Blood trickled from the wounds, dampening his hair to a sticky mess. His screams for help reverberated off the mountain ridges, ripping at her soul.

She lurched awake, sat up, and stared into the darkness, the world a blur as it had been for years.

Except that blood was as vivid as if she was watching it spill from the boy's arms and face—just as it had that night.

A sound, low and pained, echoed from down the hall. A woman crying. Softly, but so full of anguish that Ellie went completely still.

She closed her eyes and felt the woman's pain just as she had so many times this last week. She'd tried to obey the nurses and let the woman be, but once she felt the draw toward a hurting soul, she couldn't resist going to them.

Her connection to this woman was especially strong.

Why, she didn't understand.

Because they were both in this nursing home, age eating at them, bodies and minds disintegrating like dust in a storm? Both alone? Both full of regrets and suffering?

She pushed aside the blanket and reached for her cane. Gripping it with one hand, she steadied herself, then pulled on her robe over her thin cotton gown. Her bones creaked as she hobbled her way across the room and through the door.

Step by step, she followed the sound of the crying, the screech of the wind wailing outside mingling with the woman's agonized moaning. Ellie passed one room, then a second, the sobs growing louder as she neared. When she reached the door to the room, she knocked softly.

Quiet followed. No one came or invited her to come in.

She hesitated. Would she be intruding? Maybe she should go back to her room. Let the woman grieve and deal with her pain in private.

Another image flashed behind her eyes.

This time, a beautiful image. A pretty young girl. She was bent over a group of boys helping them with their homework. Long silky hair framed her slender, youthful face. Freckles dotted her nose, and her front teeth were slightly crooked, but in an endearing way. A scar marred her forehead, but the girl didn't seem self-conscious about it.

She laughed at something the boys said. Then the image disappeared, and the girl was lying in a coffin, the smile gone, her face battered and bruised.

Ellie's lungs strained for air.

No, it was more than bruised. Ugly talon marks pierced the girl's skin, leaving tracks on her cheek, almost identical to the scars on the boy's face.

Ellie choked back a moan. Was the woman crying inside that room connected to the dead girl?

Grief overwhelmed Ellie, and she brushed at the tears trickling down her cheeks as she shuffled toward the woman's bed. In Ellie's room, a chair was in the corner. She found one in the corner of this room as well.

She dragged it over by the woman's bed. The sound of her soul-filled sobs vibrated through the room, tearing Ellie up inside.

Slowly Ellie reached out her hand and laid it over the woman's. For a moment the woman went very still, and Ellie thought she might push her away or scream at her to leave.

She didn't. Instead, she squeezed Ellie's hand.

A moment later, the woman's cries quieted and her breathing softened into sleep.

◆ ◆ ◆

He traced a finger over the Mitzi doll's face, admiring the beauty in the plastic doll.

The perfectly shaped face, dainty sloped nose, rosy lips—all fake.

Just like the women who smiled at him and pretended to like him when they were only attracted to what they saw on the outside.

When all they wanted was to know what he could do for them.

When they would run if they knew the truth.

He wiped the heavy makeup from his face, his skin stinging as the light penetrated the outer layer. The scar ran deep, the skin jagged and puckered, the bones beneath slightly crooked.

His face wasn't the only part of his body that was scarred. Ruined.

He would never be the same. Never be the person he was meant to be.

For that, all of the others had to pay.

CHAPTER FOURTEEN

Dane addressed the sheriff. "Tell me what Easton has been up to today." Hopefully Kimball had seen something suspicious, maybe a reason to bring Easton in, even get a warrant to search his room and studio.

Sheriff Kimball jammed his hands in the pockets of his jacket. "He was inside, had appointments all afternoon. I did rounds, went to calm down the crowd still picketing the film, then came back here. By then he was gone."

Dane silently cursed. "So you don't know where he was this evening?"

"Someone said he left with a woman, that he was going to do a personal shoot with her at Graveyard Falls. I guess this chick really wanted the part bad."

"Did you go to the falls to look for him?" Dane asked.

"Yes, but I didn't see anyone. I drove back to the cabins. His cabin is near that McCray character's, but Easton wasn't there."

Had Easton given the sheriff the slip because he knew they suspected him? "Stake out his cabin. When he returns, find out where he was and what he was doing."

"Copy that."

"How about the woman Easton did the shoot with? Do you know her name?"

Sheriff Kimball consulted his notepad. "Neesie Netherington."

"I'll call the inn and see if she came back there." Josie stepped aside to make the call.

"On the way here, I talked to my deputy," Sheriff Kimball continued. "He said Baines went to a big party this evening."

Dane shook his head in distaste. Another party. Another easy picking ground for a predator. He wanted to go after Easton and Baines himself, but he had to find out more about this victim.

With multiple suspects now—Yonkers, Baines, Easton, and McCray—he had to delegate. "Tell your deputy to talk to everyone at the party," Dane said. "Make sure Baines didn't slip out and then come back. He could have lured our victim outside, killed her, returned to the party, then later dropped her body back at the center. I also want to know if Doyle Yonkers and McCray were there."

"I'm on it." Kimball left to follow up on Easton and Baines.

Dane conferred with the lieutenant for Patty Waxton's next of kin information, then he found Josie and they walked to his SUV together.

Josie got in the passenger side. Dread tightened his gut as he phoned Patty Waxton's brother.

Three rings later, and a woman's voice answered. "Hello."

"This is Special Agent Dane Hamrick. I'm looking for Heath Waxton."

"He ain't here. Then again, if you're really the law, you know that."

"Excuse me?"

"He's been locked up for three years," the woman said. "So whatever you want to pin on him, he didn't do it."

Dane cleared his throat, wondering about the family dynamics and what the man was in prison for. "I'm not trying to pin anything on him. It's important I talk to him about his sister, Patty."

"Patty? What's going on? He hasn't heard from her since he was locked up."

"She hasn't visited him in prison?" Dane asked.

"No, they had a falling out before he was arrested. She was pissed cause he tried to use her as an alibi, and she refused to lie for him."

Dane pulled his hand down his chin. At least Patty had some morals. Which made her death even more tragic. "What prison is he in?"

"Mississippi State Pen."

"Thanks. I'll get in touch with him there." He hung up, then phoned the prison and explained the situation to the warden.

"Has he had any visitors or communication with his sister during the last few months?" Maybe she'd met Easton or one of the other suspects before and told someone.

"I'll check."

The warden came back quickly. "Agent Hamrick, according to the visitor log the only person who has visited Waxton is his girlfriend. Same with his mail."

"All right." Dane wiped his clammy hands on his jeans. The guy might be a criminal, but hearing about his sister's murder would have to hurt. "Will you notify him about his sister's death?"

"Of course. If I can help in any other way, let me know."

Making that notification was more helpful than the warden knew. Dane ended the call, then joined Josie in the SUV.

"Patty and her brother were estranged. He's doing time, but according to the man's wife, he and Patty hadn't talked in a while."

"Poor Patty." Josie worried her bottom lip with her teeth. "I couldn't reach Neesie, so I left a message. Dane, she was from Mississippi, too. I wonder if she and Patty had met."

"If so, maybe she knows something about who Patty was with."

The problem was—where was Neesie Netherington?

◆ ◆ ◆

Josie couldn't help but worry about Neesie and the other young women in town as Dane drove toward the cabins on the river. Actresses had flocked to Graveyard Falls with big dreams—only now two of them were dead.

Her phone buzzed.

The number read as an unknown. Could it be the killer?

He'd texted before—was he finally going to talk to her in person? She punched Connect. "Hello."

"Miss DuKane?"

A woman's voice. "Neesie?"

"No, this is Bailey," the girl said in a voice laced with tears.

Josie's heart melted. "Bailey, honey, what can I do for you?"

"I don't know," Bailey cried. "I miss Charity. Do you and that detective know who killed her yet?"

Josie massaged her temple and glanced at Dane. He arched a brow in question, and she mouthed that it was Bailey. "I'm afraid not yet, honey, but we're working on it."

Bailey gulped. "Some reporter named Michaels is bugging me for an interview about Charity's death," Bailey said. "I didn't know what to tell him."

Of course the reporters would swarm. When they discovered there was a second body, they would run with it and everyone would panic.

"You don't have to tell him anything," Josie said.

Dane's expression darkened. "Tell her not to talk to any reporters."

Josie gestured that she understood. "Agent Hamrick said not to talk to the press. He's trying to protect you and the investigation."

Bailey sniffled. "I appreciate that. I want to talk about Charity, but I don't want just anyone writing about her. They might make her out to be something she's not."

"I understand. She's your sister and you loved her," Josie said sympathetically. "She deserves to be remembered for the special person she was."

"That's it," Bailey said. "I knew you'd understand, Miss DuKane. That's one reason I called. I want you to write about Charity." Her voice grew bolder. "If you do, people will see what a good person she was."

"Of course, I'd be honored." The girl's trust touched her deeply. "We'll get together when you're feeling better and make some notes."

"Thanks," Bailey said. "I just took a sleeping pill so I could sleep tonight. Last night I . . . Well, I had terrible nightmares."

Josie's breath rasped out as Billy's face flashed behind her eyes. Bailey's words sank in. "I can relate to your nightmares, Bailey. You will be okay, won't you? I mean, you aren't drinking and mixing pills—"

"No. I'm not going to do anything stupid," Bailey said with conviction. "I'm determined to land a part in this movie for Charity. She would want that."

Relief made Josie sag. "Yes, she would. I'm proud of you."

Bailey sniffled. "I figured if you can face this town after what happened to you, I can be tough, too."

Tears welled in Josie's eyes. She wanted to be an example for other young women, but she didn't deserve this girl's admiration. Not when she carried the weight of Charity's death on her shoulders.

"Anyway, thanks, Josie," Bailey said. "You have no idea what it means to be able to talk to you."

Josie wiped at her eyes. "Of course. Call me anytime day or night that you need me, and I'll be there."

She ended the call, desperately trying to gather her composure. The thought of speaking for another dead girl weighed on her shoulders. She wanted justice for Charity and her sister, though.

"Is she all right?" Dane asked.

Josie shook her head. "No, but she will be. That reporter is bothering her. She wants me to write Charity's story."

Dane's mouth twisted into a grimace. "I really wish you weren't involved. Maybe if you left town—"

"I'm not running from this, Dane. You should know that by now," she said, annoyed.

"I do, but a man can hope." Worry underscored his voice, softening his sarcastic tone.

She jammed her phone into her purse, ignoring his grim look. "Where to next?"

He checked his watch. "To check on McCray. The sheriff is looking for Easton."

The Billy Linder lookalike made Josie's skin prickle. If he'd killed Charity and Patty Waxton, she'd gladly help lock him away.

They lapsed into silence, the night sounds of the forest reverberating in the wind rolling off the mountains. Last year at this time, snow still dotted the ridges and the temperature was frigid.

The dark clouds above obliterated the moon and the stars, making the area look desolate and eerie as they drove into the heart of the mountains to the river.

Dane pointed to the corner cabin set against the forest. Shrouded by thick oaks and pines, it was more isolated than the others—a good place to hide. If a woman screamed for help, no one would even hear her.

A low light burned inside, but otherwise things seemed quiet.

Dane parked and checked his weapon. "Stay here."

"No." She reached for the door handle. "I want to see his reaction when you question him. Besides, he's been wanting to talk to me. Maybe he'll open up if I'm there."

Dane hesitated, then nodded in resignation and they got out.

A coyote howled, storm clouds rumbling. Dane ushered Josie behind him as they approached.

"He's not going to shoot at us or come out in the open and attack us," Josie said. "He likes this cat and mouse game too much."

Dane gripped his Glock by his side, planting himself in between her and the door as he knocked.

♦ ♦ ♦

Dane kept his senses honed in case McCray was combative or tried to escape out the back. He hoped to hell some incriminating evidence was on the man or inside his cabin. Seeing another woman's face butchered had made his stomach sour.

Footsteps shuffled inside, and he braced himself to guard Josie. He shouldn't have agreed to let her come here. Not with the killer taunting her, and McCray's resemblance to Linder. He could have easily sent her the message with the doll to entice her to play his game.

The wind shook the trees again, tossing twigs onto the porch and pummeling the roof. The damn wind roared like a freight train through the sharp ridges. Somewhere in the distance a dog barked, and an owl hooted—the wildlife a reminder of how deeply the town was buried in the Smoky Mountains.

The door opened, and Porter McCray stood on the other side.

Dane quickly scrutinized him—he wore jeans and a wrinkled plaid shirt. His hair stuck out in tufts as if he'd either run his hands through it or he'd been sleeping. No visible blood on his shirt or hands.

McCray squinted up at him with a scowl. As soon as he noticed Josie, he straightened, his eyes twitching Billy Linder–style. "What can I do for you now?" McCray asked.

"We need to talk," Dane said bluntly.

McCray lifted one eyebrow. "It's late. I have a callback for another audition tomorrow." He slanted a sinister smile toward Josie. "I appreciate you putting in a good word for me."

"I had nothing to do with it," Josie said, her tone indicating she was in no mood to entertain his sick fantasies.

"Yes, you did. You wrote a killer book." A dark chuckle rumbled from him at his own wordplay.

Josie glared at him.

Dane fought the urge to wring the man's neck and jammed one foot into the doorway. "Are you going to let us in, or do we need to take this chat to the sheriff's office?"

McCray rubbed his fingers down his neck, then gestured for them to enter. "I suppose I don't have a choice."

Dane surveyed the front room of the cabin. Wood floors, den and kitchen combination. Acting magazines and scripts scattered on the coffee table.

A stuffed coyote on the mantel. A raccoon on the desk. Linder's work?

"Are those yours or did they come with the cabin?" Dane asked pointedly.

McCray smirked. "The elk head and bear skin rug came with the cabin. I brought the others. Thought having some of Linder's taxidermy work would be inspiring."

Josie shuddered beside him. Dane wanted to pull her in his arms, but he had to keep it professional. Feeding McCray any personal connection between Josie and him might work against them at some point.

"Josie, you look tired," McCray said in a quiet tone, as if the two of them were intimate.

Josie offered him a bland look. "I'm tired of violence, of men hurting women."

"Where were you tonight?" Dane asked.

McCray turned his attention toward Dane. "I stayed at the community center until six when everyone finished up, mingling with the other actors. Have to get to know one's competition."

Dane needed exact time of death, but he didn't have it yet. "Then what?"

McCray folded his arms across his chest. "I drove up to Graveyard Falls and went for a hike to get a feel for the falls and the woods where Linder lived."

"Did you go to Linder's old house?" Dane asked. That place had been roped off as a crime scene. As far as he knew, it had sat empty since mother and son had been incarcerated.

"Not yet." He smiled at Josie, irritating Dane more. "I was hoping Josie might show me the house."

That was not going to happen.

Dane gestured toward McCray's shirt. He wished to hell the asshole did have blood on it so he could drag him to jail. Even if he hadn't killed the women, Dane didn't like the way he looked at Josie. "Is that what you've been wearing all day?"

"Yes." McCray's jaw twitched. "Why? What's going on?"

"Another woman was murdered tonight." Dane didn't bother to ask permission or wait for McCray to stop him. He pushed past him and walked into the kitchen.

He opened the kitchen cabinets and drawers searching for a sharp sculpting tool, knife, or scalpel that McCray could have used as a weapon, but he found nothing but standard kitchen knives that were stocked in all the units.

McCray mumbled a protest as he followed on his heels. "Wait just a damn minute. Don't you need a warrant?"

"Not if I have probable cause."

McCray fidgeted. "What cause is that?"

Dane fought a grin. McCray's slip out of character meant Dane was getting to him. "I don't have to explain anything to you."

Dane pushed past him and searched the lower cabinets, the small desk in the corner, then the garbage.

"You think that if I'd killed someone, I'd keep the weapon? That would be stupid, wouldn't it?" McCray asked sardonically.

"Not all criminals are smart." Dane flipped on the hall light. One bedroom held a bed, but the other looked as if it was being used as an office.

Rita Herron

Beside a desk sat several foldable cardboard stands filled with articles about the Bride Killer and Thorn Ripper. Photos of the victims and a large picture of Josie holding her book along with the press release for the movie were tacked on one.

Even more disturbing, another board held photos of all the female actors who'd signed up for auditions in Graveyard Falls.

Charity Snow's photo was in the middle of the board.

But the table in the corner made him suck in a breath. It held taxidermy tools and a squirrel with its eyes carved out.

Dane cursed. If one of those tools had Charity's or Patty's blood on it, he'd be able to nail the bastard.

CHAPTER FIFTEEN

Josie barely stifled a gasp at the sight of the photos. Porter McCray had immersed himself into Billy Linder's life, but seeing the gruesome pictures of the Bride Killer victims on the wall seemed wrong, even cruel.

That dead coyote's piercing eyes sent nausea through her.

Dane gestured at a book on taxidermy beside the tools. "Practicing carving up animals?"

McCray's eerie smile twisted his face. "It was a unique part of Linder's character."

A very disturbing one.

Dane walked over to examine the tools, curious at the blood dotting them. "Is that all you've been carving?"

"Yes," McCray said. "Before you ask, I didn't kill the squirrel. It was already dead."

Josie couldn't tear her eyes from the pictures. "Where did you get those photographs?" she asked. "The press never released them."

"Neither did the police," Dane said sharply.

McCray shrugged. "I did some research."

"You paid someone for them, didn't you?" Dane asked. "Someone from the police department?"

A vein pulsed in McCray's neck. "No."

"Then you had someone hack into police files," Dane guessed.

"Let's just say I did my research." McCray ran a finger over the coyote's head. "Many actors go to great lengths to learn accents for roles. They change their physical appearance, lose or gain weight, dye their hair, take classes, do special tactical training, learn different languages, even immerse themselves in different cultures."

Dane pointed to Charity's photograph. "Why is Charity Snow's picture in the middle of your board?"

McCray looked at her with interest. "I was scouting out the females who might play opposite me."

"Did you know Patty Waxton?" Josie asked, her voice cold, accusatory.

"I met her earlier today." He shrugged. "I met a lot of other people, too, Josie. You know everyone is chatty there at the center."

Dane wanted the man's attention off Josie. "Did you take her up to the falls to check out the locations of the murders?"

"No. What good would she have done me?" McCray angled his head toward Josie. "The only person I invited to go there was you, Josie. You could tell me things about Billy that no one else knows. Things that you left out of the book." His voice grew low, disturbing. "Things that were personal, like how he talked to you, how he touched you."

Memories bombarded Josie, making her lungs tighten. Billy had looked like a terrified child at the idea of his mother dying.

He was strong, though. His tentative touch had turned to cold steel when she'd thrown that gravy on him. She could still feel his hands around her neck, feel the thick ropes weighing down her arms and legs. Hear his mother's cackle of laughter as he'd tied her to the bed.

"That's enough." Dane's bark jerked her back to reality.

McCray wiggled his eyebrows at her suggestively. "That's for Josie to decide."

Josie rolled her hands into fists. "Mr. McCray, you've taken this role-playing entirely too far."

Dane shoved McCray onto the chair. "Sit down and don't move. If I find one thing in this cabin to implicate you, you're going to jail." He pulled on gloves and began to collect the taxidermy tools to send to the lab. "I'm starting with these."

McCray's bravado crumbled slightly, but he pasted on a slimy smile. "You know I'm just acting, don't you, Josie? You don't think I killed those women?"

Josie didn't know what she thought. He liked toying with her so much he could have sent those dolls and pictures to get her attention.

In her eyes, any man sick enough to stoop to frightening women was capable of murder.

◆ ◆ ◆

Dane searched the closet and desk, but found nothing.

He shot a look over his shoulder, daring McCray to move.

After all, he might be the unsub who'd brutally stabbed two women. If Betsy's death was related, possibly three.

Hope warred with caution. Dane wanted them to be the same killer, wanted to free his mother of the burden of knowing that her daughter's killer was still out there.

He needed concrete proof to make an arrest, and to appease his own mind. So far, McCray didn't quite fit with being near UT at the time of Betsy's death.

Refusing to leave Josie alone with McCray, he took her arm and strode to the second bedroom.

Josie wrapped her arms around her middle. "I can't stay in the room with that creep any longer."

"I'm sorry," Dane said. "I know this is difficult for you."

Josie offered him a brave smile. "I'm fine. Just do what you have to do."

Dane wanted to comfort her, but he admired her show of courage, and time was of the essence. He nodded, then searched beneath the bed and mattress, then the closet. If he found something, McCray's lawyer might argue that it was inadmissible because he didn't have a warrant, but Dane would argue that he saw the blood on those tools, and that he'd thought another woman might have been abducted—meaning Neesie Netherington—and that he suspected she was being held at the cabin.

Besides, the tools and photographs were in plain sight.

McCray's unnatural obsession with the serial killer Billy Linder suggested he could be honing his craft, establishing his own MO to gain fame like Linder.

"What exactly are you looking for?" Josie asked.

"Murder weapon. Also any bloody clothing or towels, his or the women's. A strong-smelling soap. I think he cleaned the victims' makeup off with it."

Josie folded her arms and watched as he searched.

Clothing from the man's suitcase had been dumped into the dresser drawers, and a plastic laundry basket held dirty clothes, although none had bloodstains or smelled of bleach or cleaning chemicals. No women's clothing either.

If McCray had killed the women, he'd disposed of their clothes somewhere else.

From the bedroom, Josie made a strangled sound, and Dane rushed to her. "What is it?"

She stood in front of the wardrobe, her back to him, and she was trembling. Dane slowly walked toward her, his heart hammering. Clothing and hats, ones that looked like costumes for different characters, overflowed the wardrobe. Pancake makeup along with two different hairpieces, hair dye, eyeglasses, and a fake mustache sat on the vanity, and a cane leaned against the wall.

When Josie turned and looked up at him, fear clouded her eyes.

Damn.

There were pictures of Josie tacked on the inner door. Photographs taken at the crime scene at Linder's house.

Where he'd kept her hostage.

♦ ♦ ♦

Neesie Netherington had a message from the author of that book, but it was too late to call her back tonight. She slipped into her room at the inn, half hoping her roommate was awake so she could talk about her evening.

She didn't bother with a light and tiptoed over to the second double bed, but it was empty.

Granted she was late herself, but where was Patty? She was more of a homebody than Neesie and usually turned in by ten. Patty insisted that lack of sleep caused you to age faster, and she couldn't afford a face-lift if she had wrinkles at thirty.

Too wired to sleep, Neesie flipped on a light and went into the bathroom. The stark light accentuated the makeup that was smeared, and her lips looked swollen, her face chafed from an evening of sex.

The memory of Eddie Easton's seductive smile warmed her, although truth be told, the photo session in the woods had rattled her nerves.

When he'd first explained his niche photography shoots—taking pictures in a setting simulating one of the scenes from this movie—it had sounded like a good idea.

She hadn't been prepared for the emotions pretending to be strangled would have on her.

For a few moments, that garter had felt so tight around her neck, she couldn't breathe. It had felt real, as if Eddie was going to choke the life from her.

She pressed her hand to her throat and examined the slight bruising around her neck. She wouldn't do that again.

Exhausted and knowing she had her audition in the morning, she stripped, pausing to study the scar on her torso. Damn her ex.

No more bikinis for her. At least not unless she did something about the scar.

If she did love scenes, it would be visible. Makeup would help.

That charming photographer Eddie had noticed and offered her a solution, a discount with a surgeon he knew. If she landed a part here, she could afford it.

She pulled the business card for the plastic surgeon from her pocket and studied it. Dr. Silas Grimley. He worked in LA but was in Knoxville for a plastic surgeons' convention.

If she got rid of the scar, maybe she could finally purge her ex from her mind.

She donned a gown, washed the makeup from her face, then took the card and laid it on the bedside table.

Tomorrow she'd call Dr. Grimley and set up an appointment.

♦ ♦ ♦

"You can't arrest me because I have a few pictures in my cabin," McCray said haughtily. "That's not against the law. It's called research."

Dane gritted his teeth. Unfortunately, the jerk was right. He needed blood, a weapon, something concrete to tie him to the crime.

"It can be considered stalking," Dane said. "*That* is against the law."

"I'm not stalking anyone." McCray narrowed his eyes at Josie. "Am I, Josie? I haven't touched you or threatened you. I only asked for consultation on the movie. I'm sure I'm not the only one here who'd like a private session with you."

"I'm not offering private sessions," Josie said firmly. "If you come near me again or bother me, I'll file a restraining order."

McCray's eyes turned menacing. "How can you do that when we'll be in the same building during the next few days?"

Dane snatched him by the collar. "Just be sure to stay away from her, or I'll find a way to lock you up." Dane leaned closer, using intimidation tactics he'd learned in training. "So, if you have nothing to hide, what is your real name? I know it's not McCray."

McCray averted his gaze, his tough façade fading. "I don't have to answer that."

"Either answer it here or down at the sheriff's station." Dane raised a brow. "If word spreads that you're a suspect, what do you think that will do to your chances of landing a part in this film?"

Steam oozed from McCray's pores. "All right. I'll tell you, but I'd prefer my name remain confidential."

Dane didn't intend to make any kind of deal with this asshole. "What is it?"

He swiped sweat from his forehead. "Lou Hiscock."

"Hiscock?"

"Yes," McCray said in a tight voice. "No one in show business would take me seriously if I introduced myself that way. It sounds like a porn star."

It did, but Dane refrained from commenting. Unfortunately, until the lab examined those tools and determined if the blood was human, he didn't have enough to make an arrest. If he'd found prints at Josie's, he could justify bringing McCray in for breaking and entering or for stalking. But he didn't have prints.

Still, if McCray made one move toward her, he'd haul him in.

He gestured for Josie to lead the way, and they left the cabin and walked back to his SUV.

He texted Peyton McCray's real name and asked her to run a search on him. Hopefully something concrete would turn up to link him to these murders. So far, all he had was a strong dislike for the guy and a few tools he'd used practicing taxidermy. The man even had a reasonable explanation for that.

At this point, Easton looked more like the viable suspect.

His phone buzzed, and he snatched it up. "Agent Hamrick."

"It's Kimball. I found Eddie Easton. He's at his place now. Says he did a photo shoot with that girl Neesie Netherington earlier, then they hooked up. No bloody clothing or weapons on him."

"What about the Netherington woman?" Dane's pulse kicked up a notch. "Any sign of her?"

"Afraid not. I left a message on her cell phone."

"I'll stop by that inn and see if she's there." He'd find out exactly what happened at that photo shoot. If Neesie had seen a scalpel or carving tool in his equipment, or if Easton had frightened her, it might confirm that they were on the right track.

CHAPTER SIXTEEN

Josie's nerves were on edge as she and Dane stopped at the Falls Inn. It was nearly one o'clock in the morning, late to call on anyone.

With two women dead, every minute counted.

Dane knocked on the door, not surprised that it took a few minutes for the owner to answer, and that she was half asleep.

"What in the world?" Cynthia Humphries muttered. "Do you know what time it is?"

"We're so sorry," Josie said. "It's important, though."

"Yes, I apologize," Dane said sincerely. "Ms. Humphries, another woman was murdered tonight. I need to talk to one of your guests. She might know something about the young lady."

Her eyes widened. "Oh my God, I can't believe this is happening. Who was she?"

"One of the actors in town for the film, Patty Waxton," Dane said. "We're wondering if your guest Neesie Netherington knew her."

"Yes, they said they'd met before coming here." She patted at her hair with a shaky hand. "Let me get her."

Dane nodded, and she disappeared up the stairs. Josie dug her hands in the pockets of her jacket, dreading the conversation they were about to have.

Voices rumbled, and a twentysomething brunette with wavy hair descended the stairs, tightening her robe with the belt as she entered the foyer. Josie introduced herself and Dane, earning a wary look from Neesie.

Dane cleared his throat. "Miss Netherington, do you know Patty Waxton?"

She paled as if she sensed bad news. "Yes, we're roommates. We met at another audition. What's wrong? Is Patty okay?"

"I'm afraid not," Dane said. "We found her body outside the community center earlier. She was stabbed to death."

"Oh my God, I was afraid something bad happened to her." The girl's legs buckled, and Josie and Dane caught her and helped her to the bench in the foyer.

"What makes you say that?" Josie asked gently.

Tears seeped from Neesie's eyes. "Because she goes to bed early, and she wasn't in the room when I got home. I haven't seen her since this morning or heard from her."

"You were with Eddie Easton earlier?" Dane asked.

She crinkled her nose. "Yes, why?"

Josie squeezed the young woman's arm. "Please, Neesie. Tell us what happened with Eddie. Where were you?"

She chewed a thumbnail for a moment. "He took me up to the woods for a photo shoot."

"What time was that?" Dane asked.

"Dusk." She shifted from foot to foot. "It was kind of eerie. He likes to take these niche pictures. We reenacted one of the murders."

Josie lifted Neesie's chin and frowned at the mark on Neesie's neck. "Did he hurt you?"

"No, not really," Neesie said. "We went to the falls, and he had me dress like the Bride Killer victims, right down to the wedding gown and garter."

Josie wiped her clammy hands on her clothes. "Then what?"

"Afterward, we went to a motel and well, you know . . ."

"You were with him all evening?" Dane asked.

"Not the entire time," she said. "I fell asleep about eight, and when I woke up he was gone. He left a note that something came up, along with cab fare."

Josie bit back a comment about not sleeping with strangers. Neesie was going to feel bad enough about Patty's death without a chastising. "Did Eddie have a doll with him? A Mitzi doll?"

Neesie chewed her nail again. "No, why?"

Josie folded her hands around Neesie's to keep her from biting her nails to the quick. "It might be important."

She worried her lip with her teeth as if thinking. "I didn't see one. But he had other props in his closet. Ones for various scenes the actresses could portray."

Josie stewed over what Neesie had said. Porter McCray was creepy, but Easton seemed more likely the killer. His fetish photography gave him the perfect opportunity to lure women to their deaths.

Even if he hadn't hurt Neesie, he could easily have killed Patty earlier and stashed her body somewhere, then slipped out, driven back to Graveyard Falls, and dumped Patty's body after everyone else had left the community center.

The poor girl had no idea how lucky she was to have just come away with bruises. She could be lying in a patch of weeds dead just like the others.

◆ ◆ ◆

Dane vacillated over whether McCray or Eddie Easton was the unsub. Easton was winning out.

McCray was stranger than fiction, creepy, and obsessed with the details of the Linder case to the point he might have crossed the line and decided he wanted to taste what it felt like to take a human life. If so, why wouldn't he have emulated the Bride Killer? Why use talon marks when he had no experience himself in taxidermy or with birds of prey? He recalled the theory about the scars. As far as he knew, McCray hadn't suffered from scars either.

On the other hand, Easton had attended UT when Betsy visited, and he'd worked with birds of prey. He'd also been scarred, had plastic surgery, had access to all the actors, and had photography sessions with many of them. The young women would easily trust him and go with him without a fight.

Just like Neesie had when she'd allowed him to dress her in a wedding dress and mimic strangling her with a garter.

Pervert.

The thought of Easton's actions made Dane want to wrap his hands around the man's neck and teach him what it felt like to be powerless.

"So how was the sex?" Dane asked.

Josie caught his arm, her brows furrowed. "Dane."

Neesie coughed. "Excuse me?"

He ground his teeth, regretting his abruptness. But he had police work to do. "I just need to know if he was dangerous. You said he posed you like one of the victims during your photo session. Did he tie you up? Make you uncomfortable? Frighten you?"

Neesie shoved her fingers in her hair and rubbed her head as if debating how to answer.

"I'm not judging," Dane added quickly. "We're looking for a man who killed two women. Did you feel like he would hurt you?"

"I don't know. Maybe." A sliver of fear shot through her eyes. "Reenacting that scene made me nervous because we were alone in the woods. He reminded me of . . ."

Josie squeezed Neesie's hand. "Of who?"

Neesie made a strangled sound. "My ex."

"What happened with him?" Dane asked.

"He was obsessed with me," Neesie admitted. "He followed me everywhere and scared off my friends. When I broke it off, he told me he'd never let me go."

Josie gave her hand another sympathetic squeeze. "Go on."

"One night he beat the crap out of me," she said. "I wound up in the hospital with a broken jaw, cracked ribs, and a slice out of my stomach. I still have scars."

Dane grunted. Men who beat up on women were assholes. "Where is this guy now?"

"I don't know." Neesie turned to Josie for support. "When I was released from the hospital, a friend helped me run away. I took a new name, a new identity. I still look over my shoulder."

"If you'll give me a photo, I'll alert the sheriff to look out for him," Dane said, his protective instincts driving him.

Neesie retrieved her phone and scrolled through some photos, then texted Dane a snapshot of the scumbag.

Dane assured her that if he was in town, he'd be picked up and questioned. "Let's get back to Easton. Did he mention anything about his past?"

Neesie shook her head. "When he saw my scars, he offered to refer me to a plastic surgeon named Dr. Grimley. He's worked on some of the other actresses and models in LA."

"Grimley." Dane committed the name to memory. He'd seen that man's business card in the basket in Easton's studio. Charity Snow had had breast implants—had Dr. Grimley performed the surgery?

"Did Patty have any cosmetic work done?" Dane asked.

Neesie gave a short nod. "She had cheek implants and a tummy tuck, and maybe something else, although she wouldn't talk about it." Neesie tugged at the belt to her robe. "I'm not sure who did it. We only met a couple of months ago. She'd already had the work done."

The fact that both victims had plastic surgery wasn't unusual in the acting world, but it still was a common denominator.

Any common denominator might prove to be a lead.

There was also a connection between Easton and Grimley. That could be significant, putting both men at the top of his suspect list.

♦ ♦ ♦

Exhaustion tugged at Josie as Dane drove to her house. Dane had to be worn out, too, but he didn't show any sign of stopping for sleep.

How could she not admire him for his dedication? He might have sounded harsh with Neesie, but she sensed he was angrier at the man who'd abused her than at Neesie.

Dane phoned the lab and left a message for his IT person, Peyton, to see what she could find out about Neesie's ex, Leroy, and Dr. Grimley.

"Grimley is a plastic surgeon," Dane said. "I need to know if he performed cosmetic surgery on our two victims. Also find out everything you can about his background and connection to the photographer Eddie Easton."

The memory of finding that doll on her bed haunted Josie as he pulled in her drive.

As she entered her house, she immediately scanned the kitchen and living room, then went to the bedroom to make sure no one had been inside.

When she returned to the kitchen, Dane was standing by the back door looking out into the dark woods. Josie had thought the forests looked spooky last year when she was here, but knowing another murderer was lurking around made her wonder if evil was drawn to Graveyard Falls.

"It's late, Dane. You must be worn out. Thanks for driving me back."

His shoulders were rigid as he pivoted to face her. "If that's your way of telling me to leave, it won't work. I'm not going anywhere tonight."

His husky voice washed over her, stirring feelings that she couldn't allow herself to pursue. For God's sake, while she'd initiated a kiss before, another woman lay dead.

She and Dane needed to focus on finding her killer.

"I'm fine. You don't have to stay."

"I know you're fine," he said with a heavy sigh. "That you're tough." He curled his hands around her arms. She glanced down at the floor, aching to hold him yet knowing she had to be strong.

He forced her to look at him. "The unsub who brutally stabbed two women was in your house earlier. For all we know, he may come back."

She trembled, and his look softened. "I'm not trying to frighten you," Dane said, "but we have to be realistic. At some point, this unsub may want to do more than just send you photographs. He may want to talk to you in person."

Josie's breath caught at the dark worry in Dane's expression. "You think he'll try to kill me?"

Dane shrugged. "I don't know, but from now on, I'm not leaving your side."

◆　◆　◆

Silas Grimley opened up his blog called *The Bird Diaries* and skimmed his last entry.

His father used to make him keep a journal cataloging the details of every bird of prey they'd rescued, any injuries the animal had sustained, and the treatment they'd given the bird.

He'd also performed experiments on the birds.

Some that'd made the birds sick and turn violent toward humans.

When the birds had died, he'd let the raptors clean the bones, then his father collected them. Together they'd made intricate collages for the walls.

Silas kept some in his apartment back in LA.

After the attack, Silas had started writing about the horrors of what had happened to him and how he'd become a collector of bones. The first stories depicted his early years when his mother left and his father became obsessed with the birds.

Silas had been terrified of the sharp talons and beaks and had shied away from helping his father.

Showing fear had infuriated the man. Determined to teach him to be strong, he'd forced Silas into the pens.

Flooded with images of the hawks and vultures circling above his head, pecking at his face and arms and hands, Silas exhaled. The memory of the birds ripping his flesh from his hands and face with their claws was so strong that he felt as if it was happening all over again. He could still smell the metallic scent of his own blood.

He placed his fingers on the keyboard and began to describe the little boy's tentativeness as his father had shoved him into the pen. His father had always worn gloves when he'd worked with the falcons, but sometimes they'd pecked through the thick fabric and clawed through his shirt.

His father had been proud of those scars.

In this story, Silas decided to make the boy fight back instead of cowering like a coward.

The boy grabbed a stick and beat at the birds, but each swing of the stick seemed to only enrage the wild animals more. Their hisses and screeched attack calls rent the air as they swarmed and descended on the boy.

Bloody and aching from the claw marks, the boy crawled to the door of the pen and managed to unlatch it. Blood dripped from his hand and arm as he shoved it open.

The birds continued to attack, tearing at his flesh as he dragged himself through the opening in the dirt. Mustering all the strength he could, he pushed the pen door open wide. They rushed to escape. They flapped and soared to the sky.

He'd freed them and saved himself.

His father's bellow boomed through the ridges, and he sagged with defeat. He'd never really be free, not until his father was buried and he could flee the mountains himself.

Just like the falcons and eagles.

CHAPTER SEVENTEEN

Shaken by the thought of this latest killer coming after her, Josie was tempted to ask Dane to crawl in bed with her and hold her all night.

Earlier, they'd almost made love.

Was he thinking about that now?

His deep breath made her look into his eyes. Desire, hunger, and . . . worry darkened the depths. She didn't know which caused her heart to pound faster. The thought of a killer after her or falling in love.

God, no.

She wasn't falling in love. She was simply feeling vulnerable and lonely. Dane was strong, protective, and noble. Unlike any other man she'd ever known. At least one whom she'd gotten close to.

"Go to bed and get some rest, Josie," Dane said in a gruff whisper.

She stifled the urge to throw herself at him, then fled before she gave in to the need building inside her.

Guilt hit her, though, and she grabbed an extra blanket and pillow for the sofa, rushed back in, and pushed them in his arms. "If you need anything, let me know."

A chuckle rumbled from him. "That's what I was going to say to you."

She did need something. She needed him.

But that was impossible.

So she returned to her bedroom and closed the door.

Wind whistled outside, beating a tree branch against the window, but she pulled the curtains tightly together, hoping to muffle the sound, then hurriedly slipped on pajamas. A quick wash of her face removed what little makeup she wore, and she brushed her hair, one look in the mirror a reminder that she didn't fit the victim's profile.

So far, he'd targeted beautiful young women—but as Dane had pointed out, both had undergone plastic surgery. Neither of those elements fit her.

Knowing Dane was in the den alleviated her anxiety over the earlier break-in, and she crawled in bed and pulled up the covers. But sleep eluded her.

Instead, a myriad of memories flooded her.

Images of Billy Linder and the skeletal frame of his mother hunched in that wheelchair, the whites of her eyes red with broken blood vessels, blue veins bulging beneath paper-thin skin.

The scent of dust and mildew and rancid body odors that permeated the cabin suffocated her, and she gasped for a breath.

Then images of the mangled doll's face and the poor women who'd been brutally murdered taunted her, their cheeks marred with the talon claw marks.

The talons belonged to birds of prey.

Was *that* the killer's message? That he was the predator stalking the town and these women were his prey?

Or could there be something else about the talons?

Billy Linder had worked as a taxidermist and was obsessed with showcasing his work.

Was this unsub obsessed with birds? Had he been raised with them?

He also collected bones. That was just as disturbing as the talon marks.

Perhaps he was some kind of scientist who studied bones, or an archaeologist or a forensic analyst?

That was another avenue to explore. But one that might lead them to the right man and stop his madness.

◆ ◆ ◆

Dane finally dozed for a couple of hours, but the minute the sun glinted through the front window, he jerked awake, his mind already analyzing details of the case.

He retrieved his computer from his SUV and decided to work before he heard from Peyton.

While the computer booted up, he rummaged through Josie's kitchen and brewed a pot of coffee.

All night the case had eaten at him.

The fact that two victims had plastic surgery, yet the killer had carved their faces, destroying that beauty, disturbed him. Whoever the unsub was, he had a grudge against beautiful women—or women who'd undergone cosmetic surgery.

Why? Because he'd been rejected?

Because he disagreed with plastic surgery for some reason—perhaps based on religion?

A cup in hand, he entered Patty Waxton's name into his laptop and ran a search. She had no police record, and no family other than the brother in jail. She'd graduated from high school and taken a few acting classes in a local community arts center.

Her headshots had been done by Eddie Easton just as Charity Snow's had. Medical records were harder to obtain, so he called the ME.

"Dr. Wheeland, it's Agent Hamrick. What can you tell me about our latest victim?"

"COD was the same as the first victim. The injuries and cuts on her face were made with the same type of instrument, which I believe was a surgical scalpel."

Dane's heart hammered.

The plastic surgeon would have a scalpel. But why would a doctor who made his living saving lives and making people more attractive kill?

Why would he maim a woman's face when his reputation was built on repairing imperfections?

He had a similar problem with the photographer's motive. Why would Easton kill the same women who fed his ego and his wallet?

Easton wasn't lacking in his own looks or female attention. Neesie Netherington had admitted that—in spite of his disturbing niche photography—he'd charmed and seduced her. He hadn't hurt her when he had the opportunity. He could easily have killed her in the woods when they were doing the photo shoot.

Dane needed more information. "Anything else you can tell me from the body? What about time of death?"

"I'd put TOD sometime between three and eight yesterday morning. Again, the victim had sex sometime earlier that day, but no signs of forced sexual assault."

"What about the tox screen?"

"She was given the same paralyzing drug as Charity Snow."

Dr. Wheeland's attention to detail was an asset. "Any trace evidence?"

"There were traces of makeup beneath her nails," Dr. Wheeland said. "I'm analyzing it now."

Frustration shot through Dane. Instead of the answers he needed, he only had more questions. "Odd, since the killer wiped her clean of makeup." Dane mentally referenced Betsy's case. There were major differences in this unsub's MO that he wasn't sure the killer's evolution could account for.

Was he trying to see connections when they weren't there?

"That's what I thought," Dr. Wheeland continued, oblivious to Dane's turmoil. "This makeup has a different consistency—it's thicker, more like pancake makeup. Who knows? She might have used it earlier and simply didn't clean her nails well enough to eliminate traces."

Dane had known a girl in high school with a port wine birthmark who covered it with pancake makeup. "Isn't pancake makeup used by people with scars or those port wine birthmarks?"

"Yes," Dr. Wheeland replied, "although actors and special effects artists use it for various roles."

The makeup artist probably had an array with him. "Did Patty have a scar or birthmark?"

"Not that I've found, but there are signs indicating she had cosmetic work."

Dane stewed over the forensics. These clues were leading away from Betsy's killer.

These girls needed justice, too, though. "If the makeup particles were a result of her contact with the killer, that means he may be covering up a scar himself. Or he could be in disguise."

"Both are possibilities," Dr. Wheeland agreed. "Or he could be one of the actors."

Like McCray. Or even Baines—the makeup artist.

He had been scarred in an accident when he was young and had more than a hundred stitches. Most of the women in attendance this week probably knew him or worked with him.

They would certainly trust him.

Although as far as he knew, neither Baines nor McCray had been anywhere near Betsy ten years ago.

Disappointed that the pieces weren't fitting the way he wanted, Dane thanked the ME, his thoughts churning as he phoned the sheriff. "Kimball, do you have anything on Baines?"

"According to my deputy, Baines worked at the community center until around eight last night, then went to dinner with a group and left the restaurant with some other guy."

"Where did they go?"

"Back to the cabin. Guy left around ten. After that, Baines went out. My deputy followed him but said he lost him on the highway."

"Dammit, so Baines had unaccounted free time last night when he could have brought a body to the center and dumped it."

A tense second passed. "That's possible, I guess. And before you get pissed, I already talked to my man about doing a better job. He's a newbie, though, and just learning the ropes."

Figured. Dane wished he could cover all the bases himself, although that was virtually impossible. "What about the early morning hours yesterday?"

"He was at his cabin, left at six for a run," Kimball said. "Went back and showered, then headed to the community center."

Of course, he could have snuck out the back at some point.

Dane's phone beeped, and he told Kimball to keep him posted, then connected the other call.

"Dane, it's Peyton. You won't believe what I learned about that plastic surgeon."

♦ ♦ ♦

Josie woke to the smell of coffee. Instead of the horrible nightmares that had plagued her for months, her dreams had been full of Dane in her bed making love to her.

If making love to him was that wonderful in her dreams, what would it be like in real life?

On the heels of that dream, the reason Dane had spent the night sent a chill through her.

Knowing they needed to get to work, she showered, then dressed in a skirt, sweater, and boots, uncertain what the day would hold.

Dane looked up as she entered, and she grabbed a cup of coffee and dumped sweetener in it, her body tingling at his perusal. Did he like what he saw?

A second passed, and his gaze returned to his computer.

She fought disappointment but chastised herself. The two murdered girls needed his attention more than she did. The killer could be stalking another victim now.

"That damn reporter Corbin Michaels wrote about the murders," Dane said. "He's named our killer the 'Butcher.'"

Josie tucked a strand of hair behind her ear. "Good grief. Giving him a name will only pump up his ego."

"I know. I'm ready to lock the jerk up until we've caught this unsub."

Unfortunately they both knew he couldn't do that, not unless Michaels broke the law.

"Did you get any sleep?" she asked.

He shrugged. "A little. Did you?"

Heat flushed her face, and she averted her gaze and scrambled for a couple of bagels to pop in the toaster.

"Josie?"

"Yes, I slept fine," she said, feigning innocence. "What's the plan for today?"

"We have a press conference at eight," he said, not missing a beat. "I'll fill you in on the way."

"Do you want to shower first?"

He raised a brow. "You don't mind?"

No—she'd like to have showered with him. But she couldn't tell him that.

She swiped at a bead of perspiration between her breasts. These close quarters and the trauma of another killer in town were driving her crazy. "Of course not. You have extra clothes?"

He pushed away from the table. "I keep a duffel bag in my car. Comes in handy on a case."

"Right." In spite of the heat simmering between them, he didn't make a move to pursue it. She should admire him for his dedication to the job.

She reached in the refrigerator for eggs. "I'll put together breakfast while you shower."

He nodded, then walked past her, brushing her arm as he left the room. Josie ordered her libido under control. Dane was not interested in sleeping with her. Any attraction between them was simply on her part.

The shower water kicked on, eliciting an image of a naked Dane standing beneath the warm water. Of his broad shoulders dotted with water, his hair wet and slick, his sex jutting out, thick and hard.

Hunger spiraled through her. She wanted to join him. To forget that another maniac killer was in Graveyard Falls.

That the killer was connected to her.

Needing something to do with her hands, she toasted the bagels, then whipped up a couple of omelets with spinach, peppers, and onions. Dane probably liked breakfast meat, but she didn't have bacon or sausage on hand.

Dane entered, freshly shaven, his hair still damp, his big body so masculine that she sucked in a breath.

They needed to eat and get moving before she did something impetuous and jumped his bones.

His dismissive attitude helped put her back on track. Charity and Patty needed her to help him find their killer.

He dropped into the seat at the table, his jaw firmly set. If she'd hoped for a compliment on the meal, he didn't bother.

Of course he had more important things on his mind.

She unfolded her napkin and spread it across her lap. "Tell me what you found out while we eat."

He dug in with his fork. "It's about that plastic surgeon, Dr. Silas Grimley. Apparently Easton sends referrals to him. He performed cosmetic work on both victims."

Josie's mind raced. "You think he's involved in the murders?"

"I don't know yet. His childhood is disturbing, though. His father rescued raptors, and he used to lock Silas in the cages with them. When Silas was young, he was attacked by the birds."

Josie's throat closed as images hit her. "My God, I was thinking earlier that the killer might have been attacked by birds. Coupled with the fact that his father allowed it, that kind of abuse could seriously alter a child's mental state. He could have suffered a psychotic break."

Dane sipped his coffee as if considering her theory. "Grimley was scarred pretty badly on his arms and legs. His face took the brunt of the attack. He spent most of his youth disfigured and cast as an outsider by other kids."

"That fits with the killer's MO." A mental profile formed in Josie's mind. The pretty girls would have run from Grimley, too. Rejected him.

Was he murdering women to get revenge for the way they'd treated him when he was young?

♦ ♦ ♦

Dr. Silas Grimley was definitely at the top of Dane's list of persons of interest.

"Thanks for breakfast." Dane polished off the omelet as if he hadn't eaten in days. "I called Dr. Grimley's office in LA, but the receptionist said he's taken a leave of absence. Apparently he's in Knoxville attending a conference for plastic surgeons."

She rinsed the dishes and stacked them in the dishwasher while Dane did some research on his computer. "Maybe someone rejected him recently. He could have gone through a bad breakup and that triggered his killing spree."

"That's possible. I called the hotel and Grimley is registered for the convention, but he wasn't in his room. I left a message on his cell phone, but so far, he hasn't gotten in touch. He could easily drive down from Knoxville to Graveyard Falls and then back."

Dane gestured toward his laptop screen. "The lab sent me a link to a blog he writes called *The Bird Diaries*."

"*Bird Diaries?*"

"Yeah." Dane had read some of them earlier. He swung the laptop around for her. "As a kid he kept a diary of his work with the raptors. He turned that experience into a series of fiction stories. They're extremely disturbing. They sound autobiographical."

"You mean he describes being attacked?"

"Yes. He blends fiction with his accounts, but he describes in detail how it felt when they clawed at this boy and ripped his skin and muscle."

Josie skimmed a couple of short entries. "That doesn't mean he's a killer. It's probably therapeutic for him, just as it was for me to write my book."

"No, but at one point he calls the boy the *bone collector* because he collects bird bones. He makes collages out of them."

Josie's face paled. "That is troubling."

"He's also written a story about a woman being mauled by vultures." He drummed his fingers on the table. "In that story, the woman's face is left scarred with claw marks."

CHAPTER EIGHTEEN

An hour later, Dane stood behind the podium in one of the conference rooms in the courthouse. Sheriff Kimball had organized a press conference to address the two murders.

He spotted Corbin Michaels in the crowd and braced himself for an inquisition. Today at least four other reporters had shown up, along with the mayor, the film crew executives and staff, actors, and the local residents.

Sheriff Kimball introduced himself and Dane. "Thank you for coming. Unfortunately, we have a situation in Graveyard Falls, and we need your cooperation."

"We heard two women were stabbed," one of the reporters shouted. "Are they related to the Bride Killer murders?"

Sheriff Kimball held up a hand to halt more questions. "First, let us report the information we have, then we'll open for questions."

Voices rumbled, people shifted uncomfortably, and Dane gestured toward the sheriff. "As Sheriff Kimball said, my name is Special Agent Dane Hamrick. Yes, two women have been murdered. The first victim's name was Charity Snow, the second, Patty Waxton."

"Did he dress the women in bridal gowns?" one of the reporters asked.

"No." Dane didn't want to divulge the women's state of undress yet. Withholding key elements and details of the MO might help later to weed out false confessions if the need arose.

"This is not a copycat crime, nor is it related to the Bride Killer or Thorn Ripper murders," Dane said. "There's no need to panic, yet at the same time, since there have been two murders bearing the same MO, we're concerned that the killer may strike again. I would like to caution all the young women in town to be careful, not to go out alone at night, and to travel in pairs. At this point, we haven't determined how this unsub, unknown subject, is luring his victims to their deaths, but we suspect that the killer is someone these women trust. He is probably in his midtwenties, and he may be connected to the film business. We also believe he's attractive and charming, so the women are not afraid to go with him."

"Were the victims sexually assaulted?" Michaels asked.

Dane forced a calm to his voice. He'd seen this reporter around bothering Bailey Snow for an interview. "There is evidence the victims had sexual relations, but no clear indication of rape."

"What about victimology?" Michaels asked. "Is the killer targeting any specific type? Blondes? Brunettes? Professional women?"

"As I said earlier, both women were actresses, but no, no definitive physical description. The women did not know each other, and we haven't found anything in common other than the fact that they were in town for auditions."

He intentionally omitted the detail about cosmetic work—he didn't want to create a panic or give the other women in town a sense of false security in case the plastic surgery element wasn't a key factor.

With the similarities in MO, the violence bordering on overkill, and the short time lapse between crimes, he suspected that this unsub would kill again.

And soon.

A female reporter waved her hand. "Do you have any suspects?"

Dane bit back a response. He had too damn many. "We have a couple of persons of interest, but we're not prepared to disclose that information." He scanned the crowded room, searching for any suspicious behavior, someone who appeared nervous, or someone watching Josie.

Josie had claimed a seat beside the casting director. Irritation nagged at Dane as Michaels sidled up to them.

"If you have any information regarding the murders, or if you see or hear anything suspicious, please contact the sheriff's department." He glanced at the women in the group, who looked panicked and frightened. "Please, ladies, be careful. Don't trust anyone."

Of course half of the women in the room wouldn't heed that advice. They were all eager to be discovered and would schmooze with industry professionals. The housing and the timing of auditions placed everyone in close proximity and created camaraderie. It also created an air of false trust and intimacy and paved the perfect ground for women to be victimized.

Worse, his prime suspects consisted of the makeup artist, the photographer, and an actor. Except for the plastic surgeon, all were an integral part of the film company. Although Easton gave referrals to Dr. Grimley, whom the women would easily trust as well.

Dammit. This unsub had a virtual pool of vulnerable targets in one location.

The question was—which one of them would be next?

◆ ◆ ◆

Déjà vu struck Josie as panic rumbled through the crowd. Two years ago, the residents of Graveyard Falls had been on edge because of the Bride Killer. Now another murderer lurked in their midst.

Corbin Michaels waved his hand again. "With the controversy over the project, do you think the killer is targeting the town as a way to protest this film?"

People in the crowd turned to stare at Josie.

Olive leaned closer to Josie. "Don't let him make you feel guilty. You simply wrote the story. People deserved to know the truth."

"Thanks, Olive." Josie offered her a smile. She felt like such an outcast in this town; it was nice to have a friend.

"No, I don't believe that's the case," Dane said. "How could one justify killing innocent women as a way to stop publicity over past crimes?"

"Serial killers are not always logical," Michaels pointed out.

"Maybe not, but there is a certain logic to their pathology," Dane replied. "The MO of these crimes indicates this unsub wants to make a point."

"He hasn't contacted the media," one of the reporters said.

Across the room, Porter McCray flashed Josie a sinister smile, reminding her of Billy Linder when he'd chained her to that bed.

Relief filled her when Dane answered for her. "That's all the questions we have time for. We have an investigation to work."

Michaels shouted his name. "Isn't it true that the killer is carving the women's faces with talon-like marks? That's his signature, isn't it? He's a butcher."

Anger shot through Dane, and he went stone still, his gaze focused on the reporter. That was the name he'd given the unsub in the paper, although he hadn't printed specifics. Now he was digging. "Where did you hear that?"

"It is true, isn't it? He carves their faces before he stabs them, then he takes a bone chip as his trophy."

Rumblings of unease and shock echoed through the crowd. Josie pressed a hand to her chest. How did the reporter know that detail?

"Is that true?" someone shouted.

"There's another serial killer in town!" a woman in the back cried.

A man pushed his way through the crowd. "Why aren't you telling us everything?"

Dane raised his hand to quiet the hysteria. "I don't know where you received that information, Mr. Michaels, but the details of this case have not been released yet. I'm asking everyone in town not to panic but to be cautious. When we have more information, I'll inform the public."

"He also leaves one of those kids' dolls," Michaels continued. "The Mitzi doll. What does that mean?"

Dane ignored him and started down the steps, but the other reporters swarmed him while Corbin strode through the crowd toward Josie.

"Did the killer contact you?" Olive asked in a hushed whisper.

Josie was tempted to confide in her, but Dane wanted to keep details confidential. "I can't discuss the investigation."

"Oh my God." Olive pressed her hand to her chest, her silver nails shimmering beneath the light. "He did, didn't he? Do you have any idea who stabbed those women?" Olive looked around the room, paranoid. "Is he in here now?"

"I don't know," Josie said honestly, although she sensed he was watching the fuss, enjoying the fear on everyone's faces.

Olive squeezed her arm. "Be careful, Josie. I'd hate to see you get hurt."

"I don't want *anyone* to get hurt," Josie said. "I'll do whatever I can to find the sick son of a bitch and put him away."

"Good for you. I admire your grit, Josie."

Josie smiled wanly. "I'm just doing what I have to in order to survive."

A heartbeat of silence passed, and Olive squeezed her arm again. "I know and that's why I like you. Please let me know if you write this story. If people show interest in this film, we might option the next one."

Olive excused herself to chat with some of the girls, and Josie squared her shoulders as the reporter approached.

Michaels stopped in front of her. "Did the killer contact you?"

Josie straightened her spine. "I should ask you the same question. Where did you get your information?"

"It's correct, isn't it?" Michaels asked.

"You need to direct your questions to the sheriff's department," Josie said. "I'm simply in town to work with the film company on my book. I don't appreciate reporters who sensationalize crime and create panic."

Disbelief filled Michaels's gray eyes. "You're the one who wrote the book, Miss DuKane. I think you know a lot more about these murders than you're letting on. You want the exclusive story, so you're cozying up to the agent in charge."

Rage heated Josie's blood. "That is a horrible thing to say. My heart goes out to these two young women and their families and friends."

"You still may profit from it."

"You know nothing about me." Guilt rose from the bowels of Josie's conscience. "I didn't write the book for money. I wrote it to help people heal."

"Yet here you are embroiled in another murder case," Michaels said snidely.

Dane appeared from the crowd, anger emanating from him. "Harassing Miss DuKane is not going to get you what you want."

Michaels glanced back and forth between Josie and Dane. "What I want is the truth, to warn women who they should be watching out for." Disapproval rang in his voice. "To be able to tell people that they can walk the streets in Graveyard Falls without fearing for their lives."

"Then we're in agreement on that." Dane glared down at the man. "Where did you get your information?"

Michaels winced slightly. "You know I can't reveal my source."

Dane snatched the man by the arm and dragged him to the side. "Listen to me, this is not just some story, you asshole. Women's lives are at stake."

Michaels gripped Dane's fists to pry them from his arm. "I'm trying to warn them who to look out for."

"*Where* did you get your information?" Dane asked again, his tone harsher.

Michaels's nostrils flared. "I told you, I can't reveal my source."

Dane shoved him against the wall. Dark clouds moved above, casting shadows across the place. People passing paused to gasp, but he motioned them to move along. "Withholding information in a homicide is against the law. If you really want to help stop this killer, start talking."

Michaels lifted his chin in a challenge. "Only if you give me an exclusive."

Dane's steely eyes met Michaels's. For a moment, Josie thought he was going to pound the man's face in.

She couldn't blame Dane if he did.

"Fine," Dane said icily. "But you can't print anything without my permission. Now spill it, dammit."

Michaels tore Dane's fingers from around his collar. "I received an anonymous text."

Josie's stomach knotted. She'd gotten a text with photographs. So why was the killer sending this reporter texts as well?

"With pictures of the victims?" Dane asked.

Michaels narrowed his eyes but said nothing.

"Show me the damn text," Dane said through gritted teeth, "or I'll arrest you for impeding a homicide investigation. Do you want another woman to die?"

Michaels snarled at him, but he removed his phone from his pocket.

Dane's gut tightened as he read the message.

All the pretty faces lined in a row,

All the pretty faces, I'll carve them as I go . . .

Dammit. The unsub had not only left a cryptic message but also sent the reporter the same photographs he'd sent Josie. Why?

Because she hadn't gone public with them, and he wanted to be memorialized?

Dane stepped aside to call the lab to see if they could trace the origin of the text.

Michaels turned back to Josie. "Did he send you pictures, Miss DuKane?"

"Leaking that information to the public was dangerous and underhanded," Josie said instead of answering him.

"People have a right to the truth," Michaels argued.

"Trust me, Mr. Michaels," Josie said, "I understand the need to know the truth and report it. Being irresponsible can cost people's lives."

Dane stepped back to them.

"I'm assuming you put a trace on my phone," Michaels said.

"You want the story, then help us and you'll get your exclusive. If I discover you're in contact with the killer and you hold back that information, I will arrest you as an accomplice." Dane handed the man back his cell phone. "Now excuse us. I have a killer to catch."

◆ ◆ ◆

Dane mentally studied the facts he had so far, trying to make one of his suspects fit Betsy's case as well.

"Why do you think the killer contacted Michaels when he's been contacting me?" Josie asked.

"Maybe he's disappointed that you haven't revealed his MO. He wants his five minutes of fame?"

Josie tucked a strand of hair behind her ear. "I guess that makes sense. It just seems odd that he wouldn't escalate in his contact with me. Do something to make me put him in the limelight."

Dane nodded, although he wasn't convinced either. Was the text legitimate?

It had to be. It also had to have been sent from the killer. Or someone who knew the killer's identity.

Only a select few people—those working on the case—had access to the details.

The ME. Sheriff Kimball. The crime team workers. Josie. Him.

Unless someone close to the killer figured out the truth, or the killer confided in them.

Josie lapsed into silence, then jotted notes on the suspects and victims, probably already planning her next book.

Still stewing, he phoned the sheriff and asked if he'd leaked the information. "Of course not," Sheriff Kimball said defensively. "I *am* a professional."

"Did you have any luck with that prisoner list?" Dane asked.

"Nothing concrete. The one prisoner who butchered his victims died in a fire. I checked prison escapees and mental patients. Zilch there as well."

So he was covering all the bases. "Talk to the CSI lead and have him verify that none of his workers were the leak," Dane said. "I'll talk to the ME."

Sheriff Kimball agreed, and Dane phoned Dr. Wheeland and explained about the reporter.

"He didn't get any information from me or my office," the ME insisted. "My people understand the importance of confidentiality."

Dane thanked him, then punched Peyton's number. He couldn't discount the connection between Easton and Betsy—Easton had attended UT. He would have been a little older than Betsy, but it was possible they'd met at the party.

"Dane, I haven't traced that text yet," Peyton said. "Our best IT guy is working on it."

"Thanks. Can you find out exactly where Gil Baines, Porter McCray, and Dr. Silas Grimley were ten years ago in May? May nineteenth, to be exact."

"That might take some time."

"I know, but it's important. Find out if any of them, including Easton, had an affiliation, even if it was just a friend, who attended the fraternity that threw the party where my sister died."

"Dane, what's going on?" Peyton asked.

"This is personal," he said, hating to share. But at this point he'd do anything to solve the case. Even ask for help. "I think this case might be connected to my sister's murder."

"All right," Peyton said. "I'll look into it."

Relieved she didn't push for more, he thanked her. "Anything on the second vic's computer?"

"Patty Waxton was more active on social media than Charity Snow. She was a patient of Dr. Grimley's."

"You accessed her medical file?"

"No, I'm still working on that. Dr. Grimley was proud of his work, and a select group of patients signed waivers allowing him to display their before-and-after photographs on his website."

"Blatant advertising—I thought that was unethical," Dane commented.

"Could be. Grimley's staff sings his praises and said the testimonials from patients make others feel more comfortable about going under the knife. His head nurse claims he is dedicated to his patients. His motto on his site is *I can make you look like anyone you want to be.*"

Dane chewed the inside of his cheek. "Patty agreed to be photographed and used in his promotions?"

"Yes."

"How about Charity Snow?"

"She wasn't on the site," Peyton answered, "but the nurse's assistant remembered her and said the doctor took special care with Charity, that she was shy, and that the implants changed her life."

Yeah, but had they gotten her killed?

"There was one problem with another patient," Peyton continued. "It happened a few months ago."

"What kind of problem?"

"A female patient had a reaction to the medication during surgery and almost died. She sued him after that and ran a smear campaign to destroy his reputation. Grimley's temporarily taken a leave of absence and went to that convention to connect with other surgeons to repair his reputation."

"Where is this woman?"

"California. Apparently Dr. Grimley was upset about the operation. He offered to repair the woman's face, but she didn't want him to touch her again. It appears that he settled out of court, and she was well compensated."

Interesting story. It didn't make him a killer. Although an incident like that could be a possible trigger.

But there was one problem with the theory. Why would Grimley, a doctor supposedly devoted to his patients, kill two of them now when the publicity surrounding the movie and the referrals from Easton could put his career back on track?

◆ ◆ ◆

Silas stared at the news reporter, his heart pounding. Two women had been murdered in Graveyard Falls.

Two women who had once been his clients.

A knot of apprehension squeezed his belly.

The last year had been hell.

That one woman's face taunted him. The surgery, her reaction . . . he'd almost lost her.

Then she'd rejected the skin grafts, and he couldn't fix her.

Save her.

Make her into the woman she wanted to be.

Instinctively he rubbed his fingers over his face. Dammit, he understood the pain of being scarred. Of wanting to be something you weren't.

Of having people look at you like you were evil just because you looked different.

Easton was supposed to be in Graveyard Falls. He was also supposed to be recruiting more patients for him. He'd lost so many because of that botched surgery. That one was fucking complicated and a mess all the way around.

The TV camera flashed pictures of the two girls who'd died, and he flinched.

Seconds later, the image of another girl surfaced in his mind. Years ago.

Young, sweet, kind. She'd befriended him when he was ugly. When others shunned him and treated him like a monster.

He'd loved her, wanted her for himself, wanted to be with her forever. Emotions clogged his throat as her cries sounded in his head.

She'd left him anyway, and he'd been all alone since.

CHAPTER NINETEEN

Josie admired the ornate trim work, marble floors, and chandeliers as they entered the convention hotel.

A cluster of men in suits had gathered for coffee at a seating area to the right. Another man passed her and gave her a once-over, making her self-conscious. "It's weird, going into a convention full of cosmetic surgeons."

"What do you mean?"

"I feel like they're scrutinizing me for flaws, contemplating how they would fix my face."

Dane paused beside her, his gaze sweeping the clusters of people in the lobby. "There's nothing wrong with your face."

Josie gave a little laugh. "Well, I don't have scars, but I'm not model pretty either. My nose is a little crooked—"

"Stop it, Josie," Dane said gruffly. "You're beautiful just the way you are."

Warmth spread through Josie, a tingling starting inside her that made her want to forget this case and ask Dane to get them a room.

Oblivious to her thoughts, Dane moved forward.

Thankfully she'd held her tongue. She normally didn't lust after a man, but the past few months she'd felt vulnerable. Seeing her mother with the love of her life made her think about her own future. About how since her abduction, she'd lived her life alone, not inviting men into her life.

Dane phoned Dr. Grimley and left a message. "Dr. Grimley, this is Special Agent Dane Hamrick. I'm at the convention hotel and need to speak to you. Please call me back at this number ASAP."

Ignoring the curious looks of another suit who seemed to be staring at her nose—probably thinking he could make it smaller—she followed Dane to the registration desk.

He flashed his badge and identified himself. "I need the room number for a Dr. Silas Grimley."

A thin twentysomething guy with big dark glasses frowned. "Sir, we can't divulge that information, but I can ring his room for you."

Bunch of fucking red tape. "Forget your rules. This is police business. I'm investigating a double homicide. Give me the damn number."

The young man fidgeted with his collar, then clicked some keys. A minute later, he scribbled the number on a sticky note and shoved it toward Dane.

Josie kept glancing around, trying to fit the man with the scars to the men she saw walking through the lobby.

Dane gestured toward the hallway leading to the bank of elevators. They rode the elevator to the tenth floor and found the room. Dane knocked and called the man's name. No one answered. "Dammit, the doctor could be anywhere in this hotel."

Sensing his frustration, Josie jumped in to help. "Let's have him paged."

They rode the elevator back down and found the same young man working the desk. This time Josie asked him to make the announcement.

"This might be a bust." Dane scanned the lobby. "Grimley might be in Graveyard Falls. This conference could be a front for an alibi."

"Let's hope not," Josie said, although Grimley could be holding another woman hostage right now.

Five minutes later, a tall man with short, neatly clipped dark hair wearing a black suit approached the desk. He was handsome, tall, and broad shouldered, with wide cheekbones and crystal gray eyes.

But he looked harried. His tie was askew, his gaze darting around the room as if searching for someone.

Or hiding?

The desk attendant motioned to Josie that it was Grimley, so she and Dane headed toward him.

Dane flashed his badge and introduced them. Grimley wasn't what Josie expected. This man appeared to be polished, and he was well dressed, his face flawless.

"Hamrick?" Dr. Grimley's voice cracked. "That's your last name?"

"Yes." Dane narrowed his eyes. "Why?"

Grimley tugged at his tie. "No reason."

Josie studied Grimley. Dane's last name disturbed the man. Maybe he'd known another Hamrick?

Grimley quickly turned to Josie. "You're that DuKane woman who wrote the book about the Bride Killer, aren't you?"

Josie tensed. If he was the killer, he probably knew everything about her. Or he could have seen one of her interviews.

Had he sent her the picture of the dead girl and left her that Mitzi doll?

◆ ◆ ◆

Dane steered the plastic surgeon toward the elevators. "Let's go someplace more private and talk. Your room would work fine."

Maybe he'd find something incriminating.

"What is this about?" Dr. Grimley asked as they waited for the elevator. "That insane patient who's trying to ruin my career?"

"No," Dane said bluntly. "It's about the murders in Graveyard Falls."

The doctor's face paled slightly. "I heard about that on the news." He clenched his briefcase as they entered the elevator and it zoomed upward. "I'm not sure what I can do to help."

The elevator doors opened, and the three of them stepped out. Grimley fidgeted with his shirt collar as he walked down the hallway and opened the door.

As they entered, Dane quickly conducted a visual sweep, searching for a Mitzi doll, photos of the victims, a broken mirror—anything implicating the doctor—but the room looked neat and orderly. Bed made, Grimley's suitcase open on the luggage stand, expensive suits hanging in the closet, bottled water on the nightstand.

The bathroom was neat as well—a toiletry bag held essentials, but nothing suspicious.

Of course, a smart killer wouldn't leave evidence lying around. He might have his tools or trophies stashed in his car.

Frustration knotted his insides. He needed a warrant to search Grimley's vehicle, but he didn't have evidence to justify one.

The doctor dropped his briefcase on the desk. "I still don't understand why you're here."

"You performed cosmetic work on the victims," Dane said.

"I have performed surgery on a lot of men and women. What does that have to do with these women's deaths?"

"That's what we're trying to determine. How long have you been in Knoxville?"

Dr. Grimley tugged at his tie. "Four days. I've been in and out of meetings at the convention all week."

"The photographer Eddie Easton gives you referrals, doesn't he?" Dane asked.

The man's eye twitched. "Yes."

Josie started to thumb through a stack of papers on the desk, but the doctor snatched them away from her and stuffed them in a drawer.

"Are you hiding something?" Dane asked.

Grimley's eyes flashed with anger. "Those are confidential patient files," he said tightly.

"May I use your bathroom?" Josie asked.

The doctor raised a brow as if to say no, but agreed, and Josie slipped inside the bathroom.

"All right, let's get this over with, Agent Hamrick," Grimley said.

Dane nodded. Hopefully Josie would find some clue about this man in the bathroom.

Judging from his attitude, Grimley was in a hurry to get rid of them. He'd bet his next paycheck that the moment they left, the doctor would be on the phone to Easton to warn him he was a suspect.

Time to get down to business. Treat him like a suspect. Play on his shaken mind-set. "Have you driven to Graveyard Falls to meet up with Easton for a consultation with any of the models and actors?"

Dr. Grimley glanced down at his hands. They were shaking slightly. "No." His voice cracked again.

Odd that he reacted to that simple question. If he was innocent, why was he so nervous? "Can anyone corroborate your whereabouts the night Charity Snow was murdered?"

A slight moment of panic lit the doctor's eyes. "I don't know. I was here, but I stayed in my room to do some research."

"What about last night?" Dane pressed.

Alarm flashed across Grimley's face as if he realized the timing was important. "I attended a session on burns. Later, I had a few drinks and retired early."

"You had drinks with someone?"

He shook his head. "No, alone." His voice rose in pitch. "You can't possibly think I had anything to do with those deaths? I'm a renowned doctor, for God's sake. I help people, not hurt them."

Josie stepped from the bathroom. She shook her head slightly as if to indicate she hadn't found anything.

She cleared her throat. "Dr. Grimley, do you know what a Mitzi doll is?"

Grimley pivoted toward Josie, his eye twitching again. "A what?"

"A Mitzi doll," Josie said. "They're popular with girls of all ages. Fashion Mitzi, Ferrari Mitzi, Bridal Mitzi."

"Oh, right." He shrugged, dismissing Josie. "I've seen the TV ads. What do they have to do with me or these murders?"

"That's what I want to know," Dane said bluntly.

Grimley looked annoyed. "I have no idea what you're getting at, Agent Hamrick."

"Your father was a falconer. You worked with him as a kid."

"Yes." The man's Adam's apple bobbed up and down as he swallowed. Then he pinched the bridge of his nose as if fighting a headache. Or panic.

Time to put the pressure on. "You were attacked by the birds when you were young, and you were scarred."

Grimley stumbled back slightly, his eyes darting from side to side. "That was a long time ago. I don't like to talk about it."

"I'm sure you don't," Dane said. "You were locked in the cage with the birds. They tore at your skin and hands—"

"Yes." Grimley rubbed his cheek. Was he feeling for the scars? "That attack is the reason I specialize in cosmetic surgery."

Dane crossed his arms and moved closer, using an intimidating stance. "Both victims we found had talon marks carved into their faces."

The color drained from Grimley's face. "Good God."

"We think the carvings were made by a scalpel."

Grimley broke out in a full-fledged sweat. "Jesus, that's horrible."

"You use scalpels," Dane said, the accusation clear.

Grimley backed away, hands raised in defense. "I didn't do it. I fix women's faces, make them prettier, repair their scars. Hell, I like transforming them into creatures to be admired. I would never disfigure someone."

"Our IT department dug up a photo of you when you were young. The claw marks on the women's faces are almost identical to the ones on your cheek before your reconstruction."

Grimley dropped his head into his hands. Dane thought he was going to be sick. "I didn't kill those women."

"If you confess," Dane said, "you might be able to plead insanity."

Rage flickered in Grimley's eyes as he gestured toward the door. "If you want to question me again, go through my attorney. Now get out."

"Don't leave town," Dane said as he stepped into the hallway.

Grimley glared at them, then shut the door in their faces.

◆ ◆ ◆

Panic seized Silas as the agent and Josie DuKane left. They were asking questions he didn't want to answer.

Talking about murder and stabbings and young women and the birds of prey.

He wiped the perspiration beading on his neck and paced back and forth, debating what to do. He'd thought he'd covered his tracks, but what if he'd messed up?

What if that agent figured out the truth?

After that doctor had volunteered to fix his face years ago, he'd tried to repent for his sins. That physical change had transformed him into a new person.

He thrived on doing the same for others.

Last year he'd volunteered with Doctors Without Borders and donated his time to help children with birth defects and deformities. Cosmetic work wasn't just for the vain. It impacted a person's future, changed his or her self-concept, opened doors to a life the individual never thought he or she could have.

Only sometimes the scars lingered on the inside. Sometimes the mind refused to let them go. Then those scars became such an intrinsic part of your psyche that they shaped your thoughts and actions.

And your nightmares.

The psychiatrist called it PTSD.

Guilt was also a part of it. Only he didn't talk about that. No one knew his darkest secret.

My mistake.

I can't tell. Not ever. No one will understand.

Frantic, he snatched his keys and phone and hurried to his Mercedes. He punched Easton's number as he barreled down the road.

Easton's phone rolled to voice mail after the third ring. "It's Grimley. That agent Hamrick and Josie DuKane just came to see me. He was asking all kinds of questions about the two murders in Graveyard Falls. We have to talk ASAP. I'm on my way."

He hung up, his heart pounding. He could see himself stabbing the girl, the blood spurting. Her scream of terror taunted him.

He jammed the knife into her chest again.

She hadn't loved him; she'd rejected him like everyone else.

She'd had to die.

◆ ◆ ◆

Josie contemplated Dr. Grimley's reaction as she and Dane drove back to Graveyard Falls. For a successful plastic surgeon, he had appeared to be awfully on edge. Not confident, as she would have expected.

He was handsome, though, neatly dressed, articulate, so women would trust him, especially if they were going to discuss a consult about cosmetic work.

His nervousness bothered her, though. He'd obviously suffered as a child. He'd also seemed sincere in his devotion to his job.

But he had been shaken when Dane questioned him about the

murders. He'd even reacted oddly at Dane's name. He had hidden those papers from her, too. Although they could have been patient files.

"Did you see anything suspicious in the bathroom?" Dane asked.

Josie shook her head. "Just the usual toiletries. No bag of scalpels or dolls or broken mirror. What did you think about the plastic surgeon?"

"He's hiding something," Dane said. "I don't know what, but I intend to find out."

◆ ◆ ◆

Neesie sipped a cup of tea as she studied herself in the mirror. She'd heard other girls bustling around leaving for the center, but she was waiting to hear from the casting director.

She couldn't get what Josie and that agent said out of her mind. McCray was weird, but so far, he'd left her alone.

Eddie Easton was a different story—the photo session at the falls had unnerved her, but Eddie hadn't hurt her. Although for a moment, she'd thought he was going to choke her with that garter.

But he had offered to help her. Eddie had said he'd talk to the plastic surgeon for her, that he was coming to Graveyard Falls this week and he'd set up a consult.

Her phone dinged, and she clicked to read the incoming text.

Callback for part of Josie DuKane. Meet me and we'll discuss the audition. Olive Turnstyle, casting director.

Excitement bubbled in her chest. Playing Josie would be a dream come true, especially now that she knew and liked the woman.

Josie would probably help her, too!

She checked her watch, then phoned Gil Baines, hoping he could do her makeup before she met with Olive. Not that Josie wore a lot of makeup. She was more of a natural beauty.

Gil Baines could make her look natural and wholesome like Josie. He'd probably have wardrobe suggestions, too.

He answered immediately and told her he'd work her in.

Psyched, she showered and dressed, then rushed outside to her car. The parking lot at the inn was empty, as everyone was at the community center, although a couple of older women were power walking on the sidewalk, and a tall man was walking his Yorkie.

A little girl and her mother strolled past, a doll clutched in the child's arms. A memory pricked at Neesie's consciousness as she fumbled with her keys. Hadn't Josie mentioned something about those Mitzi dolls?

Neesie had seen one in that closet.

She punched Josie's number to tell her but received her voice mail, so she left a message. "I saw one of those dolls you were talking about at the community center. Call me."

The wind picked up, blowing leaves across the back parking lot. Dark thunderstorms crawled across the sky adding a gloomy gray cast over the area. Somewhere a cat screeched, startling her. She looked up and saw it scramble into the bushes, a trash can lid clanging against the asphalt.

A shadow fell over her face, and she pivoted, but the sharp sting of a needle stabbed her neck.

She tried to scream but her tongue wouldn't work, and when she reached for her car to steady herself, the world spiraled out of control.

She hit the ground, her body convulsing. Fear choked her as she tried to see who'd attacked her.

Instead a dark void swallowed her into its abyss.

CHAPTER TWENTY

Josie checked her phone as she and Dane drove toward Graveyard Falls. A message from Neesie.

"Dane, Neesie called. She saw one of those dolls at the community center."

"Where was it?"

Josie's heartbeat accelerated. This might be the lead they needed. "I don't know. She didn't say. I'll call her and find out."

She punched Neesie's number, but her voice mail kicked in. "Neesie, it's Josie. Please call me. I need to know where you saw the doll. It's important."

She ended the call, her mind racing. "I'm worried, Dane. I should have told Neesie why we were asking about the doll."

"Corbin Michaels already did that," Dane pointed out.

Josie rubbed her temple with two fingers. That was true. "What if whoever has the doll knows that Neesie saw it? She could be in danger."

Dane pressed the accelerator. "I'll call Sheriff Kimball and ask him to find her."

Josie twisted her hands together. The thought of Neesie falling prey to this butcher terrified her.

♦ ♦ ♦

Dane swerved onto the highway. That doll could lead them to the unsub.

His phone buzzed. Peyton, not Neesie.

"Dane, I'm sending you a link to Dr. Grimley's latest blog. These entries are even more disturbing. One was just added that sounds like a description of the murders. The claw marks on the face are man-made instead of being caused by the vulture."

He considered turning around and running surveillance on Grimley. But Grimley was too smart to take another girl right now.

Or was he? Maybe he was so bold he thought he could get away with anything.

"I'm on the road, but I'll look at it as soon as I get back to Graveyard Falls."

"There's something else," Peyton said. "I dug around for more information on Easton. Apparently he dated a girl named Sherry when he was in photography school. She was murdered shortly after they broke up."

Dane tensed. Easton had also attended UT when Betsy had visited. And his girlfriend had been murdered.

Another coincidence that couldn't be ignored. "How did the girl die?"

"She was stabbed."

The hair on the back of Dane's neck stood on end. "Who initiated the breakup?"

"According to the girl's friends, she did. She claimed that Easton had gotten weird. He wanted her to pose in ways that mimicked horror movies."

Dane sped around a curve. That's how the damn man made his career. "Were charges filed against him?"

"No, although he was a person of interest. His alibi was shaky, but the cops never could make the case."

Just like they hadn't been able to with Betsy.

He gripped the steering wheel tighter. God, could he really be close to finding Betsy's killer and locking him up?

He needed details. "Where was the girl's body found?"

"By the river. According to Sherry's girlfriend, that's where Sherry and Easton used to meet. Unfortunately, there were no witnesses. No weapon was ever found. No DNA."

"Did she have any unusual markings on her body?"

"No, nothing distinguishable."

Dammit. They needed some concrete physical evidence to bring Easton in, not just suppositions.

The working theory fit the MO, though. The photographer had also volunteered at that nature preserve and knew Silas Grimley. He could have heard Grimley's story of being attacked by the birds and added that to his signature.

Or hell, what if Easton and Grimley were partners?

Both were troubled. They could have bonded as adolescents at that nature center and remained friends, even offering alibis to help each other get away with murder. He hissed.

He hadn't considered a team before. Having a partner was rare with serial killers, but it happened.

Was he actually looking at two different killers working together?

♦ ♦ ♦

Dane's face looked strained as he hung up.

"What's wrong?" Josie asked.

"A girl Easton dated in photography school died under suspicious circumstances after they broke up. She was stabbed to death."

Josie's lungs tightened. "You think that Easton is the Butcher?"

"I don't know," Dane said. "Things are pointing to both him and Dr. Grimley. Each of them had troubled childhoods and worked at the same nature preserve with the raptors. They could have bonded and formed a team."

A chill slithered up Josie's spine. "You know that's unusual. Although sometimes couples have murdered together, and so have a few men. Usually one is the more dominant and convinces the submissive one to help lure the victims."

"Easton could be the submissive, enticing the girls through photo shoots and then turning them over to Grimley. Grimley's childhood abuse and his disfigurement fit with the MO," Dane said. "They could also alibi each other."

"True." Josie mentally pieced together the scenario, trying to make it gel with the men she'd met and their personalities. "Although Grimley seems more the submissive type to me. He was really nervous when you questioned him."

"He *should* be nervous." Dane retrieved his tablet from the seat. "Take a look at Grimley's latest blog and see what you think, Josie. He takes the talon carvings to a new level. We might be able to use it to build a case against him."

Josie clicked on the link and skimmed a few of the earlier entries to get a feel for Grimley's style. She searched for a pattern, details he might have inserted that only the killer would know.

The Bird Diaries

By Silas Grimley

The daddy led him outside to the cages. A loud squawking erupted, and the trapped animals screamed for release.

They flapped their wings and flew from one side of the cage to the other, their cries to escape piercing his ears.

"Become one with the birds," his daddy

said. "Tame them and you will find your inner strength."

"No, Daddy," he pleaded as his father pushed him toward the cage. "I'm scared."

Daddy jerked him to a halt, grabbed both his arms, and forced him to look at him. "Fear is your enemy." Daddy's eyes stabbed at him like needles. "Conquer it and the world is yours."

Tears burned the backs of his eyelids, but he blinked them back. Crying made Daddy mad. He didn't like it when Daddy got mad.

Especially when he punished him.

"Remember what I showed you." Daddy tugged gloves on the boy's hands, long gloves that went halfway up his arms.

"Go in with me," the boy whispered. "Show me again."

Daddy shook his head. "It's time you became a man."

The boy had no choice. His daddy opened the cage just enough for him to slip inside. He dug his heels in, but his daddy gave him a shove and he stumbled forward, hit the ground, and tasted dirt.

The door to the cage snapped shut, and he stared in terror at the birds as they flapped their wings, dipped their beaks, and watched him through beady eyes.

Some of them were sick. He heard their terrible screeching. Saw them attack each other. Others were starving, his father's doing.

*He went stone still, his breath barely puffing out. If
he made a sudden move, they might perceive him
as the enemy.*

Josie shuddered as she imagined the little boy being attacked by the
sharp talons.

She skimmed several more blog entries, more stories about the
child. The details of the attacks, of the birds as they fed on the boy,
made her stomach feel more nauseous.

Why hadn't someone intervened and removed him from that home?
A good doctor or teacher should have recognized signs of abuse.
She scrolled down to a more recent story.

*The boy was an adolescent now. He bore the
scars of his work with the birds. He loved them.
He hated them.*

*They had dug so deeply into his skin with their
knife-like claws that they were a part of him now.*

*His blood carried the scent of the carrion they had
torn apart with their jagged talons before turning
on him.*

*Even though he tried to hide them, someone had
seen the scars.*

*His father hadn't meant for it to happen. Neither
had he. He'd hidden them with long-sleeve shirts
and jackets and never complained.*

Then one day the girl had noticed. She had told.

*The next week that haughty biddy with the ugly
black hat from the state had come to visit. She'd
taken him from the cages and his birds and made
him live in that other home. That was where he
met the older woman.*

She'd tried to chase his nightmares away with sweet bedtime stories and cookies and milk.

It was too late to change the past. Cookies and milk were for babies.

He wasn't a kid anymore.

He had to live with the monsters. They came for him at night like the devil rising from the grave.

The housemother sensed his bond with the falcons. She'd known they were part of him. So she'd let him work at the nature preserve where he could be close to the birds.

Then one day it happened. He made a friend. An older boy who took him under his wing. A boy who liked the raptors and carved them out of wood.

Then the girl came, too. She was older than him. So nice.

He liked her pretty smile and the way she looked at him as if he mattered. As if she didn't see the mangled flesh on his face that he tried so hard to hide.

All the other girls cared about was styling their hair and covering their faces with makeup. They were obsessed with their stupid dolls. That Mitzi doll with nail polish and eye shadow and fancy clothes and shoes.

It had all started with that silly show. Mad About Mitzi—all the girls wanted to look like the teenager who played Mitzi.

They were so shallow.

Except for her.

The sweet girl with the musical voice and kind eyes.

She was different.

At least he'd thought she was.

Then he'd seen the doll in her room. She had one just like the others.

"No!" he screamed.

His screaming did no good.

Besides, he loved her anyway.

He had to work up the nerve to tell her. She wouldn't smile at him like that if she didn't love him, too.

Dane cleared his throat, drawing her back from the reading. "What do you think?"

"I'm not finished, but these definitely could be autobiographical. He mentions a boy he befriended and a girl he was in love with."

Dane's sharp intake of breath startled her. "Does he name the girl?"

"No." Josie turned the pages to see if he called her by name later on, but didn't find it.

"The boy was probably Easton," Dane said, his voice dark. "They met at that nature preserve."

"What about the girl?" Josie asked, although she sensed she knew the answer.

"I can't be sure, but my sister volunteered at a nature center. She could have met them both there."

Compassion for Dane rose inside her along with hope. Maybe he would finally get closure.

Had Easton and Grimley bonded to the point of staying lifelong friends—and killing together?

She skipped to the last entry, the one Peyton thought pointed to Grimley as a killer. The first part described the Mitzi doll and how he'd carved its face.

The last few paragraphs made chill bumps skate up Josie's spine.

> *He had suffered from the vultures' vicious claws.*
>
> *Now it was her turn to suffer.*
>
> *He picked up his scalpel and held it above her pretty face. Her eyes widened in terror. She tried to scream, but he covered her mouth and jabbed the blade into her cheek until it connected with bone. Blood oozed from the cut, making his heart race.*
>
> *She kicked and clawed at him with her nails, but he sank the knife deeper into her cheek, marking her as the birds had marked him.*
>
> *Tears rolled down her face and mingled with the blood, painting a red river down her face.*
>
> *He lifted the scalpel and tasted her fear as her blood wet his tongue.*

The scream woke Ellie from her nap. For a moment the monsters that haunted her in her sleep were so vivid she forgot she was blind. Monsters with grotesque faces and blood dripping down their fangs. Monsters that were half bird, half human just like the man had been.

A loud cry pierced her ears. This one was real and came from down the hall. Some man shouting they were trying to poison him in this place. Another cry from a lady who'd lost her mind and insisted that she was a princess and deserved to be in a mansion. Poor girl was definitely not living in reality. Though maybe she was better off than where she'd been before she was put here.

Then the other woman, Paula—the one she'd connected to—had met monsters just like Ellie. She'd lost her daughter to one.

Ellie blinked back tears. She'd known monsters in her life. Had barely escaped one. Had tried to save the boy from him.

Not a day passed that she didn't wonder what had happened to that kid. If he'd turned his life around or if he'd become like his father.

Yesterday the nurses had been talking about the murders in Graveyard Falls. The killer marked his victims with talon marks.

He'd left a Mitzi doll with his victims. The Mitzi doll . . .

She'd found a doll in *the boy's* things one day when he was out. He'd hidden it in that duffel bag that he always kept with him, the one he'd brought from home. Inside, she'd discovered feathers from a red-tailed hawk, a picture of the cages where his father kept the birds, and the bones he collected.

Those tiny, hollow bird bones. He'd carefully shaped them into collages that he hung on his walls. He called those grotesque renditions of animal skeletons his treasures.

They reminded him of his kills. That he had control and power over something.

She'd told him it wasn't right to exert one's strength over those things smaller than you. He hadn't listened.

One cold, dark night she'd walked in on him. He was holding that doll in his hand. For a moment, he'd caressed and kissed its lips like it was a real person.

A second later, he'd picked up a carving tool and butchered its face. His hideous laugh as he mutilated the plastic had sent terror through her. It was the first time she'd been frightened of him.

Afraid he was turning into his old man. Afraid he might someday turn that rage onto a real person.

When she'd asked him what he was doing, he'd lashed out, grabbed the doll, and run.

He'd never come back.

Only now she saw those dolls in her dreams, their faces ripped apart by a sharp blade, their perfect pretty faces destroyed.

Another scream echoed in her head, and a young woman's face materialized. A brunette. In her early twenties.

Ellie had no idea who she was.

"Please don't kill me," she cried. "Please."

The shiny glint of the blade pierced the young woman's cheek, and blood trickled down her face.

Ellie clenched her clammy hands together, praying with all her might that the images would disappear. That what she was seeing in her mind wasn't real.

She didn't want to watch these innocent women die. Didn't want to hear their screams of sorrow and fear.

Didn't want to remember the fear and guilt that had choked her years ago when another young girl had lost her life.

Or the terror that seized her when she'd realized that if she hadn't been trying so hard to save the boy, the girl would still be alive.

He settled his fingers onto the keyboard. The words flowed freely onto the screen. Another blog.

> *All the pretty faces lined in a row.*
>
> *One stab, two stabs, then the pretty goes . . .*
>
> *Just like the women here in Graveyard Falls.*
>
> *Except for Josie DuKane.*

She was pretty all right. Not perfect. But she didn't seem to care. That made her even more special.

A scalpel to the dolls' faces took care of those smiles, though. One stab. Two. Another.

The plastic fell away, brittle and cracking. First the eyes, then the nose, then that mouth that could give a man such great pleasure.

And destroy him with vile words.

Empty holes behind the exterior, a hollowness inside just like the insides of the girls, so like the hollow bones that he liked to pick from the birds and add to this collection. Girls who valued their looks so much that they would pay to go under the knife.

One by one the scalpel ripped apart the damned perfect faces until the dolls lay scattered across the floor.

A deep hunger for revenge gnawed at him. It wasn't enough.

More had to die.

CHAPTER
TWENTY-ONE

Dane mulled over the blogs he'd read as Josie continued to skim them. Abuse in children triggered psychotic breaks, schizophrenia, violent outbursts, and rage.

Grimley certainly had suffered. Those blogs were enough to justify a psychiatric evaluation of the man.

Although he still wanted some concrete evidence to take to a judge.

"Peyton's right. This blog is really disturbing," Josie said. "It's about the Mitzi dolls and a boy who collects bones. He describes jabbing the scalpel into her cheek."

A mental image of the women's mauled cheeks with the bones missing flashed in Dane's head. "Morbid, but just like our killer." The pieces fit. Grimley collected animal bones from his kills and could have escalated to collecting human bones.

"I'm going to try to reach Neesie again," Josie said. "I don't like the fact that she hasn't returned my call."

Her concern triggered Dane's. What if Neesie was in trouble?

Dane pressed the accelerator, his anxiety mounting as he veered off the main highway toward Graveyard Falls. He wished to hell he had enough evidence to bring Grimley in.

If the men were partners, Easton could be kidnapping the girls. Then they'd meet up and either he or Grimley or both of them killed the victims.

Josie blew her hair from her face as she left another voice mail. "Drop me at the community center. I have to find Neesie."

If the killer already had her, it might be too late. Dane steered the vehicle to the right and pulled into a parking spot.

He had another email from Peyton. "Let me check this and I'll walk you inside."

Josie reached for the door. "Take your time, Dane. I'll go ahead."

Dane touched her arm before she climbed from the vehicle. "Be careful, Josie. Stay away from Easton and that McCray man."

"Don't worry," Josie said. "I learned my lesson with Linder. I'll keep up my guard."

He hated that that lunatic had stolen her innocence. Although at least now she was cautious and wouldn't be fooled into trusting a killer.

◆ ◆ ◆

Josie rushed inside the center, anxious to find Neesie. The last days of auditions were underway, and the crowd was thinning out, the actors who hadn't received callbacks heading out of town.

Olive stood at the board posting another round of selections. Josie hurried toward her.

"I've been wondering where you were." Olive consulted her notepad. "I'm down to three different candidates for Billy Linder. McCray fits the part better than the other two, but he still makes me uneasy."

"Me, too." Josie sighed. "Olive, have you seen Neesie Netherington?"

Olive's brow furrowed. "No. I left a message for her to meet me for a second audition, but she didn't show."

A sick feeling climbed into the pit of Josie's stomach. That didn't sound like Neesie. Something bad must have happened to have kept her away.

♦ ♦ ♦

Dane studied the police report on the murder of Easton's former girlfriend, the coed at the photography school. Her name was Sherry Bagley. She was twenty-one, from Kentucky, and had come to California in hopes of pursuing her dream of acting.

She and Easton had dated for nine months. According to interviews of her friends, Sherry liked Eddie, but after a while, she said he was creepy, that he wanted to take pictures of her in odd places. He'd wanted her to pretend she was acting out a scene in a movie and let him photograph her.

More than one scene depicted murder.

When Sherry broke it off with Easton, he'd tried to win her back, but his constant attention bordered on stalking.

One night at a frat party, Sherry disappeared. Her girlfriend claimed that he came to see Sherry, but that she blew him off.

Eddie told police that he'd stayed at the party that night until midnight, that he'd had too much to drink and passed out in one of the upstairs bedrooms, but no one could verify his story.

Police questioned Eddie's father about his childhood history, but his father praised Eddie for his artistic ability. According to Mr. Easton, Eddie was slightly antisocial as a child, but "artists often were." He'd expected Eddie to follow in his footsteps and become a sculptor, and Eddie did carve wood figurines, including faces and raptors. When his father saw the photographs Eddie took of the birds, he agreed Eddie had a talent for photography.

Police questioned his father about the coed's death, and he insisted that Eddie wouldn't hurt a fly. That was the reason he'd volunteered at the nature preserve—he wanted to save injured creatures.

Of course, most fathers would defend their sons. If Eddie was a psychopath, he could easily fool someone with an act.

Had he escalated from carving wooden figurines to women's faces?

Dane skimmed the names of the students questioned at the party, his pulse quickening when he found Silas Grimley's name listed.

Grimley had only been fourteen at the time. Why was he at that party?

The man's reaction to his last name had been odd—had he recognized the name Hamrick because he'd met Betsy?

His adrenaline spiked. Good God, this could be the connection he'd been looking for all along. He might finally get answers, get closure, save his mother.

Dane turned to the background information Peyton had sent on Grimley.

The man had lived with his father in the woods, where his father was a falconer. Due to abuse, he was removed from his father's custody and placed in a foster group home. Eventually he'd been returned to his home, where he stayed until his father disappeared one night.

Police had found human blood in the cages where the man kept the birds as well as traces of both Silas's blood and his father's. They had questioned Silas about his father, but Silas claimed that he had been staying at the foster home, and that his father was often gone for days on hunting trips.

They had never located the man or found his body, so the case went cold. For all they knew, Grimley Sr. had abandoned Silas.

While at the group home, Silas volunteered at the nature preserve where his father's falcons had been moved.

At sixteen, Silas had undergone extensive cosmetic work by a plastic surgeon. Apparently the housemother in the group home where he'd been placed had seen an article about a plastic surgeon who did pro bono work and contacted him. When he'd met Silas, he'd handled his case for free.

The surgeon's name was Dr. Bryce Kirk.

Kirk might have more insight into Grimley.

Dane texted Peyton to check with the doctor. Some physicians required patients undergoing plastic surgery to see a therapist. Peyton could find out if Silas had.

A psych report on the man might shed insight on whether or not Grimley was a killer.

◆ ◆ ◆

Josie fought panic when she couldn't find Neesie. She just prayed the young woman was safe.

She headed down the hall, but Porter McCray stormed toward her. "You told that casting director not to hire me."

Josie took a step back. "That's not true."

"Yes, you did." He grabbed her arm and shoved her up against the wall. "I asked you to practice with me, to give me insight into Linder's character, but you refused. You didn't like me from the beginning."

Josie stiffened, her pulse pounding. "Take your hands off me, Mr. McCray."

"Do as she said."

Josie breathed out in relief at the sound of Dane's gruff voice.

McCray didn't turn around, though. Instead, he squeezed her arm tighter, still in Linder persona. "You'll be sorry for this."

Dane yanked the man away from her, his look lethal. "Is that a threat?"

McCray glared at Josie, then shoved Dane and strode down the hall.

Josie was trembling as she watched him disappear. If she hadn't thought he was dangerous before, she did now.

♦ ♦ ♦

Dane was tempted to beat the crap out of McCray for frightening Josie. The damn man was off in the head.

He also wanted to drag Josie into his arms and promise her that no man would ever hurt her again.

How could he promise that after he'd failed his little sister?

He scrubbed his hand through his hair. He might not be able to promise anything, but he'd damned well do his best. "Are you okay?"

Josie nodded, although her lower lip quivered. "I can't find Neesie, though. She got a callback for a second audition with the casting director but didn't show. She might have booked a session with Easton."

Dane glared at her. "I told you not to go near him."

"I was coming to ask you to go with me," she said, her chin jutting up.

Still angry over McCray's manhandling, Dane gestured toward the door to the studio, then led the way. He knocked but didn't bother to wait for an invitation to enter. He stormed inside, wanting to catch the man off guard.

Cameras were set up, backdrops of various scenes propped in the corner, one depicting a waterfall, which he assumed was Graveyard Falls.

"He's not here," Dane said.

Dane noted a schedule posted on the board. "Neesie Netherington was supposed to meet with him this morning." God, he hoped the killer hadn't gotten to her.

Josie hurried through the room, opening doors and closets in search of the young woman. "Look at this, Dane. I didn't realize there was a back door."

Neither had he. Dane scowled as he opened it. It led to the back parking lot. Easton could have easily come and gone from the studio with no one knowing. With the hall door closed and the sign indicating he was shooting, everyone would assume he was in the room, giving him an alibi when he could have been anywhere.

Dane scanned the parking lot and surrounding area, but didn't spot Easton or his van.

Pulse racing and remembering that Neesie had said she'd seen a Mitzi doll, he went to search for it. If it was here, he'd know Easton was involved.

This time he had a chance to find the missing girl, to save her. It wouldn't make up for Betsy or the other victims, but every life mattered.

He surveyed the studio. Cameras, set props, lighting equipment. Coffee cups and soda cans littered the trash can. A closet was behind the screen, partially blocked from view. He checked it, but the door wouldn't budge.

Curious about what was so important it was locked away when the man's expensive camera equipment was left in the open, he picked the lock.

A box of props sat inside.

Josie peered over his shoulder. Her sharp gasp followed his curse.

A Mitzi doll was tucked in the box, its face carved with the talon marks of a falcon, blood dotting the cheeks.

◆ ◆ ◆

Neesie Netherington didn't want to die. She clawed for something to hold on to, for a way to escape, but her bound hands met dirt and gravel. Panic shot through her. She was tied up, outside somewhere.

Too far away for anyone to hear her scream.

"Please don't kill me," Neesie whispered.

"I'm sorry, I have to. You saw too much."

Tears blurred Neesie's eyes, and she struggled to free herself, but the ropes were too tight, and her limbs felt weak. Heavy.

Oh God. She'd been drugged.

She tried to turn her head to see where she was, but she couldn't move, and it was so dark she couldn't make out anything. The metallic scent of blood filled her nostrils. Maybe a dead animal?

Or was it a human?

Bile rose to her throat. Was this what had happened to Charity and Patty?

Time stood still, her life flashing in front of her. Her acting career. Her ex. Her hopes and dreams.

Strong hands slid beneath her arms and dragged her across the ground. Dirt and gravel ripped at her skin. She tasted dust.

She blinked, desperate to figure out where she was.

First she'd been knocked unconscious. Sometime later she'd woken up in the trunk of a moving car. Engines had roared as vehicles passed. Wind howled. The road had been curvy, then bumpy as if they'd veered onto a dirt road.

Rough hands clenched her arms harder and jerked her back to the moment.

Neesie struggled again to make out her abductor's face, but he slammed her against a tree, and her head swirled with a sickening rush.

Fear choked her.

"Just let me go," she cried. "I promise I won't say anything."

A shrill laugh rent the air, and then the sharp sting of a knife pierced her skin. She opened her mouth and screamed as the point dug deeper into her cheek. Pain ripped through her. She tasted blood.

A second later, he jabbed it into her heart. Her body jerked and bucked. She gurgled blood.

Then the world blurred into a sea of black where she was floating away. Footsteps crunched. She tried to cry out. To beg him to come back. To save her.

But the scent of her own blood wafted toward her. The footsteps faded.

He was leaving her to die.

CHAPTER TWENTY-TWO

Using a handkerchief, Dane carefully wrapped the doll until he got it to the lab to be processed. Adrenaline pumped through him. If Easton's prints were on it, he could use it to make a case.

"Josie, while I look around, page Easton to meet us."

"Sure."

"Be careful. If you see him, don't let on that we suspect him. Text me and I'll come to you."

She agreed and hurried from the studio. Dane searched the rest of the box and the closet but found nothing incriminating. Just costumes and a copy of Josie's book.

Dammit.

Still, the doll should be enough to obtain a search warrant for Easton's cabin and car. In case Easton and Grimley had talked and planned to leave town, he called Sheriff Kimball. "Put out a BOLO on Easton. He's driving a gray 2015 BMW."

"I'm on it." Sheriff Kimball cleared his throat. "By the way, Gil Baines spent the day scouting out film settings with some bearded guy in charge of sets and scene locations. They hiked around the woods and falls."

Kimball had taken initiative. Dane was glad to have him on his side now. He needed eyes everywhere. "Anything suspicious?"

"Nothing concrete. I don't think he had sex with the victims, though."

"Why do you say that?"

"Because he and this other guy have a thing."

"I see." Not that he cared about the man's sexual orientation, but since both Charity and Patty had engaged in sex before their murders, they believed the killer had had sex with the women.

The trouble was he hadn't left DNA on the victims.

"He also has an alibi for the last murder."

Dane mentally checked him off the suspect list. The paging for Easton echoed over the intercom, and Dane hung up and headed to the interior hallway where he had a good vantage point of the rooms and front door.

If Easton was in the building and tried to flee, he'd catch him and haul his ass to the station.

◆ ◆ ◆

Dane talked to the cameraman and the set director, but neither had seen Eddie all day. They'd also denied knowing Silas Grimley.

Were the two of them with Neesie? Or had they decided to run before he closed in?

"Speak to the casting director," the set director said. "She brought Easton into this project."

"Thanks." Dane left the room in search of Olive Turnstyle.

Several actresses sat whispering nervously as they waited for turns to audition.

"Where is Ms. Turnstyle?" Dane asked.

"We don't know. She was supposed to be here," one of the girls said.

A second later, the woman burst into the room, looking harried.

"Sorry I'm late," the casting director said. "I got sidetracked by a phone call."

The women murmured they understood. When Olive noticed him, she smoothed down her skirt and offered him a smile, the harried look disappearing.

"Ms. Turnstyle?" He shook her hand, surprised at her firm handshake.

"Yes, Agent Hamrick. Please call me Olive."

"All right, Olive." He motioned for her to step to the side, then lowered his voice. "I wanted to talk to you about Eddie Easton. Is it true that you brought him into the film company?"

"Yes." She jammed her notebook into her briefcase. "Actually, one of the actresses who worked on another film in LA introduced us. His unusual approach to the photo shoots caught our attention."

He wanted her personal take on the man. "What do you mean, unusual?"

"He was creative and chose different locations and settings for the shoots, not just a studio approach. If an actor wanted a specific part, he suggested they dress to fit the character. He created sets or shot at locations similar to the setting in the story line of the script." She hesitated. "Some of the pictures were disturbing, but he definitely created a niche for himself and got attention."

"Did you ever sense Easton was dangerous?"

Her eyes flickered sideways as if she was contemplating how to answer. "His intensity made me nervous. He also has a propensity for the macabre."

"Can you be more specific?"

"He kept a book of shots of women who'd suffered facial injuries." Her nose wrinkled into a frown. "Before-and-after shots."

"Before and after?"

"Yes. He's friends with this plastic surgeon, Silas Grimley. Eddie referred models and actors wanting cosmetic work to him."

He already knew that. He needed more. "Do you know Dr. Grimley personally?"

"No, but some of the actresses who've used him rave about his work. Although sometimes I thought he encouraged women to undergo drastic reconstruction that was unnecessary."

That was no surprise. Being obsessed with perfect looks came with his job. "What did you think was unnecessary?"

"He carried things to the extreme." She drummed her fingers on her notepad. "He told one woman he'd make her look like that Mitzi doll."

Another indication Grimley might be guilty. "Anything else?"

She nodded. "There was also talk about a patient he'd accidentally disfigured during surgery. I think there was a lawsuit."

"How did you know about the lawsuit?" Dane asked.

She shrugged. "Gossip. The acting community is small, Agent Hamrick."

A botched surgery would definitely feed the grapevine. Women would want to warn other women.

Had the botched case and the lawsuit triggered Grimley's desire to maim and murder these women?

♦ ♦ ♦

Three of the women Josie spoke with mentioned seeing both Charity and Patty with Eddie Easton. He also recommended they schedule a consultation with Dr. Silas Grimley.

One actress was pleased with Grimley's work, although she'd overheard an altercation about a lawsuit with a former patient while she was in the waiting room.

According to her, the good doctor broke down and left the office in an incoherent rage. The scene frightened the young woman so badly that she decided not to pursue another surgery.

Josie thanked them and went to find Dane. Just as she rounded a corner in the hallway, Doyle Yonkers appeared, his demeanor instantly putting her on edge.

She tried to sidestep him, but he snatched her arm and yanked her into a corner.

Back stiffening, Josie pulled her arm away. "What are you doing?"

"Haven't you and this movie crew caused enough trouble?" he snapped. "Our families didn't want the past dredged up and put on screen for everyone to see."

"The past was dredged up when Billy Linder committed murder. All I did was tell the story."

"You've brought more pain to the victims' families than you can imagine. Even worse, you made it sound like my sister was at fault."

"That's not true," Josie said firmly.

His eyes pierced her with condemnation. "That's how my mother felt. That you think Candy should have been friends with Charlene. That girl was weird as shit, though, and dangerous. Nobody liked her."

"She was definitely disturbed," Josie said. "And I understand this has been painful for you."

"You have no idea," he snarled. "My mother was already ill, but when she saw the news about more girls dying this week, she couldn't handle it. She took some pills and killed herself."

Josie gasped. Sorrow for him and his family filled her. "Oh my God, I'm so sorry. I never meant—"

"To do what? Tear people's lives apart?" He dragged her toward the back door. "To kill my mother? Because she's dead now and it's your fault."

Josie's sorrow quickly turned to fear as he shoved her outside.

CHAPTER TWENTY-THREE

Dane spotted Doyle Yonkers shoving Josie out the back door and took off at a dead run. What the hell was that man doing with his hands on her?

By the time he reached the exit, the bastard was pushing her down the steps toward the alley.

Dane's hand went to his gun. From his vantage point, he couldn't tell if Yonkers was armed or not.

He didn't care, though. He had his hands on Josie, and that was not allowed.

"Stop, Yonkers!" he shouted. "Let her go."

Josie spun around and pushed at Yonkers. The man stumbled and hit his back against the wall.

Dane pulled his gun. "Don't move or I'll shoot."

Yonkers went wide-eyed and threw up his hands. "Don't shoot. I don't have a weapon."

Dane stalked toward him and motioned for Josie to move away. She was already doing so, her expression daring Yonkers to touch her again.

"I wasn't going to hurt her," Yonkers screeched. "I just wanted to talk."

"You always push women into alleys to talk?" Dane barked.

Yonkers paled. "No . . . I was just upset."

"Keep your hands up," Dane ordered. He didn't trust that the man hadn't lied about being armed, so he quickly patted him down.

"Tell him, Josie, I didn't hurt you," Yonkers pleaded.

"You forced me outside," Josie said, refusing to cut him any slack. "That's assault."

Dane finished the pat down, satisfied the man wasn't carrying a weapon. He didn't necessarily need a gun to overpower Josie or any other woman, though.

"I just wanted to talk," Yonkers said angrily.

"You mean terrify me?" Josie asked, arms crossed.

"Or get revenge?" Dane added.

Yonkers averted his eyes. "It's not like that," he said, his voice lower. "I was upset. My mother killed herself." He gestured toward Josie. "All because of this movie and the publicity she brought to town. Because of her more girls are dead. My mother couldn't take it anymore. It's like the past keeps repeating itself."

Dane didn't give a rat's ass about this jerk. He had no right to manhandle a woman. "Maybe you're the one repeating the past. You want to get back at Josie, so you stabbed those other women?"

Yonkers staggered backward, shock on his face. "What?"

"Charity Snow and Patty Waxton," Dane said. "You wanted to punish Josie and make the film crew leave town, so you killed two women to scare people away."

"That's absurd," Yonkers said. "I haven't killed anyone. I wouldn't do that, especially to make a point."

Dane hissed between his teeth. He didn't think it was enough of a motive, but he had to do something to put the fear of God in Yonkers. "Why should I believe you? I saw you manhandling Josie."

Yonkers turned to Josie. "I just wanted you to stop, the whole town did, but you refused and now my mother is dead, and I've lost the last bit of family I had."

Yonkers sounded pathetic. If anyone understood the pain of losing a loved one, Dane did. But he hadn't used his grief as a reason to push people around and blame innocents like this bastard was doing.

◆ ◆ ◆

Guilt and sympathy filled Josie at the anguish in Doyle Yonkers's voice. He had suffered an unspeakable grief in his childhood, borne the brunt of survivor's guilt, as well as watched his parents bury themselves in so much grief that they'd failed him.

"I'm sorry for your loss, Doyle, and that your mother had such a difficult time with her grief," Josie said. "You must have been very lonely growing up, living in the shadow of that loss."

Dane reached for handcuffs, but Josie pressed a hand to his to stop him.

"Josie—"

"He didn't hurt me." Josie silently willed Dane to trust her. "You need to see a counselor, Doyle. Not blame me or the town. You suffered a terrible tragedy years ago. Sometimes that brings families closer together. Sometimes it tears them apart."

His face crumpled, and tears leaked from his eyes. "If you hadn't brought this movie to town, if you'd only left that day after the press conference—"

"That's the kind of logic abusive men use to justify their actions." Josie refused to fall into that trap. "You pushed me in the street that day, didn't you?"

"I'm sorry." Regret and shame flashed on his face. "I didn't want to hurt you, only to scare you so you'd stop the film."

"Did you run her off the road?"

He gave a nod. "I told you I wanted to scare her. I even stopped to make sure she was all right."

Josie's pulse pounded at his twisted logic. "I could have been killed."

"I'm sorry." Defeat weighed his voice. "I knew it was wrong after I did it."

Dane pressed a hand to Josie's waist. "Do you want to press charges, Josie?"

She rubbed her hands together. Yonkers had terrified her, but he'd had a rough childhood, and she understood that this film triggered bad memories just as it was doing for her. At least he hadn't resorted to murder. She and Dane needed to focus on finding the Butcher. "No, not now. Not if you agree to get therapy, Doyle."

He rubbed his eyes. "I've been to therapy before."

"Then go again," Josie said flatly. "I understand it's difficult to talk about what happened, but it helps. I've done it myself." She licked her dry lips. "Do it so you can move on and have a life and put all this behind you."

Just like she was trying to do. Only it wasn't easy.

He jammed his hands in his pockets and looked down at his shoes. "I will and . . . I'll go back on my meds."

Josie offered him an encouraging smile. "Good."

A car door slammed. Footsteps crunched.

Josie glanced at the parking lot. Easton was walking toward them. They needed to talk to him.

He might be the unsub carving up women's faces.

If he was, he had to pay.

◆ ◆ ◆

Dane gripped Yonkers. "If you bother Miss DuKane again," Dane said in a lethal tone, "I will arrest you and make sure you never see the light of day again."

Yonkers threw up his hands. "I won't. Don't worry."

Dane shoved him. "Then get out of here." With Yonkers off the suspect list, he could focus on Easton and Grimley.

Yonkers looked relieved at escaping arrest and darted away. Dane was amazed at Josie's compassion. He hoped she'd made the right choice in letting the man off the hook.

Dane didn't want Easton to escape, though, so he rushed toward him. He half expected him to run, but Easton was either so cocky he thought he'd never get caught—or he was innocent.

Although as Dane neared him, a wariness shadowed the man's face. "Mr. Easton, I need you to come with me to the sheriff's office."

Easton narrowed his eyes. "What for?"

"To answer some questions."

Easton glanced at Josie warily, then back at Dane, his posture stiffening. "Do I need a lawyer?"

Dane stepped forward, towering over the man. "I don't know, do you?"

"I haven't done anything wrong," Easton said in a defensive tone. "I'm not this psycho you're looking for."

"Then come in and talk with me. Maybe you can help us catch him."

Easton squinted against the sun, but agreed. Although he looked wary, he didn't seem as worried as Dane would have expected.

The ride back to the police station passed in a tense silence. Josie seemed lost in thought. Probably worry over Neesie.

He wanted to console her and assure her the young woman was fine. But he didn't believe in lies. He was worried, too. If Easton was involved and didn't confess, and the killer had Neesie, they might be too late to save her.

When they arrived, Dane escorted Easton to the interrogation room, then he checked the fax machine and found information Peyton had sent over. Josie grabbed coffee for the three of them and met him in the room.

Easton settled in the wooden chair at the table, fidgeting. He gave a suspicious glance at the coffee as if he thought it was a ploy to lift his prints—or to make him feel relaxed enough to spill his guts.

"All right, why did you bring me here?" Impatience laced Easton's voice. "I've already told you that I knew Charity and Patty. I saw them at the party, but I didn't kill them."

Dane laid a photo of each of the victims on the table. "Because we have two dead girls. And we think another is missing. Do you know Neesie Netherington?"

Easton licked his lips. "I did a photo shoot with her. That's all."

"Are you sure you didn't kill her like you did these two women?"

Easton pushed up as if to leave. "Wait just a fucking minute."

"Sit down and look at the damn pictures," Dane said in a tone that brooked no argument.

Easton did as Dane said, his gaze dropping to the photograph. A second later, he made a strangled sound in his throat. "Jesus. That reporter was right. Someone butchered her face?"

Dane tapped the photos with his finger. "Yes, you did."

Easton balled his hands into fists on the table. "It wasn't me. I like pretty girls—I take their pictures to help them get modeling and acting jobs." He paused, his beard stubble rasping as he wiped his chin. "Think about it. I would never destroy their beauty. It's how I make my living."

Dane studied him carefully. He sounded sincere, but some people were consummate liars. They could even pass polygraphs when they were guilty.

"You didn't tell everyone that the girls were left naked." Easton's tone was accusatory, but his gaze remained fixated on the gruesome pictures. "Or about that claw mark on their cheeks. You practically denied it when that reporter mentioned those details."

Dane laid the picture of the Mitzi doll he'd found in Easton's studio on the table. "We found this one in the closet in your studio tonight."

Easton's mouth went slack, his eyes wide. For the first time, he seemed to realize that Dane had evidence against him.

Easton gulped. "You found that in my studio?"

Dane nodded. "Don't tell me you don't know what it is or where it came from."

Panic streaked his face. "I know what the Mitzi doll is. Hell, everyone in the US does. But I didn't have one in my studio."

Dane gave him a disbelieving look. "Then who put it there?"

He flattened his hands, then rolled them into fists again. "How should I know?"

"A lot of little girls collect these dolls and want to be like them, just like they want to be princesses," Josie interjected.

Easton's gaze swung toward her. "Sure, kids fantasize and play pretend."

Dane slapped the picture of Easton's former girlfriend on the table. "You recognize her?"

The color drained from Easton's face. "Of course I do. That's Sherry. Why do you have her picture?"

Dane paused, letting the questions mount in Easton's head. "Tell me about your relationship with her," he said.

"She was the only girl I ever loved," Easton finally admitted. "I asked her to marry me, but then she died."

Dane gave him a flat look. "She was murdered. After being seen at a frat party with you."

Easton nodded, pain flashing in his eyes. "Yes."

"You were the last one who saw her alive," Dane continued.

"No," Easton said emphatically. "The person who killed her was."

"You two argued," Dane said.

Easton squared his shoulders. "We had a lovers' quarrel, nothing big."

"That's not what we heard." Dane paused for effect. He wanted the bastard to stew. "She broke up with you because you frightened her with your weird photograph ideas. And you stalked her afterward."

Easton clenched the table. "I didn't stalk her."

"You wanted back with her?" Dane asked.

"Yes, I loved her," Easton muttered. "I went to the party to convince her to give me another chance, but she told me no, so I got drunk."

"Yet she ended up dead that night," Dane said, the implication clear in his voice.

Easton shifted, guilt darkening his eyes. "I know, and I blamed myself. If I hadn't passed out in one of the upstairs rooms, if she'd stayed with me, she might be alive." He heaved a breath. "I didn't kill her. I would never have hurt her. I loved her with all my heart."

Dane hardened his jaw. His tone reeked of obsession. "Then who did kill her?"

"I don't know. I wish to hell I did." Easton slammed his fist on the table. "Those asshole cops fucked up by wasting their time looking at me instead of investigating."

Dane let his tirade linger in the air, which intensified Easton's agitation.

Easton gestured toward the pictures of Charity and Patty. "Now what the fuck is going on? What does Sherry's death have to do with these recent murders?"

"You were seen with all the victims shortly before they died." Dane laid a picture of Betsy on the table, his heart hammering as he waited for Easton's reaction.

Easton slumped against the seat, perspiration dotting his forehead. "God, where did you get that?"

Dane planted his fists on the table to keep from jerking the man by the neck and choking him. Was Easton reacting out of guilt? "That girl was my sister, Betsy. She went missing from a frat party at UT where you were." Dane swallowed hard. "The police found her body a few hours later. Did you kill her, Easton?"

"Shit." Easton dropped his head into his hands. "I think I need a lawyer."

♦ ♦ ♦

Josie sensed Dane's frustration. He was still agonizing over the loss of his sister. He also wanted a confession, but Easton hadn't broken.

Dane folded his arms. "If you aren't guilty, why do you need a lawyer?"

"Because you're obviously trying to pin this on me," Easton said.

Josie touched Easton's hand in an effort to implore him to cooperate. "Please, Eddie, talk to us. Another girl is missing. If you didn't hurt Charity or Patty, then help us stop this madman before he takes another life."

"I don't know how to help you," Eddie said, his voice weak. "I would never butcher a woman like that."

Dane tapped Betsy's photograph again. "What do you remember about my sister? You met her at a frat party ten years ago."

Eddie's face contorted in anguish. "Listen, Agent Hamrick, I did meet her, but not at the party. I knew Betsy before that night."

A muscle ticked in Dane's jaw. "Go on."

Eddie's hand shook as he wiped his forehead. "We met at a nature preserve."

"The same one where you met Silas Grimley?" Dane asked.

Eddie murmured yes. "Silas was fourteen, a mess, all fucked up by his old man, and your sister took him under her wing."

Dane leaned across the table to intimidate the man. "That's where you and Silas became friends?"

"Yeah. I was kind of a big brother to him, and Betsy was like a big sister."

Grief lined Dane's face. "Did Silas visit you at school?"

"Yeah, when I was at UT. A couple of times, I let him come up for the weekend to show him that he had a future." His voice grew low. "I thought it would help him see he could make it to college if he worked hard and got his shit together."

"Did Grimley meet your girlfriend Sherry?"

Eddie nodded, although his eyes became guarded, then suspicious. Josie was trying to get a read on him, but he gave off mixed messages.

"Was Silas visiting you the weekend your girlfriend died?" Dane continued.

Eddie's hand shook as he finally picked up his coffee and took a sip. "Yes."

Dane leaned another inch closer. "He was there the night Betsy was murdered?"

"Yes." Easton made a strangled sound in his throat. "You think Silas killed Sherry and Betsy?"

Before Dane could answer, Josie's cell phone buzzed.

She checked the text and went cold inside.

It was a picture of Neesie Netherington lying in a pool of blood, one hand holding a broken mirror, the other a Mitzi doll.

Bloody claw marks scarred her face.

CHAPTER
TWENTY-FOUR

Josie's stomach roiled. "My God, Neesie is dead."

The room fell into such a deafening silence that she could hear her own heart hammering in her chest.

Dane grabbed the phone and studied the picture. "Dammit, we're too late again."

Josie started trembling and couldn't stop.

Dane shoved the picture in the man's face. "Where did you leave this woman?"

Eddie jerked back at the sight of the picture. "Good God. That's Neesie."

"Hell yeah, it is," Dane snapped. "Where is she?"

Eddie shook his head back and forth vehemently. "Listen to me, I told you I didn't kill anyone."

"What about your partner?" Dane snarled.

"Partner?" Eddie lurched to a standing position. "You're fucking nuts."

"Sit down!" Dane pounded the table. "Tell me how you and Grimley pulled it off. You lure the females in with the promise of a photo shoot, then refer them to him for cosmetic work. Then who kills them? Do you take turns? Does he do the carving or do you?"

Eddie's breath rasped out. "For the last time, I'm not involved in any murders. If Grimley is, he's done it on his own." He fisted his hands by his sides. "In fact, if he killed Sherry, I'd like a shot at him myself."

Josie remained quiet, studying Easton's body language for signs of guilt.

Dane's theory about the two men working together held merit, but Eddie seemed genuinely shocked that Dane suspected Grimley of killing his girlfriend.

"Was Grimley questioned in Sherry's murder?" Dane asked.

Eddie shook his head. "He was just a kid. I thought, and the police thought, some guy she met at the frat party killed her. I saw her talking to some dopehead earlier, and I figured she'd gotten mixed up with the wrong guy."

"You and Grimley have kept in touch, remained friends?" Dane asked.

"Yes. Some plastic surgeon corrected his scars and mentored him, so Silas wanted to do that for others."

"Did you think Grimley was dangerous?" Josie asked.

"Was—you mean *is* he dangerous?" Eddie heaved a breath. "I don't know. He had some issues when I first met him."

"What kind of *issues*?" Dane asked.

Eddie rubbed his temple. "He was a loner, troubled. Sometimes he latched onto people."

"Like who?"

"Like me and Sherry. For a while he wanted to do everything with us. Then Sherry got tired of it. She said he creeped her out."

"You told Grimley this?"

"Yes." Eddie's expression slowly changed as he realized the implications. "Jesus, I told him that a couple of weeks before Sherry died."

"Did he latch onto my sister?" Dane asked.

Eddie's expression turned wary. "Yeah. Like I said, he was a screwed-up adolescent. He was in love with her."

Josie imagined the scenario—a troubled young kid, needy, craving love. A teenage girl trying to help him. He mistook her kindness and compassion for more. "Did Betsy know how he felt?"

Eddie shrugged. "She realized he had a crush and said she'd let him down gently. That he seemed fragile to her."

"Dammit, Easton." Dane shook the man. "Didn't it occur to you that he killed her because she rejected him?"

◆ ◆ ◆

Anger pushed Dane as he called the sheriff. He should have done more to find Neesie Netherington. Should have worked harder, found this unsub before now.

They had to stop this son of a bitch before another woman died. "I want Silas Grimley found immediately and brought in for questioning. Get your deputies to look for the Netherington woman's body. Josie just received another text. The young woman is dead."

Dane ended the call, then turned back to Easton. "Where's Grimley now?"

Easton threw up his hands. "I don't know. Probably back at the convention in Knoxville."

If Grimley was the unsub and killed Betsy and Sherry, those murders took place years ago. What had triggered him to start killing now? How did the doll get in Easton's closet?

Had Grimley put it there?

"Did Grimley have a recent breakup?" Dane asked.

Easton shook his head. "Not that I know of. I don't think he was even seeing anyone. He spent all his time working."

"He probably thought he'd win these women's affections and admiration with his work," Dane suggested, "but they rejected him on a personal level, and he snapped."

"Listen," Eddie said. "I can't believe he'd kill his patients and mess up their faces. He hated being scarred, and dedicated his life to making women more attractive. He's got some kind of God complex. He honestly believes he's their hero, that his work saves lives."

Dane considered his argument. It made sense. But that lawsuit had challenged his position to play God.

He retrieved another page from the file Peyton had sent and showed it to Easton. One notation said she'd talked to the plastic surgeon who took care of Grimley, and he'd recommended a therapist, but he didn't know if Grimley followed up.

"He was saving lives?" Dane said sardonically. "He was making them look like that Mitzi doll."

Easton knotted his hands together but didn't respond. Dane's phone buzzed, and he checked the number. Sheriff Kimball.

He punched Connect. "Agent Hamrick."

The sheriff released a weary sigh. "I know where Neesie Netherington's body is."

Dane's gut clenched. "That was fast. Where did you find her?"

"That casting director just phoned, upset," Sheriff Kimball said. "She found the woman lying in the bushes in front of the Falls Inn."

Dane told him he'd be right there. Then he took Easton by the arm. "Come on, you're going to stay here until I find Grimley and process this crime scene."

"What the fuck?" Easton shouted. "You can't lock me up."

"I'm still not convinced you're not working with Grimley. I can hold you for twenty-four hours for questioning," Dane said. "I don't intend to let you warn Grimley that we're onto him."

Easton cursed again, but Dane led him to a cell and locked him inside. Then he and Josie hurried to his car.

♦ ♦ ♦

Josie couldn't help but recall Doyle Yonkers's accusations as she and Dane drove to the inn and parked.

Sheriff Kimball's police car sat in front on the curb, and a crime van was already on the scene while another deputy monitored the spectators who'd gathered to watch the horrid events unfold.

Now three young women were dead, their dreams and futures cut off at too young of an age.

If she hadn't written this book and sold the movie rights, and the film crew hadn't come to this town, would these three women still be alive?

Was it her fault they were dead?

"Why don't you wait in the car?" Dane asked, his voice gruff. Tender.

She shook her head. "I'll do whatever I can to help stop this bastard. I don't like the fact that he's using the town and people here as his hunting ground."

"Did you believe Easton?" Dane asked as they walked up to the inn.

"I don't know," Josie said. "After Billy Linder, I don't trust my own judgment anymore."

Dane paused and looked at her for a moment. The wind blew his hair back, ruffling the ends and making him look impossibly sexy in the waning light.

Sexy and dangerous to her heart.

She could fall in love with Dane so easily.

Hell, she was already in deep lust.

She ached to run her hands through his hair, to beg him to take her back to his cabin, light a fire, and make love to her long into the night. To make her forget that she might have brought more murders on a town that had already suffered enough.

Someone shrieked from near the front door, jerking her attention back to the scene.

Dane squeezed her arm. "Hang in there, Josie. We'll find this lunatic and lock him away just like we did Billy Linder."

Sorrow filled Josie. Even though they found the killer, a lot of people had suffered in the meantime. The victims' families were still grieving, just as Dane had never stopped hurting over the loss of his little sister.

Bailey Snow and another young woman were huddled together, consoling each other, while a chuffy guy tried to snap a photo with his camera. Sheriff Kimball jerked his phone away.

"Take a picture and I'll arrest you," Kimball snarled. "Show some respect to this woman and her family. They haven't even been notified."

Josie's pulse clamored. The crime scene crew had roped off the area while two deputies worked to contain the small crowd. Their questions couldn't be silenced.

Neither could their whispers of shock.

"Was she killed by the same person who murdered Charity and Patty?" a woman shouted.

"You didn't tell us those girls were left naked, that he butchered their faces," another girl cried.

"What kind of sicko does this?"

"When are you going to catch this maniac?"

"We're doing everything possible," Sheriff Kimball said in an effort to calm the rising hysteria. "If you see or hear anything that might help us, please contact my office. If you knew this woman personally or saw her earlier today and can shed some light on her movements during the last twenty-four hours, that would be helpful."

Dane spoke to Lieutenant Ward, but Josie waited outside the crime scene tape, respecting the fact that they didn't want the scene contaminated.

Grimley's past actions and the timing certainly pointed to him. There were also connections between Dane's sister and Easton's girlfriend that couldn't be ignored. Easton also had that doll in his closet.

She studied the crowd. Something about the interviews didn't mesh. If Easton or Grimley had contacted her, she'd expect at some point for them to give her a sign. Some kind of signal that they'd sent her the photographs. That they were interested in her focusing on them.

She hadn't detected anything like that. Easton appeared to be cocky, sure of himself, but stunned that he was a suspect. Grimley vacillated between a show of confidence and vulnerability.

Had they somehow connected to merge their strengths and weaknesses and become the Butcher?

Or were she and Dane on the wrong trail?

♦ ♦ ♦

Dane jammed his fists into his pockets, wishing he had hold of the son of a bitch who'd killed Neesie Netherington. The poor woman had been left in the bushes beside the inn, her limbs contorted at an odd angle just like the first two victims.

Naked and alone, left in the elements as if no one gave a damn about who she was. The shattered glass of the compact mirror glinted against the darkness. Blood had already congealed on her chest and dried on her cheek.

Remorse engulfed him. While they'd been running around chasing leads, she'd already been dead.

"COD appears to be the same as the others," Dr. Wheeland said. "It also looks like he used the same type of instrument to carve the talon marks on her face."

Easton's comments about Silas Grimley echoed in Dane's head. He'd been scarred from the attack. He had known Betsy and Easton's girlfriend and had been at the college when both of them were there.

"Anything look different?" Dane asked.

"Nothing that's evident. The stab wounds look similar, so does the carving. I don't see bruising on her thighs or fluids, but I'll run a rape kit anyway as I did with the others."

Dane zeroed in on her wrists and ankles. "She was restrained."

"Yeah. Maybe she was more of a fighter, and he had to tie her up."

Dane strode over to talk to the sheriff. "It's time to bring Dr. Grimley in." Dane filled him in on the man's background and the details he'd uncovered.

"I'll issue a BOLO and alert bus and train stations as well as airports. Two deputies are canvassing the crowd to see if anyone saw anything."

"Good. Keep me posted." Dane quickly phoned Peyton. "I need a search warrant for Dr. Grimley's car and belongings."

"I'm on it."

"Did you find out the whereabouts of that guy Leroy Weaver?"

"Yeah, he's been in a rehab facility for the past three weeks. Nearly died of an overdose and family committed him."

Dane hung up. So Weaver hadn't found Neesie.

Cynthia, the owner of the inn, stood by the casting director, one hand fluttering across her chest as if she felt faint. Josie had joined Olive, who looked shell-shocked.

Dane slipped up beside Josie and squeezed her arm. She gave him a grateful look, which compounded his guilt. He should have stopped this guy by now.

His gut tight, he resorted to business. He was much better at that than personal relations. "Ms. Turnstyle, you found the body?" Dane asked.

Her hand trembled as she adjusted her glasses. "Yes, when I arrived and was going inside, I heard a noise."

"She was still alive?" Dane asked, confused.

Olive shook her head. "No, I'm afraid not. It was just a cat."

"There's a stray that hangs around," Cynthia said. "I leave out food for it on the back stoop."

"Anyway, it sounded like the cat was injured and it was in the bushes, so I ran over to look for it." A tear rolled down Olive's face, and

Josie put her arm around her to comfort her. "I saw her legs poking out of the bushes," Olive finished.

"This is just horrible," Cynthia murmured as she gaped at the scene. "I can't believe someone left that poor girl out here."

"Did you see anything?" Dane asked the innkeeper.

Cynthia shook her head. "No. I was inside tidying up the rooms and chatting with a couple of the other girls. Everyone's been so upset about these murders that I hold a nightly prayer session for the guests who want to pray with me."

Dane glanced back at Olive. "Did you notice anyone lurking around when you arrived?"

Olive shook her head. "No. I'm so sorry, I wish I could be more helpful."

"You're doing great," Josie assured her.

Olive rubbed two fingers to her temple. "I told you earlier Neesie was supposed to come for a callback and never showed. Now I understand the reason."

The panic Josie had felt earlier mixed with regret. "I know, I'm so sorry. I wish I could have done something to save her. She seemed like such a sweet girl."

"She was." Olive cleared her throat, pulling herself together. "Under the circumstances, I'm going to talk to the director and request that we postpone this film. I can't stand to see anyone else hurt because our crew is here."

Josie nodded. "I think that's a good idea."

Dane didn't know how to respond.

Yonkers came to mind. If someone had wanted to run the film crew out of town, they'd succeeded. But the brutality of the crime indicated a stronger motive, a pathology that had nothing to do with something as simple as stopping a movie production.

If he wanted to kill again, he would find another victim.

Dane scanned the people huddled around the house and crime scene.

Was the killer standing in the crowd, watching the town and police scurry around in shock and fear at his latest kill?

The killer was focused on Josie. Would she be his next target?

Cold fear washed over him at the thought. He was lying to himself if he said he didn't care about Josie.

He cared too damn much.

CHAPTER
TWENTY-FIVE

Wind hurled debris and leaves across the road as Dane drove Josie home. Dread knotted every muscle in her body.

Would she find another butchered Mitzi doll at her house?

It was probably best they were shutting down the film project. At least temporarily. The mood in the town and among the actors and film crew had definitely grown somber.

Dane parked, and they walked to her porch together, both as desolate as the gray skies. Josie froze and clutched his arm. "Oh God, Dane. Look, another doll."

Dane cursed and tenderly squeezed her arm. "We will get him," Dane said in a comforting tone.

Josie sighed. Yes, but when? And how many more had to die?

She had to focus on the details. This time the doll lay on the porch, its butchered face taunting her with blood. The blood on the other dolls had been the victims'.

She shivered. This was probably Neesie's blood. "Easton didn't do this," she said in a raw whisper. "He's in custody."

"We can't be sure," Dane said. "We've been gone all day. He could have watched and dropped it off as soon as you left earlier."

Josie leaned against him, surprising him. "That's true, I guess."

"The killer must be shaken up." Dane clenched her hand for a moment, lingering as if he wanted her to know he was on her side. "The fact that he didn't take the time to break in means he was in a hurry."

Disappointment tugged at Josie when Dane released her hand. She wanted to hang on to him and let him keep her grounded. Safe.

Guilt returned on its heels, reminding her that she had to keep working and help Dane.

"If Easton and Grimley are partners, Grimley could have left it to throw us off."

Josie nodded, although despair and frustration made her chest ache. "If he thinks we're closing in on him, he might run."

"I don't think so. He likes the game too much." Dane gestured toward the dark house. "Let me check inside in case he wanted to fake you out by leaving the doll outside."

Josie stiffened at the thought. Dane drew his gun and opened the door. The house was quiet, the windows rattling from the wind, a tree limb scraping the glass panes somewhere in back. Storm clouds shifted and moved, making the sky even more gray and dreary.

Dane slowly crept inside, and she followed on his heels. She glanced in the kitchen and living area, but nothing seemed amiss.

Bile rose to her throat when they stopped at the doorway to her bedroom. Dane had been wrong.

The Butcher had been inside.

Blood was smeared across her white comforter in the jagged lines of a claw mark, just as it had been smeared on Neesie's face.

♦ ♦ ♦

Dane phoned Lieutenant Ward and asked him to send another crime team to Josie's house. He hated this bastard for toying with her. Josie didn't deserve this.

She looked pale and fragile as they watched the two investigators search the house and dust for fingerprints. The bloody comforter and doll went into a bag for analysis.

"Grab a few things, Josie," Dane told her. "You aren't staying here tonight."

Josie frowned at him for a second, then nodded without arguing, a sign she was frightened.

She gathered her toiletries and tossed some extra clothes into an overnight bag.

Dane's phone buzzed as they headed to his SUV.

"It's Sheriff Kimball, Agent Hamrick. Knoxville airport security spotted Grimley buying a ticket to Mexico."

Dane's pulse jumped. "Tell them not to let him board that flight. I'll be there ASAP." He ended the call and relayed the news to Josie.

Josie clutched her purse strap. "So he's running?"

"I must have been wrong. It appears he is. He probably found out we detained Easton and knew we were close to making an arrest."

Josie sank into the seat and fastened her seatbelt. "I'm surprised he'd leave Easton to take the fall."

"He was locked in a cage as a kid. He's probably terrified of being locked away again."

Sympathy registered on Josie's face. Dane had none, not for a cold-blooded man who carved up women's faces for fun.

Adrenaline pumping, Dane sped toward the airport, cursing at the traffic as he veered onto the interstate leading to Knoxville. He blinked against the glare of lights—weaving in and out of traffic and passing the slower cars, his siren roaring.

Josie clutched the door handle, unusually quiet.

Dane rubbed her shoulder. "You okay?"

"As all right as I can be with another death on my conscience." Josie twisted her hands together. "I feel so helpless. Like I should have done more."

"That's the story of my life, Josie. But you're not at fault here, so stop blaming yourself." Although he, of all people, understood guilt. "You didn't have anything to do with this psycho or his crimes."

"Logically I know that," Josie said. "But he's sending me those pictures. Do you think he wants to punish me for writing about the Bride Killer?"

Dane gritted his teeth in frustration. "He's demented. He takes some kind of sick pleasure in hurting women and taunting you. He wants you to make him famous like Billy Linder."

Dane turned off the interstate and drove toward the airport. Siren wailing, he sped around traffic heading to the main terminal and parked in front of the building.

A policeman met him at his vehicle. "Sheriff Kimball phoned and explained the situation. I've alerted security throughout the airport."

"You know where he is?"

"Yes, he's waiting at the gate for his flight," the officer said. "He has no idea we flagged him and that we're holding the plane until you arrived."

"Thanks." Dane and Josie raced inside and met with an airport officer who led them through security and the crowded halls.

When they finally reached the gate, Dane spotted the plastic surgeon pacing by the window, his movements agitated, cell phone pressed to his ear. Dane motioned for the officer to stand back and guard the area, and two more security guards arrived as backup.

Dane kept his eyes trained on Grimley. The intercom blared with announcements for flights that were boarding. Grimley paced, his movements agitated as he kept checking his watch and the flight schedule.

"Stay here and out of sight. We don't want to alert him that we're here," Dane told Josie. "If he runs, get out of his way and let the police handle it."

Josie nodded and stepped into the corner of one of the airport stores. Dane silently thanked her. He was more concerned about her safety than anything else.

And that scared him. But he didn't have time to analyze his reaction.

If Grimley panicked, he might try to take a hostage, and he didn't intend for Josie to get caught in the middle.

Dane cut through the crowd, keeping his head low and Grimley in sight. He needed to get closer before he charged the man.

Anxiety knotted his shoulders. A family of four elbowed their way through to the gate in need of seats, and a group of college kids appeared, laughing and hauling backpacks and fast food. An airline attendant pushed an elderly man in a wheelchair in front of him.

All slowing him down.

By the time Dane had cut through the throng, Grimley had spotted him. Instant panic flooded his face, and he shoved his phone in his pocket, abandoned his rolling bag, and took off running away from the gate.

"Dammit." Dane motioned to the guards to cover the exits, and gave chase.

Grimley shoved a young woman and her baby out of the way. Dane caught the lady just before she stumbled and fell. He gently steadied her, then raised his badge and shouted for people to move.

Grimley jogged down the corridor past the food court, then jumped onto the escalator going toward the baggage claim and ground transportation. Dane broke into a sprint, waving the guards forward, one of whom was speaking into a mic on his lapel, alerting security to stop Grimley from leaving the airport.

More crowds piled onto the floor as a flight unloaded, and Dane shouted again to clear the area as he jogged down the escalator and raced after Grimley. The man paused at a restroom to glance back, saw Dane, and darted toward the exits.

Dane veered around a group of tourists gathering to catch a hotel van. Two officers stepped to the door to block Grimley from leaving.

Grimley screeched to a stop and frantically searched for another exit, but Dane caught up with him, jerked his arms behind him, and snapped handcuffs around his wrists.

"Dr. Silas Grimley, you are under arrest for the murders of Charity Snow, Patty Waxton, and Neesie Netherington." Dane patted him down to make sure he wasn't armed, but the man was clean.

"You can't do this, I didn't murder anyone." Grimley swung his hands wildly. "I'm being set up!"

Dane clenched his jaw to keep from slamming the bastard against the wall. "Shut up, it's over, you bastard."

Then Dane shoved him through the exit to a police vehicle waiting to take him to jail.

♦ ♦ ♦

Josie met Dane at his SUV.

"Where's Grimley?" Josie asked when she saw the empty vehicle.

"The county police are transporting him to jail," Dane said. "I wanted to search his luggage and car."

Thank God Grimley hadn't escaped. Maybe they'd get to the truth now.

Dane unlocked the SUV, his jaw tense. "Letting him sit and sweat in a cell for a while will be good for him. Maybe he'll be ready to talk once I interrogate him."

Knowing Dane, he wouldn't be happy until he got a full-fledged confession.

Another officer appeared dragging a rolling suitcase, then settled it in front of Dane.

"Did your security team locate Grimley's car?" Dane asked.

The officer spoke into his mic, then nodded. "Third level, extended parking."

"Looks like he planned to be gone a long time." Dane opened the trunk bed of his SUV, then pulled on latex gloves, set the luggage inside, and picked the lock.

Dane quickly rifled through the contents. Two designer suits, a pair of dress shoes, ties, a photo album. Dane glanced at her with a raised brow, then opened the photo book.

Her stomach clenched at the sight of the pictures—there were pages and pages of the actors who'd come to audition in Graveyard Falls.

Billy Linder had kept a Bride's Book with photos of his victims, pictures taken after their death.

This book held headshots and photos of actresses in various situations depicting scenes from her book. Granted the scenes she'd written were dark, but they were based on fact. Seeing these reenactments suggested he was exploiting the story line for his own demented pleasure.

A sick feeling washed over her. Did Grimley have copies of the photos he'd sent her? Was he the Butcher?

"I'll take everything to the lab," Dane said as he closed the book.

Josie spotted something jammed in an inside pocket. "What's that?"

Dane unzipped the compartment, then scowled. "A picture of Grimley and Easton together at the nature preserve."

"You really think he and Easton are partners?" Josie asked.

"I don't know," Dane said. "Don't you?"

Josie bit her lip. "I don't know yet either. A lot of things point to them working together. And Grimley definitely fits the profile."

Dane finished searching the suitcase and closed it. "Well, I intend to find out."

He climbed in the driver's seat and drove into the parking garage for extended parking. Grimley's Mercedes was locked, so Dane retrieved a crowbar from his SUV and opened the passenger door. Josie stood back on pins and needles as he searched the interior. If they found the bones from the victims, they could seal the case against Grimley.

The dash and front seat held nothing important: insurance information, a couple of magazines on the latest plastic surgery techniques, and handouts from the conference he'd just attended.

Dane found the lever to unlock the trunk and popped it. A duffel bag had been stuffed inside.

When he opened it, Josie leaned forward to examine the contents. Gym clothes, underwear, extra dress shoes.

Dane dug deeper. Several scalpels were wrapped inside, tucked in a side pocket.

Along with a butchered Mitzi doll identical to the ones left with the victims.

◆ ◆ ◆

Dane sped back toward Graveyard Falls, emotions churning. He'd considered having Grimley detained in a Knoxville jail, but decided it might be advantageous to have Grimley close to Easton in case he needed to use extra persuasion to coerce Grimley into a confession.

Josie fidgeted with her phone. Hopefully they had the killer or killers in custody, and no one else would die.

His cell phone buzzed, and he snatched it up. "Agent Hamrick."

"It's Peyton. Listen, Dane, I spoke with the counselor who worked with Silas Grimley as an adolescent. She said Grimley denied the abuse. When he was questioned about his father's disappearance, he clammed up. She even suspected that he might have killed his old man and buried him somewhere on their property."

Dane should have figured that out. "Have a team search the area for a grave or body."

"I'm on it," Peyton continued. "Grimley suffered from social anxiety and tended to become obsessive about friendships."

Dane swallowed hard. "Did he talk about my sister?"

"She didn't mention a name, but she confirmed that he had an unhealthy obsession with a girl who volunteered with the adolescents." She paused. "I'm sorry, Dane. You think that was your sister?"

"Yes." Dane ignored her sympathetic tone. Rage at Grimley had taken over. "I've wanted answers for a long time. Locking up this bastard will at least mean closure." Then maybe his mother would heal and return to the living.

Peyton's sigh punctuated the air. "There's one more thing. The text the reporter received came from a phone belonging to Grimley."

Now they were getting somewhere, racking up the evidence they needed to seal Grimley's coffin.

He thanked Peyton, then ended the call and filled Josie in.

"I'm so sorry, Dane," Josie said softly. "I understand this is personal to you."

His hands tightened around the steering wheel. Josie's sweet voice threatened to bring his emotions to the surface. He didn't have time for that. "Damn right it is. That sicko is going to pay." Bitterness welled inside him. His sister had wanted to help people, but her loving, giving heart had gotten her killed.

Josie rubbed her temple. "You think he may have told her how he felt, or she figured it out. Even if she tried to let him down easy, he was unstable and could have snapped."

Dane nodded, desperately trying to rid his mind of the images that bombarded him. Betsy's shock when she realized the boy she was trying to help was violent. The terror and betrayal she'd experienced when he'd turned on her and stabbed her.

Imagining her last minutes was so painful it could bring him to his knees. It had at one time. He'd bawled like a fucking baby.

No more.

"Dane?" Josie laid a gentle hand on his arm. "Are you all right?"

He shook his head, reigning in his emotions. "I will be, though. Once Grimley is locked away for life."

They reached the sheriff's office and jail, and he parked. Josie squeezed his arm again, but he was too torn up inside to do anything but force his legs out of the car.

She followed him, her presence giving him more comfort than he wanted to admit. For a moment when she'd asked if he was all right, he'd almost yanked her into his arms.

Hell, he wanted to bury himself inside her and let her sweet body help him forget everything. Her lips could give him relief. Her body could replace his aches with pleasure.

But he had to focus. Tie up the case.

Make sure Grimley never saw the light of day again.

As he entered, the officers were handing Grimley over to the sheriff.

"You can't do this," Dr. Grimley shrieked.

"Shut up." Dane jerked him by the collar of his starched shirt. "Sit down and be quiet while we process you."

The plastic surgeon gave Josie a pleading look as if he thought she would help him, but pain wrenched her eyes. Pain this man had caused.

Dane steeled himself. If he'd killed Betsy, he didn't deserve sympathy.

Sheriff Kimball had already patted him down, and Grimley's personal belongings lay on the desk. Dane rifled through his wallet. A few hundred dollars in cash.

Debit and credit cards. A one-way ticket to Mexico.

Then a folded photograph Grimley had tucked inside.

It was Betsy. Fucking son of a bitch had kept it all these years. Did he look at it at night and think about her? Did he sleep with it like some pervert?

He grabbed Grimley from the chair. "You killed my sister, you bastard."

Grimley's eyes widened in fear as Dane hauled him through the doors to the interrogation room.

CHAPTER TWENTY-SIX

Dane shoved Grimley against the wall. "You twisted freak. You killed Betsy."

The fury and anguish he'd lived with for so long boiled over. He wanted to snap the man's neck in two and hear the bones pop.

Grimley's legs buckled. "You're hurting me!" he cried.

Dane slid his hands around the man's throat and squeezed. "That's nothing compared to what you did to Betsy and those other women."

Grimley coughed for air and tried to pry Dane's hands from his neck. "I didn't kill them—"

"Dane, stop it, this isn't the way." Josie's soft plea barely registered above the noise of his hammering heart.

He cursed. He hadn't realized she'd come into the room.

Footsteps pounded, then Sheriff Kimball appeared beside him. "Let him go, Hamrick. We'll do this, but we're going to do it the right way."

Pain throbbed in Dane's chest. His fingers were frozen around the man's neck. He couldn't move them. "You don't understand, he killed my little sister."

A soft hand stroked his back. "I'm sorry, Dane," Josie said, "but you can't let him turn you into a killer. Betsy wouldn't have wanted that."

"You don't want this case to get thrown out because you were related to the victim and mishandled it," Sheriff Kimball said.

Dane's throat thickened, making it impossible to talk. His hands shook with the force it took not to completely crush the man's windpipe.

An image of Betsy at nineteen lying dead taunted him.

Then when she was twelve. Betsy with pigtails and knobby knees, grinning, poking her tongue out at him.

Betsy at eight playing dolls and dress-up.

Then at fourteen, Betsy playing soccer and raising money to help feed hungry kids.

Betsy in that coffin, her complexion milky white and unnatural, the light gone from her eyes, the smile replaced by tight lips the damn mortician had glued together.

The world spun, rage and grief blinding him.

"Come on, Dane," Josie said gently. "Let him go and you'll get justice for your sister."

The sheriff shot him a warning look while Grimley sputtered for help. Dane clenched his jaw, gave Grimley's neck one last squeeze to scare the bastard, then jerked his hands free.

Grimley flailed his arms to stay upright. Sheriff Kimball quickly ushered him into a chair. "Sit down and stay there," Kimball ordered.

Josie rubbed slow circles along Dane's back, a reminder that good did exist somewhere in the world. Yet she'd seen the violence just like he had and lived through it.

Dane stepped away from her touch, his unleashed fury like air trapped in a bottle about to explode. Hurt darkened Josie's eyes, but she didn't speak.

He couldn't talk either, couldn't explain all that was going on in his head. Everything was wrong. His mother's anguished face. Betsy's lost life. His fight to find her killer.

Had he finally achieved that goal? If so, what then? For ten years, finding her killer had consumed his life.

Grimley rubbed at his throat with long, thin fingers. Fingers that were adept at using a scalpel to carve women into beauty queens.

Yet he'd also shattered so many lives.

Grimley would not get out of jail, not ever.

The sheriff laid Grimley's briefcase on the table. Dane took the cue and regained his professional air. He'd get a confession out of this creep, then lock him up forever. One by one, he laid excerpts from the man's blog on the table. He stabbed a finger at the last story about the birds.

Grimley folded his arms and body as if he could collapse inside himself. Yet his eyes twitched back and forth, a sliver of pride in the depths. He recognized the entries. They were part of his story. His life.

"Here it is, you cocky bastard," Dane said. "You describe exactly what you did to those women. Now tell me about it yourself."

♦ ♦ ♦

Josie studied Grimley's body language, mentally profiling him.

Just as Billy Linder had been abused, so had Grimley. His abuse wasn't sexual, but physical and mental. Living with those horrific scars and being shunned by peers, especially women, was reflected in those stories. In his career choice.

Probably in every aspect of his life.

A myriad of emotions played across the plastic surgeon's face. Fear. Panic. Anger. Guilt.

Although his demeanor changed as he studied the last entry.

"Good God," the doctor muttered. "I didn't write that story."

Josie straightened, analyzing his tone. He sounded sincerely shocked.

"Don't bother to lie, Grimley," Dane said. "We read through all of your entries. This last one describes the way you carved the talons on the young women's cheeks."

He shook his head in denial. "Wait, you don't understand. I wrote the other blogs, but not this one. Don't you see? Someone's trying to frame me."

"I don't fucking believe you," Dane said. "You killed my sister and Easton's girlfriend, then you came to Graveyard Falls and murdered three other women just for fun." Dane jabbed his finger on the blog entry. "You collected bones from the animals you killed, and now you're collecting them from the women you murder."

Grimley gaped at him. "The killer took a piece of bone from the victim's faces?"

Josie twined her hands together, waiting for his response.

Dane slapped his hand on the table. "Yes. What did you do with them? Are you making a collage out of them like you do the animal bones?"

"I—this is not me. I didn't do this." Grimley looked ashen-faced and confused.

Josie mentally reviewed the facts to determine if they had the right man.

All the evidence pointed to Grimley as the Butcher.

A history of abuse. A horrific trauma during childhood.

He'd tried to turn his life around by giving back to those in need, but like an amputee suffering a missing limb, Grimley probably still felt those scars and reacted as if others saw them as well.

The patient mishap could have triggered his old insecurities. He was admired by the women he'd made beautiful, yet the lawsuit threatened to end his career—he was in danger of losing that admiration.

If Betsy had been his first kill, he'd probably reacted out of jealousy. Even if she'd rejected him gently, that rejection triggered the pain of the other times he'd been rejected by girls, and he'd exploded.

Although Josie had to consider Grimley's age. An adolescent would have had the strength and power to kill another teenager. And with his intelligence, he'd climbed the ranks of his profession awfully quickly.

Grimley pushed the journal entries away. "I want a lawyer."

Sheriff Kimball glanced at Dane. Dane cleared his throat. "All right, but, Grimley, if you cooperate and help us, we might arrange a deal to keep you off death row. If you lawyer up, that deal goes away."

The corner of Grimley's mouth twitched. His hands were still cuffed, the metal clanging as he fidgeted.

Dane didn't wait for a response. He slapped the photographs they'd found in Grimley's car on the table, spreading them out for the man to see the brutalized faces of the women he'd carved.

"Three victims, all who knew your buddy Easton, all who had cosmetic work done by you—all butchered by a surgeon's scalpel."

Grimley's pallor turned green, his hand trembling badly as he rubbed his forehead.

"Look at them," Dane ordered. "Those talon marks remind you of anything?"

One by one, the doctor traced a finger over the claw mark on the victims' cheeks. When he looked up at Dane, horror darkened his eyes. "I made these women pretty. Why would I destroy my own masterpieces?"

Dane hesitated, but a muscle ticked in his jaw, indicating he was barely controlling his rage. "Because you wanted more from them and they rejected you. Like my sister did."

A shadow fell across Grimley's face, and he looked down at the handcuffs again.

Dane slid his sister's picture in front of the man. Josie's lungs tightened.

Betsy was so young and beautiful, a softer, feminine version of Dane, a kid who'd had her future snuffed out by a vicious crime.

"You recognize her?" Dane asked coldly.

Grimley dropped his head into his hands and moaned.

The temptation to soothe Dane tugged at Josie, but she didn't dare interfere with the interrogation. Pressuring the suspect was part of the process.

"There's no use lying," Dane growled. "You met her at that group home, then she volunteered at that nature preserve and met Easton."

Grimley pressed the heels of his fists against his eyes as if he could obliterate the images. "I loved her," he said in a choked whisper. "Betsy was the first girl who was ever nice to me. She didn't care about my scars."

Josie clenched her hands together, wishing she could help Dane through this part. Grimley's expression bordered on childlike, his adoration for Betsy glittering in his eyes.

"You loved her, but you killed her anyway," Dane said with a condemning stare. "You took her life when all she did was to be kind to you."

"You don't understand what it was like," Grimley said brokenly. "I had nightmares about being locked in the cage with those birds. They tore my face and arms and hands apart. Then Betsy came along and . . . she didn't even notice them."

Dane stood, shoulders rigid as he paced the room.

Sheriff Kimball stepped in front of Grimley, and for once, Dane allowed him to take the lead. That was a big step for Dane, one Josie admired.

"Go on," Sheriff Kimball said. "What happened?"

"I . . . tried to make up for what happened," Grimley cried. "I got counseling and learned to control that rage."

Dane's boots clicked as he strode back to the table. Hands braced on the surface, he leaned forward, pinning Grimley with an intimidating stare. "What do you mean—you tried to make up for what happened? You can't *make up* for ending someone's life."

Grimley rocked himself back in the chair, one hand rubbing at his jaw as if feeling for the scars he'd once had.

"Tell me, dammit," Dane bellowed. "My mother is catatonic because of my sister's death. The grief and agony of knowing her killer was free while Betsy lay in the ground completely destroyed her."

Grimley startled, then squeezed his eyes shut for a brief second, his face strained.

Josie sensed Dane was hurting. She had to do something to help. She walked over to the table and slid into a seat across from Grimley.

The sheriff gave her a questioning look, but she gestured for him to let her try to reach the man.

"It's time to tell the truth," she said softly. "In your heart, Silas, you know that you'll feel better once you relieve yourself of this burden. I have a feeling you've wanted to do it for a long time."

"I have. I felt so bad, so guilty, I hated myself." His voice broke. "I never meant to hurt Betsy."

Dane started to speak, but Josie held up a warning hand. "Let him finish. He wants to tell you what happened." She patted the doctor's arm. "Don't you, Silas? You loved Betsy."

He nodded and pinched the bridge of his nose. "It's true, I loved her so much, but . . . in the end she didn't want me, and I just lost it and I . . . killed her."

◆ ◆ ◆

Nausea churned in Dane's stomach.

He reached out to choke Grimley, but Sheriff Kimball held him in place. "Let him talk, Hamrick. You don't want his confession to get thrown out of court."

The sheriff's words jolted Dane back to reality.

Hell no, he didn't.

He was face-to-face with his little sister's killer, the man who'd stolen her life and destroyed his and his mother's. He wanted the man to suffer the way he had.

The way his mother still was.

Tears leaked from Grimley's eyes. "I didn't mean—"

"You stabbed her," Dane said bluntly. "How can you not mean to do that?"

Grimley's glazed look suggested he'd slipped back in time. "I loved her," he said. "She was so nice and sweet, and pretty. Not model gorgeous but she was lovely inside and out."

"Yes, she was," Dane said in a low voice.

Grimley used both hands to claw at his face. "I was a fucked-up kid back then, and for the first time in my life, I thought I was lovable—she made me feel that way."

Tension vibrated in the air as Dane struggled not to slaughter the man.

"Go on," Sheriff Kimball said.

Grimley heaved a breath. "The last time I saw her, she told me she was going away to college, and I panicked. I couldn't lose her. She was everything to me. So I told her how I felt. I thought if I declared my love, she wouldn't leave, but she said I was too young for her, that I needed to date someone my own age like she intended to do."

Dane's chest ached from trying to control his rage. He'd been waiting years for this. Yet the man in front of him was pathetic, like a sick puppy.

"She met Eddie Easton at the nature preserve, too, and I thought she was going to hook up with him, so I followed her to that party," Grimley continued. "I saw her talking to Eddie. They were laughing and having fun. They didn't care that I was hurting inside."

Dane steeled himself. "So you confronted Eddie?"

"No, it turned out that Eddie was meeting his girlfriend, Sherry." Grimley rocked back in the chair, the wooden rungs creaking. "I got all excited then. I thought I had another chance. Then Betsy started flirting with other guys, and I couldn't stand it."

Dane gripped the chair edge to keep himself from bolting from the room. He didn't want to hear this. But he had to stick it out, had to hear for himself exactly what had happened.

"She went outside, and I followed her." Grimley's right hand trembled so badly he dropped it to the table and covered it with his other hand. "Instead of being happy to see me, she told me to go home, that we would never be anything but friends. Then she started to walk away, said we shouldn't see each other anymore, that she was cutting out her work at the nature preserve. I couldn't let her leave me, so I grabbed her arm to keep her from going." He gave Dane a childlike look as if he thought he'd understand.

Dane's body tensed with rage. Josie gave him an encouraging look, a reminder that she and he were on the same side.

"But Betsy got upset and I . . . lost it." Grimley's voice cracked on a sob. "It was as if I blacked out, like it was someone else in my body. I had that knife, and I was shaking her, and she told me I was crazy, and I . . . must have stabbed her." He held his hands in front of him as if they were foreign objects. "Blood was spurting everywhere, and she was crying, then she doubled over and went limp in my arms, and my hands were bloody."

Dane couldn't move, couldn't breathe. The scene Grimley painted played over and over in his mind like a bad horror show.

"I didn't know what to do then," Grimley continued. "Suddenly I realized what I'd done, and Betsy, my dear sweet Betsy, was looking up at me in shock, and she had this sadness in her eyes like she knew she was going to die. I . . . I couldn't save her."

A dark coldness settled over Dane as the man wailed like a baby. "You tried to save her?"

Grimley nodded, a wildness in his eyes. "I tried to stop the bleeding, but it happened so fast and her aorta was ruptured, and I couldn't."

Dane leaned closer, resuming his intimidation tactics. "You didn't call nine-one-one."

Grimley's eyes glazed over as if he was reliving that day. He rocked himself back and forth again to soothe himself. "No, and I . . . I hated what I'd done."

"You hated it, but instead of calling for help, you ran and left Betsy alone," Dane said. "You left her in an alley like she was nothing."

A self-deprecating sigh escaped the man. "I was scared. I knew the police would lock me up, and I'd been locked in that cage with the birds so many times that I couldn't stand to be trapped like that again."

Dane stared at him with all the rage and hatred he'd kept bottled since the police had knocked on the door and informed him that his sister was gone.

Grimley wiped at his eyes. "I'm so sorry, I hated myself, I really did. I decided I had to make up for what I'd done, that I'd turn my life around, and I'd never hurt anyone else again. That I'd spend my life as a doctor, taking care of other people, making them better."

Dane tapped each of the victim's photos—Charity, Patty, then Neesie. "Except you did hurt again," he said, not bothering to hide his disgust. "You killed Betsy, then decided you liked it and you killed Eddie's girlfriend and now these women."

Grimley shook himself as if he needed a jolt back to reality. "I did kill Betsy, and I hated myself for it, but I didn't kill those other women. I swear."

Dane gave him a hate-filled look. "I don't believe you."

"It's true. I told you I made a vow to help people." His voice rose a decibel as if he could convince Dane he'd redeemed himself. "That's why I became a doctor."

"You aren't saving lives. You do cosmetic surgery," Dane hissed.

"I am saving people," Grimley insisted. "You don't understand what it's like to be damaged, scarred. To be laughed at and pointed at and ostracized because you're ugly."

Dane scoffed. "So you're rationalizing murder by saying that your scars drove you to kill?"

"No . . . no," Grimley stammered. "I'm just saying that being scarred can be emotionally and mentally crippling. I give people a chance to be the best they can be."

"You're a sick pervert," Dane snapped. "You have this idea of the perfect woman, and you try to create her by performing surgery on women to make them look like that damn Mitzi doll."

Grimley gripped both sides of his head with his hands as he shook it in denial. "No . . . no . . . no."

Dane pressed on. "You whetted the taste for killing when you were a teenager. Your father was a cruel man, and you turned on him and killed him so you could escape."

Shock registered on Grimley's face. "What? No, you're wrong. I didn't kill my father. He ran out on me."

"That's what you wanted everyone to believe," Dane said. "I know that he was cruel, and he's the reason you were scarred. One night you couldn't take it anymore, and you murdered him."

CHAPTER TWENTY-SEVEN

Josie shifted, absorbing all the doctor had said.

Dane was furious, but a calm came over him. Not that that calm wasn't full of unleashed rage, but the seasoned agent had returned. His shoulders became more relaxed, the seething look in his eyes fading to resignation. He had Grimley now. He had succeeded.

No wonder he was so good at his job. The controlled man was just as menacing as the enraged one.

"I didn't kill my father," Dr. Grimley said. "I can't believe you'd suggest a thing."

"Why not? He was the root of all your problems, wasn't he?" Dane asked. "He abused you. Put you in that cage and treated you like you were an animal."

"He was only trying to make me strong. To help me learn to bond with the animals. As he did."

Disgust at Grimley's father made Josie's throat thicken. Grimley represented a classic case of abuse—he defended his abuser, even made excuses and blamed himself for the abuse.

Of course, most likely he was parroting what his father had told him.

"When you got rid of him, you could finally leave that place," Dane said. "You had a chance at a real life."

"I was put into a group home for misfits—that's not a real home," Dr. Grimley said bitterly.

"If you didn't kill your father, what happened to him?" Dane asked.

Dr. Grimley rubbed the back of his neck. "I don't know. I kept thinking he'd come back for me, but he never did."

Dane took pleasure in watching the man squirm. "What about Sherry, Eddie's girlfriend?"

Grimley studied his nails. His despair seemed to have dissipated quickly. "What about her?"

"Eddie Easton was your buddy. He had a girlfriend, and you were jealous," Dane said. "You thought he was going to cut you out of his life for Sherry, so you killed her?"

"No." Dr. Grimley dropped his hands to his lap. "Eddie loved Sherry like I loved Betsy."

"You loved Betsy so much you killed her," Dane said coldly. "So Eddie loved Sherry like that?"

"No, no, that's not what I meant," Grimley stammered.

"Eddie killed her. Then the two of you traded stories about killing Betsy and Sherry, and you bonded and became partners. Later, you decided you could murder again, maybe even take turns. It was the perfect plan. You provided alibis for each other to throw off the police."

Denial bled through the doctor's eyes. "That's crazy."

Dane showed him photos of the scalpels they'd found in his car. "You always carry a bag of scalpels with you?"

The man's face paled again.

"We also traced the message you sent to Corbin Michaels, the reporter who leaked the MO of the killer." Dane leaned into his face. "Only the killer would know those details."

The doctor gasped. "You traced it to my phone?"

"That's correct," Dane said.

"That's impossible. Check my phone and you'll see." He fumbled in his pocket, then seemed to realize the sheriff had confiscated his belongings.

Dane made a low sound of disgust. "Of course you wouldn't do it on the phone you carry. You're smart enough to buy another one or use a burner phone like you did when you sent pictures to Josie."

Grimley rocked the chair back again. "I didn't send any pictures to Miss DuKane. I didn't send a message to that reporter either."

Dane recited the phone number of the phone Peyton had traced.

Grimley stood, hands shaking, handcuffs clinking. "I lost that phone months ago."

"Lost it?" Dane asked, mocking him.

"Yes, just ask my secretary. I was frantic that day. Someone had been in my office while I was out. I don't know who, but things were moved around and that phone was missing."

Josie tried to read Grimley again. He'd admitted to killing Betsy, so if he had murdered Charity, Patty, and Neesie, why not take credit for those murders as well?

◆   ◆   ◆

Dane scoffed at Grimley. "Convenient excuse, you lost your phone."

"It's true," Grimley said. "I remember the exact day because I was running late. I had to catch a flight for Africa. I do volunteer work on children with birth defects."

Dane simply stared at him. If the bastard thought he was going to redeem himself for Betsy's murder by his Good Samaritan work, he was wrong.

Sheriff Kimball shoved a pad in front of Grimley. "Write down everything you told us about the night you killed Betsy Hamrick."

Grimley's hand trembled as he picked up the pen. He stared at the blank page for a moment, then tapped the pen on the pad and began to write.

◆ ◆ ◆

As they left the sheriff's office, Dane released a weary breath. "I have to go tell my mom."

"I'm sure she'll be relieved to have closure," Josie said, her heart breaking for him.

Dane shrugged, his jaw tightening as he drove her back to her house. "She hasn't responded to anything in months. The nurse says she believes Mom can hear me, but she's too lost to speak."

Josie squeezed his arm. "Maybe this news will shake her from her depression."

"I hope so, but I'm not counting on it. Putting Grimley away still won't bring my sister back."

"No, but at least you both know that her killer didn't escape. There is some peace in getting justice. Putting Billy away helped me."

Dane nodded, but the anguish in his expression lingered. She didn't push, though. It would take time.

He veered down her drive and killed the engine. His eyes darkened as he faced her. "I need to see my mother tonight. The nurse says sometimes she has nightmares and wakes up screaming Betsy's name."

"I understand about nightmares," Josie admitted.

Dane took her hand in his, then planted a soft kiss on her palm. "I know you do."

They sat in silence for a moment, her heart racing at the fierce hunger in his eyes. She wanted him to come inside. She wanted to hold him and soothe his pain and purge the tension vibrating between them.

Her heart tripped. If she wasn't careful, she'd find herself in love.

She didn't want to end up with a broken heart. Dane was completely devoted to his job. Except for an occasional one night in his bed, a woman had no place in his life.

Maybe one night would be worth it.

He didn't give her the chance to invite him inside.

He pulled his hand away, released a shaky breath, then squared his shoulders. In spite of his pain, Dane was still the strong one. The one who took care of everyone else.

But who took care of him?

She wanted to be that someone.

First he needed to talk to his mother. So she opened the car door.

He caught her hand and squeezed it again. "Call me if you need me."

She offered him a small smile. "I was going to tell you the same thing."

Their gazes locked, heat and emotions simmering between them.

She had to let him go.

She slid from the car, walked to her door, and waved good night.

♦ ♦ ♦

Dane clenched the steering wheel in a white-knuckled grip. He wanted to go inside with Josie, strip her clothes, and climb inside her warm body.

He'd seen a flicker of heat that indicated she wanted the same thing.

He remained rooted to the spot, though. How could he lose himself in sex when his mother sat in a catatonic state because she had no answers about her daughter's death?

The wind picked up to an ominous level, ripping twigs and limbs from trees and hurling them across the road. Tornado season had started out with a twister in Georgia, and the sky and freakish storms and temperatures indicated one might be headed their way.

By the time he arrived at the nursing facility, dark clouds had moved in, obliterating the stars and painting the sky black.

He parked in the lot by the nursing home, anxious to see his mother. For so long, he'd hung on to the fact that arresting Betsy's murderer would make a difference, that his mother would come out of her depression, that he didn't know what he'd do if she didn't.

Memories of her making chocolate chip pancakes for him and Betsy for breakfast teased his mind. His mother had loved to bake. While he was growing up, his house had always smelled like peach pie and cinnamon or chocolate. He could still see Betsy licking the brownie bowl.

He checked to make sure his weapon was secure and hidden beneath his jacket, then fought the wind as he braved his way to the front door. He was a grown man, but entering this place made his stomach churn like he was a kid heading to the doctor for a shot.

He signed in at the nurses' station, wincing at the sound of the medicine cart rattling by.

"We weren't expecting you today, Agent Hamrick," the nurse said.

"It's important I see Mother tonight. How is she?"

A sympathetic look tugged at her slim face. "About the same, I'm afraid. She had another nightmare this morning."

Maybe those could stop now.

"The good news is that she's made a friend."

"A friend?"

"Yes, a blind woman named Ellie who lives down the hall," the nurse said. "Your mother doesn't talk to her, but she seems comforted to have a visitor sit with her every day."

Dane breathed out. Maybe that was a good sign. His mother had always been social. That made it twice as hard to see her so withdrawn.

"I appreciate you telling me. I worry about her being so alone."

The nurse squeezed his hand. She was pretty, in a quiet kind of way, and a great nurse. She'd also expressed interest in him before.

She didn't stir his blood like Josie DuKane.

No one did.

The sound of a patient crying jerked Dane back to reality, and he thanked the nurse again, then strode down the hall.

As usual, he inhaled a deep breath before entering, bracing himself for the pale, fragile woman who'd once thrown baseballs with him and laughed when he'd chased lightning bugs.

She was sitting by the window in a wheelchair, her hair twisted into a neat bun, a shawl wrapped around her arms. Though she was only in her midfifties, she seemed much older. Her hair had grayed, something she never would have tolerated if she hadn't been so depressed.

He padded over to her and called her name, not wanting to alarm her. She didn't respond, but he pulled a chair up beside her.

Her hands were twined in her lap, and he picked them up and placed them between his own. Hers were cold, limp, her eyes vacant as she stared into space.

"Mother, I had to see you tonight," he said softly. "I finally did it. I caught Betsy's killer."

He waited a second, and when she didn't respond, he spoke again. "I promised you I would find him, and I did. He's in jail right now, and he's never going to get out."

A slight twitch of her fingers against his palm made his heart jump. Had she heard him?

"Did you hear what I said, Mother? Betsy can rest now. The man who took her life won't hurt anyone else."

Another twitch, then she blinked and her eyes focused slightly. A small smile tugged at her mouth. Or maybe it was a twitch as if she was trying to speak.

He held his breath, waiting.

But a second later, her eyes glazed over again.

Once again, she was gone.

◆ ◆ ◆

Silas paced the cell, his heart beating so fast he thought it would explode out of his chest. Maybe it would, and his blood would fly against the dirt-stained, graffiti-covered walls.

Down the hall, voices rumbled. He wasn't the only prisoner in the Graveyard Falls jail.

What kind of scumbag had they put in here with him? Didn't they realize he was a noted, respected doctor? That he had skills?

Those skills made you a suspect, he reminded himself.

It wasn't just the skills. It was those ugly claw marks on the young women's faces.

Time dragged him back into a vortex of bad memories, and he swayed, so dizzy he could barely stand.

He wrapped his trembling fingers around the bars of the cage. The birds were squawking, flapping their wings, and screeching their attack call.

He sank to the floor and covered his head with his hands to fend them off, but dozens of them flew at him, pecking his skin and tearing at his flesh. The metallic scent of blood hit him. It was dripping down his arms and face.

Pain seared his cheek, and he tried to scream and fight off the raptors, but they were vicious, and he must smell like carrion because they swarmed him, enjoying their feast.

Betsy's sweet face floated through the terror, then an image of her lying on the ground, blood oozing from that knife and her chest.

Images of the other girls followed, Charity, Patty, Neesie . . . they all looked the same. All like perfect Mitzi dolls, their pretty faces a disguise for the ugliness beneath.

Cold terror enveloped him, and he doubled over.

He'd called his attorney, but he hadn't answered, so he'd left a message.

God dammit, he had to call Josie DuKane.

She'd told the Bride Killer's story so everyone would understand.

Hopefully she'd do the same for him.

He licked his lips and tasted blood—he'd clawed at his face with his own nails until he'd drawn blood.

Betsy's blood had tasted so much sweeter, but his tasted like the monster that he was.

CHAPTER TWENTY-EIGHT

Josie jotted down notes on Silas Grimley the way she had done on Billy and Charlene Linder. There was a story here to tell, the truth about the Butcher murderer, but she still sensed something was missing.

She needed details of each victim to get to the heart of the story. Needed to know more about Charity, Patty, and Neesie. Their likes and dislikes, their family history, their dreams.

They were innocent victims and the ones the public would relate to and want justice for. Their future had been robbed by a man who, although abused himself, had inflicted unspeakable pain on each of them and their family and friends.

What had their thoughts been before they died?

A chill swept over her. She remembered her own—worrying about her mother and the grief she'd experience when Josie was gone. About the people she would miss. About the family she would never have.

Dane's face materialized, an image of the two of them together planting itself in her mind.

Only Dane didn't want her.

Shoving thoughts of him aside, she turned back to her notes. The plastic surgeon intrigued her. His experience with the birds of prey and his abusive father, his bone collections, and his rejection through the years had set him up for mental health issues. No wonder he chose plastic surgery. The stigma of being scarred in a world where magazines, TVs, and movies plastered photographs of perfect people that no normal individual could live up to had inspired him to help others.

All noble. Except for these murders.

Her phone jangled, and she checked it, hoping it was Dane. The sheriff's number appeared on the display.

She pressed Connect. "Hello."

"Josie," Sheriff Kimball said. "Is Agent Hamrick with you?"

"No. Did you try his phone?"

"Actually, I really wanted to speak with *you.*"

Josie frowned. "With me? Why?"

"Dr. Grimley's lawyer showed up, but Grimley is insisting on talking to you. He says that you'll listen to the truth, that Agent Hamrick won't."

"Dane's just so close to this," Josie said in defense of Dane.

"I know, and I understand the reason now. But Grimley responded to you. Maybe you can help."

Josie tapped her pen on her notepad. Dane wouldn't like it.

He was satisfied that he had the Butcher in custody. He'd suffered so much already.

Although if there was something Silas was holding back, and she could get that information, she had to try. "All right. I'll come over in the morning."

He thanked her and disconnected. Outside, a car engine rumbled and headlights gleamed through the front window.

She rose from the table and went to the door. Dane had parked and was walking up the drive, his head bent.

A strong gust of wind hurled leaves across the yard, tossing his hair in disarray, making him look wild and unkempt.

And so handsome that her lungs squeezed for air.

She opened the door, anxious to know what had happened with his mother, praying it went as he'd hoped.

When he looked up at her with anguish darkening his expression, she knew it hadn't.

◆ ◆ ◆

Dane cursed the circumstances. He'd thought solving his sister's case would bring his mother back to life, but he'd left her looking just as listless as before.

Josie gently touched his hand. "Dane?"

"I saw her." He barely managed the words past the lump in his throat. "I told her, but I don't know if she heard."

Josie's eyes flickered with compassion. "She heard. Give her time, Dane."

Time was supposed to heal, but he felt rawer tonight than ever.

Grimley's confession had opened up the wounds again, resurrected memories and images of his sister, images so painful it was as if he'd just received news of her death again.

He hadn't known what to do with himself. Where to go.

Except that he'd wanted to be with Josie.

Josie took his arm and coaxed him inside. "Do you want food? A drink? To talk?"

He shook his head. The only thing he wanted was to forget the pain for a little while.

"Dane?" She pressed her hand against his cheek. "Tell me what you need."

His gaze latched with hers, hunger spiraling through him, and he slid his arms around her waist. "I need you," he said gruffly. "I want you."

A soft smile curved her mouth.

"I know that's not fair," he finished. Would he be using her?

"Life isn't fair," Josie said. "What happened with me and Billy Linder wasn't fair. All the murders in this town, those young women dying—that wasn't fair." Her voice turned husky. "Losing your sister and your mother shutting down wasn't fair."

Emotions made his body tremble.

He didn't speak, though. He didn't have to. Josie understood.

Desire and heat flickered in her eyes as she led him to her bedroom. His breath rushed out as she cupped his face between her hands.

When she stood on tiptoe and pressed her lips against his, he felt humbled. Honored.

Starved for her touch.

She tasted like sweetness and sin and salvation all at the same time. He moaned low in his throat as he wrapped his arms around her and deepened the kiss.

Josie threaded her fingers in his hair, urging him closer, and he trailed his fingers along her shoulders and down her back, settling her into the vee of his thighs. His cock hardened, throbbed, ached for her touch.

He wanted to tear her clothes off, sink himself inside her, and lose himself in the pounding of their bodies together.

Instead he forced himself to go more slowly. To let his fingers linger around her waist, to drop kisses along her neck, and to tease the sensitive lobe of her ear. Her body moved against him, her hands clinging to his arms as if she might collapse if he didn't hold her up.

Her breathing grew rapid as he unbuttoned her blouse and parted the delicate fabric. White lace barely covered her generous breasts, taunting him with the promise of firm, ripe nipples beneath.

He groaned as she began to unbutton his shirt. Heat fired his blood, his passion growing with every touch of her fingers on his hot skin. She slid his shirt off his shoulders, and he did the same with hers, pausing to admire the golden skin of her cleavage and the flesh peeking beneath the sheer lace.

Excitement mounting, he lowered his head and trailed more kisses along her neck and throat, then lower to her cleavage. She moaned, soft and husky, and he walked her backward toward the bed until they stood against it.

Her chest rose and fell with her rapid breathing, and he teased her nipples through the lace. She kissed his jaw and clung to his arms as he eased her jeans down her legs, and she stepped out of them.

She looked so damn beautiful clad in sheer lace that his heart gave an odd pang and his cock throbbed to be inside that luscious body.

She shoved at his jeans, and he grabbed a condom from the pocket, then tossed his pants aside. A devilish twinkle sparked in her eyes, and she cupped his ass in her hands and ran kisses over his chest until he thought he would die from bliss.

Unable to resist any longer, he unfastened her bra and released a pleasured sigh as her breasts spilled into his hands. He rolled them in his palms, then dipped his head to tug one ripe nipple into his mouth. She moaned and whispered his name, then threw her head back in abandon.

The invitation was all he needed.

He trailed tongue licks down her belly to her heat, then stripped her panties, dropped to his knees, nudged her legs apart, and flicked his tongue along her sweet, damp center.

◆ ◆ ◆

Erotic sensations pummeled Josie as Dane swept his tongue along her sensitive folds. She dug her hands into his hair, trembling with pleasure as he brought her to the brink of an orgasm.

Sweet release teetered on the surface.

She whispered his name, aching to have him closer, but he plunged his tongue into her heat, and she groaned as the first waves of euphoria caught her and carried her through the ride.

Seconds later, he eased her back onto the bed. He stripped his boxers and crawled above her, then rolled on the condom and nudged her legs apart with his thick length.

Her body convulsed in mind-numbing pleasure again as he stroked her body with his shaft. She lifted her hips, meeting him thrust for thrust, then gripped his hips, desperate to have him deeper inside her.

He braced his hands on each side of her, his breath rushing out as he drove deeper and deeper, building a frantic rhythm that they rode together until another orgasm rippled through her.

His followed, the intensity in his groan lifting her heart with the fact that she'd given him pleasure in the midst of his pain.

He called her name, his head thrown back, his body slamming into her again and again, the passion as fierce and undeniable as the love soaring in her heart.

Love?

She tensed, mentally battling the emotion. He must have realized her hesitation because he paused and searched her eyes.

"Josie?"

The insecurity in his voice obliterated any reservations she had, and she licked her lips then smiled and drew his head down for another kiss.

He closed his mouth over hers, and she tasted her own desire mingled with his hunger, spiking her orgasm to a fever pitch that nearly brought tears to her eyes.

She'd thought Billy Linder had ruined her for wanting to be with a man, for trusting, for allowing herself to be vulnerable again.

To love.

Dane had given that back to her.

◆　◆　◆

Dane closed his eyes, battling emotions as he rolled sideways, slipped from the bed, and stepped into the bathroom. A desperate hunger and need had driven him to Josie's bed.

That need made him want to go back and never leave her.

How long had it been since he'd allowed himself to feel pleasure?

Josie called his name, and he stripped the condom and then crawled back in bed beside her and pulled her into his arms. His chest heaved for a breath, and his heart pounded with the aftermath of sensations still shooting through him.

He had never made love to any woman who made him feel like Josie did.

He wanted to do it all over again.

That thought scared the shit out of him, but he forced his fear aside. He and Josie had both needed the release.

It was more than that, and you know it.

He squashed that voice. Sex was all it could ever be. His life was his job, and that job was too damn dangerous to chance being with a woman long term.

Besides, loving someone and losing them hurt too damn much.

Josie rubbed slow circles over his chest with one finger, a gentle gesture that aroused him and made his heart tug painfully at the same time.

He stilled her fingers with one hand. "Josie?"

"Yes," she said softly.

"Thanks for tonight."

A tense second passed. "You don't have to thank me." She lifted her hand and placed it against his cheek, forcing him to look at her. "I wanted you, Dane. I still do."

Her honey-like voice did something to him, and he kissed her again, hunger consuming him.

She rolled him to his back and climbed on top of him, and he teased her nipples to stiff peaks with his fingers. She groaned, threw her head back, and moaned as he tugged one into his mouth.

She looked so damn beautiful, he wished he could freeze the moment. He mentally snapped a picture, storing it away to remember when he was alone at night.

She cupped his cock in her hand, stroking him from base to tip, making his cock throb. He shifted, undulating his hips, and tried to pull her back on top of him. He wanted inside her. Now.

She had none of it. Instead, her head moved south, and she flicked her tongue across the tip of his penis, swirling her tongue over his engorged length until he thought he would explode in her mouth.

Needing to feel her body quivering around him, he finally dragged her back on top of him, cupped her hips in his palms, and guided her to his sex. She lifted her body and impaled him, then moved on top of him. He gripped her hips, pumping his cock inside her until he lost control and the two of them were overcome with sensations. Need and passion reached a crescendo, and they climaxed in each other's arms again.

Both breathing heavily, she collapsed on top of him.

Grimley was in jail. Josie was safe tonight, and so were the residents of Graveyard Falls.

They fell asleep, both sated and exhausted.

◆ ◆ ◆

Ellie sat beside her new friend Paula Hamrick, her heart fluttering as Paula squeezed her hand. It was the most movement she'd felt out of the woman since they'd met.

Something had changed today. Paula had learned the truth, that Silas had killed her lovely daughter.

Ellie wanted to tell her that she was sorry, that she should have stopped Silas, but he'd been just a boy, and she hadn't understood her visions, that she'd had a premonition of what he'd do.

By the time she had, it was too late.

Although when she'd seen Silas cleaning the carcass of the birds he'd killed, washing and bleaching the bones then making collages out of them, she'd known he wasn't normal.

Lord have mercy on them both. She didn't want to believe he was evil.

No matter how awkward and strange he'd been, she'd been drawn to him because he had no mother.

She might be touched in the head, but the devil had possessed his daddy and given him a mean streak. He'd connected more with those godforsaken birds than he had with his own flesh-and-blood son.

Truth be known, she'd felt sorry for Silas.

She'd been naïve.

She'd thought being kind to him, loving him, showing him patience and understanding would help fix the broken boy, but her love hadn't been enough.

"I heard what your son told you," she said to Paula. "I know he arrested the man who killed your daughter. I'm so sorry for how you've suffered."

A small sound erupted from the woman's throat as if she was trying to speak, but then quiet fell. The woman's pain suffused Ellie as if it was her own.

Some other emotion bled through the pain. A peacefulness washing over Paula.

Ellie squeezed Paula's cold hand in hers, needing the human touch as much as she sensed her friend did.

Although Paula wouldn't be friends with her if she knew the truth.

She might hate her.

A dozen gruesome images flooded Ellie, flashing behind her eyes. The sharp blade of the scalpel twisting and digging into the women's faces. The hand holding that scalpel carving the sharp lines of the talon.

Only Silas wasn't holding that scalpel.

He wasn't killing those three young women in Graveyard Falls.

There was someone else.

She couldn't see the person's face, but evil had stolen his soul just like it had Silas's daddy.

CHAPTER TWENTY-NINE

Dane woke with a jolt.

His arm was asleep.

He shifted, then realized Josie was lying curled against him, her long hair draped across his chest, her breath feathering his neck.

Pleasure shot through him as he remembered the night before. He'd awakened twice, and they'd made love again both times.

It wasn't enough.

He wanted her this morning. Today. Tonight. Maybe always.

Wind whistled through the eaves of the house, banging the roof and hurling twigs against the windowpanes.

The wood floor felt cold against his bare feet as he forced himself from bed.

He needed the cold to tamp down his morning erection. Because he had to put a stop to this insanity of bedding Josie. If he didn't, he'd never be able to leave her.

He had to leave her. Didn't he?

His cell phone buzzed, and he checked the text. The sheriff.

Michael's story about the arrest hit the morning news. Press conference this morning at eight.

Dane responded that he'd meet Kimball at the press conference.

Where had that reporter gotten his information?

He brewed a pot of coffee and showered, hoping to scoot out before Josie woke. When he emerged from the shower, she was sitting up in bed, arms folded, holding a cup of coffee. She gestured that she'd poured him one.

Damn, he could get used to this.

Josie half-naked, sleep tousled, and sexy in the morning after he'd loved her all night, coffee in bed.

He couldn't get used to it.

He had a case to tie up.

Using every ounce of restraint he possessed, he picked up the mug and took a sip, the awkward silence steeped in unspoken memories of their intimate night.

"Leaving?" Josie asked in a husky whisper.

He steeled himself against caring. "I'm meeting the sheriff for a press conference. Apparently that reporter found out we made an arrest and already printed the story."

Josie threaded fingers in her hair and swept it back from her face. "How did he find out?"

"I have no idea, but I intend to ask him." He didn't like the possibility that someone was leaking information. Or that the killer had contacted Michaels. If Michaels had held back information that could have helped them save the girls, he deserved to be punished.

Josie threw her legs over the side of the bed. Beautiful, sensual legs that she'd wrapped around him while he'd driven himself inside her.

God. He wanted to do it again right now.

"Dane, last night before you got here, Sheriff Kimball called. Dr. Grimley wants to talk to me."

He strapped his gun inside his jacket, stalling to control his anger over the man's audacity. "Just like we thought. He wants you to make him famous."

Josie grabbed her robe. "I'm not sure about that, but I have to see what he says."

He narrowed his eyes. "Then I'll sit in on it."

She shook her head. "He asked to speak to me. Alone."

A scowl darkened Dane's face. What was the man up to? "He's dangerous, Josie."

"He's in custody, Dane. Besides, maybe I can get him to open up more. I'll record our conversation."

Dane checked his watch. "All right, but one of the deputies needs to stand guard. I don't want you in the room with him by yourself."

Grimley was a sick, cold-blooded killer who'd taken his sister's life. If he touched Josie, Dane would kill the bastard.

♦ ♦ ♦

A half hour later, Josie drove to the police station. A deputy met her and explained that Dane had phoned with orders.

Not only was Grimley in a cell, but Eddie Easton was still in custody as well.

Hopefully forensics would discover something concrete to help solidify the case. Dane had also contacted LA police and asked them to search both men's homes.

Josie squelched the spark of sympathy threatening when the deputy led the plastic surgeon into the interrogation room. His hair was sticking out in all directions, his eyes were red rimmed and swollen, and he'd clawed at his face until he'd drawn blood.

She schooled her reaction. She refused to allow him to manipulate her, not when he'd torn Dane's family apart.

"You said you wanted to talk to me," Josie said, maintaining a neutral voice.

The confident plastic surgeon with the gleaming white teeth and perfect smile had vanished.

In his place sat the insecure, traumatized, abused adolescent who'd been starved for love to the point of transferring his affections to the one person who'd been kind to him—Betsy Hamrick.

Josie removed a recorder from her purse and set it on the table. "You want me to tell your story, then talk to me," Josie said. "I plan to record our session. I assume that's all right with you."

"Fine." He raised his bleary eyes toward her. Dried blood dotted his face and fingernails. "I know you and Agent Hamrick think I'm a monster, but I'm not this maniac they call the Butcher."

Josie simply stared at him, refusing to react, even though revulsion at the images of the victims gripped her. He had carved bones from animals he killed. He had stabbed Betsy Hamrick. He had written those gruesome stories. "You killed Betsy Hamrick?"

He gave a nod. "I didn't mean to. I loved her—"

Remorse tinged his admission. Betsy was still dead, though. "So you said. You still took her life."

"I know." He dropped his head forward on a groan and rubbed his eyes. "If I could go back and change one thing in my life, it would be that. I'd jab that knife in my own chest before I'd hurt her again."

Silence stretched between them, the doctor's regret palpable.

"You did kill her," Josie said. "Because you had pent-up rage inside you from your own childhood."

He kept biting his lip as if he'd developed a tic. Probably one he'd had when he was younger, his reaction to stress. "That's what my therapist said."

"So you confided in your therapist?"

"Yes." Grimley's voice sounded weak, defeated. "She's the one who suggested helping others would enable me to forgive myself."

"*Did* you?"

"Forgive myself?" He made a sarcastic sound. "No. How could I when I killed the only girl I ever loved? I've thought about Betsy every single day since. I wish I'd died that day instead of her." He picked at the dried blood on his face, opening up the wound, a definite tremble in his hand. "If I could trade places with her now, I would."

Josie breathed out deeply. "What about Eddie Easton's girlfriend?"

"I was jealous of her," he admitted in a self-deprecating voice. "I looked up to Eddie. I flipped out because she told him that she didn't want me around. That I was strange. Spooky."

Josie tried to picture where he was going with this. Had he decided to confess to Sherry's murder? "Did Eddie defend you?"

"No, Eddie just laughed. He told her I was harmless. A freak, but harmless." His last word sounded bitter as if he resented Eddie's description of him.

"That must have made you angry."

"Yeah, it did. He made me sound like a psycho." He studied his hands. They were scarred. And trembling. When he looked back up at her, his eyes were clear, though. "I didn't kill Sherry. I saw her leave with another guy. Eddie was pissed, but he didn't go after her. He got drunk and hooked up with another girl."

"So who killed her?"

"I honestly don't know," Grimley said. "Rumor was that she'd messed around with some junkie and that he killed her."

"Did the police pursue that lead?"

He nodded. "Yes, once they stopped considering Eddie as their only suspect. They found the junkie dead behind Sherry's dorm. He had Sherry's wallet on him, so they thought he killed her for money."

Josie stewed over what he said. That scenario sounded plausible. "Tell me about you and Eddie."

His brows drew together. "What do you mean?"

Josie decided to run with Dane's theory. While Grimley was opening up, hopefully he'd tell her everything. "He meets the women through his business and refers them to you. Then you perform the cosmetic work and give him a kickback."

Dr. Grimley shrugged. "That's only fair."

"His photography studio is a great way to solicit new clients," Josie said. "It also could be the perfect way to take advantage of young women."

"That's not the way it is," Grimley said. "I help people be the best person they can be. Most of the women who come to me have self-image problems. Cosmetic work gives them confidence and changes their futures."

Josie bit back a comment about vanity. Someone born with a deformity or scarred from an accident definitely deserved cosmetic work. She had to steer him back to the facts. "We found a Mitzi doll in Easton's closet. Judging from the photographs on your website, you fashioned women to look like her."

"Not to look like *her*, to look their best," Dr. Grimley said. "That doll is just a personification of the fact that women strive for physical beauty and perfection."

"You repair those flaws so they won't be imperfect anymore?"

"We've already discussed this," Dr. Grimley said. "How can you think I could desecrate a woman's face like this Butcher?"

"You and Eddie were the last people to see these women alive," Josie said. "Just look what you did to your own face."

He frowned as if he had no idea what she was talking about. She gestured toward his nails and pulled out her compact, then handed it to him.

When he saw his reflection, he gasped. His hand shook harder as he wiped away the blood. "God . . . I did that?"

"Yes, you did," Josie said, contemplating his mood changes. He pinged back and forth between the injured, insecure boy and the self-confident surgeon.

He shoved the mirror toward her. "Take that thing away."

"You don't like mirrors, do you?"

"No. At least, I didn't when I was young. I don't mind them now." He looked down at his bloody finger.

"Is that why you left a broken mirror with each victim?"

Surprise flickered in the doctor's eyes. "The killer left a mirror with the victims?"

Josie nodded, playing along with his denial. "A broken one. As if he wanted us to know that underneath the women were too ugly to look at."

Brows furrowed, Dr. Grimley stood and began to pace, chewing his lip more frantically with each step. The deputy gave him a warning look and pointed to the seat.

Grimley cursed but sat down, his movements agitated.

"Listen, Miss DuKane, Agent Hamrick is too blinded by the fact that I killed his sister to really look for the truth about the Butcher."

Dane was emotional, but he had a right to be. "He's an excellent agent, and he has evidence that points directly to you."

"I don't give a damn what he has. It's not true. Someone is framing me. I think I know who."

◆ ◆ ◆

Dane braced himself to deal with the press again. As much as he despised them, the residents of Graveyard Falls had a right to know they could rest easy in their beds tonight.

A small group of press members, the mayor, half the residents of Graveyard Falls, and the film crew had gathered for the press conference.

Michaels's story had hit the morning news, and everyone in town wanted confirmation that the Butcher was in custody.

Unfortunately, some were starved for the grisly details.

"Yes, we have made an arrest," Dane said.

Whispers echoed through the crowd, and several people raised hands to get his attention.

"We'll address questions in a minute," Dane said. "First, I'm sure you're anxious to know who we have in custody. We arrested a man named Dr. Silas Grimley. He's a plastic surgeon who received referrals from the photographer Eddie Easton. At this point, no charges have been placed against Easton, but we have detained him for questioning."

Although that twenty-four hours would be up soon, and if he didn't make a case against Easton, he'd have to release him.

"I'm not at liberty to disclose key pieces of evidence we have against the doctor for his alleged crimes, but suffice to say, it was adequate for a warrant, and we are putting together a case now. Dr. Grimley also confessed to a prior murder, which we believe is linked to his history of violence."

"Did he admit he killed Charity?" Bailey Snow asked.

Dane met the young woman's gaze through the crowd, his pulse hammering. He wanted to respond yes, but he couldn't lie. "At this point, no. I promise you that as soon as more information is available, we will inform the public."

Corbin Michaels eased his way to the front of the group. "Why would a plastic surgeon deface women when he spends his life enhancing their looks?"

Dane slanted the reporter an irritated look. He'd agreed to give him an exclusive, but Michaels had violated his trust when he'd printed the story this morning.

"We're still working on establishing motive," Dane said.

Michaels pressed on. "If Dr. Grimley is the Butcher, what triggered his desire to kill now?"

Betsy's sweet face materialized, making Dane's gut churn. "A psych evaluation will reveal more about him and provide insight into his mental state."

Hands shot up with more questions, the crowd murmuring amongst themselves.

Dane gestured for the sheriff to take over, and he jogged down the steps of the stage and headed straight toward Michaels.

When he reached the reporter, he motioned for him to step aside. "Where the hell did you get your information about the arrest?"

Michaels gave him a cocky look. "I can't reveal my source."

Michaels had previously received a text from the killer. Grimley was in custody last night, and his phone had been confiscated—he hadn't divulged anything to Michaels.

Dane jerked him by the collar of his white shirt. "Tell me the damn truth."

Michaels lifted his chin. "I received an anonymous text. Just two words—*Butcher arrested.*"

"Listen to me, Michaels, if you've been holding back pertinent information that could have helped us solve this case and save the victims and I find out, you're going down."

Michaels reared his head back in defense. "If I'd known who the killer was, I would have come forward."

Dane locked stubborn stares with the man, still unsure if he could trust him. The first text Michaels received had come from Grimley's phone. He'd have tech trace this one. One of the deputies could have given Michaels the tip.

His phone buzzed.

Josie.

Hoping Grimley had confessed to all the murders, he strode toward the parking lot as he called her.

◆ ◆ ◆

He smiled from the edge of the crowd. That agent was convinced that Silas Grimley and Eddie Easton were responsible for the butchered girls.

Good.

Except now the killing would have to stop.

That would be hard to do.

There were so many other women out there who needed to be punished. To be exposed for the ugliness beneath. For looking at him as if he didn't belong.

Jail was not an option. Neither was getting caught.

Besides, watching the plastic surgeon and the photographer rot in prison gave him great joy.

Not as much as watching the girls scream and seeing their blood spurt, but it would do.

At least for now.

Once the dust settled, he could find a new hunting ground.

CHAPTER THIRTY

Josie dreaded this conversation with Dane, but she had to be honest. Another woman's life might depend on it. "I understand you need closure for your sister's death, and Grimley admits to her murder. It definitely was a crime of passion. He reacted out of anger. But these other murders, they were planned."

"He evolved," Dane said tightly. "He whetted his appetite for blood with Betsy."

"He doesn't behave like an attention-seeking killer. He actually seems to have remorse for stabbing your sister."

"Remorse doesn't bring my sister back," Dane said, bitterness sharpening his tone.

Josie tensed. She understood his anger and wanted to help. "He's going to prison for the rest of his life for your sister's murder, so why not confess to the others?"

"Listen, Josie. We have the right man. Grimley is a sick bastard who killed Betsy and those other women, so don't stir up some kind of excuse to get him off."

A tense heartbeat passed before she responded. Could Dane's emotions be clouding his judgment?

"That's not what I'm doing," Josie said, biting back a retort. "I want the truth, Dane, and I'm not sure we have it."

"What? Grimley isn't enough of a story for you?" His sigh of disgust echoed over the line.

Josie winced and started to explain, but he cut her off.

"We have his scalpels, the same type that he used to carve the victims' faces. He also had pictures of the victims and modeled his surgeries by that damn Mitzi doll." He paused for a breath, then continued. "You read that blog. Those stories describe exactly what he did."

"That's just it," Josie said, desperate to get through to him. "He told me he didn't write those last two entries, and I think he's telling the truth. They were different, the language, the flow, the syntax—"

"Stop it," Dane said. "You are not going to mess up this arrest, Josie. I've been waiting years for justice, and I won't let anyone interfere. Especially you."

Hurt swelled in Josie's chest. Last night she'd thought they were close. She trusted him and thought he trusted her.

That he might even have feelings for her.

"I understand you're upset," she said, pushing her hurt aside, "and you want to blame everything on him, but he told me about this lawsuit against him, about this patient he accidentally scarred. He said she hates him, that she might be behind this."

"Of course he's going to offer up another suspect," Dane said, "he wants to get off."

"But—"

He cut her off again. "Think about it, Josie. Why did he ask to speak to you instead of me or the sheriff? He knows you're soft, that you're emotional." His voice turned harsh, cutting her to the bone. "He thinks he can charm his way into your good graces so you'll believe him just like you believed Billy Linder was an okay guy."

The breath whooshed from Josie's lungs. His comment played to every insecurity she'd ever had.

That she was a fool, that it was her fault that she'd been abducted, that she had poor judgment when it came to men.

That maybe she wasn't smart enough to do her job . . .

"Go to hell, Dane. You do your job. I'm going to see if there's any truth to his statement." Josie didn't wait for a response. She disconnected the call.

His words taunted her, though, resurrecting her doubts. She dropped her head into her hands for a minute, grappling for control.

What a fool she'd been to believe that Dane might care for her. Last night had been about sex on his part. Yes, she'd fantasized about more, that it meant something to him.

She couldn't—wouldn't—make that mistake again.

She would accept that Dane didn't love her and pursue what Dr. Grimley had told her.

The truth was more important than her pride.

If someone had framed Grimley, the women in Graveyard Falls were still in danger, and she was obligated to uncover the truth. If she didn't figure out the killer's identity, another woman might be carved up just like the others.

She couldn't live with that.

Dane pinched the bridge of his nose as he settled into his vehicle. He needed to question Easton again.

He'd push Grimley until he confessed to the other murders.

Josie's voice taunted him, though. She believed Grimley had been framed.

But the bastard had confessed to murdering Betsy.

Damn Josie for making him doubt himself. He was good at his job. She was emotional.

So are you, especially about your sister.

He dropped his hand to his lap. Good God.

Was he right? Had the man charmed her into trusting him?

Or had he lost his objectivity? Was there some truth to Grimley's statement?

The fact that the doctor was being sued didn't sit well. That patient might be bitter enough to frame him.

Fuck.

He didn't *want* there to be anyone else involved. He wanted to wrap up this damn case, charge Grimley for all the murders, find out if Easton was involved, and leave town before he fell too hard for Josie.

You already have.

No, he couldn't be in love with her. Caring about someone was too dangerous. He'd already lost too many people he loved to open himself up to that kind of pain again.

His phone buzzed.

Loving Arms.

Seeing the number for the nursing care facility where his mother was staying on the display box, he quickly connected the call. "Agent Hamrick." He held his breath, praying his mother hadn't taken a turn for the worse.

"Agent Hamrick, you don't know me, but my name is Ellie. I'm a friend of Paula's."

Dane tensed, trying to place her. Was she another nurse? "What's happened? Is she all right?"

"Yes, I'm sorry. I didn't mean to alarm you. She and I had a nice visit this morning."

"What?" Maybe she was a volunteer. "Who are you again?"

"My name is Ellie. I'm in the room down the hall from your mom. Paula and I struck up a friendship the last few days."

The truth dawned. "Yes, the nurse told me about you."

"Good. I need to see you right away. It's important. It's about your sister's death and the Butcher case."

Dane's pulse jumped. How did this woman know about that? From the news? "Excuse me?"

"Just stop by Loving Arms please."

"I'll be there as soon as possible." Dane hung up, then spun the vehicle toward the nursing home, curious to see if this woman had information about the case. A thread of fear wormed its way through him, though. What if Josie was right and Grimley wasn't guilty of all the murders and the killer came after his mother?

Suspicions ate at him. He knew nothing about this stranger who'd suddenly come into his mother's life.

A few minutes later, he parked and hurried inside. The attendant at the front nurses' station directed him to Ellie's room. As he walked down the hallway, the scent of cleaning chemicals and medicine filled the air.

Precious met him in the hall. "Hi, Agent Hamrick."

"How's my mother?"

"Actually, her therapist is strolling her outside. She seems more relaxed since your last visit. Almost as if she's slowly coming back to us."

Hope budded in Dane's chest. Maybe his mother was turning a corner for the good.

"Precious, tell me about this lady, Ellie, who made friends with my mother."

Precious smiled. "Miss Ellie is a little odd, but she's a sweetheart. I think she's really helping Paula."

Dane relaxed slightly. He thanked her and headed to Ellie's room. It was two doors from his mother's. He knocked and a voice called for him to come in. The room was darker than his mother's, but otherwise held the same type of hospital bed, two chairs near the window, a small TV.

A frail-looking gray-haired lady sat in one of the chairs, her face in the shadows as she stared out the window. She turned slightly as he entered. "Agent Hamrick."

"Yes."

She patted the chair beside her. "Come in. We have to talk."

As he walked over to her, he scrutinized the way her delicate hands worked, clicking knitting needles together as she spun what looked like a baby blanket from yarn. He didn't know what he'd expected, maybe for her to have pictures of the dead girls, but he was surprised.

When he sat down and she faced him, her eyes were glazed.

She was blind.

How in the world had she befriended his mother when she couldn't see and his mother didn't speak?

He trusted Precious's opinion enough to hear her out, so he claimed the chair and then cleared his throat. "You said you have information for me?"

"Yes." Tension thickened the air as she paused in her knitting. "I heard you arrested Silas Grimley for your sister's murder."

Dane curled his fingers around the arm of the chair. "Yes."

"I knew Silas when he was young," Ellie said, surprising him. "I was the housemother in the group home where he lived after he was removed from his father's care."

Dane let the silence stand. He didn't want to hear some sob story about the young boy Silas.

Silas had stolen too much from his family and him.

Besides, there were a lot of people who suffered trauma in their lives who didn't use their past as an excuse for violence against others. Josie was the perfect example. She used her ordeal to help others.

Regret for the way he'd talked to Josie engulfed him, but Ellie laid a frail hand over his, and he focused on her. "Agent Hamrick, I understand the hate in your heart, but please hear me out. Silas was a troubled kid, abused and scarred so badly that he lived in his own world of hurt and shame."

"If you want me to feel sorry for him or go easy on him, this visit is over." He started to stand, but she gripped his hand with gnarled fingers.

"Please don't leave yet. I understand your anger and your mother's."

Again, Dane waited.

"I'm so sorry for what happened, for Silas and what he did to your sister. I never forgave myself for that."

Shock bolted through Dane. Anger followed. "You knew he killed her and covered for him?"

She hesitated. "I didn't know, not at first. Later, I had visions and saw him. He was out of his mind when it happened."

She must be a nutcase. "What do you mean, you had visions?"

"This probably sounds crazy to you, but after I lost my sight, my other senses became stronger. Sometimes I have premonitions or see things, things that are happening. Just the way I saw into your mother's mind and realized she needed a friend. Someone to share her pain with. That's when I started visiting her."

"If you knew Grimley murdered Betsy, why didn't you come forward?"

Ellie wiped at a tear with her arthritic hand. "Because I loved Silas. He was torn up about what he did. He needed guidance, and if I'd turned him in, he'd have gone to prison, and he'd never have amounted to anything."

"Do you realize that by allowing a killer to go free, you endangered other women's lives?" Dane asked in an incredulous voice. "My sister had a future and was a good person. She wanted to help people. For God's sake, she tried to help *him*."

She pressed a hand over her chest. "Maybe I should have told, but I thought Silas needed a chance. He'd already suffered so much." She reached for his hand again, but he pulled back.

"My sister suffered," Dane said through clenched teeth. "My mother suffered and still is."

"I know. I feel her pain. I wish I could change the past, but it's too late. I have been a friend to your mother, though, and I'm helping her work through her grief."

"She wouldn't have suffered if you'd done the right thing and turned Grimley in when you first suspected he was dangerous." Dane curled his hands into fists. How dare this lady pretend to be his mother's friend when she should have come forward years ago. Now three more women's deaths were on her head.

"I know what you're thinking, that those other women wouldn't have died if I'd turned Silas in," she said, as if she'd read his mind. "That's the reason I have to do the right thing now."

"The right thing?"

"Yes, please hear me out. Silas is not a serial killer," Ellie said, her voice growing stronger. "He didn't murder those women in Graveyard Falls."

Dane barely controlled his animosity. "Yes, he did. He started with my sister. No, his first kill was actually his father."

The woman set her knitting aside. "He didn't kill his father."

"How do you know?"

She angled her head, and even though she was blind, Dane sensed she could see him, that she was watching his reaction. "Because I did."

Dane simply stared at her. She was slight in size, five-two, at the most a hundred and ten pounds. "You killed him? How did you overpower him?"

"I had a shotgun," she said as if relaying a story she'd heard somewhere else, one that didn't involve her. "When I realized Silas's daddy was abusing him, I tried to convince him to relinquish custody of Silas to me and get help for himself. He refused. After a while, the court decided to put Silas back in that home to be tormented all over again. I couldn't stand the thought of that kid being hurt anymore."

"You didn't want to go to jail yourself," Dane said, his voice accusatory. "That's the reason you didn't tell the police about Silas."

"That's partially true, but not for the reason you think. I wasn't afraid of prison. It's just that I couldn't have helped Silas if I was locked away, and he needed me." She rubbed at the knots on her left hand. "Besides, that vile man who spawned him didn't deserve to live."

"I have no doubt about that," Dane said. "By protecting Silas, you let him get away with murder. Once he'd killed one woman, his appetite was whetted."

"You're wrong. He changed after Betsy died." Her voice grew sad. "He was overcome with grief and self-hatred. And he felt so guilty that he tried to make amends. He went to medical school to help others, and with his intelligence, he sailed through. He even volunteered with Doctors Without Borders."

Dane didn't want to hear another word about Grimley's childhood. "Miss Ellie, I understand if you're loyal to Grimley, but we have evidence that points to him as the Butcher. We found scalpels in his possession, as well as photographs of all the victims."

She pushed to her feet and reached for his arms, her fingers digging into his skin as if she was determined to convince him she spoke the truth. "He didn't kill them, I tell you," Ellie said earnestly. "I saw those murders, and his hand wasn't holding the scalpel."

"You saw the murders? How is that possible?"

She breathed out deeply. "I told you, I have visions."

"For God's sake." Dane pried her hands from his arms.

"You don't have to believe me, but if I'm right," she said, "the Butcher is still out there. Do you want that on your conscience?"

Dane took a step back, struggling with the idea that he might actually be wrong. That this crazy lady might know something. Grimley had confessed to Betsy's murder. "My conscience is just fine."

"But it won't be if I'm right," Ellie said. "I know because I was in denial about Silas for years, and I've had to pay for my denial. Don't make that mistake, Agent Hamrick."

That statement got to Dane, triggered his doubts.

The woman continued. "You already blame yourself for your sister's death. You think that your mother blames you, but she doesn't. She loves you."

Dane's chest hurt with the effort to breathe. He did think his mother blamed him.

He blamed himself.

"She wants you to know that she forgave you, that she's still inside that shell and that she's coming back to you." She patted his shoulder in a motherly gesture. "It's time you forgive yourself. Your mother and sister want that."

Dane backed toward the door. What kind of charlatan was this woman?

"You can think what you want of me, but you have to keep looking." Ellie's voice rang with sincerity and confidence. "Silas is not the Butcher. The hand I saw was smaller, more delicate, almost feminine."

Dane had had enough. "You're suggesting the Butcher is a woman?"

"Yes."

That was impossible. The profile fit Grimley. The evidence pointed to him. The killer would have needed physical strength to carry the victim to the dump site.

Josie's comments about Grimley echoed in his head. Josie hadn't had premonitions. She had doubts based on her study of criminology.

If he was wrong, the killer was still out there.

He couldn't live with himself if the Butcher took another victim.

Josie's thoughts vacillated back and forth. One minute she believed Silas Grimley, the next she faltered. Damn Billy Linder for making her doubt her own judgment.

Damn Dane for doing the same thing.

If Grimley wasn't the Butcher, then more women might die.

Compelled to find the truth, she parked, but before she went in, she reread Grimley's blogs, analyzing the tone, the language, the syntax, even the slant of the story lines.

The first few entries consisted of stories about a little child and the raptors he worked with. They were disturbing in that they portrayed Silas's life as a young boy.

He had been an odd child, had been interested in science, had liked dissecting animals, and had collected bones from dead animals, especially birds.

In the last two entries, the boy had grown into an adult who'd become an artist through his plastic surgery. He crafted women's faces to resemble photographs of anyone the patient wanted to emulate, as well as the Mitzi doll that little girls idolized.

He also had a sick sadistic side, liked to fantasize about carving the women up and showing the ugliness beneath the skin.

The writing style was different than the original entries, revealing a demented man whose delusions had turned to murder. In the last story, he described a cage where he planned to hold his victims.

A cage filled with raptors. He wanted the women to feel the pain he'd felt.

She sighed. If Grimley had written that story, he should be locked away from society.

If someone else had penned the stories and framed Grimley, another woman's life hung in the balance.

◆ ◆ ◆

Dane phoned Peyton to tie up loose details and see if police had discovered anything at Grimley's or Easton's LA residences.

"Easton's residence was pretty clean," Peyton said. "According to the detective who searched it, he had tons of photos of women, all ones he'd taken. Some were in bizarre settings, and a couple mimicked rape scenes, but there were no scalpels or Mitzi dolls. They spoke with Easton's neighbor, who said he was a womanizer, but she'd never considered him violent." She paused. "The neighbor confirmed that Dr. Grimley visited Easton, and she said the two men were friends, but that was all she knew about them."

Dane rubbed at his forehead, antsy for more. He wanted to tie Easton to the crimes.

Peyton's nails drummed against her desk in the background as they always did when she was onto something. "Go on."

"Dr. Grimley's house was a different story. The LA detective reported finding an assortment of scalpels along with a personal wall of photos of all the women he'd treated with cosmetic surgery."

That was no surprise. "Anything else?"

"Yes. Apparently Grimley collected bird bones. He made a collage out of them for his home."

That tied in with the unsub's MO. "Maybe he was going to do the same with the bones he removed from his victims' cheeks." They needed to find those bones to cement the case.

"Quite possible. I also spoke with Dr. Grimley's receptionist about that phone he claimed was stolen," Peyton continued. "She confirmed his story. Apparently he was leaving the country that day and didn't want to go without the phone, but he couldn't find it."

If Grimley hadn't lied about the phone, had he been telling the truth about being framed? "So someone could have stolen it and used it to send that text to Michaels?"

"It's possible."

He squeezed his eyes shut, an image of those talon carvings mocking him.

"What about that lawsuit? Did you learn anything more about the woman who filed it?"

"Yes, and that's disturbing." A tinge of excitement laced Peyton's voice as if she thought she was onto something. "Dr. Grimley is in the early stages of Parkinson's and has developed a tremor. The investigator who worked on the lawsuit said Grimley didn't want anyone to know, but that tremor could have affected his dexterity."

"He was still operating," Dane said, putting together a mental picture of what had happened during the surgery and afterward. Grimley thought he was a god. The fear of losing his practice could have tipped him over the edge.

"Yes, although his lawyer kept that fact hushed. He settled the lawsuit out of court. Even so, the patient was extremely bitter and went on a campaign to destroy Dr. Grimley's career. She posted accusations online and showed up at his office several times shouting at the other patients that Dr. Grimley was a butcher."

Dane's blood ran cold. "A butcher. Were those her exact words?"

"Yes." She paused. "It gets more interesting, too. Medical records are confidential, but I hacked into this patient's computer and found something."

"What?"

"The surgery involved facial reconstruction, but also encompassed a transgender operation."

Dammit to hell. Ellie's comment about seeing a woman's hand holding the scalpel taunted Dane.

They'd assumed the killer was a male because he'd have to be strong enough to carry his victim. If this transgender client was born a male, he might have had the strength to do it. And he could have dressed like a man to throw suspicion from himself. "What is this person's name?"

"She calls herself Naomi Leakes. Although her original name was Nate. I'm sending you her photograph now."

A sick feeling welled in Dane's chest as the picture came through.

Good God. He recognized her. Him. He'd seen her at the community center.

Josie's face flashed in his mind. She'd been determined to keep investigating. She was probably at the community center asking questions.

He had to warn her before it was too late.

CHAPTER
THIRTY-ONE

Josie's phone dinged with a text as she parked at the community center. She threw the car into park and retrieved the message.

Meet me to discuss the final casting. Olive.

Josie texted back that she would, although she'd thought the film crew had put things on hold. Then again, Dane had held a press conference announcing Grimley's arrest, so they were probably back on schedule.

She jammed her phone in her purse and hurried inside. A handsome man with neatly clipped black hair wearing a gray suit smiled at her as she entered the lobby.

"Josie, hey, I wanted to talk to you."

She frowned but came to a halt. She didn't recognize the man. Was he part of the film crew? "Excuse me?"

His gray-blue eyes skated over her. "You don't recognize me, do you?"

His voice sounded familiar, but she couldn't place his face.

"No," she said, annoyed. She didn't have time to play games. "Have we met?"

A chuckle rumbled from him. "Yes, but I was in character. I'm Porter McCray." He gestured toward the board listing the cast chosen for the film. "I got the part of Billy Linder."

Pinpricks of unease tiptoed up her spine at the sound of Linder's name.

"You look totally different," she said, shocked at the transformation.

He laughed again. "I told you I totally immersed myself into my part. It worked."

Josie studied his face. Gone was the beady look in his eyes, the spooky air that he wasn't quite normal, the tic at the corner of his mouth.

"I guess congratulations are in order."

"Thank you. Maybe I could buy you a drink," he suggested.

"Sorry. I'm meeting someone now. I need to go." Worried the killer was still at large, she crossed the main lobby. Voices echoed from down the hall, and then three girls came around the corner. One girl was crying, the other two consoling her.

"There'll be other parts," one of them said.

"Yeah, who wants to play a dead girl?" the brunette murmured.

Josie was tempted to warn them that the Butcher might not be finished, but Dane wouldn't want her spreading rumors. She had to have something concrete to prove she was right.

Her phone dinged that she had a call. Dane. He probably wanted to talk her out of asking more questions, so she ignored it.

Olive exited Eddie Easton's studio. She looked frazzled as she darted into her office. Sympathy for her new friend surfaced. She'd been dealing with disappointed and irritated actors who hadn't been cast all day.

Josie paused at the door of the woman's office. She didn't want to disturb Olive if she was upset about something.

Although Olive *had* asked to meet her. If she was finished casting, perhaps she wanted to have coffee or a drink.

She glanced through the crack in the door. Olive pivoted to face the mirror on the closet door, her back to Josie.

A second later, Olive slammed her fist into the mirror and shattered the glass.

Josie covered a gasp. Blood dotted Olive's hand as she lifted it.

Then Olive lifted a Mitzi doll from a bag in the closet and traced one bloody finger across the doll's cheek, painting a talon mark across the doll's porcelain face.

Cold fear washed over Josie. Olive had the doll. Olive had drawn talon marks with blood on the doll's cheeks.

Olive had pretended to be her friend.

Only she didn't look like Olive right now—her eyes had turned menacing.

A deep tremble started inside Josie as doubts assailed her. Could Olive be the killer?

Legs weakening at the thought, she backed away. She had to phone Dane.

Then Olive looked up and saw her, and any semblance of friendliness disappeared.

Rage distorted her face.

"Ah, Josie," Olive said shrilly. "I wish you hadn't seen that."

Josie shook her head in denial. "I don't understand," Josie whispered.

With her bloody hand, Olive pulled a gun from her pocket and took aim at Josie's chest.

◆ ◆ ◆

Olive Turnstyle, the casting director, was Naomi Leakes, aka Nate.

Dear God. She'd befriended Josie.

Had Josie figured it out?

Dane's heart hammered as he cranked his car and barreled from the parking lot. He had to get to Josie.

Questions assailed him as he veered onto the street. How had Olive/Naomi/Nate known so much about Grimley's past? Had she known he'd murdered Betsy? She could have hacked into his computer to add to Grimley's blog, but how had she planted evidence in Grimley's car?

He slammed his horn at a truck that pulled out in front of him and sped around it. He tried Josie's number again as he raced toward the community center.

Please answer the phone, Josie.

His last conversation with her rolled through his head. He'd been harsh.

Even if she was okay, she might not speak to him. Not after the way he'd talked to her earlier. Regret burned in his gut.

They'd made love last night, all night, and that had freaked the hell out of him—he'd wanted to stay in bed with her all day.

Then she'd suggested that he might be wrong about Grimley.

He hadn't wanted to be wrong. He had Betsy's killer and that was what mattered.

Except Charity and Patty and Neesie deserved the same justice.

He cursed himself. Josie was right. He'd allowed his rage against Grimley to cloud his judgment.

If she was hurt or in danger because of him, he'd never forgive himself.

He swung into the parking lot, threw the door open, and hit the ground running. Thunder boomed above, and lightning zigzagged across the gloomy sky.

There were very few cars left in the lot, a reminder that the film crew was leaving town until they returned in a couple of weeks to start filming.

He spotted Josie's car in the third row.

It was empty.

She must be inside the building.

A camera crew was loading cameras into a van, and the limo that had brought the bigwigs of the production company to town was pulling in.

The van Easton used to transport his equipment was still parked in front. Dammit, he didn't know what kind of vehicle Olive drove.

She might have Josie now.

He jogged up the steps and inside. The entryway, which had been crowded before, was empty. Instead of the chaos of dozens of actors waiting in lines and gathering to discuss the script and their roles, an eerie silence echoed through the building.

Dane's instincts jumped to full alert.

When he reached Olive's office, no one was there.

Josie's purse was lying on the floor, the contents spilled out, her cell phone beneath the edge of a chair.

Panic seized him.

He yelled her name, then Olive's name, terrified. His voice boomeranged off the empty walls.

Frantic, he searched the closet, his stomach churning at the sight of the broken mirror and the Mitzi doll.

A doll with a talon drawn on its face out of blood.

His pulse quickened. Was that Josie's blood?

Please, God, no.

He couldn't lose Josie, not when he'd just found her.

♦ ♦ ♦

Josie's heart banged in her chest as Olive jammed the gun in her side. "Walk, Josie. And don't you dare make a noise or try anything. I'll blow your head off and anyone else's that gets in my way."

Josie couldn't believe her ears. She'd been so foolish, hadn't once considered Olive.

Olive pushed her through the back door of the community center toward Eddie Easton's van. Olive kept Josie close as she waved to the crew leaving. "My God, Olive, it was you? You killed those women. You butchered their faces and left them like they were trash."

"They were only pretty faces," Olive hissed.

Josie choked back a sob. "No, they were young women with futures ahead of them. With dreams."

"What about my dreams?" Olive growled. "What about who I wanted to be?"

Josie had to stall. Maybe someone would see them and figure out something was wrong. Maybe Dane would. "Who did you want to be?" Josie asked.

"A woman like them, but if they knew the truth, they would never have been friends with me."

"You left me those dolls," Josie said, the pieces clicking together in her mind. "You smeared blood on my bed, and you took my underwear."

A twisted smile lit the woman's eyes. "I wanted to know what it was like to be you. To have people admire me and like me for what I am."

"But they might have if you'd given them a chance."

"No. I didn't fit anywhere." She pushed Josie into the van, but Josie dug her heels in.

"Olive, please, you don't have to do this."

Olive's eyes turned to ice chips. "I'm sorry, really, Josie. I like you. You're not like all the others."

"Then let me help you. We'll get you a therapist—"

"It's too late for that," she said, her voice shrill. "You saw me, the mirror. You know."

"Know what?" Josie asked, desperate to connect with her. "That Dr. Grimley hurt you, that he scarred you? Or did someone else hurt you first?"

A low wail came from Olive as if anguish overpowered her.

"What is it about the mirrors?" Josie pressed.

"My mother . . . I used to play in her makeup and look at myself in the mirror, to dress in her clothes. She called me a freak. I told her then that I was a little girl inside this boy's body, that I was meant to be a girl." A sob escaped Olive, and her hand shook as she waved the gun. "She found me in her underwear one day and slammed my face into the mirror. The glass shattered."

"It scarred you," Josie said, sickened by the image. "That was a horrible thing for a mother to do."

A terrifying wildness streaked Olive's face. "Dr. Grimley promised he could fix anyone, make you be the person you wanted to be. He lied. He made all those other women pretty, but look what he did to me!" She wiped a thick blob of makeup from her cheek, revealing rigid, puckered skin. "That's not all he did either. He was supposed to make me a woman, but he botched it up." Her voice rose, sounding crazed. "You should see what I look like down there. I'm ruined."

"I'm so sorry." Josie had to calm the woman. "But killing me won't change that."

"Shut up and get in the van. I promise to make it painless for you." Olive aimed the gun at Josie's head, then shoved her into the back of the vehicle. Josie considered fighting, but one bullet would end her life, and she wasn't ready to die.

"Please, Olive," Josie said sympathetically. "You need help."

A maniacal laugh escaped her. "What I need is for everyone to think that Silas Grimley is the Butcher because he butchered me." She slid her hand inside her pocket and removed a hypodermic.

Fear crawled through Josie. Olive had subdued her other victims with a paralyzing drug.

You are not going to be a victim. Lord help her, she'd survived the Bride Killer. She would survive this.

"Please, Olive," Josie pleaded. "Give me a chance to write your story. I'll make people understand. You can be a role model for others in your situation."

A sad look flickered on Olive's face, but resignation followed. "It's too late." Olive raised the needle, and Josie's instincts kicked in. She pushed at Olive's hand, but the woman jammed the gun in her face.

Josie froze.

A second later, the needle pierced her skin, then everything went dark.

◆ ◆ ◆

The panic clawing at Dane mimicked the fear he'd had the night he'd called Betsy for hours to check on her, and she hadn't answered.

She'd been dead.

His lungs squeezed. Josie couldn't be.

He found the security guard who'd worked at the center and explained the situation. "Did you see Olive Turnstyle or Josie DuKane?"

The guard shook his head no.

"Help me search the building. If you see either one of them, don't try to stop them yourself. Call me. The Turnstyle woman is dangerous."

The guard went one way, and he hurried the opposite direction, searching every room in the building. Nothing.

Which car belonged to Olive?

He phoned Peyton. "Issue an APB for Olive Turnstyle, aka Nate or Naomi Leakes's vehicle."

The sound of keys clicking in the background told him she was at work. "On it. She drives a 2015 Ford Escape. Gray."

Dane ran to the front of the building and searched the parking lot. Fuck. "Her car is still here."

"She must be in the building."

"No, I've searched inside." He scanned the lot again, his pulse hammering. "Wait. Easton's work van is gone. She could have taken it. Find the tag number."

Jesus, God, the van had been there when he'd arrived. He'd just missed them. "Copy that." Keys clicked again. "Hang on, Dane."

He jiggled his foot. They had to find Josie in time to save her. "Check and see if the Turnstyle woman or Leakes owns any property, a house, cabin, someplace she might take Josie. Someplace she could have killed her other victims."

"Doing it as we speak."

"Thanks. I'm going back to the jail to question Easton and Grimley again. If they know anything, I'll make them talk." Hell, he'd beat the answers out of them.

The security guard shook his head as Dane approached. "I didn't find anyone. The place is empty."

"If either of them shows up, call me." He shoved a business card in the man's hand and jogged toward his car. The last victim had been left at the Falls Inn.

He phoned the owner as he drove toward the jail and explained.

"I can't believe that nice young woman would hurt anyone," Cynthia said. "She was so sweet."

"Let me know if she or Josie turns up." Panicked, he slammed down the phone and hit the accelerator.

Josie's argument about Grimley being framed taunted him. If only he'd listened, hadn't been so stubborn, so sure he was right. But they had been looking for a man, and Olive had dressed and presented herself as a woman.

The woman she'd wanted to be.

She'd also befriended Josie. Probably so she could keep abreast of the case.

She'd cleverly orchestrated everything, planting false clues along the way to lead them to Grimley.

When he reached the jail, he swerved into a parking spot and hurried inside. Sheriff Kimball was on the phone, but Dane motioned for him to hang up. "I need your help, Sheriff."

Kimball nodded. "Just tell me what to do."

Dane relayed what had happened. "Back me up."

Kimball nodded again and went to get the prisoners.

Both men remained shackled and chained as they shuffled in the interrogation room. Grimley looked ragged, a shell of a man, his professional façade gone.

Easton appeared slightly calmer, although animosity simmered beneath that calm. "When are you letting me go?" Easton said. "You've had your twenty-four hours."

Dane folded his arms. He had to release the man, but he needed him to talk first. "Tell me about Olive Turnstyle."

"What?" Easton frowned, and Grimley looked baffled. Having to turn to the man who'd killed his sister made Dane's stomach sour. But he had a job to do, and he'd damn well do it or more lives would be lost. Josie's, for one.

She was too important to let his animosity toward Grimley get in the way.

"Her real name is Nate/Naomi Leakes," Dane said. "Something happened during her surgery, and she was left scarred." He directed his gaze toward Grimley. "How am I doing so far?"

Grimley drummed his fingers on his leg. "She had a bad drug interaction and—"

"And you'd developed a tremor so your hand wasn't steady," Dane said. "You shouldn't have been operating."

Grimley squeezed the bridge of his nose with his fingers, the tremor evident. "It was an accident, a mistake. I . . . My insurance settled."

"Leakes wasn't satisfied with money, was he—she?" Dane asked sarcastically. "She wanted to be one of the pretty girls you made beautiful."

Grimley merely nodded.

"She was scarred and knew she'd lose roles." Dane relied on logic—at least as he saw it through Leakes's eyes. "Now she's stuck on the sidelines casting other women in roles she wanted to play."

Easton cleared his throat. "What does this have to do with me?"

Dane turned his gaze on the photographer. "You played into these women's fantasies and referred them to Grimley. My guess is that you referred Naomi to him."

Easton shifted uncomfortably, his handcuffs clanging. "So? Those women wanted cosmetic work. They wanted to stand out. And Nate—Naomi—wanted help. I figured it would be challenging, but Dr. Grimley is the best."

"Only he botched it," Dane finished.

Grimley became agitated, rocking his chair back and forth as he turned to Easton. "You knew Naomi was here? That she was this Olive woman?"

Easton muttered a curse. "Yes, but I felt sorry for him—her. She was trying to get her act together, trying to move forward. She used a different name so no one would know about the transgender surgery." He threw up his hands, his voice emphatic. "Good God. I never suspected that she'd kill anyone, or that she was framing you for murder."

Silence fell for a full minute, each man working to figure out if the other was lying about his knowledge of Olive. Dane was doing the same thing.

He'd never once considered the casting director as a suspect, never suspected she was a man. Because he'd been looking for Betsy's killer, and Easton and Grimley both had connections to his sister. He had been so focused on that aspect that he'd missed the signs that the killer wasn't the same.

Guilt threatened to bring him to his knees. Josie was in danger because of him.

"How did Olive know about your past, Grimley?" Dane asked. "About how you got your scars?"

"Fuck," Easton said in a strangled voice. "I told her."

"You did what?" Grimley shot up from his seat. "That was confidential."

"I'm sorry," Easton said. "We had drinks and got to talking. She asked how I knew you, and the story just came out. I thought it would help her forgive you."

Grimley dropped back in his seat and pressed the heels of his hands against his eyes.

"That explains that," Dane said. "This is the important part." He leaned forward, hands on the table. "I believe she's abducted Josie DuKane and that Josie is in danger. Where would she take her?"

Easton and Grimley exchanged confused, blank looks.

"I don't know," Easton said.

"She's based solely in LA," Dr. Grimley said.

Dane rapped his knuckles on the table, fighting despair. "Think, is there any place significant to her?"

Grimley shook his head. "No. She didn't have family that I know of."

Dane's phone buzzed that he had a text. He quickly checked it.

Easton's van spotted driving east into the mountains. Have alerted authorities.

Dane clenched the phone in a death grip. "She's been spotted driving your van, Easton, heading into the mountains."

"Good God," Grimley muttered.

Dane gritted his teeth. "What?"

"I know where she's going." He paled. "To the house where I grew up."

Dane's blood went cold.

To the place she'd described in the blog she'd written under Grimley's name.

To the cage where she planned to watch her last victim die.

CHAPTER
THIRTY-TWO

Josie stirred from unconsciousness and blinked against the darkness. The wind must be strong now because the van was blowing all over the road.

Cold terror seized her as reality returned.

Olive was the Butcher.

She blinked and tried to move her arms and legs, but they refused to work. Olive had injected Josie with that paralyzing drug so she couldn't fight back.

Charity and Patty and Neesie must have felt this same fear.

The van bounced over a bump, jarring her teeth, and she fought a scream. No one could hear her. She'd have to bide her time, pick the right moment to fight.

Only how could she fight if she couldn't move?

Where was Olive taking her?

She choked back a sob. She had to stall until Dane could find her.

Dane. Did he even know she was missing?

Despair threatened to swallow her. Dane believed he had the Butcher in custody. He hadn't wanted to hear what she had to say.

For all she knew, he could have already moved Grimley to a federal facility and left town himself.

Tears pooled in her eyes and trickled down her cheeks, but she was helpless to wipe them away.

She didn't want to die.

◆ ◆ ◆

Dane turned onto the dirt road leading to Grimley's childhood home, praying he was right, that Olive was taking Josie to that house.

Wind swirled through the trees, shaking them and kicking up dust. The mountain ridges still held hints of snow on the sharp peaks, yet the sky looked gloomy, dark storm clouds rolling across the mountaintops, the air chilled and filled with the smell of impending rain.

Or a tornado.

The SUV's tires churned over the uneven dirt and rocks, leaving Graveyard Falls behind and taking him farther into the mountains and away from civilization. Trees rose like giants, some so close together, their branches thick and wound together as if they'd linked arms to keep intruders out. At one point the big limbs twisted and intertwined, creating a tunnel effect, as if he was driving into a dark forest where he might be swallowed and never emerge.

Grimley's father must have liked the isolation. He'd needed space, land, the wilderness, to rescue and raise the raptors. Living off the grid had also afforded him enough privacy so no one would see how he was treating his son.

Dane pushed aside sympathy for the way Grimley had been tormented as a kid. It didn't excuse his crimes, and it certainly wouldn't keep him from prison.

Thunder rumbled louder, and lightning streaked the sky in jagged lines. He pressed the accelerator, eating the miles as he delved deeper into the woods.

His phone beeped. The sheriff's number. He connected. "Agent Hamrick."

"Are you there yet?"

Dane checked the GPS, his agitation rising. "No, but I'm getting close."

"I'm behind you a few miles."

Dane thanked him and hung up. He wanted backup, but he couldn't wait. It was his fault Josie was in trouble. If only he'd listened to her, hadn't cut her off, hadn't been so intent on putting Grimley away on as many charges as possible, he would have seen the truth.

The memory of her drawing him into her arms and comforting him the night he'd talked to his mother made him ache. She had been so loving and generous, so compassionate and—passionate.

He wanted to hold her again. To comfort her and soothe her nightmares and make up for pushing her away.

He wanted to make love to her.

If he lost her to this madman—madwoman—he'd never forgive himself.

He checked his weapon, battling despair. He would not lose her.

But if Olive had hurt her, he'd kill her.

♦ ♦ ♦

Josie tried to lift her finger. Move a toe. Her hand. Her body was weighted down as if it was asleep. She tried to scream, but even her vocal cords seemed paralyzed.

Olive grabbed her by the arms and dragged her from the van. Josie's body hit the graveled dirt with a thud. She looked up, eyes pleading with Olive to let her go.

Olive simply jerked her along like she was a sack of potatoes, heedless of the dirt and rocks tearing at Josie's skin and clothes.

Out of her peripheral vision, Josie spotted an old shack, then a big cage.

This was the house where Dr. Grimley had grown up. The cage where he'd been locked like a wild animal, where he'd been attacked.

The cage was empty now, but if Olive killed her, the vultures would sniff her blood and have her for dinner.

Olive gave her a twisted smile. "I really hate to do this, Josie. I liked you. You weren't like all those wannabes with their fake boobs and plastic smiles. You were real."

Josie tried to speak, but her voice came out as a moan.

"I know what you're thinking, that if I let you go, you won't talk. Only you will talk. You're the type that has to be honest, that has to fight for justice. I like that." Olive's voice wavered as she dragged Josie toward the cage. "That's the reason I had to come after Grimley. I needed justice, too."

"P-Please," Josie cried, although the word was a mere screech.

Olive shoved the door of the cage open with one foot and dragged Josie inside.

"I know Grimley is in jail, and when they find your body, the police will realize that he didn't kill you. No one will find you out here. At least not for a while. By then I'll be long gone."

A tear spilled over onto Josie's cheek, then another and another.

Olive was right.

"Besides, if I'm lucky," Olive said in an almost wistful tone, "there won't be enough left of your body to identify you."

Josie's heart clenched with fear as Olive tied ropes around her feet and hands and attached them to the posts of the cage. Terrified, she struggled again, but to no avail.

Olive moved over her and raised a scalpel. "Don't worry, Josie, I won't leave a scar on your face. I'll make this as quick and painless as possible."

Dane spotted Easton's van parked in front of the old wooden house, then a cage and Olive standing over Josie. The damn woman was holding the scalpel, ready to strike.

Terror coiled inside him, and he sped his vehicle down the drive and screeched to a stop near the cage.

One quick wound to the aorta and he wouldn't be able to save Josie.

He threw his car into park, grabbed his gun, checked the ammo, then jumped from the driver's side. "Stop it, Olive, it's over!"

She didn't react. She seemed too focused on what she was doing—or lost in a world of delusions.

The wind blew dust up, swirling it like a funnel cloud. Taking advantage of the fact that she didn't realize he was there, he eased inside the cage.

Olive lowered the scalpel and traced it over Josie's chest, ripping her blouse open and drawing blood.

His heart nearly stopped beating altogether. Josie was tied spread-eagle on the ground, her eyes full of fear. He motioned to her to be quiet, but Olive jerked her head toward him.

He aimed his gun at her, but she lunged forward, waving the scalpel at him. He knocked it from her hand and sent it flying across the ground. Olive dived for it with a bellow. He fired a shot, but she rolled out of the way, grabbed the scalpel, and swung it at his leg. It nicked his ankle and blood seeped from the cut, but he ignored the pain and raised his weapon again.

"Olive. It's over."

"Grimley got what was coming to him," she shouted.

"Maybe, but Josie doesn't deserve to die." Neither did the other women she'd killed. He couldn't save them, though.

"Move and I'll shoot."

"Go ahead." She raised the scalpel toward herself. "My life is over anyway."

"It didn't have to be that way," Dane said. "You chose this path."

Josie made a strangled sound, and Dane glanced at her to see if she was all right. Olive moved quickly, tearing at his face like a wild animal.

Dane didn't hesitate. He pulled the trigger.

Shock darkened her eyes as her body bounced back. Blood gushed from her chest. She clenched the wound with one hand, then collapsed onto the dirt. Dane patted her down to make sure she didn't have another weapon.

Josie cried out again, a sob escaping her. All Dane could think about was going to her.

A car rumbled up the drive a second later, and the sheriff appeared. He climbed out and rushed toward them.

"Call an ambulance," Dane yelled. He knelt by Olive. "How did you plant that evidence in Grimley's car?"

A twisted chuckle rumbled from her. "It was easy. I flirted with the valet, told him I wanted to leave a surprise for my boyfriend, and he gave me the keys." Her sinister laugh faded to a hollow sound. "He believed I was Grimley's girlfriend."

She looked pale and glassy-eyed, her body convulsing. He doubted she'd make it, but he didn't care.

All he cared about was Josie.

◆ ◆ ◆

Josie sobbed, well aware the sound resembled an injured animal's cry more than her own voice, but the drugs still held her prisoner.

Any effort she made to move was futile.

Dane knelt beside her. "It's okay, I'm here. An ambulance is on its way."

She blinked to let him know that she understood. His poor mother must feel this way, trapped in a world of pain and silence.

He stroked her hair away from her face. "I'm so sorry I didn't believe you, I'm so sorry."

She understood that, too. She just wanted to be set free. She used all her energy to move, and finally her fingers fluttered.

Dane yanked a knife from his pocket and quickly cut the ropes. Then he lifted her beneath her shoulders and pulled her into his arms.

Tears of relief spilled down her cheeks as he rocked her in his lap and held her.

◆ ◆ ◆

Dane paced the hospital waiting room, anxious about Josie's condition. Even though the doctors had identified the drug and assured him that she'd recover, he couldn't erase the image of her lying helpless in that damn cage.

If he'd been a few minutes later . . .

You made it in time. She's all right.

Was she? Would she be plagued by more nightmares?

If she were, it was his fault.

Voices echoed in the hall, then footsteps, and Josie's mother, Anna, and her husband, Johnny, raced up. Mona, Josie's half sister, and Cal followed on their heels.

Anna looked panic-stricken. "Where is she?"

Mona grabbed his arm. "Is she okay, Dane? What did that crazy woman do to her?"

"She's going to be all right." Dane explained about the paralyzing drug. "The doctor said it will wear off soon."

"I have to see her," Anna said, frantic.

Mona nodded. "Me, too."

They hurried to the nurses' station while Cal and Johnny remained in the waiting room with Dane.

"I heard you cracked the case," Cal said. "Good for you."

Self-recriminations screamed in Dane's head. He didn't deserve accolades. He just wanted to get to Josie. See that she survived. "Actually, Josie figured out Grimley wasn't the Butcher. I almost got Josie killed."

On the way to the Grimleys' old homestead, he'd realized just how much Josie meant to him.

How much he loved her.

He'd prayed she was alive so he could tell her.

Now looking at her family and knowing that his stubbornness had put her life in jeopardy, he kept his mouth shut.

He had no right to ask for forgiveness, much less love.

Josie blinked back tears as her mother and Mona doted on her. She'd assured them that she was okay. She'd survived Billy Linder.

She would survive this.

Where was Dane?

He was probably furious with her for going to the community center by herself. He'd said she was naïve, and she had been.

She'd trusted Olive completely. Hadn't seen beyond the surface, beyond what Olive wanted her to see.

Johnny poked his head in. "Everyone all right in here?"

Anna stroked Josie's hair. "Yes. Josie's going to be okay."

"Where's Dane?" Josie asked.

Johnny frowned. "He said he had to go, honey. Do you need me to get him?"

Emotions swelled in Josie's throat. Yes, she wanted him.

But he didn't want her. He simply cared about the job. For a while she'd helped him, had been his partner. He didn't want a partner, though. He'd told her that in the beginning.

She'd have to learn to live without him just as she'd learned to live with the nightmares.

CHAPTER
THIRTY-THREE

It had been three days since Dane had seen Josie.

Every day was torture.

He'd never thought he'd love anyone else in his life, much less want to spend every waking moment with a woman.

He wanted to spend every moment with Josie.

Josie had become an obsession. Missing her was all he could think about.

Even knowing he'd closed the case didn't quiet his need for her. His want.

Unfortunately, Olive Turnstyle had died in the ambulance on the way to the hospital. Justice was served, yet she'd died without having to face her victims' families. That didn't seem fair.

Grimley had been moved to a state facility. He'd made a plea deal to avoid a lengthy trial and was given a life sentence. After thirty years, he was eligible for parole. Dane doubted the man would make it that long. His Parkinson's disease had already begun to progress.

Dane packed his things at the cabin. He was ready to leave Graveyard Falls.

The good news—his mother was slowly emerging from her catatonic state and starting to speak and interact. Maybe one day she'd be strong enough to leave the nursing facility.

Apparently she and Ellie had discussed sharing an apartment. He was glad she had a friend, even if that friend professed to have visions. For a brief moment, he'd considered turning Ellie in for killing Grimley's father, but under the circumstances, he decided justice had been doled out after all.

His suitcase in the SUV, he headed out of town. Back to his life. Another case.

Only a few miles down the road, and the itch to see Josie one more time overcame him.

He spun his vehicle around.

Ten minutes later, he found himself sitting in Josie's driveway. He stared at her house, remembering when she'd called him about the photograph. She'd been scared and shaken but so gusty he'd liked her on the spot.

He cut the engine, an image of her standing up to him, insisting that she needed to help with the case, stirring. Then he saw her taking his hand and drawing him to bed when he'd needed her warm, sweet touch to stave off his own nightmares.

A few weeks ago he hadn't cared about anything but his job and finding Betsy's killer.

He'd been driven by guilt. In the end, he'd found the truth, but he'd almost gotten Josie killed.

He owed her an apology. He was a man who believed in taking ownership of his mistakes and in saying he was sorry. He couldn't leave town without doing it now.

Nerves clanged inside him, but he opened the door and climbed out. A fresh storm was brewing, tornadoes touching down in other parts of the South. Tornado warnings had been issued for the rest of the day and night, and one had been sighted in North Georgia.

Wind swirled leaves and debris across the drive, tossing twigs in his path. The sky turned dark, a funnel cloud in the distance spinning as if a tornado was headed this way. He'd been caught in the eye of the storm himself for so long that he'd forgotten how to live.

He'd emerged a different man.

A man who wanted more than a job. A man who wanted love and someone to share his life with.

Determined to learn from his mistakes, he strode to the door and rang the bell. His shoulders knotted with anxiety as he waited for Josie to answer. Her car was here. She had to be inside.

Finally she opened the door. He took one look at her and lost his breath. She looked so damn beautiful he wanted to drag her in his arms and never let her go.

An image of her tied spread-eagle in that cage flashed back, and emotions clogged his throat.

"Dane?" Her eyes searched his. "I thought you'd already left town."

He gestured toward his SUV. "I'm packed and on my way. How about you? What's going on with the movie?"

"The film company decided to hold off production until things settle down. Maybe in a few months . . ."

"So you're leaving town?"

She bit down on her lower lip. "Yes. I don't think I can stay in Graveyard Falls. I'm a reminder to all the locals that I brought another serial killer to town."

"*You* didn't bring a killer to town," Dane said, his voice firm. He couldn't—wouldn't—allow Josie to blame herself. "Olive was on a path to destruction before this film fell in her lap. She used you, the town, and the movie to get her revenge."

Josie blinked, her eyes moist. "I know, it's just hard to forget."

He would never forget it either. "I'm sorry for what I said, for putting you in danger." God, he had to spit it out. "You were right that day. I let my emotions over my sister's case cloud my judgment and lost my objectivity. I should have at least investigated Grimley's claims."

Josie reached out a hand as if to touch him, but then pulled back. "Don't beat yourself up, Dane. You had a right to be emotional. I'm just glad that you found your sister's killer." She paused. "How's your mother?"

"Better. She heard me tell her about the arrest and is making progress."

"She must have felt trapped," Josie said softly. "That's the way I felt when I was given that drug. I could see and hear everything, but I couldn't move or speak."

Regret made Dane flush with heat. He had to look away. Too much guilt.

Stand up and be a man. You have no right to look away. You have to face her. "Are you having nightmares again?"

"Some," she admitted. "Don't worry, though. I'll be okay."

He nodded. Of course she'd be okay. She was tough. She didn't need him. "You're going to write this story, too?"

She rubbed two fingers against her temple. "I have to. It's my way of coping, of making sense out of the violence."

He gave an understanding nod. "Maybe I should have written about Betsy."

"We could do that together," Josie offered. "That is, if you want."

God, yes, he wanted it. He wanted her sweetness and compassion and intelligence and tenacity. He wanted her in his arms any way he could have her.

Most of all he wanted her beside him and in his bed.

Dane forgot all the reasons he wasn't supposed to fall in love, because he was already knee-deep in it. Josie was smart and beautiful and strong, and he needed her.

The wind picked up, roaring as if a freight train was coming.

"There's a tornado warning," Josie said, her brows furrowed. "You shouldn't be on the road."

"I'm not afraid of a storm," he said quietly.

Josie's gaze met his. "What are you afraid of, Dane?"

He swallowed hard. "I was afraid of falling in love," he said. "Of caring about anyone. I shut down after Betsy died, and then when my mother lapsed into that silent world, I thought I'd lost her, too. I thought that she hated me, that she blamed me."

She licked her lips, her voice a whisper. "Your mother loves you."

He shifted, barely able to keep his hands from reaching for her. "When I thought Olive might have killed you," Dane said gruffly, "I realized I'd fallen in love with you. I can't go back to not caring, Josie." He swallowed the lump in his throat. "It's my fault you almost died, and I can't expect you to forgive me—"

"I already have," Josie said softly. "I love you, too, Dane."

Hope mushroomed inside Dane as Josie took his hand, pulled him inside, and led him to her bedroom. Slowly they stripped their clothes, then fell onto the bed together.

Outside the storm raged, the wind howled, and tree branches snapped and beat against the house. The clouds opened up, dumping rain on the earth, the force of it shaking the windows.

They were oblivious. Josie was safe in his arms, and he loved her. That was all that mattered.

♦ ♦ ♦

Three weeks later

Josie stood in front of the priest wearing a long, satiny white gown. She was thrilled to have her mother, her half sister, and her stepfather present to watch her marry Dane.

Even more wonderful was the fact that Dane's mother had begun talking. Today she and her friend Ellie were attending the wedding.

The ceremony was short and sweet, but when Dane kissed her, she kissed him with all her heart. She would love him for the rest of her life.

Toasts were made at the reception, but she barely sipped her champagne. She and Dane had been looking for a quiet moment to share their news with his mother.

Her mother and Mona already knew.

While the guests began to serve themselves from the buffet, she and Dane joined his mother and Miss Ellie.

Dane leaned over to kiss his mother's cheek. "I'm so glad you're here, Mom."

She squeezed his hand, then smiled at Josie. "You look beautiful, dear."

"She's positively *glowing*," Miss Ellie said with a smile.

Josie laughed. According to Dane, the blind woman claimed to have visions. Maybe she knew Josie's secret.

"Mom, Josie and I have something to tell you," Dane said with a squeeze of her hand.

Josie scooted into the seat beside his mother while Dane claimed the opposite side. "Mrs. Hamrick—"

Dane's mother smiled warmly. "Please call me Paula."

"All right, Paula, we have a surprise." Josie squeezed the woman's other hand. "We're going to have a baby."

His mother's smile lit up. "Oh my word, a baby."

"It will be a girl," Miss Ellie said with conviction.

Dane's mother laughed and hugged Josie and Dane. "You know, there's some truth to her visions," she whispered.

Josie blushed. "Well, if it is a girl, we're going to name her Betsy. That is, if it's all right with you."

The baby would never take Dane's sister's place, but they wanted to honor his sister's memory. A beautiful girl whose life was taken too soon.

Tears glistened in his mother's eyes. "Yes, I'd like that." She rubbed a finger over the locket around her neck. "Betsy would have liked it, too."

They hugged again, then the music cranked up.

Dane stood and extended his hand to Josie. "Time for our first dance as husband and wife."

Josie laid her hand in his, and together they walked to the dance floor.

Dane wrapped his arms around her, and she leaned into him, savoring his solid warm body as they swayed to the music together. His tender caresses and kisses had chased away all her nightmares and filled her with happiness.

Sadly, murder had brought them together, but love would see them through any storm, because they would face it together.

ACKNOWLEDGMENTS

Thanks to the amazing team at Amazon Montlake for their support for this series and for taking a walk on the dark side with me!

My sincere appreciation to my developmental editor, Mallory Braus, for her enthusiasm, encouragement, and for pushing me to make the book better during the revision process. (Thankfully she couldn't hear my cursing in the wee hours of the morning as I implemented her changes!) I hope we do many more projects together. Yes . . . I really do.

As always, I have to mention my fabulous agent, Jenny Bent, who thought I was a sweet Southern girl until she read my books—then represented me anyway.

Also, a special thanks to New Orleans Police Chief Scott Silverii for answering endless law enforcement questions. You are the greatest!

I especially want to give a shout-out to the real Precious, a wonderfully sweet and compassionate young woman who showed great kindness and tenderness to our family and my mother last year during her stay at a nursing home/rehab facility. God puts people in our lives when we least expect them and need them the most—and Precious was definitely a godsend.

I can't write thanks without mentioning my critique partner of twenty years, Stephanie Bond, who, like a good husband, has stuck with me through all the highs and lows of the business and my writing career. It's the greatest of marriages—she never complains when I plot murder over a glass of wine, and I don't even have to pick up her dirty socks.

And last but not least, thanks to my fabulous husband and three great kids for their support. Even though they are sometimes shocked at my sinister stories, they love me even when I frighten them.

Happy reading in Graveyard Falls!
Rita

ANOTHER GRAVEYARD FALLS
NOVEL BY RITA HERRON

All the Dead Girls, coming in Fall 2016

PROLOGUE

She had to run away.

JJ Jones had been planning it ever since she'd learned what would happen on her thirteenth birthday.

She would become a substitute for her foster father's wife.

Her stomach roiled at the thought, and she slipped from bed, retrieved her backpack, then tiptoed over to Sunny's bed.

Sunny was two months younger than JJ, but small for her age, frail, and terrified of her own shadow.

JJ couldn't leave Sunny to face Herman's wrath when he discovered JJ had left.

She gently shook her foster sister. "Wake up, Sunny, it's time."

Sunny groaned and rolled to her side, but JJ made her turn back toward her, then whispered as loud as she dared. If he caught her, she'd be punished.

He liked to punish.

"Come on, Sunny, we have to go."

Sunny's eyes slowly opened, confusion clouding them. "What? I was dreaming."

Probably of a better place to live. Clean clothes. A real family.

JJ had given up on those things a long time ago.

She pressed her finger to Sunny's lips to remind her to be quiet. "Remember, I told you about my birthday. I won't let that man touch me. We have to go *now*."

Fear flickered across Sunny's face, but she nodded, threw her covers aside, and dropped to the floor. They'd packed their backpacks the night before and slept in their clothes. Not that they had many clothes. Herman and his wife, Frances, used the money the state gave them to support their booze habit.

JJ grabbed her jacket and shrugged it on, then tossed Sunny hers.

The wind howled outside, thunder rumbling. JJ's adrenaline kicked in. They had to get to the bus station before the storm hit.

She jammed her feet into her boots, and Sunny did the same. They threw their backpacks over their shoulders, crept to the window, shoved it open, and crawled outside. The fresh air was refreshing compared to the stench of the dirty house and the smell of liquor.

JJ had repeatedly phoned the social worker for help, but the woman had such a big caseload, she ignored JJ's calls. She didn't know what else to do but run.

Sunny's legs buckled as she hit the ground, and JJ steadied her. A noise echoed from inside. JJ froze, terrified he'd woken up.

She motioned toward the woods in back, then mimed the word "Go." Sunny nodded, and they ran toward the woods. JJ had stolen a flashlight from the house, and once they were far enough away not to be seen, she flicked it on and used it to light their path.

The coach's son had promised to meet them at eleven. She hurried Sunny along, wincing as the bitter wind ripped through her and raindrops began to pelt them. She and Sunny yanked their jacket hoods over their heads, then picked up their pace, slogging through the woods as fast as they could.

A half mile down from the house, she cut to the right toward the street, and they jogged toward the Dairy Mart where she was supposed to meet the boy. The lights were off inside the ice-cream shop, and the parking lot was empty.

JJ ushered Sunny beneath the awning to the side of the building, and they huddled in the rain, waiting.

Seconds dragged into minutes. Minutes bled into an hour. Disappointment and despair tugged at JJ.

"He's not coming," Sunny said, shivering.

JJ wrapped her arm around her friend and rubbed her arms to warm her. A chill had wormed its way through JJ, too, and her teeth were chattering. She hated to admit it, but Sunny was right.

Lightning zigzagged across the sky, crackling as if it had struck a tree. Rain turned to hail, the icy pellets pounding the concrete.

They couldn't stay here all night. Sooner or later the local cops might show or someone would see them.

Then they'd take them back to *him*.

No way would JJ let that happen.

She grabbed Sunny's hand. "We're not giving up. We'll walk."

Sunny dug her heels in. "But it's miles. I'm tired and cold."

Anger seized JJ. "Then let's hurry." Sunny balked, but JJ shook her by the shoulders. "Listen to me, you'll be thirteen in two months, then he'll want you."

Sunny's face paled, ghostly white against the dark, gloomy night. "Where are we going?" Sunny whispered.

"My grandmother's. She lives in Nashville."

"I thought she didn't want you," Sunny said in a choked voice.

JJ's heart clenched in pain. Sunny was right. Her grandmother hadn't wanted her as a baby. But JJ refused to let that stop her from finding a better place to live. A safe one.

"She was sick when I was born," JJ said. "When she hears what Herman planned to do to me, she'll let us stay." At least she hoped she would. Otherwise, she had nowhere to turn.

"What if she lets you stay but won't keep me?" Sunny cried.

The fear in Sunny's voice tore at JJ. She had no idea how her grandmother would react. Thirteen years ago, she'd told social services she couldn't raise an infant. Would she feel the same about a teenager?

No, JJ would convince her she could take care of herself. All she and Sunny needed was a roof over their heads and for people to leave them alone.

"Don't worry, I'll work it out." She gave Sunny a reassuring look. "I promised to take care of you and I will."

Sunny wiped at a tear, then gripped JJ's hand, and they headed down the street together. The country road had no streetlights, and the clouds shrouded the moon. Sunny stumbled, and JJ flicked on the flashlight again.

She didn't know the exact mileage but guessed it was about ten miles to the bus station. Thunder rumbled and the rain beat down, pounding the ground and soaking them to the core. Mud and water seeped into JJ's shoes, adding to the chill.

A half hour later, Sunny complained that her legs were hurting. Occasionally a car passed, but JJ quickly turned off the flashlight, and they ducked behind some trees to hide.

Another mile and despair threatened. Sunny tripped over a tree stump, collapsed to the ground, and cried out in pain. "I hurt my ankle."

JJ wiped rain from her face, willing herself not to cry, too. They still had a long way to go. She stooped and shined her light on Sunny's foot. It was turning red and swelling.

Panic streaked through her. What were they going to do?

The sound of an engine rent the night, and she pivoted. A truck was coming toward them. The headlights nearly blinded her, and she slid an arm around Sunny's waist to support her and help her stand.

"I can't put weight on it," Sunny whined.

Brakes screeched. The driver must have seen them. He slowed, gears grinding as he veered to the side of the road. The passenger door opened with a screech. JJ squinted through the bright lights.

"You girls need help?"

She couldn't make out the man's features, but a girl sat beside him. And there was someone else . . .

JJ's lungs squeezed. Surprise filled her at the familiar face.

A loud clap of thunder rent the air. Sunny startled. JJ helped her up, pushed Sunny into the cab first, then hauled herself onto the seat.

As she closed the door, JJ turned to see who the man was, but it was too dark inside the cab to make out his face. The cab smelled, though, like some kind of men's cologne. A cologne she'd smelled before . . .

"I'm sorry," the girl said in a low voice.

JJ frowned. What was she sorry for?

A second later, the man shoved a rag over JJ's mouth and nose, and the world swirled to black.

CHAPTER ONE

FIFTEEN YEARS LATER

6:00 a.m., Thursday, April 2—Graveyard Falls

No one in Graveyard Falls knew the real reason Sheriff Ian Kimball had moved to this town. Hopefully, no one ever would.

Not unless he found what he was looking for.

Depending on the answers he got, he'd tell them and let the cards fall where they may.

The truth shall set you free, his father used to say.

A bitter chuckle rumbled from him. Except his dad had insisted he'd told the truth fifteen years ago, and no one believed him. He'd gone to prison anyway. And Ian's family had been destroyed.

Hell, the truth might destroy Ian again, but the guilt was already doing that, so he might as well keep digging.

At the moment, none of that mattered, though.

Right now he had a real mess on his hands. On the heels of a serial killer stalking the town, this F-3 tornado was too damn much.

The devastating damage from the nearly two-hundred-mile-per-hour winds and flooding that had swept over the Southeast thirty-six hours ago, hitting them with a funnel cloud that had ripped up trees by their roots and flung houses and cars as if they were ping-pong balls, had left the town shaken and picking up the broken pieces of their homes and shattered lives.

"Shit, I can't believe this." Deputy Whitehorse's boots dug into the muddy earth where they stood assessing the damage at the trailer park outside Graveyard Falls.

Metal, glass, household items, clothing, underwear, lamps, kitchen utensils, dishes, linens, broken furniture, and children's toys lay scattered across miles of soggy soil. Ancient oaks and pines were split in two, ripped from the ground, and branches and limbs that had once been large and sturdy now lay in piles like kindling.

Ian had already walked the town square. Most of the businesses and residents in the city limits had fared better than the outskirts, but the Falls Inn had lost its roof, a live oak had fallen through the kitchen at Cocoa's Café, and numerous homes had flooded.

"How many casualties?" Ian asked.

"Three so far. A woman trying to get home to her kids was struck by a tree when it crashed into her VW."

"Jesus, poor family."

Deputy Whitehorse pushed his ponytail over his shoulder. "Ninety-year-old Marvin Mullet tried to save his chickens and got thrown against his tractor on the way to the barn. He died instantly."

"If only people had heeded the warnings we issued," Ian said, hating to hear about the old man. "Who else?"

"Elderly woman in the trailer on the end. Neighbor said she'd lost her hearing and was confined to a wheelchair. He tried to convince her to let him take her somewhere safe to wait out the storm, but she refused to leave her home. Rescue workers found her dead beneath the kitchen table. She was holding a Bible, a picture of her husband, and a tin of snuff."

He pointed where the trailer had once stood, but all Ian could make out was a few pieces of metal, broken china, a needlepoint family tree, and a damp photo album that probably held precious mementos of the woman's life.

Sorrow for the families struck him, but he didn't have time to dwell on it. There was too much to do. The governor was flying in to visit the area and hopefully issue orders for state help for the residents and town.

Rescue crews had been working overnight to help residents escape their flooded and demolished homes and uncover victims who might be trapped. The community center that had been used to stage auditions for a film crew making a true crime movie about the serial killer cases in Graveyard Falls was now ironically being used to house the homeless. The Red Cross had rushed in with emergency supplies, blankets, clothing, food, water, and flashlights. Utility companies were working around the clock to restore power.

Ian's phone buzzed. He snatched it from his hip, dread balling in his gut when he saw the name. His other deputy, Ladd Markum. The last twenty-four hours had been nothing but bad news. "Sheriff Kimball."

"Sheriff, you need to get over to Hemlock Holler."

Ian frowned. Hemlock Holler was a desolate stretch of land by the river surrounded by hemlock trees. Rumors claimed nothing would grow on the stretch because the land was haunted. Once a prison had stood on the grounds, but it had been destroyed in another flood years ago. Like the legend of Graveyard Falls where locals swore they could hear the screams of three teenage murder victims echoing off the mountain, those same residents insisted you could hear the prisoners' shouts for help in the holler. "What's going on?"

"We've got a problem. A *big* problem." The deputy's voice cracked a notch. "The pilot from that search and rescue team called. They spotted something suspicious, so I drove over to check it out."

"And?"

"You have to see for yourself."

"I'll be right there." Wiping sweat from his forehead, Ian punched Disconnect, then addressed Deputy Whitehorse. "I have to go. Let me know if there are any other casualties."

Whitehorse nodded grimly. "I'll keep you posted."

Ian rushed to his police SUV, jumped in, hit the siren and lights, and sped toward the holler. Debris and tree limbs in the road slowed him, and he had to drive around a utility truck working on downed power lines, but finally he made it.

Early morning sunlight fought to find its way through the aftermath of the dark storm clouds and lost the battle, an oppressive gray clouding the sky. The deputy's vehicle was parked at an overlook on the mountain where tourists often stopped to enjoy the scenic view—or hear the so-called ghosts.

Ian swung his SUV in beside it, dragged his jacket up to ward off the chill, and hiked down the hill. Wet dirt, gravel, and rocks created a slippery path. Ian latched onto trees and broken limbs to keep from falling and careening down the embankment.

His deputy waved him toward where he stood by a patch of mangled trees that created a V shape. Locals called it Rattlesnake Point because a bunch of teens had been hiking here once and stumbled on a bed of rattlers that had sent three of them to the hospital with bites.

A hissing sound filled the air, and Ian hesitated, gun drawn as he searched for the snakes.

The tangled weeds and brush were so thick, though, he couldn't see.

Deputy Markum tilted his hat to acknowledge Ian, but the man's face looked pale, almost sickly.

Ian rubbed his hand over his bleary eyes. He was going on thirty-six hours with no sleep himself. "What is it?"

"The storm was nothing. Just look." The deputy lifted his flashlight and shined it across the ground.

Ian followed the path of the light, a cold engulfing him like nothing he'd ever felt before. At Rattlesnake Point, he'd expected to see a bed of snakes the storm had unearthed.

This was more disturbing than snakes. A sea of white that resembled ghosts bobbed up and down on the surface of the flooded valley.

He narrowed his eyes, trying to make out what he was seeing. The prison ghosts the locals gossiped about?

No. The white—Jesus, it was a river of thin, white gauzy fabric. On further scrutiny, he realized the fabric was nightgowns. Gowns mired in mud and dirt and leaves.

Gowns like women wore.

"What the hell?" He moved his flashlight across the murky water with a grimace. More sticks and twigs, broken branches?

No.

The truth hit him like a fist in the gut.

Bones.

The ground was covered in bones. *Human* bones. They floated in the water, protruded from the earth, clung to the white fabric, and lay scattered over the ground where the water had receded.

He swallowed back bile. Good God.

His deputy coughed. "Someone was buried here."

Ian ground his teeth. "Not someone. There are dozens and dozens of bones." He removed his hat and scrubbed a clammy hand through his hair. "This is a damn graveyard."

ABOUT THE AUTHOR

USA Today bestselling author Rita Herron fell in love with books at the ripe old age of eight when she read her first Trixie Belden mystery. Ten years ago, she traded her job as a kindergarten teacher for one as a writer and now has more than ninety romance novels to her credit. She loves penning dark romantic suspense tales, especially those set in small Southern towns. She earned a Career Achievement Award from *RT Book Reviews* for her work in Series Romantic Suspense and has received rave reviews for the Slaughter Creek novels. Rita is a native of Milledgeville, Georgia, and a proud mother and grandmother.